Confessions
From the Pumpkin Patch

by
Karlyle Tomms

Edited by Vaughanda Bowie
Cover Image by Karlyle Tomms

TigerEye Publications
P.O. Box 6382
Springdale, Arkansas 72766
www.TigerEyePubs.com

Confessions from the Pumpkin Patch

Copyright © 2014 by Karlyle Tomms

All rights reserved. No portion or part of this book may be reproduced, copied or transmitted in any form, electronically or by mechanical means, including photocopying, recording or by any information storage and retrieval system without the written permission of the author.

This is a work of fiction.

ISBN: 978-1503169401

Printed in USA

DEDICATION

I would like to dedicate this book to Marcia Hayden Young who not only taught me to believe in myself but taught me to cherish and express my creativity.

Prologue

I've heard it said that any life worth living is worth living well. Perhaps they should have said, "*any* life is worth living." At least I believe that. If you are here, it is because you are meant to be here. Maybe we are all here just to live our own story, only that. Maybe the only thing we have to do is watch our story unfold as though we are watching a movie we have never seen before. It's our movie and we have the starring role, but we have no idea how it is going to turn out, not really. I don't know that my story is special in any way, no more special than anyone else's. It seems to have manifested the way that it did despite my plans and intentions to play it out a different way.

There is a term in psychology called "scripting." It has to do with how various influences in our upbringing script us into a certain story, a certain path that we subconsciously follow. It could be that, in a way, we are all scripted to become what we become, that our thread in the fabric of humanity is already colored before it is woven. We may have little or no choice over the patterns in our thread, but we can choose how we weave it into the patterns of life. We all have choice, but no matter what decisions we make, no one controls their destiny. Choice combines with destiny to create each unique story.

I'm fascinated by the idea that there are billions of people on the planet and each one of us has our own unique story. Some of us write our stories, however, most only live them. All of us talk about the little stories that make up the novel of our lives, whether in a cocktail conversation or a talk given at a ladies luncheon. Our stories intertwine and weave the fabric of humanity. All of our stories create a pattern of existence that includes all the stories that we each experience and all the stories of those who have gone before us. This is the one tiny thread that I have woven into the fabric of humanity.

For what it is worth, this is my story.

Confessions

From the Pumpkin Patch

To Barbara Booth
Get your groove on Baby!!!
Blessings

Chapter 1

My name is Lovella Titwallow. Don't laugh. I married into the name. I have to say that it was a significant improvement over my maiden name, Fuchs. Yes, I know how it looks. That's not how it is pronounced. The "u" is long. Fuchs as in "F-you-chs." I learned over time to put a line over the "u" when I signed my name in an attempt to tip off the reader that the pronunciation is not to be confused with that other four-letter word which is so popular in human language. It did no good. People still pronounced it the way that it looks. Perhaps it is because I myself enjoyed the other word so much.

I was born in 1948 and I am from a small town known as Climax, Pennsylvania and right now you are thinking, "What a coincidence." The town itself, if it can be called that, is merely a bump in the road just a couple of miles from New Bethlehem which is itself nothing but a very small town.

Very funny. It's all very funny isn't it, the little tricks that life plays on us, the little scripts we seem doomed to play before we ever realize what is really going on. It was Shakespeare who said, "All the world is a stage and the people merely players." The old boy knew a little something, didn't he? How could he know what a drama my small town life would become?

When I was in elementary school, I dreaded the first day of class when a new teacher, who had perhaps never seen my name or failed to be warned ahead of time, would call first roll. It would go smoothly until she or he stumbled into the space between the E and the G. Even then, Foster, Forrest, or Freed fell off the tongue like apples off a tree. Then my name would follow, and there was the inevitable silence as a teacher pondered exactly how to pronounce it. There was the "Fa-chez" pronunciation, the "Feu-kees," the determination to say anything but "Fucks" even though that pronunciation was obviously the first to pop into the unsuspecting educator's brain. If I possibly could, I would try to get to the teacher before class and give the correct pronunciation of my name. This was my effort to redeem myself after the first grade teacher mispronounced the name saying it, for some reason, exactly the way it looks. No sooner had the words fallen off her lips when Johnny Sigmund shouted, "My Daddy told me that's a dirty word!" The teacher's purple face and rapid stuttering attempt to cover what she had just said led me to realize that there was something drastically wrong with my name.

Karlyle Tomms

From that point on, all was lost. Of course, everyone in class wanted to know why it was a dirty word. Some went home, used the incorrect pronunciation, and asked parents why it was a dirty word. They didn't get much, but those who asked older siblings came back to school edified and cruel. After that, any time the name was mispronounced, there followed a room full of cackling children, all of them gleeful at my embarrassment. The giggles would begin even if I dared to raise my hand to try to get the teacher's attention before a tragic mistake was committed. I therefore learned to sit there in silent indignation and embarrassment.

Outside of class the taunting began. Boys would comment as I walked by, "Hey, I hear Lovella Fuchs." They pronounced the name correctly in their taunt, but the meaning was obvious. Another boy might say, "Yeah, that's right, I fuched her last night."

I would either keep walking in silence, attempt to ignore it, or I would turn to them and shout, "Fuchs you!" Eventually, I decided that I would embrace my name and all the implications therein. I would honor the word, appreciate it, live up to it and use it as often as I felt necessary. Who cared whether there was an "h" or a "k" in the name. I would treat it as though it had always been a "k." By the time I was in high school when boys would say, "Hey, I hear Lovella Fuchs." I would turn, smile and say, "Damn right, and good at it!"

My father, John Fuchs, worked in a peanut butter factory and was an alcoholic. He spent his days in the factory and the family was never lacking for peanut butter. He held his drinking for the weekends, at least early on. He was a short man, 5' 6", and he had a round little belly that protruded over his belt like a basketball. His belly did not flop over his belt, which is good I suppose because he liked to wear the most gaudy and outlandish belt buckles. His hair was mousy blonde and made a horseshoe around his bald head. Thankfully, he opted out of a comb-over, still there was one tiny little tuft of hair growing just in the middle above his forehead, and he always let it grow too long. Often, I begged him to cut it. Once I caught him passed out drunk, so I shaved it off. When he came to, he almost cried as he looked into the mirror. I never considered what insecurities that little tuft of hair might have been covering. I felt so guilty that I never touched it or mentioned it to him again, but I was forever at a loss to understand why that little patch meant so much to him.

My Mother was a church lady, of sorts. She was more a cross between a church lady, a fashion model wanna-be, and Satan himself. Her name was Drucella. The "ella" has been a part of female names on her side of the family for as long as time I suppose. It was a tradition that all female children should have a first name ending in the "ella." Who knows why?

Confessions from the Pumpkin Patch

Hence my name Lovella. My grandmother was Claudella. My aunts were Johnella, and Cloella, and so on, and so on. The "ella" was like some sacred script that must be added to the name of any newborn female if she was to be considered a true part of the family.

My mother was in church every Sunday and every other time the door was open for any church or church-sponsored activity. I don't think there was ever a Bible study or a pot luck that she ever missed. She wore her hair, which was near jet black when she was young, high above her head. I would say in a "bee hive." However, it was more like a hornet's nest. Her temper, like a hornet nest, was swarming with venomous stings. Sometimes she would sting and you never knew what hit you until it started to hurt. When she was really angry the swarm would overwhelm you into either fleeing or submitting. Sometimes all you could do was duck and cover. Over time, I learned to swat.

As mother began to age and health diminished ability, her hair came down in a salt and pepper rats nest. She had given up the bee-hive before that time, yet she kept it stacked above her cranium for all of my childhood. It seemed like a warning that at any moment the swarm might be released. I have to say, however, that when she finally got rid of that stupid stack above her head, I was both shocked and appealed.

I was an adult and married before I ever saw her with her hair down like a normal woman and then again after she had lost her mind and had been placed in the nursing home. When she was younger, she was the utmost of prim and proper. She was slim and at least three inches taller than Daddy, almost skinny, and very careful about her food. Her cheek bones were high enough to provide an extra support for her yellow plastic rimmed glasses. Never a hair was out of place, and she wore a dress and high heels for everything, even when cooking or cleaning house, and, oh yes, she always smelled of vanilla or cinnamon.

I was an only child, pity's sake. How I longed to have a brother or sister, who might share the torment with me, but it was never to be. I developed a fantasy that after the consummation that produced me my Mother never allowed coitus again. I could imagine her saying to herself, "That was disgusting. I'll certainly never do that again."

I was both adored and tortured as a child. On one hand, my father was anything but perfect and on the other hand, my mother demanded absolute perfection. Daddy's love was always diluted by alcohol and perfection was the price I paid for Mother's love. I suppose one of the reasons I speak the way that I do is because Mother was constantly picking at me, training my words, my diction, my accent so that I could be her perfect little offspring. The shame of her Kentucky heritage was to be remedied I suppose by perfect diction.

"Ar-tic-u-late, Lovella!" Her words will forever ring in my ears. It is a wonder I didn't develop a tic from all the harassment. Instead, I developed a very precise manner of speaking from a very young age. It was the one gift, I suppose, that I could give her. In time, it may have been her gift to me.

In the evenings, after a perfect dinner on Mother's perfect china and after the dishes were washed and put away, we would sit in the living room and watch shows like Red Skelton through the static of a preliminary model of black and white TV. Of course, we had one even though many at the time did not. Mother was going to see to it that we had the best and the latest regardless of whether we could afford it. I could have cared less. I would sit in my corner chair reading and occasionally look up when Mother would cackle in laughter at a joke that, even as a child, I found inane. Daddy would usually fall asleep on one end of the sofa as Mother sat on the other end, perfectly upright, sipping her iced tea.

In his sleep, Daddy would often snore and fart and this would gather a quick dart of the eyes from Mother and a momentary microsecond of disgust on her face. Then her eyes went back to the television as she watched every moment, every second of everything that came across the screen. Even if it was a complete failure of broadcast and nothing but snow and hiss she would watch intently expecting the picture to return at any second.

At precisely 9:00 PM Mother would turn off the television and begin jabbing my father in the ribs with a long scarlet painted fingernail. "John! Get up! It's time for bed!"

He would moan, growl, open his eyes, take a breath like some kind of horror film monster and stretch before staggering off to bed. I often wondered if he had tiny little scars on his rib cage from being poked with that fingernail.

As for myself, Mother would merely give me a stern look and I would go to bed. However, I would often read until late in the night with a flashlight under the covers so Mother wouldn't catch me. Then I would struggle to wake up the next morning. Nonetheless, I would always get up at first call for I did not want little fingernail scars in my own rib cage.

Breakfast would be ready before Mother called me to get up, and by the way, she would never allow me to call her Mom or Mommy. I was required to call her Mother, and nothing else.

The way she cooked, I thought it must be a torture for her to stay so skinny because the breakfast table alone would consist of pork chops, bacon, or sausage, with hash browns, eggs, buns, pancakes, or French

Confessions from the Pumpkin Patch

toast and this was every morning. She sat there and nibbled bits of everything, but never what appeared to be a full serving of anything. At the same time, she would consistently admonish my father and me to eat.

By the time I was ten, I was allowed coffee, and this became something I looked forward to every morning. What a godsend. It was liquid alert. I would pretend to be more awake than I was as I watched the steaming black miracle fall into my cup. If I had my way, breakfast would have been coffee and a few bites of egg. However, Mother rationed the coffee as though it was a prison camp commodity.

Mother always drove me to school and Daddy to work. She would state that she absolutely had to have our one car during the day as she had meetings to attend and things to do. It was more likely that she had to have control. She would get us up early enough that breakfast would be put away and dishes would be done before we left the house. I never understood why this could not wait 'til after she returned to the house after dropping us off, but it was part of her perfection and her routine. She never left the house without everything being perfectly in place first.

On most days, I think the car simply sat in the driveway after she had delivered us, but she did often go to the church during the week to sit on some ladies committee or something. How everything looked was very important to Mother, and church was part of her plan to appear in the best possible light. She was a Methodist, a church she must have chosen like the story of "Goldilocks and the Three Churches" because it was just right, not too ritualized like the Catholics and not too fundamentalist like the Baptists.

On Wednesdays the battles began. Daddy would tell her that he had arranged a ride home with a friend after work on Friday. Of course, this meant that he was going directly to a bar with one or more of his drinking buddies. He would make up some kind of story about having to help someone fix their vehicle or something, but Mother and I both knew what he intended to be doing. Mother would make plans every Friday night to have a family from the church over for dinner and insist that he would have to be there. This would then become among the strangest of arguments as she would announce her plans at breakfast on Wednesday morning.

"Johnnnnnnnn" she would say, dragging the name out as though it was the last note of a ballad, "I'm having the Millers over for dinner on Friday. I know that you will want to spend time with Mr. Miller as he owns a burgeoning company, and I'm sure that he will be able to help you in the development of your career."

"Well Sissy," Daddy would respond. "You see, Honey, I have plans for

Friday, and I just can't be here." Sissy was his nickname for her. I'm not sure why.

"Oh really, dear?" she questioned through lips that teetered on the brink of being pursed. "What plans would those be?"

"Well you see Sissy, there is this fellow from work who knows this fellow who is one of the big wigs over at the factory and he is sure that this fellow he knows can get me a better paying position, maybe even foreman."

"Oooh."

The singsong note would drag out long and slow, and there would be the slightest little pop at the end.

"What would this fellow's name be?"

"Well, uh."

Daddy would stumble, searching his mind for the right words, for he was never quite smart enough to rehearse before Wednesday morning and, therefore, not very good at lying.

"I don't know the name of the other fellow that this fellow at work knows, but the fellow at work, his name is Jim."

The angrier Mother became, the more it sounded as though she was singing rather than talking, or perhaps it was more like the buzz of the hornets.

"This fellow—Jiiiim—" she would twitter, "If this person he knows can provide high powered positions, why isn't he procuring the job for himself?"

"Well you see," Daddy continued, "there's two jobs open, and Jim likes me and likes to work with me and he wants both of us to talk to this fellow so we can both move up in management and make more money."

The more intimidated Daddy became, the more his voice would wheeze.

"Weeellllll," Mother would sing, "I don't think I can cancel the dinner with the Millers for it has been planned for some time now, and it seems to me that Mr. Miller, as an entrepreneur, would be in a better position to further your career."

"But Sissy, now," Daddy would plead, "this is planned too and Jim is expecting me to be there."

When Mother's song of anger came to a crescendo the insults would begin.

"I would think, Joooohhhhnn, if you were the kind of man who wanted to present a good example for his impressionable daughter, you would want to have dinner with good church-going people, instead of rallying about the whims of a factory worker who, if he could advance anyone's career including his own, obviously would have done so!"

Confessions from the Pumpkin Patch

This would go on between them over breakfast until one of them gave in or there was a stalemate. If one of them gave in, there would be weeks of subtle resentment to follow that would be expressed in trite little insults on Mother's part, and something usually like farting at the dinner table on Daddy's part. More often than not, there was a stalemate. I hated when that happened for it meant that the argument would continue every moment that they were awake together until Friday evening. I would watch in silence, more as though I was watching a living television show rather than the life of my family.

When there was a stalemate, it would go on to the last minute on Friday. Mother first picked me up from school. Then she would drive immediately to the peanut butter factory so that she could stalk and spy on Daddy. My torture would be an hour to an hour-and-a-half sitting in the car with Mother as she repeatedly expressed her displeasure about Daddy. As we waited for him to emerge from the building, Mother would pontificate about how much he had wronged her. She never could seem to accept the fact that Daddy's drinking was more important to him than any career opportunity.

"I don't know why your father insists upon doing this every weekend, week in and week out."

By this time, the singsong quality of her voice had been replaced with a sharp piano-key tone like a child pecking out one note at a time, and rarely being able to put melody to it.

"I do everything I can to give you and your father a lovely home. I keep it spotless. I make sure that there is a lovely meal on the table—on time, every time. The laundry is done. The cupboards are kept well stocked. I have no idea why he wants to do this to me. Doesn't he know that everything I do, I do for my family—and God, of course? I must put God first, but I never let my church activities interfere with what I do for my family and your father doesn't seem to care at all. I make a lovely nest for him so you would think that he would want to come home to his family every day, not just week days."

The first time that I recall her doing this stalking thing when the factory let out, Daddy came out of the building, unsuspecting, chatting with his drinking buddies. Mother was lying in wait and trotted up to him in her perfect high heels as fast as she could. "John! John!" she exclaimed. "We have to go! There's been an emergency at the house. Lovella has been hurt."

She had insisted that I hunker down in the car seat so Daddy could not see me. The window was down, so I could hear their conversation and I was peeking up over the door frame. I thought it was going to be a joke, but soon learned that Mother did not really have a sense of humor.

"What?" Daddy responded, face filled with shock, for no matter what else, it was a fact that Daddy loved me. "What is it? What's the matter?"

"We have to go now, John!" Mother went on. "We have to take her to the emergency room."

"Well why haven't you already taken her to the emergency room?" he asked. Suspicion peaked.

Mother went on with her lie.

"She was crying for her Daddy, John! She wouldn't go without you."

The first time it worked, but that would be the last time. Each time Mother tried a ruse she would have to make it more complicated and better thought out than the last one.

Daddy began sneaking out of the factory a different way. He didn't change his behavior. She didn't change hers, and he delighted in telling her that his co-workers would frequently tell him that he was married to a real "nut case."

This went on for years, stalking Daddy at the factory, and sitting in the car silently as Mother both complained about Daddy and rehearsed her deception.

"Your father knows I love him. He has always known that I love him. I only want him to be the man he was meant to be. I only want him to succeed in life and where is he every Friday night? I have taken such steps to introduce him to good people, people who can help him, help us, people who are pillars of the community. He always has something else to do every Friday night. Regardless how I try, he is still working at this factory. He says he has meetings he has to go to on Friday evenings. I just don't believe there are any real meetings. After all these years working at a factory, he has never even gotten a slight promotion. He should have at least gotten some kind of promotion by now. I don't know what he is thinking going off every Friday night when he could be home with his family, and with good friends—good people who could help him get somewhere in life."

I learned to read a book and tried to ignore her. The truth is she knew exactly what he was thinking and so did I. She pretended that I didn't know and would make all manner of excuses for him at the same time that she was trying to force him to make a different choice. One day in the car when I was about twelve, during her ranting I said, "Mother, does it ever occur to you that Daddy likes to get drunk?"

"Lovella Chevon Fuchs!" she exclaimed. (Yes my middle name is Chevon.) "Whatever would possess you to say such a thing?" Mother was so very dramatic. I suppose I got that from her although my drama is a

Confessions from the Pumpkin Patch

little different and I would like to think, a little more sophisticated.

"Mother," I said, "he's drunk every weekend. You know it. I know it. Why pretend that we don't know it? Maybe he just likes to get drunk."

She was stunned for a moment in silence, breath held, and then released like a balloon held tight for far too long. After a moment she said, "Perhaps you are right dear."

Nothing else was said. I was stunned that she would ever admit that anyone else could be right. She sat there, silent, spent, as though exhausted from all those years of trying. For a moment, it seemed as though she was going to cry, but she didn't. I never saw my mother cry until after she was in the nursing home, mindless and vulnerable.

After a moment she started the car and we drove home. I don't know what kind of reaction Daddy had when he came out of the factory to find that she was not there. Perhaps he thought it was one of those nights when he managed to trick her and sneaked out a different way, but he didn't come home.

Mother and I arrived to an empty house. She had long since stopped actually inviting anyone over for Friday dinner. She found that Daddy, if she could get him home, would inevitably get drunk anyway and would simply embarrass her in front of her church friends. That night we walked silently into the house. I sat down in my chair. Mother sat in her place on the end of the sofa. After a while, she turned to me and said, "Dear, what would you like to have for dinner?"

I looked up from my book, stunned and speechless. For the first time ever in my life, my mother asked me what I wanted.

"Surprise me," I said, as I stuck my nose back into my book.

Karlyle Tomms

Chapter 2

I met my best friend in the first grade. Her name was Gretta Tannenbaum. At the time, she had stringy brown hair that her mother always braided into neat little pigtails standing way too high above each ear. She had no front teeth, a pug nose, and black rimmed glasses with lenses thick enough to be used as submarine windows. We met because the bitch stole my swing!

It was recess and I had gotten a nice swing toward the middle of the steel giant swing-set that was just outside the first grade classroom. I was swinging along when I noticed what I thought was a quarter laying on the gravel. I stopped the swing and went to investigate. It turned out to be only a bottle cap. When I turned to reclaim my swing there was Gretta with her skinny little ass in the very swing I had claimed. I ran immediately up to her, grabbed a pigtail in each hand and yanked her backwards out of the swing. Then it was on. I dragged her to the ground, topped her and began slapping her with both hands. She retaliated by grabbing my hair with her one free hand and pulling me by the hair to one side.

In those days, my hair was very long and black like Mother's. Mother insisted that I let it grow long and called it my "glory." She would also never put it up like hers for she clearly distinguished between adult and children's hairstyles. In this case, it turned out to be my liability. Gretta was able to use it to yank me over and the next thing I knew she was on top of me with slobber drooling from her mouth. Unimpeded, without teeth to block its way it fell into my face as I twisted from one side to the other in disgust. Thankfully the teachers were soon there to pull her off me.

Next, we sat in the Principal's office, chairs side by side facing his desk. He was a bloated man with jowls that hung on each side of his face outlining his thin little lips. I sat there imagining him to have the nose of a pig. His name was Mr. Buckner. He was a kind man, I suppose, and always seemed to be well intentioned. His voice would squeak occasionally when he talked between a light whisper-wheezing like tone.

"Now girls," he proclaimed. "We don't fight in school. It isn't nice. It isn't lady-like and I am sure that your mothers have taught you how to be young ladies."

"She stole my swing!" I shouted!

10

Confessions from the Pumpkin Patch

"Did not!" exclaimed Gretta.

"Now girls," Mr. Buckner went on. "We don't shout either. It isn't nice and I know you both want to be nice girls, don't you?"

"Well, she did steal my swing," I pleaded again.

"I thought she was done with it," said Gretta.

"Now girls," responded Mr. Buckner. "We must learn to share. We must take turns with the swings. There aren't enough swings for every child to have one all the time. We must share. Don't you think it is nice to share?"

Gretta and I looked at each other more in confusion at his approach than anything else. If my mother had been handling this, it would have been quick and simple. She would have pinched my ear hard enough to leave a bruise and she would have stated firmly though clenched teeth, "You will not behave in this manner!" Those were simple, clear instructions. Enough said. I would have gone on about my business until the next infraction. I later learned that Gretta's mother would simply have turned it over to her father who would have lectured her incessantly about how she was embarrassing the family.

Mr. Buckner folded his fat little fingers in front of his pig face. "I am not going to punish you this time, since it is the first time, but I'm afraid if you do this again there will have to be consequences. Now I want you to give one another a hug and say that you are sorry."

We both looked at him with shock and horror. He said he was not going to punish us, but what greater punishment could there be than forcing me to hug and apologize to the bitch who stole my swing. We looked at each other with identical horror and disgust.

"Now girls," he continued, "We must make amends and apologize for wrong doing. I want you to hug now and say that you are sorry for what you did."

Neither of us moved.

"Go on girls. Do as I say."

Slowly and silently like repelling magnets, we rose from our chairs and stood before one another.

"Okay, girls. Big hug."

We embraced one another rather like two porcupines attempting to avoid the other's quills.

"I'm sorry I pulled you off my swing," I said. I did not give up claim to the fact that it was my swing.

"I'm sorry I drooled in your face," she said, and at this moment, Mr. Buckner applauded slapping his fat little hands together as he chuckled in his airy, little voice.

"Oh, thank you, thank you, girls. That was very sweet," he said. "Now wait in the hall and I will call the hall monitor to escort you back to your class."

As we stepped outside the door of his office Gretta leaned toward me and said quietly but clearly, "Doody head!"

My response was to lean back to her and whisper, also ever so quietly, "Bitch!"

Once outside the door she said, "I can't believe you called me that. I would call you that but my mom says I shouldn't use dirty words."

"Oh?" I said. "And you think doody head is not a dirty word?"

"Well it's not as dirty as bitch," she said.

"Doody means shit, doesn't it?" I growled. "Isn't shit a dirty word? You just called me a shit head."

She looked at me, eyes wide like a startled owl and then a smirking smile crawled across her face.

"I can't believe you are saying those words," she giggled.

"Why not?" I said. "They are part of the English language aren't they? Who made the stupid rule that it is okay to use some parts of the language but not others?" Never mind the fact that I would never in a million years (at least not at that point in my life) have allowed Mother to hear me using those words or that argument.

"I never thought of it that way," she said. Then she looked at me, eyes darting to either side to be sure no one else was listening as she giggled the word, "Bitch." She quickly covered her mouth with the tips of her fingers as the following embarrassment hit her.

"Twat!" I said in immediate reply and she cackled out loud.

From that point on we were the dearest of friends. We had found common ground. We always shared the swing after that, not because Mr. Buckner had admonished us to do it, but because we wanted to. In addition, we became quite a team and very skilled at intimidating others on the playground to give up whatever place we wanted.

By the time we were in the third grade, our mothers would occasionally allow us to sleep over at one another's home on a weeknight. Daddy would not be drunk through the week and so Mother felt safe enough to allow it. I would later have to beg her into allowing weekend sleep-overs which she seldom ever granted for fear that Daddy would embarrass her or that stories about the truth in our family would get out.

When Gretta came to my house, we left Mother and Daddy to the living room as we retreated to my room to play. Mother required at least an hour be devoted to home work so we would at least pretend to be doing homework until she stopped checking on us about 7:00 PM. Then we would sing songs and play games like patty-cake or play with dolls. What

Confessions from the Pumpkin Patch

girl doesn't love dolls? Sometimes we would play the "secret game." The game always began with a little rhyme and after the rhyme, the person who sang the rhyme would tell a secret to the other. By the time we were teens there was practically nothing that we did not know about each other.

The first night we played the game after Gretta taught it to me, I sat on the bed and sang. "I have a secret that I must not tell. If I tell it to you, you must not tell." Then I said, "My Daddy gets drunk every weekend."

She gave me a very curious look and said, "What's drunk?"

I could not believe that she didn't know this. I said, "Well, do you know what whiskey is?"

She said, "No."

"What about beer?" I said.

"Oh," she said, "that is the stuff that grown-ups can drink but kids aren't allowed to drink."

"Yes," I said, "And beer contains alcohol and whiskey is a hard liquor which is a stronger alcohol and when people drink it they get drunk."

She giggled a witty giggle and said, "When I have a lollypop, I'm a hard licker."

I couldn't help but laugh and said, "No, it's not that kind of licker. It's liquor." I spelled it. "L. I. Q. U. O. R."

We went to the dictionary where we found: "Middle English licuor, from Latin *liquor*, from *Liquere*. Date: 13th Century: **A:** a usually distilled rather than fermented alcoholic beverage. **B:** a watery solution of a drug." We knew little more than we knew in the first place. What I knew at the time was that alcohol, whatever kind he happened to consume depending on his mood, made Daddy drunk.

"Okay," she said, "but what is drunk?"

We went back to the dictionary where we found: "a period of drinking to intoxication, or of being intoxicated." I hated dictionaries for this very reason, having to look up word, upon word, upon word because each word that was used to define something was more complicated than the last. Finally we looked up intoxication where we found: "an abnormal state that is essentially a poisoning."

This set me to tears. I never realized before that point that my daddy was poisoning himself every weekend and I began wondering how soon he would die.

Gretta grabbed me, and hugged me. "What's the matter? What's the matter?" she exclaimed.

Mother having ears like a bat heard me from the living room. The next thing we knew the door to my bedroom opened and there she stood. "Is everything alright in here?" she questioned.

13

Karlyle Tomms

I slammed the dictionary closed, sniffled back my tears, and quickly made up a lie. "We were just reading about a bunny who lost his mother," I said.

"Aw, that's so sad," she said. Then she smiled a crooked little smile, closed the door and retreated back to her television.

I took a deep breath and said to Gretta, "My daddy is poisoning himself. What am I going to do?"

"I don't understand how," said Gretta.

"He gets drunk every weekend," I said. "It says here that drunk is an abnormal state that is essentially poisoning. We have to stop him."

"But we're just kids," said Gretta. "How can we do that?"

"Maybe I just need to talk to Daddy," I said. "Maybe if he realizes what he is doing he will stop."

I realized in that moment that Mother's stalking every Friday night was her attempt to stop him and it didn't work. I resolved that the following day I would talk to Daddy about his drinking, but first I had to make sure that Mother wasn't around.

Gretta and I talked for another hour or so and then went to bed, early for me. She slumbered quietly beside me but I didn't sleep. I had to come up with some way to make sure that I could get Daddy alone to talk to him. Finally, I decided to ask Mother for a red velvet cake to have over the weekend. I knew that she would have to shop for ingredients and I would tell her that I had to study for a test so I would not be able to go to the grocery store with her. The next night was Thursday and it would be a perfect time, but I had to make sure that I told her after we picked up Daddy or she would just drag me to the store between school and picking him up.

The next afternoon we were sitting at the factory waiting to pick Daddy up. There was no problem with this on any day but Friday.

When Daddy came out of the factory, I got out of the front seat and into the back. Daddy spotted our car in the usual place and I waited for him to get into the front seat. I knew he would not want to go to the store or wait outside for Mother to shop.

Shortly after Daddy got into the car I said, "Mother, I have a math test tomorrow. If I make a really good grade, can I have a red velvet cake for this weekend?"

"How do I know you are going to make a good grade?" she questioned as she drove us home.

"Well a red velvet cake would make me try harder." I said.

"I don't even have the ingredients to make one," she continued.

"Well, can you stop and get them?" I questioned. I knew this would get

Confessions from the Pumpkin Patch

Daddy and sure enough it did.

"Hold on there now," he protested. "I've had a long hard day and I don't want to be diddling around a grocery store after work."

"But Daddy, please," I pleaded.

"No! Now I told you, I'm tired!" he exclaimed.

Mother knew where this was headed and more to keep the peace than to please me she offered, "Why don't I just drop you off at home, John. Then Lovella and I can shop for cake supplies."

"But Mother, I have to study for my test," I replied. The test, which I had known was coming, was merely a ten question weekly but Mother didn't have to know that, at least not until after I got what I needed. It worked.

"Okay, then," she submitted, "I will drop the two of you off at home while I run by Safeway to shop."

"Thank you, Mother," I said, gloating in my victory.

Daddy and I were not long inside the house when he plopped himself on the sofa and was about to turn on the radio to listen to the evening news. Even though we had a television he still preferred the radio news. I knew I had to catch him quick before Mother got back. I sat down on the sofa beside him and said, "Daddy, I have a problem and I really need to talk to you about it."

He stopped with his hand halfway to the radio knob and turned back to me. "What's up, Punkin' Patch?" he said as he jostled my hair. Daddy always wanted to listen to the news after work, but he also loved me very much and would never hesitate if he thought I was truly in need.

"Well, Daddy," I began, "last night, I was looking in the dictionary and looking up words, and I know you get drunk on weekends, and—"

"Hold on there now," he said protesting with guilt, "We don't need to be talking about that. That's not stuff kids need to talk about with parents."

"But Daddy," I persisted. "I looked up the word drunk and it said it was poisoning."

"No it's not," he said. "It is just getting a little off your feet once in a while. It's just a way to relax and blow off a little steam after a hard week."

"But Daddy, why would the dictionary say that it was poisoning? That means it could kill you."

"Honey, it's not going to kill me," he said. "Alcohol has been around for thousands of years. Lots of people drink. It doesn't hurt anybody."

"Then why can't kids drink it?" I questioned.

He grunted with exasperation. "Because it is not for kids," he said. "Some things you got to be mature enough to handle."

Karlyle Tomms

"But if it's not good for kids, it must not be good for you," I continued.

"We don't let you drive yet do we?" he went on. "There's nothing wrong with driving. You're just not big enough to do it yet. It's like that. You have to be an adult first. Some people drink and some people don't. It doesn't hurt anyone."

"Well, I know Mother serves sherry to the Millers when they come over, but they only have one little glass and they don't get drunk."

I continued to plead with him. "Daddy, sometimes you don't come home all night on Friday, and when you come back on Saturday, you look sick, all puffy and red, with swollen eyes and stuff."

"Ah, that's more from not getting enough sleep than it is from whiskey," he said. "You stay up late. I've seen you at breakfast about to fall asleep in your hash browns. Sometimes we both stay up a little too late, don't we?"

"You're not going to die?" I questioned.

"Well, I hope not," he replied. "I've got a lot of living yet to do. Now you go on and study for your test and worry about kid stuff, and don't worry about grownups. We will take care of ourselves. Besides, it's our job—your mother and I— to take care of you, not the other way around."

"You promise you are not going to die." I pleaded.

"I promise, honey," he went on. "I am not doing anything on Friday night but trying to blow off a little stress from the work week. That's good for me."

He hugged me and said, "Now, go study."

I smiled a nervous smile and went to my room. I closed the door with trepidation. For no matter what Daddy said I worried about that word, "poisoning."

I got an 'A' on my test and got my red velvet cake. When Mother got the graded paper she shook it at me. "Lovella! This is just a weekly test. I thought you had a big exam. How dare you put me to all that work for something that you do every week and can practically do in your sleep?"

"I'm sorry, Mother." I said. "I was just really worried about this one. It's mostly division."

She let out a sigh more like a steam engine releasing the brakes. She slapped the paper down on the kitchen table and glared at me. "Well. I'm glad you got an 'A'. You did very well." She grabbed her apron from the hook and set about preparing dinner. I took my paper and my books to my room.

After dinner that night, I sat in my chair reading while Daddy snored on one end of the couch and Mother sat upright on the other. My mind, however, was not on the book. Although I loved Daddy and defended him with all my might, and though I wanted ever so much to believe him when

Confessions from the Pumpkin Patch

he said that he was fine, some years later I came to the painful realization that he was wrong about alcohol poisoning him.

In the meantime, that little worry was occasionally forgotten—but usually nagged at the back of my mind.

I went on as usual and loved him as best I could.

Karlyle Tomms

Chapter 3

Mother always insisted on church every Sunday morning, tedious as it was. When I was small, I simply obediently complied and rather enjoyed the separate time for children coloring pages of Jesus and such. However, as I matured and was forced to enter the main service, I found it difficult to distinguish from yet another day of school. Add to this the fact that I was obliged to disagree with anything that I thought Mother wanted. Therefore, church was a condition of circumstance that I was doomed to despise.

By the time I was twelve years old I had begun a regular Sunday morning protest starting at the breakfast table where I knew I could employ Daddy's defense. Apparently, through all the years of their marriage he had also obediently complied with her expectation that the family would dutifully show up at Sunday service. Although it must have been difficult for him to rise on Sunday morning, he probably had managed to sleep off his inevitable hang over on Saturday afternoon.

Mother dressed Daddy for church. She would have nothing of his gaudy belt-buckles on Sunday mornings. I suppose he should have counted himself lucky that she tolerated them through the rest of the week. Sunday was a time for her to show off her family and display her pretentiousness to the community. Mother was all about the show. No matter what might be going on at home, she was going to display nothing more than absolute perfection to the community. She had scraped together enough money on Daddy's small salary and her own fund-raising (usually yard sales) to buy him two well-appointed suits, a few ties and a couple of white dress shirts, and every Sunday morning she insisted that he wear them against his constant protest. However, this did not come until after breakfast.

The Sunday table was displayed with the same opulence as every other morning and we were both summoned to the table. The consolation was that it was the only morning of the week that we were allowed to eat in our pajamas. Mother had perhaps learned her lesson about this when Daddy happened to spill a cup of coffee across the front of one of the hard-earned suits she had purchased for him. She would never make that mistake again. From then on, breakfast time was moved up thirty minutes and dressing for church came afterward.

I knew Daddy hated going to church. He hated dressing in those suits. It

Confessions from the Pumpkin Patch

simply was not him. Rather than find and marry the man she wanted, Mother had found it more of a challenge to marry a pig's ear and attempt the miracle of making him into a silk purse. I suppose if she were to succeed, this would mean that she was indeed truly good. Nonetheless, despite all her efforts and Daddy's occasional willingness to act the part, he remained forever who he was, a simple man who wanted little more out of life than to enjoy it.

My first attempts at getting out of church were through faking illness. Of course this didn't work for Mother was determined that she would stay home and care for me if I didn't feel well, and then I would hear the dialog of her resentments about missing church repeated over and over as I was pretending to be ill. Daddy on the other hand was quite pleased to have a day with no suit, and he would either go back to bed, or to his work shed near the house which was his sanctuary from Mother.

For the longest time it was easier simply to go. After breakfast, I would retreat to my room to put on my Sunday dress. I could hear Daddy complaining from their room. "Drucella! Now, Drucella, that tie is too tight. You don't want me to faint right out in church."

"John!" she would demand, "the tie is not too tight. It is simply pulled up to the collar where it is supposed to be."

"Well," Daddy protested, "don't you think we could just leave the top button unbuttoned and kind of pull the tie up over it?"

"I will not have you looking like a hobo who found a suit coat in a dumpster!" she would shout, and I knew that she was at that moment pushing the tie up to his throat in a gesture indicating that he would either comply or she would hang him with it then and there.

After I dressed, I would come out to find Mother, always in her finest, standing there with a hairbrush and a bow. It was off to the bathroom where she would sit on the commode and have me stand in front of her as she pulled that toothed, plastic demon through my hair.

"Aowaoh! Mother!" I would complain, "That hurts."

"Well, Lovella," she lectured, "if you would occasionally brush your own hair and keep the tangles out of it, we wouldn't have such an ordeal to go through to make it look nice for church."

By the end of it all, my hair was smooth as silk and the top tied back over the underflow with a bow that perfectly matched the dress that Mother had set out for me earlier. Then it was off to the living room to gather Daddy who would be sitting sullenly waiting to follow her instructions.

Her pretentiousness didn't wait for church. It began right there in the living room on Sunday morning. "John, would you please pull the car around?" She would say this every Sunday morning.

This meant that he was to pull it from the driveway out to the street and wait for our descent down the front porch steps. He was never allowed to pull it to the street ahead of time because that would have looked unseemly for him to be sitting in the car all that time. Instead, he had his instructions to wait in the living room and go out to pull the car to the street at just the right moment so that Mother and I, hand in hand, could descend down the porch steps and across the walk where he would be waiting like a chauffeur to open the passenger door for us. Mother would cross the walk with her head up as though she was a movie star navigating the red carpet before her adoring fans. I, on the other hand, considered it absurd even as a young child. Yet, this was our ritual every Sunday morning. I would be guided to get in first so that I could sit in the middle between them. Then Mother would enter the car, seat herself like a Queen, and carefully brush her dress as though the mere act of movement might have soiled her. Daddy would then carefully close the door, as he was not allowed to slam, and would come around to the driver's side. Then it was off to church.

I think this was the only time that Daddy was actually allowed to drive. The rest of the time Mother did all the driving.

There wasn't much of anything that Mother considered worthy in Climax, so we attended church in New Bethlehem. On the way there, she would verbally prepare us.

"John, last week I noticed you nodding a little during the sermon," she chided. "Please make every effort to stay awake. I wouldn't want you to miss something that might save your eternal soul." On she went. "And Lovella, Mrs. Dickens said you were giggling in Sunday school last week. Please do try to be appropriate." Daddy would drive in silence. I would usually try to bring a book to read—and I would occasionally pretend to listen.

The local Methodist church was a rustic but ornate brick building with a tower on either side of the front steps. The steps crossed the entire front of the building in a wide expanse with a rail down the middle. Atop each tower was a cross. I suppose that having two steeples and two crosses somehow made it better than other churches having only one and I could imagine Mother choosing it for that very reason. If there had been no church in the area with two steeples, she would probably have chosen the one that had the tallest steeple regardless of the denomination.

There were two front doors leading into a single large alcove with marble flooring. This then led to a center arched double door that led up

Confessions from the Pumpkin Patch

the center isle of the sanctuary. On either end of the alcove were smaller doors that led to the outside isles near the windows.

The sanctuary was filled with burgundy carpet, and flanked on either side by tall, arched, stained glassed windows. Oh, what a glorious setting for a Savior, who lived on handouts, admonished the care of the poor, and protested the corruption of wealthy rabbi in ancient Jerusalem. As a child, I thought it was all so very pretty, but as I aged and actually read the Bible, I came to think of it as yet just another example on a long list of hypocrisies. I was determined that I would never be a hypocrite. If nothing else, one day I would be honest.

When I was young, the minister was a tall handsome man by the name of James Martin. He was at least a couple of inches past six foot. He had dark, straight hair, a square symmetrical jaw and blue eyes. After service, he stood at the arch leading from the foyer and greeted the parishioners as they left the building. Mother would collect me from Sunday school and insist that Daddy hold my hand as we filed down the center isle toward the exit. I came to assume that this was so she could have both hands free when she greeted Reverend Martin.

She kept her lace hanky out all through the service to touch her face and show that she was moved by the sermon. As we approached the Reverend she would stuff it inside her left hand, and lay three fingers of her right hand across his palm as a "lady-like handshake" and tell him how much she enjoyed the service.

"Reverend Martin, as always," she would begin, "it was both empowering and simply touching. What an inspiration you are to us all."

Daddy and I would smile and nod, rarely ever saying anything ourselves. I imagined Mother wishing that she had married a man like Reverend Martin rather than Daddy.

By the time I was twelve, the Methodist church, as Methodists are prone to do, had traded Reverend Martin for Reverend Zimmar, a funny looking little man who left much to be desired in the looks department. He wasn't much over five feet tall and had buckteeth protruding slightly over his lower lip so that he had the appearance, somewhat, of a chipmunk. When he spoke his name, he drew it out at the end as though trying to make sure to emphasize the last of the two syllables. "How do you do, I am Reverend Zimm-aaaaaaaar."

After this my desire to go to church completely faded. At least when Reverend Martin was there, I might have enjoyed looking at that pretty face for an hour. When Reverend Zimmar came around it was at the same time I left Sunday school and began attending regular services. That clinched it. I was through with church. Reverend Zimmar's sermons were about as entertaining as watching paint peel. I could find little context in his sermons to get excited about, and except for drawing out the ends of some words in a way that was similar to how he pronounced his name, he spoke in a sedative monotone. Daddy and I would both nod before the end of his sermon and Mother would attempt to keep attuned to the service with a painful pinch, a big perfect smile, and a dart of the eyes toward the podium. Yet I knew she was just as bored as we were.

There came a Sunday when I was nearing my thirteenth year that I decided I had been pinched enough. I determined that I was not going to go to church anymore and I announced this at the breakfast table the following Sunday morning. I could have announced it at any time through that week but I knew that I needed to take her by surprise and I knew that I would need Daddy's support.

On the Sunday following my decision Mother had made her usual opulent breakfast. I sat at the table eating my eggs and biscuits, sipping my coffee, carrying on as though there was nothing out of place from any other Sunday morning. About a third of the way through the meal, I announced. "Mother, I've decided that I am not going back to church."

She looked up from picking tiny pieces off her plate as though she had just heard a joke and said, "You most certainly are going to go to church, dear." She smiled as she took a sip of her coffee.

"No, Mother," I went on. "Indeed, I have decided that church is not for me and I will not be returning to Sunday services."

Daddy looked like a deer caught in headlights. His eyes grew wide as he watched the standoff begin. He must have known that there would be no way for him to escape being drawn into it.

"Lovella!" Mother rolled my name off her tongue with a growl in the tone. "You will not defy me, young lady! You will go to church and there will be no more argument."

I turned to Daddy who was nervously cutting his ham. "Daddy, you don't like to go to church either do you?" I questioned, knowing what the answer would be if he told the truth.

"Well, I—I believe you have to listen to your mother, Punkin' Patch."

"But what's the answer to my question, Daddy?" I persisted.

"Well, I…" He was glancing over at Mother as she glared at him like a lion stalking a rabbit. "I, ah, can't say that it's my favorite thing to do on Sunday morning."

"John Fuchs!" Mother exclaimed, "Don't encourage that child."

"Well, I was just saying how I feel about it, dear." He receded. "I know it's good for the soul and all."

"Mother," I interjected. "I am almost thirteen years old. I have reached

Confessions from the Pumpkin Patch

the age of accountability and it is my decision that I will not go back to church."

Mother stood up, leaned over the table hands flat to the table top and said, "Lovella, how dare you speak to me in this tone?!"

"I am simply saying that I have the right to make my own choice about this," I calmly continued.

"No, you do not have the right to make your own choice about this!" she exploded. "You are a child and you will do as I say."

Daddy's need to protect his little girl finally kicked in as I had hoped it would. "Now, now, Drucella," he pleaded, "There is no need to get all hot under the collar about this. Teenagers get like this. You know it's all part of growing up."

"What?!" Mother twisted toward him. "What did you just say?"

I half expected Daddy to back down at this point but the rabbit stood up to the lion.

"Kids reach a point where they want to think for themselves," he continued. "It is a normal, natural, part of growing up."

"You have got to be kidding me!"

Mother grabbed her plate, paced to the sink, threw it in, food and all, and then turned. "She is not even thirteen years old yet. She is not old enough to make that kind of decision, and besides her soul will burn in hell. Is that what you want? Do you want your only child's soul to burn in hell?"

"Now, Drucella, you're getting a little extreme there now," said Daddy as he turned in his chair. "You don't know that she won't change her mind in a few weeks and go back. She's just expressing a little rebelliousness that's all."

"I'm not going back," I said. "Neither one of us goes to church because we want to. Neither one of us goes because we want to save our soul from damnation. Daddy you go for the same reason I do, because every Sunday Mother insists on it, demands it. This is not about saving our soul. It's about Mother trying to pretend to be hoity toity for everybody in town."

At this point Mother went into a full-blown tornado rage. The hornets were out. She spun across the kitchen and up to my face as I sat leaned back in the kitchen chair. "Why you insolent, ungrateful, little brat!" she screamed. "I have given my life to this family! I have kept this house, sent you to school, cooked, ironed, cleaned, and saved coupons, and for what!? So you could sit here and disrespect me and say such horrible things to me!?"

Suddenly she caught herself, as though murder was not far from her thought, and she stood back. Calmly, but quite deliberately, she said, "You cannot believe how much effort it is taking for me not to slap you right now."

She looked over at Daddy who sat there silent and shocked. "Very well," she said, "The two of you no longer have to go to church. God forbid that you should feel that I am forrrrrrcing you."

She pulled herself up as tall as she could stand, "I will go to church on my own, by myself, and when people ask me where my lovely family is I shall tell them that I am widowed and childless."

She turned and marched stoically out of the room pausing for a moment at the door as though waiting for us to shout, "No, please wait!"

We said nothing, and Mother left the room. Daddy and I continued to sit at the kitchen table half in shock, half in glee. We finished our breakfast and I did the dishes while Daddy sipped more coffee and read an old newspaper.. Later, we heard her cross through the living room and stop before opening the front door. We heard her release a long and defeated sigh. Then the latch clicked, the door closed, and she was gone.

After church, she behaved as though nothing had ever happened.

Confessions from the Pumpkin Patch

Chapter 4

If you were not a member of the family, you would never know that Mother smoked. In an age in which it was considered to be glamorous, the habit of the stars, Mother treated it as her own private little sin.

When she smoked, it would be on the back porch in the summer and in the laundry room during the winter. When the weather was cold, she would lock herself in the laundry room to suck down one or two cigarettes. Then she would destroy the evidence before she came out. Her ashtray could not be found nor could her cigarettes, but the wafting smell of tobacco smoke would ooze beneath the door of the laundry room. Sometimes Daddy liked to taunt her.

"Sissy!" He would bang on the laundry room door as though there was some emergency, "What are you doing in there? I'm afraid the house might be on fire."

Daddy and I would snicker at each other silently outside the door as we teased her about it.

"You sure you're not burning the ironing?" Daddy would continue. "I smell smoke."

"Oh for Heaven's sake, John!" she would eventually cry out, "Leave me alone and let me have a little bit of peace to myself!"

In the summer, if either I or Daddy happened to step out onto the back porch, she would quickly snuff out her cigarette and stuff the ash tray into the back of a ceramic cat that sat by her chair. Finally, one day I said, "Mother, why do you do that?"

"Do what dear?" as though she had completely fooled me.

"Hide your cigarettes like you think Daddy and I don't know you smoke," I said.

"Why, for heaven's sake, Lovella," she replied, "I don't know what you are talking about."

As I had gotten older, I had become increasingly more defiant of Mother and the hypocrisy that would ooze from her periodically. "Well," I said, "why don't I come over there and see what you just shoved up the ass of your ceramic cat."

"Lovella Fuchs!" she exclaimed. "How dare you use language like that in front of me?"

"You prefer I use language like that behind your back?" I said. "Come

25

on, let's take a look in that cat and see what we find."

She stared at me silent and intimidating as though she was going to be able to stare me away and make me forget about it.

Finally I said, "You wouldn't lie, would you Mother?"

"All right!" she confessed as she straightened her collar like a guilty witness being called to the stand, "I smoke. There you have it. You have heard me say what you already knew. Are you happy now?"

I continued to interrogate. "What I don't understand," I said, as I sat in the chair across from her, "is why you think you have to keep it a secret."

She stared off at a bundle of tall garden phlox that was blooming by the porch. "It's just not a habit that a lady should have," she said finally.

"But lots of women smoke," I protested. "Betty Davis smokes. Most of the actors and actresses smoke. What's the big deal?"

"I don't care if other women smoke or if all of Hollywood smokes," she said, "I just hate it that I do."

"But why?" I questioned.

"Because it's nasty," she said as she looked at me pleadingly. "I wish I had never started it, and I hope that you never will. It makes my mouth taste like a smokestack. It creates a nasty mess to clean up. Sometimes it makes me cough. I hate it."

"Then why do you do it?" I continued.

"Because I can't help it," she said. "I started smoking when I was very young and now I feel like I have to do it. If I don't do it, I get nervous and grumpy."

"Oh, can we blame all that on being out of cigarettes?" I smirked.

"Don't be crass," she snapped as she went on. "Lovella, you know I like to keep clean. You know I like to keep a certain—" she paused briefly, "quality of character about me. Smoking interferes with that and yet I can't seem to quit doing it. It's like I'm hooked on a drug or something."

In those days there hadn't been much said about cigarettes being addicting. In fact, cigarettes were advertised everywhere even on television.

"It would seem to me," I pondered, "that all you would have to do is not buy any more. If you don't buy them, they are not here, and you won't smoke them."

"Lovella, it's not that simple," she said. "I don't know if I can explain it to you, but it's not that simple. Please just take my word for it, that it is a nasty, terrible habit that is hard to break, and promise me that you will never do it."

Whoops! She said the wrong thing there. Whatever Mother did not want me to do I seemed to be hell bent on doing. It might have been different

Confessions from the Pumpkin Patch

when I was younger but by the time I was a teen I had the bug. I had to try everything that was displeasing to Mother. For some reason, I had this devilish need to be whatever she didn't want me to be.

"Promise me, Lovella," she said as my mind wandered off into a vision of myself leisurely drawing down smoke like one of the Hollywood actresses.

"Why is that so important?" I questioned.

"Because I don't want you to have to fight the battle that I am fighting right now." She leaned forward and took my hand. "Promise me that you will never smoke."

I took a big sigh and lied. "I promise."

She turned loose of my hand and sat back in her chair. "Why don't you run on now," she said.

"Why?" I questioned, knowing full well that she wanted me to leave so she could smoke alone.

"Just go on, dear." She looked away and I could seem to palpate her shame.

"So you can smoke?" I continued. "I don't see what the big deal is. If you can smoke alone, why can't you smoke in front of me? It's not like I'm going to tell."

"Lovella, please," she pleaded. "I would really just rather be alone. You know my secret, okay? Now, please, just go play."

I couldn't see much reason to continue torturing her that particular day, so I did as she said and went on my way. However, I determined that I was going to find her cigarettes and I was going to try one. I had to find out what the big deal was about. I knew that I wouldn't be ashamed of it like her. I knew I wasn't like her, all prissy and perfect. I didn't have to be like her. I didn't want to be like her. So when I smoked I determined that I would flaunt it. After all, why should anyone make a secret of such a silly thing? I had friends whose parents smoked and they didn't hide it away like it was some secret shame. Why should I?

I never did find Mother's cigarettes. Every time I caught her out of the house, I looked in what I thought was every possible hiding place. I even sneaked into her bedroom one night while she was watching television and went through her purse. Nothing! I found a cigarette lighter in her purse but that was it.

This went on for weeks until I finally figured out that I was never going to find them. Oddly enough Daddy didn't smoke. You would think that he would, given that he drank so much and that he spent so much time in bars but he simply never cared for it I guess. However, Gretta's father did smoke and I finally decided that I would have to enlist her in my quest if I was ever to score that elusive first cigarette. Gretta and I had exchanged overnight visits with one another ever since we were in the second or third grade. When I was at her house, we would spend most of our time in her room and the same when she came to my house. We would have plenty of private time to talk about it, and I determined that I was going to bring it up with her the next time I was over.

So about two or three weeks after my talk with Mother I got to stay over at Gretta's house. It was a simple little ranch just like ours. Gretta wasn't an only child like me, however. She had a pesky little brother named Calvin and we would often have to put a chair under the door knob to her room to keep him from coming in to harass us. Her father managed a hardware store and, oh my, was he handsome. I tried to restrain myself from the horrible betrayal of lusting for my best friend's father, but by the time I had reached my early teens I couldn't seem to help myself. Had he not been married and the father of my best friend I would have thrown myself at him like the brazen harlot I was destined to be.

Mr. Tannenbaum was a tall rugged man with dark brown hair and eyes like polished onyx. His stiff firm jaw supported the most kissable mouth I think I have ever seen. His lips were plump and soft and when he smoked they caressed the filter of his cigarette. He never hesitated to smoke right there in front of everyone and I loved to watch it. He would pull the cigarette to his lips and draw upon it sensually. When he blew the smoke from those plump lips, it was like a sigh after a long sweet kiss. I have to admit I had a crush on him. When I finally confessed that to Gretta years later she said, "Ewweeewwwweeeeh! That's my Dad! Gross!"

That night after dinner, Gretta and I retired to her room and I began my query.

"Gretta," I began, "I have something so important to tell you."

"What?" she questioned as though we were acting out the plot of a television teaser.

I looked around the room as though to be sure there was no one lurking about and then I whispered soft enough not to be heard outside the room but loud enough for Gretta to hear as she sat on one side of the bed and I on the other. "I caught Mother smoking."

"Really?" she said, "I never knew your mother smoked."

"I knew it," I said, "but I had never confronted her about it. She always hid it. She would smoke in the laundry room or on the porch when she thought no one was around. I got her to confess that she does it. "

"Wow." said, Gretta, "Why doesn't she just smoke in front of people like my Dad?"

"Because she is ashamed of it," I said. "It doesn't fit the proper image

Confessions from the Pumpkin Patch

that she works so hard to maintain."

"But why?" questioned Gretta. "Lots of people smoke."

"Well apparently Mother thinks that it is some kind of terrible nasty thing," I said. "She made me promise I would never do it."

"That's just silly," said Gretta. "What difference does it make if you smoke? Dad really seems to enjoy it."

"I know," I said rolling my eyes to the ceiling. "I love to watch your Dad smoke." Then I caught my glee and pulled back to the moment lest she realize that watching her father smoke was a sexual turn-on for me. "I mean, why shouldn't anybody just smoke and enjoy it if they want to?"

"I know," said Gretta. "Mom or Dad have never told me I shouldn't smoke.

"Have you ever tried it?" I gleamed.

"No," she said. "I actually never thought much about it."

"Well, I want to try it," I said. "I mean, it is such a pleasure for your Dad, and such a secret for my Mother, I really want to find out what it's all about."

"Well, you are not supposed to smoke unless you're an adult," she said, acting the part of the trained and obedient daughter.

"Do you always do what you are supposed to?" I taunted.

"Well, no," she replied in a kind of sing-song voice. "I say bitch, or shit, or damn sometimes."

We both giggled and I said, "Well listen, bitch, we gotta score some cigarettes."

"How are we going to do that?" she said. "They won't sell them to kids."

"I swear, Gretta," I said. "Sometimes you are so dense."

"What?" she questioned.

"We don't have to buy them. Your Dad has them lying around. We just borrow some of his."

"Oh, I don't think that would be a good idea," she pleaded. "My dad would not like that. He is very much against stealing."

"Did I say we were going to steal them?" I pushed. "We are just going to borrow them and try them."

I was actually a bad influence on Gretta, but her parents wouldn't know that 'til much later. Still, she turned out all right.

"What's the difference?" she replied. "Besides, why don't you get some of your mother's cigarettes?"

"I tried," I said. "I've been searching for weeks. She's got them hidden somewhere and apparently a darn good hiding place cause I can't find them anywhere."

Karlyle Tomms

"My dad doesn't hide his," Gretta said.

"I know," I said. "He wouldn't miss a couple. We could just take a couple out of the pack when he is not looking and just go somewhere and try them. When we are old enough to buy cigarettes we'll buy him a whole carton to make up for it."

Oh but the forbidden fruit is sweet indeed. Gretta's eyes began to light up as she said, "We could go down under the Hetrick Road culvert. No one would ever know. I could get a couple of mom's kitchen matches. When do you think we could do this?"

"How about tomorrow?" I said.

Over the summer Gretta and I would sometimes spend two or three days together running around each other's neighborhoods before we had to go back home. The Hetrick Road culvert happened to run underneath the street a few blocks from her house at a place where the street curved. It was long and in a kind of a wide "V" shape underneath the street level. There was a little creek that ran through it, but plenty of room on either side to walk. Gretta and I had often explored it in the past.

"When do we get the cigarettes?" she probed.

"Where does your dad keep them?" I asked.

"He usually just leaves them lying on the end-table by the sofa," she said.

"Okay." I planned. "We wait 'til your parents have gone to sleep. We sneak into the living room. One of us will keep watch down the hall by the kitchen and the other will take a couple of cigarettes out of his pack. Then we will get a couple of kitchen matches. You know where your mom keeps the kitchen matches right?"

She nodded and I went on. "So we get the matches, we bring them back up here, and tomorrow we have them in our pocket as we go out to play. No one will know."

"But what if we get caught taking them?" she considered.

"We won't get caught," I told her. "If anyone comes out, we just tell them that we were thirsty and we came out to get a drink of water. We both have pockets in our nightgowns. We put the cigarettes in there and no one will ever think we are not telling the truth."

"Okay," she assessed. "Good plan."

Later that night we waited about an hour and a half after we heard her parents go to bed. We tiptoed out in the darkness of the house with just the light of the street lamp showing through the living room window. As I recall now the sounds that were coming from her parent's bedroom I realize what I didn't know at the time. They were in the middle of love making and quite distracted from anything that we were doing.

30

Confessions from the Pumpkin Patch

There on the end table, where Mr. Tannenbaum always sat was a cigarette pack. Unfortunately it only had three cigarettes in it. I was watching the hall and Gretta had gone to get the cigarettes. The next thing I knew she came tiptoeing back over to me and whispered, "There are only three cigarettes in the pack."

"So," I whispered back, "we only need two."

"But with so few," she continued, "he'll know that someone took them."

"No, he won't," I lectured. "He would probably just think he smoked more than he thought or that your mom borrowed a couple."

"My mom doesn't smoke," she whispered on.

"Look!" I muttered exasperated. "Just get the two cigarettes. If anybody says anything we'll throw them out the window and deny it. Now go on."

Finally, she went back over and took the two cigarettes. Then we were off to the kitchen to get a few matches. Into our pockets they went and we went back to bed with no one the wiser.

After breakfast the next morning, we told Gretta's parents that we were going to go out and ride our bikes.

"Be back by eleven thirty girls. I don't want you to miss lunch," her mom said as we went out the door.

In those days, especially in a small town, no one worried about a couple of teen girls riding bikes around their neighborhoods. It was safe and we played with a certain innocent abandon.

We rode down to the Hetrick Road culvert straight away. We pushed our bikes down the grassy embankment near the culvert and parked them just inside the culvert entrance.

"What do you think it will be like?" Gretta considered as we walked carefully over the rough edges of the culvert by the water.

"I don't know," I said, "but it has got to be good if so many people are doing it."

We reached a place near the center of the culvert, sat down on a couple of basketball-size rocks and took our cigarettes out of our pockets.

"You first," Gretta said as she looked to me for inspiration.

"Okay," I replied cigarette in hand.

I had seen Gretta's father smoke enough that I knew basically what to do. I clutched the cigarette between my fingers, struck the match against a stone and put it to the end of the cigarette as I sucked on the filter. Immediately my throat burned and I heaved a hoarse and growling cough.

"Are you alright?" pleaded Gretta as she placed one hand on my arm.

"I'm fine," I said half-choking. Then I pulled the cigarette back to my lips as I had seen Mr. Tannenbaum do and attempted to make love to it as he would. I drew the smoke into my mouth, foul tasting as it was, opened

31

my lips just slightly and breathed in. The smoke went curling into my lungs and I felt a slight dizziness as I coughed it back out.

"Your turn," I coaxed as I turned to Gretta.

"I don't know," she backtracked. "It doesn't look all that enjoyable the way you do it."

"I'm just starting," I said. "I'll learn how. Come on. Try yours."

She hesitantly pulled the remaining cigarette from her pocket, but after two or three tries she had not been able to light it.

"Here let me," I said as I snatched it from her hands. Within a moment, I lit the cigarette and handed it back to her.

"What do I do?" she reviewed as though she had never seen it done before.

"You've seen your dad smoke your whole life," I said. "Just put it in your mouth and suck on it."

She put the cigarette to her lips and sucked on it like a straw. The smoke went into her mouth and she blew it out as though she had accomplished something grand.

"I didn't cough," she announced.

"That's because you didn't do it right," I said. "You are supposed to draw it into your lungs."

"Why?" she questioned.

"I don't know why," I said, "but if you watch that's what everybody does when they smoke. Look," I went on, "like this." Again, I drew the smoke into my mouth, opened my lips slightly and pulled the air and the smoke through my lips into my lungs. This time, I only barely coughed as I released the smoke. Gretta did as I instructed and then heaved in a gagging cough. I started to giggle.

"Bitch!" she said and I laughed even harder.

"Whore!" I exclaimed as I put the cigarette back to my lips and drew it in like a pro.

Before it was over, we were pretending to be actresses discussing our upcoming movies. In those days, cigarettes were Hollywood-glamorous and many of the big stars smoked on screen and off. It would be many more years before the public would understand them to be more deadly than romantic.

"In my next film," I moaned in a deep sultry voice as I drew the cigarette to my lips, "I'm going to star with Bing Crosby in a little musical dance film called, 'From There to My Titties'."

"Oh really," snapped Gretta, not to be outdone as we were doing our best to be naughty. She put the cigarette to her mouth, popped it in and puffed it back out in a snap. "I'm starring with Marlon Brando in an action

Confessions from the Pumpkin Patch

thriller called, 'Long Road to Pussy Canyon'."

We giggled and carried on long after the cigarettes had burned down to the butts. After they were gone, we picked up sticks and pretended to be smoking as we broke the rules in hilarious abandon.

After that, it was all over for both of us. If we were not yet physically hooked on cigarettes, we were at the least hooked on the novelty, the crime, and the intrigue of the cigarettes. Gretta continued to swipe cigarettes from her dad for a while until it seemed we needed more of them more often. Then we began stealing them from the local market. One of us would act as a distraction as the other would pocket the cigarettes. This went on for a while 'til we found a store where a young clerk caught us one day and said, "Look, I'll sell them to you if you want them, but if I catch you stealing them again, I'm going to call the cops." From that point on we picked up bottles beside the road to redeem for the deposit money and used our allowances to buy cigarettes.

A little over a year later when I had just turned fifteen Mother knocked on the door of my room one night as I was lying in bed studying my history book.

"Lovella, may I come in?" she questioned as she tapped lightly on the door.

"Yes, Mother," I replied and she entered rather sheepishly.

She came and sat on the edge of my bed and said, "I found this stuffed behind the commode." She then held out her hand to reveal a half smoked pack of cigarettes.

"Did you forget where you hid them?" I taunted, knowing full well that she knew they were not hers.

"Lovella," she went on, "I always know where my cigarettes are hidden and besides I haven't smoked in six months now."

"Congratulations," I said, "I know that you wanted so much to quit."

"Don't be coy with me," she continued, "I know this means that you are smoking."

"What of it?" I said as I glared at her over my book.

"You know that I don't want you to smoke," she said long since having realized that she had raised a daughter who was at least just as stubborn as herself.

"Yes," I said leaving the subject open.

"If you are going to quit," she pleaded, "you need to do it now while you are young. The longer you wait the harder it becomes."

"I have no desire to quit, Mother," I crooned as I folded my book and set it aside. "I enjoy it."

"Very well," she said as she rose and walked to the door. "I will place these back where I found them. Please continue to do this privately."

The next morning I lit up a cigarette at the breakfast table, took a long slow drag, and flicked the ash into the saucer of my coffee cup. I watched as Mother continued to nibble at her breakfast as though she hadn't seen a thing. I was so disappointed that she didn't scream.

Chapter 5

By the time I was sixteen, I had read the Kinsey Reports and the Kama Sutra cover to cover. I first discovered the Kinsey Report on male sexual behavior published in 1948 at our local library when I was thirteen. Why it was in a small town library I will never know, and why our stupid librarian allowed a thirteen year old girl to check it out I will never know except that she probably had no idea what it was about. However, as soon as I stumbled on it and pulled it from the shelf I knew that I was on to something. A year or two later, I found the Kinsey report on female sexual behavior.

If I had waited for Mother to talk to me about sex, I would still be waiting. It was never going to happen. When I first got my period at the end of my twelfth year, before I found the books, I was terrified. I rose from the commode after urinating to find it filled with bloody water. I ran to the bathroom door and screamed, "Mother! Mother! Come quick! Please hurry!"

She trotted dutifully through the bathroom door and said in a less than slightly excited tone, "Why dear, what is it?"

Having learned it from Mother, I suppose I was always prone to drama. I grabbed the sleeve of her dress and shouted, "I'm dying, Mother! I must have cancer!"

Now seemingly annoyed she exclaimed, "For Heaven sake, Lovella! What are you talking about?"

"Come see!" I said as I pulled her by the sleeve to the open commode to see the carnage of my urination.

She glanced in, flushed the commode, and said, "Wait here." She then went to her bedroom and returned with a box of feminine pads.

"Here," she said thrusting the box at me, "the instructions are on the box." She then made a controlled exit without another word and went on about her business. I put the commode lid down, sat down and began reading the instructions. There wasn't much to it, no explanation, just how to use the product. I applied it as instructed and went to find Mother. She was in her bedroom mending one of Daddy's shirts.

"Mother?" I questioned handing her back the box of pads. "What is this?"

Karlyle Tomms

"They are feminine protection pads dear. They will keep you from spotting your clothing with blood. Now, go on. I'm busy." She sat the box of pads on the dresser near where she was sitting and went immediately back to her sewing.

"Well Crap!" I thought to myself, "I'm going to have to go to the library!"

It was a lucky thing for me, since I enjoyed reading so much, that our library was only about ten blocks from our house. When I was smaller, Mother would take me there on summer afternoons more as a way of occupying me so that she didn't have to deal with my boredom than anything else. When I was a little older, I would ride my bike there and sometimes read for hours.

I decided that afternoon that I would try to educate myself on what had just happened. I went to the library and began to explore the medical section. I found some books explaining the female reproductive cycle and was satisfied with the knowledge, although I resent to this day that Mother could not have just explained it. The messy process of having to deal with menstruation is the only thing I resent about being a woman.

That was the day, when I was returning one of the books to the shelf, that I happened to glance at a title that indeed intrigued me now that I was suddenly becoming so aware of, and knowledgeable about sex. It was the Kinsey report on male sexual behavior. I took it from the shelf and returned to one of the nearby tables to read.

In one afternoon, I learned more about sex than I had been taught in my previous twelve years combined, and I probably ended up learning more about it than a good many adults of the day. I had never thought of the words heterosexual or homosexual before, but there they were defined in the Kinsey Report. Mr. Kinsey had studied a fairly large population of men and had concluded that most men engage in a variety of sexual activities and many with both men and women. I thought that was very interesting.

I was intrigued by sex, even though I found the idea of Mother and Daddy engaging in such activities to be far-fetched. I could somehow never imagine that Mother would ever consent to having her body penetrated by Daddy's "dirty part" much less allow him to ejaculate into her. Still, I was proof that she had sex, at least once. I also found myself wondering if Daddy had ever engaged in sex with others besides Mother, maybe even men. Maybe that was what those Friday nights with the "boys" was all about. Maybe drinking was just a way to hide it. "No," I thought to myself, "not Daddy. He enjoys drinking too much for it to be anything else."

Confessions from the Pumpkin Patch

At first I thought it was dirty and disgusting but the more I read the more I found myself getting excited about the whole idea of sex and wanting to learn more. I read as much as I could find and when I had exhausted the information available to me, I had to resort back to my more traditional reading pursuits of novels and short stories. I would occasionally re-visit the medical section of the library to see if any new books had come in. Then a couple of years later the library obtained a copy of the Kinsey Report on female sexual behavior and my interest was renewed. I learned that twenty-six percent of females engaged in their first intercourse before the age of fifteen—and I was about to turn sixteen when I came across the information. I learned about female masturbation and decided I would give it a try. When I did, I was hooked.

I made the mistake of trying it the first time just after retiring to bed on a school night. I had read about orgasm, but I had no idea that it would make me feel like my entire body was on a pleasure roller-coaster and that the plummet from the peak would force me to scream. It was only a few seconds after my breath-halting scream that Mother came knocking at, and opened my door. Luckily, I was under the covers as I was recovering from the aftermath of that first climax.

"Good grief, Lovella!" Mother implored, "Are you alright?"

"I'm fine Mother," I panted, "I just had a bad dream."

"Oh, you poor dear," she said as she sat on my bed and put her hand to my cheek.

"I'm fine, Mother, really," I said, just hoping she would go away.

"Well, go back to sleep, dear, and have a better dream this time." She rose and turned to give me a quick glance as she closed the door behind her. I concluded in that moment that Mother must never have had an orgasm. She must have been like some of the women I read about in the report who just didn't ever get there. "What a shame," I thought. I turned over in bed and found myself drifting off to sleep.

I wondered if there might be any information about the history of sex throughout time and I began exploring from another perspective. This was the time I came across the Kama Sutra with all its elaborate drawings of sexual positions. I soon concluded that there must be something even more wonderful about the actual physical contact than mere masturbation and imagination could grant me. From that point on, when I was fifteen, I began seeking a way to find out.

There was a boy who lived up the street from me by the name of Tommy Smith. The family had moved in about a year before my fifteenth birthday. Tommy was about a year older than me and not bad for looks as teen boys

Karlyle Tomms

go. He didn't have the usual face of a teen boy pock-marked by acne. There was the occasional zit, but nothing too gross. His hair was blond and curly, his jaw square, and his eyes were hazel. On some days, I would see him out mowing the lawn shirtless and wearing worn jeans. I decided that he would be the object of my planned seduction.

One sunny weekend afternoon, I heard a lawn mower in the distance and decided to investigate. I told Mother and Daddy that I was going to take a walk around the neighborhood and I then strolled directly toward the Smith house. On the way there, I unbuttoned the top two buttons of my blouse to reveal cleavage, which I had in ample supply as those parts had matured early. When I got there, I leaned over the front gate of their white picket fence and watched as Tommy mowed.

He was intent on his work and it was a few minutes before he happened to look up and see that I was leaning over obviously gazing at him. He stopped the mower and came to the fence.

"Hello, Lovella." he said as he wiped the sweat from his brow with a handkerchief that he had tucked inside his back pocket. He had met me when he first moved in as Mother had dragged me to the Smith house with a cake and a neighborhood welcome. Since then, there had been little more than the occasional hello in passing between neighbors.

"What's going on?" he questioned as he stood there squinting in the summer sun.

"Oh nothing," I said. "I just heard the mower and thought I would come down and watch you mow." As I said this, I deliberately scanned down his body to his crotch and back up to his waiting eyes.

He gave a sheepish grin and said, "You must be really bored."

"Not so much bored as interested," I said as I brushed my hair back using all five fingers to comb it down to the last strand. "I thought you might show me your—technique."

His face went bright red as I caught his eyes locking for a moment on my cleavage. "Well," he said surly knowing full well my intentions, "I don't know that there is much technique to show. I just push it back and forth till I'm done."

"I'll bet you do," I said only slightly under my breath, yet almost so silently he couldn't hear it. Then I twisted my body upward to give him a better look between my breasts and said, loud and clear, "Fascinating — I'm looking forward to seeing you push it back and forth until you're done."

"Uh, okay." He gave a nervous laugh.

"Tommy, come here." I said as I curled my finger. "I have a question I need to ask."

Confessions from the Pumpkin Patch

He walked directly over to the fence and stopped.

Closer," I whispered, as I searched his face with my hungry eyes.

He leaned over the fence and I breathed a whisper into his ear, "Have you ever had sex?"

"Uh. Ha. " He leaned back embarrassed. "Uh, well—uh—yeah."

"Liar," I said tauntingly as I curled my finger again calling his ear back to my lips.

This time he looked to the left and right before leaning over the fence, suddenly afraid he might get caught knowing that the increasing bulge in his pants might reveal what he was thinking. Then he leaned back over and this time I whispered, "Do you want to have sex with me?"

"Oh Jeez!" he sighed as though he had just had the breath knocked out of him. "Jeez!" he sighed again as he did a little squirm where he stood. "Uh—yeah—uh—." He nervously looked around as though the sex police were about to spring from behind a tree and arrest him for having lascivious thoughts. "Uh—well—yeah—uh—," he continued nervously, finally culminating in, "When?"

"When you finish your mowing take a shower. I'll be waiting under the Hetrick Road culvert." I grinned at him as I turned and pranced away knowing full well that he was watching my swaying ass until I was out of sight.

I had already stashed a blanket and a pillow under the culvert. I sat there on a stone smoking until I heard him call a soft and questioning, "Hello?" from the other end of the culvert.

"Hello," I called back and he followed my voice to the middle of the culvert.

I put the cigarette out as he sat down beside me and started to speak. He didn't have time to get the words out before I grabbed the back of his head and kissed him. I felt him start to pull back in a startled resistance and then I felt him relax into the kiss as his hand moved over my breast. We kissed a long and lingering kiss when he pulled back with an anxious whisper, "I—uh—I don't want you to get pregnant."

"I have another week before my period," I said. "I think we're safe."

With that he began unbuttoning my blouse with nervous hunger as we moved over to the blanket. I had taken the liberty to unfasten my bra before he got there. I didn't want fumbling hands to interfere with the moment. The bra was soon away and his mouth was on my breast as he pushed his firm erection against my thigh. It seemed like an eternity before we were both disrobed and then he pressed his penis first against my opening and then pop, it went inside me. I winced in a brief moment of pain, which was quickly replaced by the pleasure of flesh against flesh as he pushed his hips to my pelvis. There could not have been more than six or eight thrusts of his hips before he suddenly moaned and fell in a lump on top of me. He didn't move. At first I didn't know what was happening. I kissed his cheek and undulated my hips against him and he then rolled over on his back beside me. I became quickly aware, that was it. He had climaxed and it was over. No roller-coaster of pleasure for me, no lying to Mother about having a bad dream. The roller-coaster had barely started to click up the first elevation when the ride ended. My imagination had been infinitely better.

"Wow," he said, half panting. "That was wonderful. I never knew it would feel so good to be inside a girl."

I propped my head up on one elbow and said, "I'm glad you liked it. It was a bit disappointing for me."

"Disappointing?" he queried.

"Yes," I said. "You had a climax. I never reached mine."

"Wow," he said in near total ignorance. "You mean girls cum, too?"

"Well, of course girls cum," I said as I poked a finger into his chest playfully. "Why would we want to have sex if it didn't feel good?"

"I don't know," he responded. "I guess I never thought of it. My dad said the main reason a woman has sex is to have kids. You don't need to cum for that."

"Do you think that was the reason I came to your house this morning?" I interrogated him. "Do you think I have acted like someone who wants to have a kid?"

"Yeah, I know," he said as he looked around the culvert. "It's a dumb idea, isn't it?"

I lay there in silence and looked at him. He looked back at me then right into my eyes and said, "So what do I need to do to get you to cum?"

"Are you up for round two?" I smiled as I stroked his face.

"Maybe after a nap," he said as he pulled me down beside him.

We fell asleep together and then sometime later I awoke to his kisses as his hands were running down my body. The sun had begun to set and the culvert was near dark. This time when we made love he lasted a bit longer before he climaxed but he didn't stop pushing after he climaxed and shortly afterward I climaxed too. It wasn't quite the reeling pleasure of my roller-coaster orgasm from masturbation, but it was nice. Afterward we dressed. I rolled up the blanket and we walked together to the opening of the culvert. I turned to him and said, "We better walk back separately. Wait here for a while and give me a head start." "Okay," he said and I gave him a quick peck on the lips before I turned to climb up the

Confessions from the Pumpkin Patch

embankment to the street.

When I was almost to the top I heard him call: "Lovella?"

I turned back to him. "Yes."

"This won't be the last time will it?" He looked up at me with a pleading look on his face.

"No," I said as I smiled. "It won't be the last time."

Then I climbed the rest of the way up to the street and glanced back at him one more time before I walked home.

Chapter 6

The next time I met Tommy in the culvert I brought a copy of the Kama Sutra.

"Oh my god, Lovella!" he said as he thumbed through the illustrations, "where did you get this?"

"From the library," I said.

He turned to me in astonishment.

"From the school library?" he asked.

"No silly," I said, "I checked it out at the public library."

"Still," he said amazed. "This is like—I can't believe they would have anything like this at even the public library."

"The book is thousands of years old," I said. "It is from ancient India."

"Dang!" he said not realizing his oxymoron. "They sure were progressive thousands of years ago."

"What do you think of it?" I said as I leaned over his shoulder.

He released a long deep breath "I mean—" he said. "Is it even possible to get in some of these positions?"

"I am certainly willing to try," I said as I caressed his arm. "But we have got to be a little more careful."

"Careful?" he inquired.

"Yeah," I said, "about not getting me pregnant. Have you ever heard of a condom?"

"A what?" He looked puzzled.

"A rubber," I said.

"Well, yeah," he replied. "My dad told me about them. We kind of had this father and son talk and he told me that I was probably going to want to have sex and that I would probably want to use protection, and—"

"Could your dad get us some?" I questioned eagerly.

"Well, I—I guess I could ask him," he said seeming embarrassed at the idea of asking his father.

"Great!" I said. "Ask him and next time we meet here bring the condoms."

I started to walk out of the culvert.

"Take that home and read it," I said, over my shoulder, "but be sure to get it back to me cause it's checked out to me and I don't want a fine—or my Mother finding out that I've read it."

Confessions from the Pumpkin Patch

"But wait," he called after me. "Aren't we going to do it?"

"Not today," I called back. "When you get the condoms."

I knew that would give him a little more motivation.

Apparently Tommy's dad considered it to be a teen boy's rite of passage to have sex, and he had no problem supplying us with condoms, although he did not know just who Tommy was having sex with.

Soon Tommy and I were meeting in the culvert a couple of times a week 'til the weather started to get cold again. By the time autumn rolled around, he had not only learned several wonderful positions, he had learned to hold himself off until after my orgasm. It was that summer of my fifteenth year that I learned I could have more than one orgasm. In fact, on a good day, I might have three or four, and Tommy became an increasingly adept lover.

We met in the culvert on a Sunday afternoon in late September with full intentions of making love all afternoon, but a cold front was moving in and by the time we had barely gotten started, the temperature was falling off into the low fifties. I could use some stupid cliché' like "we made our own heat," but the fact is, it was too damn cold to have sex. He was intent regardless of the cold but I finally made him stop.

"I'm too cold," I said, "We need to go someplace warm."

He began pondering but to no avail. Both our parents were home and there was really no other option available to us. Tommy was about to turn seventeen at the time and had gotten his driver's license over the summer.

"Why don't you go borrow your father's car?" I speculated. "And then we could drive somewhere and make love while we leave the motor running."

"I can't do that," he said. "What would I tell my dad?"

"Tell him you just want to practice," I insisted. "He knows you have sex. You don't have to tell him exactly what it is that you need to practice."

"He doesn't like for me to have the car out by myself in the evening," Tommy said as he pulled his pants back on.

I had started to dress as well, no longer being able to tolerate the chill bumps rising across my back. Finally, I looked at him. "You know," I said, shivering as I began, "if we were dating you would probably be able to take the car on weekends and we could have it for sex."

He looked at me startled. "Well, I don't want to take the car just for sex," he said as he eyed me up and down.

"So I suppose I'm just for sex then," I snapped. "I'm not the kind of girl you would want to date even though you are the boy who took my virginity."

43

"That's not what I meant," he replied. "But I thought that was what you meant, that all you wanted was sex."

"Sex is wonderful," I said. "But I like you too. I mean I was using you just because I wanted to try sex but I think there is more to us now than that."

"You were using me just because you wanted to try sex!" he snarled. "What kind of girl does that?"

"This kind," I snapped back as I poked my finger into my chest. "What's wrong with that? What were you doing it for, and don't tell me it was for love. The bottom line is that you wanted to get laid as bad as I did."

"Yeah," he replied, "but it's different. I'm a guy."

"So, does that really make a difference?" I retorted. "What's wrong with a girl wanting sex too? Oh, I forgot, you didn't even think women could have an orgasm 'til you met me. In fact you didn't know crap about anything. I might not have ever had sex before, but I taught you more about sex this summer than most guys learn in a lifetime!"

He dropped his head and then looked up at the ceiling of the culvert which was actually, when he was standing, only about an inch away from the top of his head. "You're right," he said. "I guess it's not fair. I like you. I enjoy having sex with you but I don't know that I love you. I mean, if we hadn't done this, I might even have asked you out sometime. You're pretty, but it just feels like we got the cart before the horse here, like we did it all backwards. That's what I get for being in such a hurry."

I sighed and looked away. "I guess that's what I get too," I said.

There was a very long and unpleasant silence when finally he spoke.

"So, this dating thing, how do we do that?"

I turned back to him and smiled. "Why don't you come to my house sometime this week and ask me out in front of my parents?"

"Do you think that will work?" he asked.

"Either it will or it won't," I said, "but that's what I would suggest."

We walked hand in hand out of the culvert and I walked home ahead of him.

On Tuesday evening about 6:00 PM, there was a knock on our front door. Mother was in the kitchen cleaning up as we had just finished dinner. I was sitting in my chair in the living room with my nose in a book. Daddy went to the door. When he opened it there stood Tommy nervous as cat.

"Good evening, Mr. Fuchs. I'm Tommy Smith," he said. "May I come in?"

"Certainly, young man, come on in."

Confessions from the Pumpkin Patch

Daddy ushered him in and motioned to one of the chairs for him to sit. Then Daddy sat back down on his end of the sofa. By this time Mother, hearing the commotion, had come from the kitchen with a dish towel in her hand.

"Oh, hello," she said politely. "You're the Smith boy aren't you?"

"Yes, Ma'am, Tommy Smith," he replied as he fiddled with the zipper on his jacket.

"May I get you some iced tea?" Mother said as she darted her eyes back and forth between us

"No thank you," replied Tommy. "I don't want to take up your whole evening. I just have a question I would like to ask and then I'll be on my way."

"You've got a question?" Daddy interjected as though he hadn't just heard what Tommy had just said.

"Yes, sir," Tommy replied as he fixed his gaze on Daddy and tried not to look at me.

"You have a question for me?" Daddy popped. "Is it about peanut butter? I can get you a free case from the factory you know."

Daddy tried to give everyone peanut butter. We had so much of it in our house when I was growing up that I'm surprised my tongue is not permanently stuck to the roof of my mouth.

"Ah, no, well ah, yes, but not about peanut butter."

Tommy's anxiety was obvious. It seemed as though he realized that my parents somehow knew what we had been doing all summer.

"Well, it's a question for you and for Lovella if you don't mind."

Mother smiled suddenly realizing that he was probably going to ask me out.

"What would you like to ask Lovella?" she said.

This was the kind of proper behavior and formality that delighted Mother which is precisely why I asked him to do it.

"I was wondering," said, Tommy, his voice half cracking with anxiety, "if you don't mind." He darted eyes to both parents. "And if Lovella doesn't mind," he said glancing back at me, "if I might take Lovella out on a date some time?"

I resisted the urge to taunt Mother by shouting, "Date me when you've already fucked me?"

"Lovella is only sixteen," Daddy exclaimed. "Too young to date."

"At least I'm sixteen, Daddy," I spouted, "and a lot more mature than most girls my age."

Daddy snickered. "That you are, Pumpkin Patch."

He turned back to Tommy. "How old are you?"

45

"Sir, I'm seventeen," Tommy said as he adjusted himself upright in the chair.

"So you're about the same age," said Daddy as he turned to Mother. "Drucella, what do you think?"

Mother was leaning against the door facing us as she turned to Tommy. "You know I don't know much about you, Tommy. I recall that when your family moved in Lovella and I brought a cake down to welcome you to the neighborhood but I have never gotten an opportunity to get to know your family."

"The cake was delicious, Mrs. Fuchs. Thank you." Tommy continued to fiddle with the zipper of his jacket. "We enjoyed it very much."

"Well," said Mother in her air of superiority, "Your Mother was very polite, but I didn't get the feeling that she wanted to get to know her neighbors."

"My mother is very shy," said Tommy.

I caught his eye and mouthed the words, "Don't lie."

He caught himself. "Well, she is shy around some people anyway. I'm sure she would like you very much if she got the opportunity to know you better."

Mother stared him down. "Do your parents know that you are asking Lovella out?"

It began to look as though he was going to tear the zipper loose from the fabric when he finally tossed it aside and clasped his hands together.

"They said it was okay for me to date," he said finally, "but they don't know that I planned to ask Lovella out specifically."

"How did you two meet?" interrogated Mother.

"We met when you took them the cake," I interjected quickly. "Besides I like to go by their house when I take my walks."

"Lovella," Mother said firmly. "I asked the question to Mr. Smith, not you."

"Well, she does walk by my house," said Tommy, "and I work in the yard a lot, and we just said hello one day, not much more than that, and she seems nice and she's pretty."

"What do you think, John?" Mother said as she looked over at Daddy cutting Tommy off in mid-sentence.

"Oh, it would be fine with me," Daddy replied.

Mother looked directly back at Tommy. "Tell me about your family, Tommy," she said as she glared down at him.

"My dad works at the cattle feed mill on the south side of town and my mom is a stenographer," he replied.

"Oh, your mother is a secretary?" Mother continued. "Where does she

Confessions from the Pumpkin Patch

work?"

"She works for one of the managers of Nathan's retail down town," Tommy replied.

"And what does your father do at the feed mill?" Mother interrogated further.

By this time, I was getting boiling mad at her. This had nothing to do with whether it was okay for me to go out with Tommy. This had to do with Mother's socialite-wanna-be hypocrisy as well as a way of pestering me.

"My dad is in charge of shipping and receiving," Tommy said as he looked around the room to see if anyone else had an interest.

"That's very nice," said Mother satisfying her social fang. "How about we have your parents over for dinner this Friday night and we will discuss allowing you to date Lovella."

It was all I could do to resist bolting from my chair and strangling her down to the floor until she could no longer breathe. Friday night had nothing to do with me going out with Tommy either. It was another one of Mother's attempts to make sure Daddy was home instead of out drinking while she sucked up to whoever she could suck up to in the community and it was about being in control.

"Now, now, Drucella," Daddy began to chirp. "I have probably got plans for Friday night, and it is probably too late in the week to be changing plans."

"Don't you think you could make an exception for Lovella, dear?" she sang in her sarcastic little tone.

"Well, now, you know I love my daughter, but—"

I chimed in quickly. "Mother, don't you think some other evening of the week would be nice. What about Thursday or maybe even Sunday?"

"Oh, Lovella," she crooned, "you know that Friday is the most optimal time for working people to visit. It leaves the rest of the weekend open and doesn't tax one during the work week."

Tommy must have realized something was going on because he said, "I think Friday is mom and dad's bowling night."

"Wonderful!" Mother turned back to him, her demon eyes glaring brightly. "Perhaps we could join them. Wouldn't it be nice to go bowling, John?"

Daddy, cornered as usual, began his protest. "Oh Lord, I don't even remember the last time I went bowling. I don't even know if I remember how to hold the ball. I—Uh—"

By this time I'd had enough. I stood up and yelled, "Stop it!" Then I stormed over to Mother and screamed, "How dare you turn this into

47

another one of your manipulations of Daddy! This is not about you! This is not about Daddy! This is about me! Me! Mother! You have no right to try to hold Tommy's parents hostage to your conniving just because he wants to go out with me!" I then stormed off to my room and slammed the door. About twenty minutes later, there was a knock at my door.

"Leave me alone!" I yelled.

From the other side of the door I heard Daddy's voice.

"Punkin' Patch, now I don't want to intrude on your time, but I would like to come in for a little while, if that's okay?"

If it had been Mother, and I had suspected that it was, I would have wedged a chair against the door and set fire to my own bed before I would have let her in. She probably knew that, so she sent Daddy.

I got up and unlocked the door and then threw myself back onto the bed. "What is it, Daddy?" I inquired as I looked at him. If nothing else, I always knew that Daddy would rather cut off his own hand than to hurt me.

"Well, sweetheart," he began. "We sent Tommy home and then your mother and I had a talk. You know you hurt her feelings there, don't you?"

"Daddy, I don't care if I hurt her feelings," I puffed in reply. "She doesn't seem to worry about hurting my feelings."

"Now, now, Punkin'," he pleaded. "Your mother loves you. You know that she does. I mean you know she is a bit stern and proper sometimes, but you know she loves you."

"I guess," I said, not really wanting to have the conversation.

"Well," he went on, "your mother and I talked it over and we decided that it is okay if you want to go out with this boy. We just have a few rules to follow that's all."

I deliberately avoided the bubbly and probably expected response of, "Ooooooh, you mean it Daddy? Oh, boy!" Instead I said, "Thank you, Daddy. What are the rules?"

"Well, Punkin' Patch," he continued. "No dating on school nights, be in by 11:00 PM, and no going up to Climax Point."

Climax Point, oddly enough, was the local place where lovers went to park and make out. The police would usually cruise through there several times a night. I suspected that was more due to their own voyeuristic needs than to catch anyone breaking the law.

"I can live with that, Daddy," I said as I gave him a hug.

The following Saturday night Tommy picked me up at 6:00 PM. He took me out for a burger and we went directly to the drive-in movie. He parked on the far right side in the back where we made out for much of the movie

Confessions from the Pumpkin Patch

and climbed over into the back seat of his father's car to finish it off.

The drive-in movie seemed to work perfectly except that I had to get a summary of each movie from one of my friends before I went home because Mother would inevitably question me about what I had seen.

Somehow, however, our frequency didn't seem to be enough. It was only once a week after all and we had started out having sex two or three times a week. So we began to look for other ways to get together and we became increasingly more daring.

Mother developed a new habit of going grocery shopping every Saturday afternoon. I would sneak Tommy into the house while Daddy was out in the shed and we would make love in my room without either of them knowing about it. This was fine, except that we would usually go out to the movies on Saturday night, so it didn't leave much space between one episode of love-making and another.

We had sex in his parent's garage a couple of times. Then over the summer, we went back to the culvert but that had lost its appeal after we got used to having sex in a nice bed. Nonetheless, we sought the novel. We did it in a cemetery where he bent me over the headstone of an old man who died in 1877. We did it in a changing room at a clothing store. Then, one late afternoon in July while Daddy was at work and Mother was away at some ladies luncheon or something, we did it in the laundry room of our house.

Tommy came by right after Mother had left for her luncheon. I stuffed Mother's wringer-washer full and set it to run. In those old washers, when the agitator swished the cloths back and forth, it created a very nice vibration. Tommy had me pushed up against the washer in a standing position. I had my legs wrapped around him as we used the combination of the vibrations of the washer and the thrust of our love-making to achieve our excitement. We were moaning and panting furiously when suddenly the door to the laundry room opened and there stood Mother in her perfect dress. Her face dropped immediately from smiling curiosity to a look of abject horror. She gasped as one of her white-gloved hands flew up to her mouth. She tried to shout my name but hyperventilation hit her before she could get it out, "Lov—Ell—a— Fa—Ah!—Ha!—Fa—Fa— a—a—!"

I watched gleefully as she fell, panting, away from the door collapsing into a chair at the kitchen table, which was just past the laundry room door. Tommy had come to a full stop and turned to look as well. Hanging on with one arm around his shoulders, I grabbed his chin with my one free hand and twisted it back toward me.

"Finish!" I panted.

"But your mom," he said

"Finish!" I demanded again. "This is the last time she'll let me see you. Finish!"

He began to thrust again, and in only a few more strokes I reached the most exhilarating climax of my life right there in front of Mother. Tommy's nervous whimpering cum briefly followed.

Mother had of course refused to look and had turned white from hyperventilation. Her eyes squinted and she turned her head toward the floor in the opposite direction of the laundry room door.

After we dressed, Tommy walked quietly past Mother and out the back door. I went and pulled a chair up knee-to-knee with Mother. She was still reeling from her panic attack and fanning herself with one glove she had removed.

"Are you okay?" I said feigning concern.

She looked up and horror had turned to rage. Abruptly, she stuck a pointed finger in my face and shouted with purple veined, jaw-clenching growl. "Lovella Fuchs, how dare you desecrate our home and my reputation like this?!"

I sat back calmly watching the havoc, content in my power, smug in the knowledge that I had shaken her to her core. "Desecrate is a strong word don't you think, Mother?"

"I swear you are a demon!" she shouted. "I don't know how I even gave birth to you."

"That's easy, Mother," I said smugly, "you gave birth to me by doing the same thing that Tommy and I were doing in there. You fucked my Daddy."

"Don't you even compare yourself to me!" she screamed. "You cannot compare that—that—sin to the sanctity of the marital bed."

Now, at seventeen, I found that I had less and less fear of Mother and I cared less and less for what she thought. I smiled as I said, "Sex is sex whether it is sanctioned by the church or not, Mother. Fucking is fucking."

The veins in her neck swelled to at least twice their normal size. For a moment, I thought she was going to slap me. Then I thought she might have a stroke—and for a moment, I almost wished that she would.

"I forbid you to ever see that boy again! EVER!" she raged. "He will never set foot in this house again, and you will have nothing to do with him! Do you understand?!"

"Yes, Mother," I said calmly and confidently. "I understand."

It didn't matter. I knew I would do as I pleased when I pleased. There might be only a few obstacles that would ever stop me, and Mother would never again be one of them.

Chapter 7

To say that I was grounded after the laundry room incident would be an understatement. It was three months before Mother would allow me out the front door without her escort except for school. I saw Tommy at school and explained to him how Mother was taking it. I told him I didn't expect him to wait. After all, he was going to graduate that year anyway and I think that both of us finally had to admit that it really was just about the sex.

Gretta had known everything all along. In a way, she was envious. I half believed there were times she wished she could join us. I regret that I never thought of it at the time. I knew she found Tommy attractive and soon I caught the two of them stealing glances at one another between classes. It wasn't long before he asked her out. It was no bother to me. I was done. One adventure down, a whole world to explore.

I could have marched out or sneaked out any time I wanted but I abided by the rules of the grounding, if for no other reason than to give Mother the illusion that she still maintained some control. As soon as Mother would let me go out again, I took Gretta to the public library and introduced her to the books. At first she fanned through the Kama Sutra with the same wide-eyed fascination that Tommy had when he first saw it. She pointed at pictures and bit her knuckles. She giggled and blushed. But with me as her guide and Tommy teaching her what I had taught him, she was soon just as hooked on sex as I was. But there was a huge difference in the way her relationship with Tommy started and the way that mine did. There was something there much deeper than the physical, and I could see that they were falling in love.

Gretta wasn't one to get in trouble like I was. I suppose, perhaps, because she had a good relationship with her parents and she tended to do pretty much as she was told. She would never get caught fucking a boy in her mother's laundry room. Besides, she never had a need to piss anyone off the way that I needed to piss off Mother. She cherished her time with Tommy, whereas I cherished the sex.

Tommy calmed down quite a bit after the laundry room incident as well. Maybe that is because I no longer had my evil influence over him. Of course, his parents never found out what happened. Mother was too embarrassed to tell anyone, not even Daddy. She told him I was grounded

Karlyle Tomms

for stealing a pack of cigarettes from the market. I knew that she wouldn't tell. She thought that keeping me away from Tommy was a punishment for me. I never let her know otherwise. She also knew me well enough to know that I had been the instigator, not Tommy. Yes, everyone's reputation was safe—even Mother's.

By the time Tommy graduated, he and Gretta had dated several months. That next summer she dropped out of school and married him. He went to work for the feed mill where his father worked and Gretta got a job as a waitress in a local truck stop. Tommy's dad bought him a blood-red Chrysler Imperial convertible for his graduation gift, and when they married, he co-signed for them to buy a little house. Before she was eighteen, Gretta was pregnant. I couldn't help looking at it all and thinking what a waste.

They were doing what most kids did in those days, they got married and started a family. I had no such plans. I had dreams. I had exploring to do. I had read books of far-away places and I wanted to see them all. Gretta and Tommy could have the small town life, the scraping by, and raising kids. I wanted none of it. I would see the world. I would get a college degree and I might even get a job at the Kinsey Institute, but not necessarily in that order. I knew that I was too smart to be stuck in a rocking chair with a baby on my tit. My plan was to go to college as soon as I graduated high school. I assumed that one must have an education in order to see the world. It certainly wouldn't hurt to be well-versed if I was going to hob-nob about the globe. Mother, of course, thought I should do as Gretta; meet a nice boy, get married and have babies. However, she would have wanted to handpick the boy herself and make sure that he lived up to her delusional standards of quality and future promise. The mere fact that Mother wanted me to get married was enough to turn me against it. So, despite her nagging me about all the opportunities to "have a nice, secure home" in my "own little hometown," I applied to several different colleges and took my entrance exams early in my senior year of high school.

My senior year was dull. For one thing, if a boy asked me out, Mother would do everything to sabotage it unless he was from a "reputable family." If he met her standards, she would try to shove him down my throat all the way to his shoe laces. After all this time, after knowing that I despised every idea she ever had for me, she still labored under the delusion that I would come around to her way of thinking. She ran off more boys from "reputable families" by pushing them at me than she did the less-acceptable boys who she deliberately tried to run away. When she liked a boy, you would have thought she was trying to sell him her prized

52

Confessions from the Pumpkin Patch

cow. The boys simply thought she was weird, and I didn't really care. Besides, I would find a way to screw any boy who struck my fancy. They were lucky to experience my skills and, as time went on, my sexual talents expanded.

Of course, I got a reputation. Boys talk, don't they? I even enjoyed having the reputation of a slut around school. I relished the idea that some little whisper of it would eventually make its way to Mother's ears and her torment would linger. However, I wasn't a slut. I wouldn't sleep with just any one. I just slept with everyone I wanted. By the time I graduated there was not a single boy in that school I didn't have if I wanted him. The others were beggars and wishers. The more they tried to get up my skirt, the more I took pleasure in tossing them to the curb. There were some who would stand back and act aloof, pretending that they didn't want me. But let's face it, I was beautiful and they were horny little high school boys. Acting aloof was something that none of them could pull off very well, or for very long. I always knew who wanted me. If I wanted them, I would pick the time when I was ready. Then they never knew what hit them.

Ultimately, school was a bore. I couldn't wait to get my diploma and get out of there. Despite everything else, my grades were excellent and I managed to get a scholarship to Penn State University where I planned to major in reproductive biology, of course. I had found my muse and my muse was between my legs. I was determined to learn everything I could possibly learn about it. I learned later that reproductive biology wasn't really an option, so I had to settle for plain old biology.

When Mother discovered my intended major she nearly had a heart attack, but she consoled herself with the illusion that it could count as a pre-med degree. She then began telling everyone she knew, those she only half knew, and many she had never previously met, that I was going to be doctor.

I grew sick of hearing her bantering over the phone. "Oh yes, yes, our daughter, Lovella, is going to Penn this fall. She is going to be a doctor. Oh yes, we are sooooooo proud of her."

One day I sat in the chair across from the telephone and deliberately wore no panties under my skirt. I watched as she was cooing over my upcoming medical degree and waited for a glance in my direction. As soon as it came, I spread my legs and flashed the muff-dragon full in her face. It roared silently from between my legs and had the exact frightening result I had hoped it would have. She didn't quite scream but the shrill undertone of her gasp caused a shift in the conversation.

"Oh, nothing," she whimpered as she shook her scornful finger in my

Karlyle Tomms

direction.

The muff-dragon flared and roared again! I even added my own sound effects this time. "Rooaar!" I exclaimed as I reached down and parted the dragon's lips. I was barely able to contain my laughter.

She gasped again in her disgust, angrily whispering as she clamped her palm over the mouthpiece, "Stop it!" Then she returned to her call. "Oh, I'm fine, really. It's nothing. I sat on a bobby-pin." She then held her hand over the phone again and in a shout-whisper exclaimed, "Lovella! Stop that nonsense this instant!"

The muff-dragon could not be contained and soon I was laughing hysterically. When she finally made an excuse and hung up the phone she shouted, "Lovella Fuchs! Do you have one single solitary ounce of decency in you!? What if your father had walked in?"

On one hand she wanted to throttle me, or ground me forever, but on the other hand, I was going to college to be a doctor.

"I think that Daddy would have been quite amused, Mother," I smiled. "Where is your sense of humor?"

"That is not the least bit funny!" she growled.

"Daddy told me that he was proud of me," I said. "He told me, just me, not the whole town, not everyone he thought would possibly listen, he said, 'Pumpkin Patch. I'm so proud I could pop, or did he say, poop? Either way, he told me he was proud of me."

"I might be proud of you too!" she stammered, "if you didn't act like such an infidel all the time!"

"Infidel? That's a very strong word, Mother, Mommy," I continued. "Anyway, Daddy said he wished that he was as smart as me and I told him, 'Daddy, you are as smart as me or Mother or anyone else. Just because you didn't go to college doesn't mean that you aren't smart.' "

"Yes," she said, crossing sides, "I've always tried to convince your father that he was meant for something greater."

"There you go again," I said.

"There I go again, what?" She actually looked puzzled.

I sat up in the chair, crossed my legs, and adjusted my posture into a lady-like position. "You really don't get it, do you, Mother? You honestly, in your heart of hearts, don't understand."

A revelation had just hit me.

"All this time, I thought you were just being a bitch, but you really believe this shit. You honestly have thought all these years that you could make Daddy into something he's not. I guess we really are from different worlds aren't we? I love Daddy for who he is. I have no need to make him into anything."

Confessions from the Pumpkin Patch

The puzzlement on her face expanded as she stood there in silence.

Finally, I said, "Go on, Mother. Tell all your friends I'm going to medical school. Take an ad out in the paper if you want to. It's okay. I get it. It's okay. You think that one day something is going to happen to make you finally feel good about yourself, but rather than trying to change yourself, you have tried to change your family."

She turned and walked out of the room looking like a Neanderthal who had just discovered a working television in the woods. It was beyond her.

Mother kept doing what Mother always did and she was determined that I was going to meet the right young man and we would all live happily ever after, or at least she would. She must have put an ad in the paper: "Wanted, young men between the ages of sixteen and eighteen to annoy my daughter. Must be from a good, upstanding, worthy family, and it's a plus if you are ugly."

By the time spring rolled around all the preparations were going into graduation. I had senior photos taken and Mother picked her favorite. We bought class rings and ordered caps and gowns. I just went along with it. Whatever she wanted, I accepted. Then there was senior prom.

At least six weeks before the prom, Mother began asking me if I had a date. The problem was that boys were not as likely to ask out the girl who had rocked their world sexually. Instead, they were looking for "Little Miss Sweet and Pretty." I didn't fit the bill, not that I wasn't pretty enough, or could have the manners if I wanted to, but I was the girl they fucked. I was the practice model they used to learn the ropes while they were looking for a virgin.

Not only had I matured early sexually, but I had matured early mentally and physically. By the time I made it to my senior year I needed a double-D bra to carry around the load I was packing. I still had a nice size waist of 28 inches but the average prom dress just didn't seem to be made for me. I was taller than most girls at 5'10", and my feet, unfortunately, were large enough that I had to start special-ordering shoes. Mother said I must have gotten the height from Uncle Walter on her side of the family. Lord knows, I didn't get it from Daddy's side. I was a big-beautiful, big-busted girl, and I just didn't think there was a prom dress out there for me, nor did I care.

Nonetheless, Mother was determined that I was going to be the "Belle of the Ball" during senior prom. She began dragging me to dress shops and insisting that I could go to the prom even if I didn't have a date. On the rare occasion that there actually was a dress I could wear, it was hideous. Once she made me put on this baby-pink floral thing with enough lace and ruffles to construct a commercial fishing net. Despite the fact that there were so few that actually did fit, still she beamed when I walked out of the dressing room. "Oooooooh—darling—you—look—stunning!"

"Oh, stop it, Mother!" I exclaimed. "I look like Little Ms. Muffett in her damned Easter dress. All we need is a tuffet and a spider!"

"Oh, no, no, no, no, honey. Don't be like thaaaaat," she cooed as she glanced around to see if anyone had heard me say damned. "Why, when we do your hair and make-up, that dress will make you look like the princess that you are."

"Mother," I snarled, "you are going to make me puke. I am not wearing this dress!"

"But, honey," she continued to coo, "I hate to say it but you are a little hard to fit, and we have looked at so many dresses, and this one is really very, very pretty." She grabbed the sleeve of a woman who happened to be passing by. "Excuse me. I was just wondering if I could get your opinion."

The woman turned around half-stunned and then collected herself. "Yes? What?"

Mother pulled her in my direction, "Don't you think my daughter looks just absolutely stunning in this dress? She said half pinching the woman's arm.

"Mother!" I snapped, "that's a leading question and totally unfair. Besides, I look like a cartoon whore."

The woman was now acting quite nervous, realizing that she had just been pulled into a family argument. Mother completely ignored me and kept her focus on the woman. "Go on," she pleaded, "Your honest opinion. How does my daughter look in this dress?"

The nervous woman darted her eyes searching for an escape, "Well, I, well—"

"No, please," Mother continued to plead. "Honestly, what do you think?"

The woman shored up her courage, "Well, the dress is, well, it's a bit frumpy looking, don't you think?"

I laughed out loud. "You see, Mother!" I proclaimed between giggles, "I'm not going to the prom. I'm going to meet Shirley Temple for candy-wandy, and then we are going to go pick up lollypop sailors and dance a little jig on the pier."

Mother looked at the woman dismissively, "Thank you for your opinion," she said politely but tensely, "I believe you are right."

The woman walked away and Mother turned to me with one of her glares. I was still laughing while I pranced in the awful thing in front of the mirror. I tried to ignore her but she walked over to me, leaned into my

Confessions from the Pumpkin Patch

face, and whispered crossly, "Alright Lovella. What do you want me to do? We have been to every shop in three towns and you have found nothing that either you or I can agree on."

I turned to her and smiled. "Mother, I don't have to go to the prom. I don't care. This seems like it is more important to you than it is to me."

"Well, it should be important to you too," she said as she fluffed her hair in the mirror and straightened her collar. "This is one of the most important events of your life, of any girl's life. Lovella, in just a few months you are going to go away to college and then after that only the Lord knows where you will end up. You may never see these kids again and you have grown up with them. The prom, the prom—" She searched for words. "The prom is a milestone in life, a memory maker, an unforgettable moment in time."

She took my hand and led me to a chair. Then she sat across from me and leaned in.

"Here it comes," I thought, "the motherly talk." I was right.

"Lovella, honey," she smiled as she patted my hand. "A prom is so much more important than a dance. It is a rite of passage and I think just as important as your graduation. It says that you have arrived as an adult. You have made it through and so you are going to have a party with your classmates and mark the occasion of your transition."

I sighed. "So I'll go to the prom with a boy who I will go out with for one night and probably one night only. All I will get out of it is some punch and cake and then I'll spend the rest of the evening on the dance floor repeatedly removing his hand from my ass. Why bother?!"

"Lovella, please don't use that tone, or that language," she pleaded. "Believe me you will end up regretting it later and wishing you had gone if you don't go to your one-and-only senior prom, dear."

"Mother!" I crackled. "I don't even have a date, and if you think I'm going to go publicly anywhere wearing something like this you are sorely mistaken."

She leaned back in her chair. "How about we have a dress made for you? Mrs. Newall at church is an excellent seamstress. I'm sure she could make a dress that would fit you perfectly. All we have to do is find a pattern and she can alter it to your measurements. It might cost a little more, but like I said, honey, this is your time to shine."

I hated it when Mother talked to me like a little girl.

"Okay, Mother, fine," I bargained, "but I get to pick the pattern and I get to pick the material."

Mother agreed and then it was off to some sewing stores to look at dress patterns. She wasn't happy that I picked out a pattern for a simple strapless gown with clean lines and no frills.

"Lovella, you are too big!" she gasped. "Honey, your bosom will pop right out of that thing."

"Maybe that's just what I want it to do," I taunted. "They are kind of like wild horses. They were never meant to be corralled."

"More like planets that should be orbiting the sun," Mother said, under her breath thinking that I wouldn't hear. When I glanced at her she shot me a quick and pert little smile. Mother finally convinced me to let Mrs. Newall make a neck strap for it, "just in case."

I picked out a gray fabric that had silver threads giving it just a bit of sparkle. I thought it was very glamorous but, of course, Mother had to put in her two cents for pink or white satin. I would have nothing of it. I held her to her bargain and I got my silver evening gown for the prom. I had not known that Mother had ordered a pair of white pumps for my big feet before she ever took me out shopping for a dress. I guess she assumed that I would end up wearing what she picked for me. The gown, I thought, would have looked much more fashionable with black stiletto heels, but in the end the white shoes looked fine.

It was many years after those last few months of high school before I realized that Mother was trying to make peace with me. The end result of those shopping trips for my prom dress was a compromise between us that seldom ever occurred. Too often, we would end up in a stubborn stand-off. But as I look back, I do have to realize that Mother had her moments of insight and understanding. My prom, after all, was going to be a defining moment in my life, yet not the way Mother intended.

When Mrs. Newall delivered the dress, it fit perfectly. I put it on in my room and came out to the living room to show everyone. I will never forget, as long as I live, the look on Daddy's face when I walked into that room wearing that dress. It was as though he had fallen in love for the very first time.

"Ohhhh, Punkin' Patch," he cooed. "Don't you look like a dream walking?"

I smiled knowing that it pleased him. Mother and Mrs. Newall were also both just as pleased and just as complementary.

Mother had taken care of everything. She had thought of everything right down to the last little detail. There was nothing that she hadn't thought of. That night, about 3:00 AM I bolted straight up in bed. "Oh my god," I said aloud, "she's thought of everything! The bitch has picked my date!"

Chapter 8

After prepping me for prom Mother did not mention boys at all. I found that suspicious. I knew that she had to have something up her sleeve. I expected that she would bring someone around to show him off to me but there was nothing. So I began to think that maybe I was wrong. Maybe she was going to allow me to go alone, let Daddy drop me off and pick me up. When I would ask her about it she would say, "Don't you worry about it, honey. I've got it all taken care of."

"Mother," I demanded, "I don't want any surprises!"

"Well, your Daddy is going to be there for you on prom night," she would humor me. "Aren't you, John?"

"Oh, yeah! Yeah!" he acquiesced. "Got it all taken care of."

After all, prom was on a Friday night and if Daddy was willing to give up his drinking night to be there maybe it was all taken care of. Maybe Daddy was going to drop me off at prom like I had hoped. There was nothing I could do, but wait. She had beaten me on this.

I should have trusted my gut. On prom night, after I had dressed, put on make-up, done my hair, and was ready to go, Mother asked me to sit down at the kitchen table. She sat in the opposite chair, took my hand, lightly patting it, and I thought, "Oh Shit! Kill me now! Does anybody have a loaded gun?"

"Lovella," she snickered like a sneaky little kid. "I have a surprise for you."

"What Mother," I glared, "you're secretly lesbian?"

"Oh, no, no, no," she grinned offering none of the usual, or expected, reproaches for my comment. My mind did flips inside my head. "Oh my god!" I thought. "She didn't even take the bait. She didn't scold me. She didn't even grimace. Oh god! This is bad. This is very, very bad."

I was right. It was very, very bad.

She took a very deep breath and said, "Guess what? You have a date for the prom!"

Every superlative in my head was battling for expression. What shall I say? "Fuck me over a meat saw!? Goddamn!?"

It was all too much. I felt my cheeks turn hot like someone had just thrown coffee in my face. I wanted to scream but I knew it was too late. She had me. I was in the clutches of the Cunt from Hell! Again, I wanted

Karlyle Tomms

to scream. I wanted to explode, but all I could do was sit there and tremble.

"Oh, John," she sang, "loooook how nervous the poor thing is, bless her heart. I know her heart is just a-flutter." She did not gather that I was trembling with rage not twittering with anxiety.

"Isn't that wonderful?" Daddy chimed. "Mother got you a date."

You would have thought from their expressions that their deformed child had just taken her first steps from the wheel chair. At any moment I expected Mother to shout: "Praise Jesus! It's a miracle!"

I was finally able to squeeze words through the vice grip of my vocal chords. "And who would be my date—M—Mother?"

In my mind's eye, I saw myself rising from the chair, butcher knife in hand, stabbing her repeatedly as I screamed with insane rage. Shades of Hitchcock darkened my mind. Perhaps it is a good thing that we choose not to act on some thoughts.

"Well," she replied. "Actually, he is going to be arriving here at any moment. I don't think you know him because he is from Grove City. His father is a doctor and he plans to be a doctor also. Isn't that wonderful? With your interest in medicine, you'll have so much to talk about."

"Mother," I jeered, "you are expecting me to go to my prom with a boy I've never met, who I don't even remotely know? Oh, my god!"

"He is a very sweet boy, Lovella," she continued. "I met his family at a church function. They are wonderful people. It's just a blind date, honey. I'm sure you'll like him."

"Mother," I shouted, just trying to get her to shut up. "Have I ever, even one time, shown any interest in a boy you liked?"

"No," she said, "but that's just because you like to be a little rebellious, that's all. If you had ever, stopped being so obstinate and just tried to spend a little time with those boys, I'm sure there were several of them you would have liked once you got to know them."

About that time the doorbell rang. I felt like an animal in a trap, half willing to chew my leg off rather than be caught, but there I was.

"John dear, would you get the door please?"

She continued to pat my hand, perhaps not knowing that what I really wanted was that hand and the other one around her neck, chocking her till her tongue turned blue.

"Well, hello, young man," I heard Daddy exclaim from the living room and I knew this farce had to go on.

"Come on now, dear, let's go meet him."

Mother stood but never let go of my hand. She must have known that given half a chance I would have darted out the back door and run screaming frantically into the darkness. She led me to the living room and

Confessions from the Pumpkin Patch

I found myself walking like a zombie under the control of its master. When we rounded the corner, there he stood: A dream? Yes. A nightmare!

He was at least six foot three, gangly and slightly chubby at the same time. He looked like his large, flat, ass had been glued on top of a couple of long, old lady legs that narrowed at the ankles from too many years of wearing super tight knee-high stockings around fat calves. He wore a baby-blue tuxedo with pants too short so that the cuff barely reached his ankles. His hair was black, and I counted at least three distinct cow -licks swooping in different directions. He must have had allergies because he kept a handkerchief, which he repeatedly pulled from his pocket, to wipe his red nose. I didn't know whether to puke or faint.

As soon as he saw me he waddled over, stretched out his hand, and proclaimed in a nasal clog of a tone, "Oh, hi! Hi! I'm Nathan. You must be Lovella. It is so nice to meet you."

I hesitantly extended the three fingers of Mother's lady-like hand shake hoping to have minimal contact just in case the snot was a cold and not allergies. "Yes," I said quietly.

"Oh, look at her," proclaimed Mother. "Isn't that sweet? She is usually not this quiet, Nathan. She is usually just talk, talk, talk, aren't you, dear?"

"Yes, Mother," I hissed through clinched teeth.

"Oh, before you go," she reveled in her triumph. "John, get the camera. Let's get some pictures."

Daddy rushed to the end table by the sofa where he had the camera. He had a box of flash bulbs ready to blind us as Mother pushed us together and arranged a pose. I don't know why he insisted on keeping that old camera. Many of the newer models had flash cubes so you didn't have to change the bulb every time you took a picture. However, he insisted that he had a good camera and there was no use in "changing horses in mid-stream" whatever that meant. Suddenly, "pop" went the flash bulb and the room filled with a flash of blue white light. Daddy quickly wound the camera 'til the film clicked in place for the next shot, replaced the bulb, and got ready for another as Mother exclaimed, "Oh, here, let me get in this one. I want a picture with my little girl on her special night." Mother quickly posed herself into the picture and "pop" we were blinded again. It would be at least twenty minutes, I thought, before we would stop having a navy blue spot in our vision. The blinding flash was sufficient to cause me to want to run but when Mother's antics were added to the scene, I began to feel like a cat at a fireworks display. I had to get out of there.

"Come on, let's go," I said, as I grabbed Nathan's hand and pulled him toward the door.

"But don't you want to get a couple of more pictures?" Mother queried.

Karlyle Tomms

"No," I exclaimed. "Don't want to be late, do we, Nathan?"

And without too much more clamor, I was able to drag Nathan through the door. He waddled down the sidewalk as Mother and Daddy came out on the front steps to wave good-bye.

When we arrived at the car, he stepped to the passenger side door, opened it, bowed slightly, and motioned with his opposite hand for me to enter the vehicle as though he was a valet for the fucking Queen of England.

"Cut the shit," I growled low through clenched teeth. "Just get in the damn car."

I looked back and dutifully smiled at the parents as Nathan did what he was told, and moved quickly around to get in on the driver's side. To think Daddy had actually given up a drinking night for this horseshit. Nathan pulled away from the curb as we waved one more time at the parents.

I have to admit it was a very nice ride, a new Cadillac in fact, plush and comfortable. As soon as we got in the car, I couldn't take it any longer. I reached into my purse, took out a cigarette, and popped the car lighter in to heat.

"Nice ride," I said, "yours?"

"No," he replied. "It belongs to my dad. I guess your mom told you he's a doctor. He does alright."

The lighter popped out and as I reached for it to light my cigarette he said, "You know, some of the new research is beginning to indicate that smoking can be detrimental to your health."

"Really," I replied sarcastically. "Research probably also indicates that a bullet to your head can be detrimental to your health. Wanna try it and see?"

He giggled. He actually giggled. "You know you are really funny."

"Well thank you very much," I continued with my sarcasm. "That's just what a girl wants to hear from her prom date. Find me a gun and we'll test my theory."

"Well, you're pretty too," he went on, oblivious. "When your Mom told me you were pretty, I thought, oh, she's just pulling my leg to get me to go out with you cause all the pretty girls have dates for the prom and I thought you must really be a troll, or something, and that's why your mom was trying to set me up with you. But you're pretty and I'm glad I let your mom talk me into this."

"Well, she didn't tell me a fucking thing about you," I snarled, "and guess what?"

"What?" he questioned still oblivious.

Confessions from the Pumpkin Patch

"Never mind."

I stopped myself from saying "cause you *are* a troll" not wanting to be that cruel. After all, he was genuinely innocent in all this. Instead, I cooled my heels and took a long drag from my cigarette.

"So," I said deliberately blowing smoke in his direction, "tell me about yourself."

"Well, like I said," he blabbered, "my dad is a doctor, a family doctor in Grove City, and I grew up there. I have two sisters, one older than me, like seven years older than me, and I have a younger sister, who is about eighteen months younger than me. It's like my parents had Claudia, my oldest sister, and then nothing for seven years and then, blam!, blam!, there's me and Bernadette, my younger sister. I have like been around my dad's clinic my whole life and I love science and medicine and so I'm going to study medicine, so I'm starting Carnegie Mellon next fall with a major in biology/pre-med. Oh, by the way, our prom at my high school is next week, since I came over here to be your date for your prom, wanna come over to Grove City to be my date for our prom?"

"No," I said quickly as I popped the lighter in for another cigarette. "I think one prom is more than enough for me."

I had the feeling it was going to be a night of chain-smoking. Mother had picked the boy she wanted me to marry, a rich doctor's kid destined to become a rich doctor. Never mind the fact that he was more annoying than a gang of flies at a picnic.

"Anyway," he went on oblivious, "my sister Claudia is a nurse. She works in Pittsburgh, so I guess this medical thing is all in the family. Say, you know, I don't really know how to get to your school."

"Great!" I thought to myself, "I get to spend the night wandering around Climax listening to this idiot babble."

"Well, you have actually missed the street and you are going to have to circle around. Take a right up here," I said as I pointed with my cigarette between two fingers.

Eventually, we got there and I was sure to get out of the car before Sir Galahad could run around the car and gallantly throw open the door. I straightened my dress and adjusted my purse as I walked ahead of him hoping no one would see me with him. There was no such luck. Just as we were entering the doorway, Jane Murphy, one of the cheerleaders and her date Mike, one of the football players—how very, very, cliché— intercepted us.

"Oh, Lovella!" she exclaimed. "You look stunning in that dress! Mike, doesn't she look stunning?"

Mike grinned and eyed my cleavage. I had taught him a thing or two. I

Karlyle Tomms

could see that he was missing it.

She went on. "Oh, is this your date?"

Nathan had caught up with me and she eyed him up and down like a farmer eying a pig for slaughter. She extended her hand. "Hi, my name is Jane and this is Mike."

Nathan took her hand and between sniffles said, "How do you do, my name is Nathan."

"Well, pleased to meet you, Nathan," she said as she turned to walk into the gym. Over her shoulder she chirped, "Lovella, you really know how to pick the men don't you?"

"Fucking bitch!" I thought to myself. Then I turned and chirped back at her. "Well, at least you know how to pick your nose, dear." I smiled a sarcastic smile and walked on. She said nothing but I know she was thinking "bitch!" or worse. I avoided the insecure brag of telling her his father was a doctor.

Our school had an area that doubled as theater, meeting hall, and study hall. It was a large expanse with a stage at one end. There were hardwood floors throughout and columns up the middle to support the high ceiling. For events like the prom, the band was set up on stage and the school desks were all moved out to open a dance floor. At the opposite end of the room from the stage was a refreshments area and chairs had been lined against the walls where people could sit if they chose. The theme for the prom was "Memories of the Beach."

I nearly gagged when I first heard this and was not disappointed by the spectacle when I got there. The walls were lined with construction-paper palm trees, and the refreshment table was covered in tacky Tiki masks, which doubled as candle holders. Beach blankets had also been used in the decoration. I couldn't help thinking that it had all been Jane's idea. I caught myself snickering as I strolled around the room with Nathan tagging after me like a puppy.

"You want to dance?" Nathan pleaded as we strolled.

"I think I'll have some punch first," I said as I headed for the refreshments table. I wondered if, and hoped that, someone might have spiked the punch, but there were teachers chaperoning the table quite carefully.

Nathan had to be the gentleman, so he ladled me a cup of punch as I picked up a finger sandwich. "Thank you, darling," I said politely and half sarcastically as I began to sip and look away. The punch tasted like melted sherbet and was ten times too sweet, but it was a distraction momentarily.

Nathan poured himself some punch and then trotted along faithfully behind me. I scanned the room and thought, "What am I doing here? I've

Confessions from the Pumpkin Patch

gone to school with most of these kids since the first grade and have only cared for the company of a very few actually, really not more than two." Those two were Gretta and Tommy, neither of whom was there.

Nathan babbled some inane crap about progress in the medical field and I gave the occasional gesture or grunt to feign listening but my mind wandered.

It was the autumn of my junior year when JFK was assassinated. The loud speaker at school announced the event and the kids collapsed into a variety of reactions, mostly shock. School let out early that Friday. I called Mother to pick me up and when I got in the car she was stone-faced and silent, something I certainly was not used to from her. When Daddy came home from work that night he sat and cried as he watched the TV news. Mother never said a word about it, but Daddy fretted for months afterward. The following Monday, gangs of students crowded around this very room trying to watch the broadcast of the funeral as we huddled to try to get a view of the one TV in the room. There were two or three TVs in the school so some classes had gone to the gym and others to the cafeteria to watch as America changed forever. For a moment then I felt like we were all friends, no picking on each other, or cheap shots, or snide remarks to one another. Not everyone had liked President Kennedy, but I think almost everyone felt the loss, and we grieved together.

Over a year later, that was almost forgotten. LBJ had completed Kennedy's term and then had been sworn in as elected president in January. Now, it was May and graduation was around the corner. There was a feeling of unrest that had begun to filter through the country, especially the younger people, who were beginning to become frightened about the future.

As I looked around the room, I wondered how many of the boys who were there that night would end up dying in Vietnam. I had tried so hard to avoid politics, or much of anything that had any relevance to the future, but there I was thinking what I was thinking, and I realized that I was changing, too. I turned to Nathan and said, "I'm ready for that dance now."

It happened to be a slow dance as he led me to the floor. He pulled me up close to him and I thought, "At least he is tall enough for me." I had this fear when Mother told me that she had a date for me that he would be just tall enough to bury his face in my tits on the dance floor.

We had not been on the dance floor for thirty seconds before Nathan pulled one hand around to cup my breast as he whispered in my ear, "I really want to fuck you."

In total shock at the unexpected, I found myself shoving him backwards with so much force that he fell into another couple on the dance floor. "WELL, I REALLY WANT YOU TO GET FUCKED!" I screamed, loud enough for everyone to hear. "FUCK OFF, YOU ASSHOLE!"

As I turned and huffed my way out of the building, I found myself wondering if my reputation had made it all the way to Grove City. I found myself wondering if the only reason he allowed my Mother to set him up with me is that he heard about the slut from Climax. I didn't realize at that moment that most of my anger was displaced.

I went around the building, hiked up my dress and sat on the steps of the side entrance that was closed that night. It was dark over there and I think I got around the building fast enough that the creep would not be able to find me. I reached in my purse and pulled out a cigarette and then went digging for a light, but there were no matches and no lighter to be found. I had no idea what I had done with them. "Shit!" I said as I threw the purse down on the step. I sat there for a while trying to figure out why that little incident had made me so angry. Most of the time I would have taken that kind of thing in stride, would have made some kind of off-the-cuff remark, put him in his place, and gone on. This time was different. I didn't have a real boyfriend like most of the other girls. I didn't want to be there. And I was just acting out Mother's fantasy, not mine. I suppose I could have fucked him. Big deal! What difference would it have made? He probably wouldn't have lasted thirty seconds anyway. I just found myself being pissed at everybody and everything. I hated that damn school, that damn small town, most of the people in it, and I hated my life. I couldn't wait to get out of Climax and see what the real world was like.

I started imagining what it would be like to go to college in the fall. Unlike Nathan, I couldn't afford a private college. I was going to Penn State. In my mind, I recalled photographs on the brochures. I wondered what interesting people I might meet and how an education might change my life. However, the longer I sat there, the more I felt the need for a cigarette.

After a while, I decided that I would walk home. This meant that I was going to have to come back around the building to the front entrance. I didn't want to see or deal with Nathan, so I went sneaking to the corner of the building to peek around. When I did, to my delighted eyes, there across the parking lot sat Tommy's Chrysler Imperial. The top was down and Tommy stood there leaning against the car with Gretta tucked up under his arm while they talked to a couple of boys. They were not officially attending the prom. Neither of them was still a student. Gretta had on loose jeans and a baggy T-shirt but her pregnant belly was still quite visible.

Confessions from the Pumpkin Patch

I looked around for any sign of Nathan and then went trotting across the parking lot toward Tommy and Gretta. I had no sooner stepped into the light when Nathan, who had apparently been waiting at the door came running after me.

"Lovella," he called, "there you are. I've been looking all over for you. I'm sorry. I'm sorry."

I turned on my heels and shouted viciously, "WHAT PART OF FUCK-OFF DON'T YOU GET!?"

"I'm sorry," he said. "I was very rude in there. I don't know what got into me."

"WELL YOUR DICK IS NOT GETTING INTO ME ASSHOLE!" I shouted, "SO TAKE YOUR TROLL DICK BACK INSIDE AND SEE IF YOU CAN FIND YOURSELF A BIG UGLY TROLL GIRL TO FUCK!"

"Wooooha, Lovella!" Tommy shouted, "I've never seen you talk to a guy that way.

"Shut up, Tommy!" I shouted as I turned back on Nathan and marched decidedly in his direction. He began to back up as I started my litany. "JUST WHO THE HELL DO YOU THINK YOU ARE? YOU THINK THAT JUST BECAUSE YOUR FATHER IS A DOCTOR AND YOU HAVE MONEY THAT I'M SUPPOSED TO FALL ALL OVER MYSELF, KISS YOUR ASS, SUCK YOUR DICK, OR DO ANYTHING ELSE YOU WANT? YOU THINK BECAUSE MY MOTHER SET US UP, I'M SOME POOR PATHETIC LOSER WHO CAN'T GET A DATE?"

"No, no," he was saying as he backed away.

"LISTEN UP, JACK-ASS," I continued, "JUST BECAUSE I DON'T HAVE A DATE FOR THE PROM DOES NOT MEAN THAT I'M DESPERATE! IF I WANTED A FUCKING DATE FOR THIS STUPID BASH, I COULD HAVE HAD ONE. I CAN HAVE, AS A MATTER OF FACT HAVE HAD, PRACTICALLY ANY BOY I WANT!"

"Well, I was, I was," Nathan nervously stammered.

"SHUT UP, ASSHOLE!" I screamed. "WATCH THIS!"

I turned and looked around the parking lot where quite an audience had now gathered. As I did I started calling out names. "John Coonts," I started. "Have I had you?"

John Coonts was standing there with some of his friends while his date had gone to the powder room. "You sure did, Lovella!" he laughed and shouted back. "You had me in about every position I could possibly get in."

"Whose idea was it, John, yours, or mine?" I shouted back.

"You came after me," replied John. "I was too shy to ask a girl for a date 'til you came along."

"Terry Dawson!" I went on. "Have I had you?"

"I think you had me a couple of times, Lovella," he responded. "I've been hoping you would have me again."

"Tommy Smith!" I shouted as I looked back over my shoulder, "Have I had you?"

"Hell, Lovella!" he shouted. "Not only have you had me, you taught me everything I know."

Then Gretta shouted as she planted a big kiss on him, "And I'm damn glad you did."

"Gene Sutterfield!" I shouted. "Have I had you?"

"Well, I....I," he stammered. His date was standing right beside him.

"Come on! Tell it, Gene!" someone shouted, and then others egged him on as well.

Finally he shouted back, "Yeah, Lovella, you've had me."

His date slapped his arm and pranced away and I'm not sure if he followed her or stuck around. After that, I turned back to Nathan and sneered. "You see there asshole. I've had all those guys and they have had me. Not only have they had me, but they are proud of it. But you are not going to have me. You are not going to have any part of me. As a matter of fact, the only thing you are going to have tonight is your hand! The good news is that even if you are a troll, as long as you have a hand, you have a lover. Enjoy it, asshole, cause that's probably the only lover you'll ever get!"

I then turned on my heels and marched toward Tommy and Gretta. "Get me the fuck out of here!" I exclaimed as I hiked up my dress, climbed into the car, and sat in the back seat. Tommy immediately put Gretta into the passenger's seat and popped around the car to the driver's side.

One of the guys they had been talking to said, "Hey, you mind if I go?" and the other chimed in with the same question. I had never seen these guys before. Apparently they had come just to hang out with Tommy and Gretta in the parking lot. Tommy said, "I don't mind if Lovella doesn't mind."

"You mind if we go, Lovella?" one of them said.

"Sure!" I said, "Climb in boys, why not? Who knows, you might get laid tonight."

They both hopped over the side and into the back seat, one on either side.

As Tommy started the engine and began backing the car out of the parking space he asked, "Where to, Lovella?"

I said, "Anywhere but here, Tommy. I don't care."

Confessions from the Pumpkin Patch

Tommy shouted from the front as he began to drive away, "That was quite a show back there, Lovella. You should take up theater."

I responded with a quick but cooled down, "Oh fuck off and drive!"

"By the way," Tommy continued, "These two guys work for my dad over at the mill. This is Jason and Rick."

"Pleased to meet you, Lovella," said Rick.

Jason continued with, "The pleasure is all mine."

At this point Gretta leaned an elbow over the back seat and said, "I don't think I've seen you that upset since our fight in the first grade. Honey. What did that boy do to you?"

"It wasn't that big a deal," I said, having begun to calm down. "I shouldn't have been so mean to him. I'm not that mad at him. It's just this whole fucking town, especially that fucking conniving witch I have for a mother."

"Uh, oh," she queried, "what did your mom do to you?"

"What has she done to me my whole fucking life!?" I snarled. "What does she do to everybody? She has to control everything. No one else is allowed a choice. If she doesn't outright take control, she manipulates it. I had gone along with her about going to the prom. I didn't even really want to go. I don't care. I just want out of Climax! So, okay, she had a dress made for me, at least I got to pick the pattern."

"By the way," Tommy interrupted, "you do look stunning in that dress."

"Oh yeah!" grinned Rick.

Jason echoed with an, "Mmmmmm. Hmmmmm."

"Shut up. I'm talking to Gretta," I demanded and then continued my story.

"Anyway, so I got dressed for the prom fully thinking that Daddy would drive me over and drop me off for a while. I could visit with a few friends and go home, you know? But, no! She did exactly what I was afraid she was going to do, except that she didn't even give me the option of trying to back out. She had made arrangements with this boy from over at Grove City. He showed up at the house and it's, 'Oh, by the way, here's your date!' I wanted to fucking choke her right then and there, but there would have been witnesses to the crime!"

"Oh, jeeez," Gretta sighed. "Honey, I'm so sorry. I want to say I can't believe she would do something like that to you, but I know your mom well enough to know that she would." She paused for a moment and said, "Well, we kind of figured you would be at the prom alone if you came and thought we would stop by and say hello for a while. We had no idea we would end up rescuing you."

"I'm damn glad you did," I said as I finally relaxed into the back seat.

69

Karlyle Tomms

"How about Climax Point?" Tommy questioned. "We can go up there now, Lovella, I have my own car."

"Yeah, but you aren't going to get laid this time," I teased.

"Don't count on that," said Gretta and she snickered in Tommy's direction.

"It just so happens," said, Tommy, "that I have a twelve-pack of Budweiser on ice in the trunk."

"Oh you devil!" I teased. "I've never really drank before. Is this my chance?"

"This is your chance," he continued as he made a turn to head for Climax Point.

"I almost forgot, I wanted a cigarette," I blurted, digging in my purse. "Somebody pop the lighter in. I don't have a light."

Gretta obliged as I fumbled around for the cigarette I had taken out earlier. "Where is that damn thing?" I finally found it and pulled it from the purse with it already positioned between my fingers. About that time, the lighter popped out, hot and ready. Gretta handed it to me over the seat. I pulled the sweet smoke into my mouth with the lighter on the tip of my cigarette. I lay back in an awaited smoke-filled breath of relaxation. I handed the lighter back to Gretta.

"You boys don't mind if I smoke do you?" I taunted the men who sat on either side.

"Oh, no, no," said Jason. "I smoke myself every now and then."

"You do not," Gretta ragged.

"Oh, I do," Jason defended, "but usually only when I drink."

"Yeah, well, that makes sense." Gretta replied in a half-sarcastic tone. "I quit myself, at least for now."

"Well, when did you quit? And why?" I challenged as I puffed away.

Gretta took a deep breath as though she was going to have to defend her decision. "I quit when I found out I was pregnant. I was reading a magazine in a doctor's office that said there is some research that it isn't good for you. So I figured if it's not good for me, it's not good for the baby."

"Yeah!" I hissed through a clouded exhale. "Dick-head, the asshole, was telling me about that on the way to the prom. Well, good for you. I'm glad you're taking care of yourself and the baby."

By this time Tommy was winding up a tree-lined little road and then off to the side, barely a rut in the grass. He pulled the car almost to the edge of a bluff where the lights of town shimmered in the valley.

"How did you know about this place?" I said.

Tommy laughed. "You're not going to believe it. My dad brought me up

Confessions from the Pumpkin Patch

here and showed it to me after I started getting serious with Gretta. He said he heard some guy at work talking about how he and his wife used to come up here when they were dating and he thought I might enjoy the view from here as well. I think he and Mom used to go parking somewhere when they were dating back in their teens. Kind of nice to get off the beaten path from where most folks go to park up here."

"Well, good for dad!" I exclaimed as I pushed myself into the seat. "Where's the beer?"

Tommy popped the trunk open, lit a couple of lanterns that he then hung on some tree branches near the car, then he pulled an ice cold beer from the cooler, took the church key to it and handed it to me.

"So," I said, as I held the cold can in my hand and eyed it like a lab specimen, "my first taste of beer." With that I took several very long gulps before I removed the can from my lips.

"Whoa, there now," said Tommy, "slow down. You don't want to drink too much too fast now."

"Why not?" I said. "I'm thirsty."

I had read enough to understand how to deal with alcohol. It had been one of my projects where Daddy was concerned. But, at that moment, I wanted to get drunk. I wanted to get slobbering, falling down drunk just like Daddy. The way to do that was to drink it fast.

"Here's to you, Daddy!" I shouted, as I downed the rest of the can. I handed the empty can back to Tommy and said, "I'll have another, please."

"Only if you promise to take this one slow," Tommy pleaded as he held the beer out away from my reach and pulled it back each time I lunged for it.

"Okay!" I said finally. "I'll take it slow...er."

"That's a promise," said Tommy.

"Okay, that's a promise," I said, already beginning to feel the effects of the first can that I had slammed.

He handed me the beer and then got beer out for everyone else. We all sat on the rim of the convertible in a half-circle facing inward with our drinks.

"So boys," I said, as my head bobbed between Rick and Jason, "tell me about your selves."

"Ah," Rick started finally, after casting glances at Jason. "We both grew up in Rimersburg. We were friends in high school and just looking for some work after we graduated. Then we found an ad in the paper that the feed mill in Climax was hiring, so we applied and that's how we got to know Tommy. Ah, we work together."

"Fascinating," I said as I gulped the beer a little faster than I had

Karlyle Tomms

promised. "So, when did you graduate?"

"Well, Rick's a year older than me," chimed Jason, "he graduated three years ago and I graduated two years ago."

"Oh," I said as I lifted my beer can into the air, "so you're not breaking the law by doing this like I am?

"No. Rick's twenty-one, but I'm twenty," said, Jason. "I guess he is the only one not breaking the law, 'cept I think he bought the beer for Tommy."

"Oh, so not breaking the law except for contributing to the delinquency of a minor," I responded as I swallowed more beer. "I'm cool with that."

Gretta quit after one beer. When Tommy went back to the cooler and she refused the second beer I exclaimed, "I'll have hers." And I thought that was the end of the twelve-pack. Gretta had one, the boys all had two, and by that time I had four. I didn't realize that there was one left in the cooler.

I was probably not quite as drunk as I wanted to be, but I had never had beer before and I did, despite my promise, drink them pretty fast. "I need another cigarette," I exclaimed as I motioned to Gretta to pop the lighter in again. She handed it back to me shortly. I fumbled to pick the lighter from her fingers without burning either of us as my coordination had become quite impaired by that time.

While I was lighting up I began to tempt Rick and Jason. "You know you boys are both kind of cute, and I don't think I've ever been with two boys at once—at least not in the Biblical sense."

Jason was turning red and getting nervous but I could tell that Rick was enticed. Jason stuttered, "Well, uh, yeah, but don't you think two guys at once is a little queer?"

I slurred through drunk lips, "Well, you know the Kinsey report on male sexuality says that about a third of all men admit to reaching orgasm with another man so maybe it's not as queer as you might think."

"Apparently," Rick said, "from what those guys were saying back at the school you are quite a lover."

"I am!"

I grinned as I kicked off my shoes and hiked my dress almost to my crotch. "It's hot out here, don't you think? Aren't you a little warm?"

Rick's eyes scanned my body like a road map. Jason was sneaking glances and when I would catch him he would have a coy grin as he averted his gaze.

"No, I'm fine," said, Rick. "Not too warm at all."

"So, back to what you were saying," I persisted. "Yes, I am quite a lover. I have been training myself in the arts of love since I was very young, and

72

Confessions from the Pumpkin Patch

yes, I have many…" I paused and stared at the sky for a moment and then back at Rick, "carnal talents."

Tommy was laughing at me. "Lovella, I think you are trying to seduce that guy."

"No," I clamored over my words. "I'm just reciting my curriculum vitae of passionate talents, and besides, I'm trying to seduce both of them."

"You want to tell them about your smoking habits?" Tommy taunted.

"Tommy! Stop it!" Gretta intervened.

I stared at him for a moment and then said, "Yes, I believe I do want to tell him about my smoking habits, merely one of my many talents." I turned back to Rick and Jason. "You see…I can…smoke a cigarette with my…" I pointed to my crotch. "Well, my favorite word for it is my 'muff-dragon.' It may not breathe fire but it can blow smoke."

"Oh, hell!" exclaimed Jason as he drew back and almost fell off the car.

"Well, that sounds like a very interesting talent," said Rick without missing a beat.

"Would you like to see?" I quizzed as I waved my cigarette in the air above my head.

"Oh, holy hell!" Jason exclaimed again as he darted his head back and forth torn between his morals and his sexual curiosity.

"No! That's enough, Lovella," Tommy pleaded, knowing that I would do practically anything.

"Come on, honey," Gretta joined in, "there's no need to get graphic. We're just having a nice visit and a little fun."

"Well, I think Rick and Jason would like to see," I said as I leaned unsteadily toward the front of the car and whispered. "You guys can look away if you want and I'll just give these guys a little private demonstration."

Tommy took a deep sigh. He knew I would do it anyway. I never was much on gaining approval from others or worrying about being open with my body. "All right," he surrendered. "Go ahead."

Rick and Jason were both gleaming in anticipation as I stood up and pulled my hosiery and panties down past my knees. However, Jason remained obviously nervous.

Actually, Tommy and Gretta had both seen it before, so it was no surprise to them. That's why Tommy brought up my smoking habits in the first place, but he should have known not to dare me even if I had not been drinking. I sat back down pulling my dress up to my belly-button with my left hand fully exposing the muff-dragon. I ceremoniously took the cigarette to my other lips, drew in the smoke, removed the cigarette, and released the smoke in one little puff.

Karlyle Tomms

"Oh, great god almighty!" Jason exclaimed as he watched in amazement. But, the next voice I heard was from neither of the boys.

"All right, what's going on here?" It was not a familiar voice and it was coming from behind me.

When Rick and Jason heard the voice they both scampered off to the opposite side of the car and went running into the woods. The next thing I knew a policeman was standing there on the passenger's side staring directly at me, flash light in hand.

"Hello, officer," I said as the muff-dragon spewed another little puff of smoke from between my legs. The look on his face was priceless, but unfortunately unforgiving.

"Looks like a few beer cans lying around here," he said. "You kids been having a little to drink?"

"Why, officer," I said slurring my drunken words and placing the cigarette between my facial lips to take a long slow drag, "Whatever gave you that idea?"

I released the sultry smoke from my lungs, lower lip extended to blow it toward the sky. I leaned over to rest my hand on the side of the car, cigarette still in hand, and flashed him an enticing grin. However, my hand missed the firm surface and I half fell into the back seat before retrieving myself and pretending that he had not seen it. He walked around to the cooler which was now sitting on the hood of the car. He looked up at me as he nudged back the half-open lid and then he glanced inside to see the last beer floating on melting ice.

"I think you kids are under arrest," he said as he lifted his eyes from the cooler.

In that moment, I thought to myself, "I got the bitch back. Without an effort, intent, or malice aforethought, I got her back." Mother, I knew, would not be pleased.

Confessions from the Pumpkin Patch

Chapter 9

We were hauled to the Armstrong County Jail over in Kittanning about 15 miles from Climax and since we were all under age our parents were called. Gretta and I were placed in women's-holding and I assume that Tommy went to men's-holding. I didn't see him again for a while after that.

Jail was an interesting place. The building itself was a plain, little, unassuming, brick structure. The windows were crossed with strands of metal between the glass and the exterior bars were slightly ornate covering the windows like a cluster of cast-iron spiders bolted to the brick. But I wasn't there to admire the architecture and spent very little effort thinking about it before I got to experience what it is like to be behind bars.

They stripped us of everything except our clothes, including our shoes, and even took bobby pins out of my hair. Those were the days before they had orange suits for prisoners to wear. They took everything except for basic covering then led us to women's-holding.

After we had gone through booking and were sitting in the "drunk-tank" Gretta was crying like a baby and shouting "Oh my god!" over and over until finally I screamed, "For god sakes, Gretta, shut up!"

"But we are marked criminals," she whined.

"No we are not!" I scolded. "Don't be stupid. You don't think the cops find teenagers doing this silly crap all the time? Besides, I'm the one getting charged with indecent exposure. All you are getting if anything is a charge of underage drinking. Whoop-te-dooooooo."

She caught her sniffles and straightened up. "My parents are going to kill me," she continued.

"Your parents are going to kill you?" I pranced around her with elaborate sarcastic gestures. "Look at you! You are a married woman. You are pregnant with your first child. You are an adult. Hell, for that matter, we are all adults. So the stupid state has some archaic law that says adults can't drink 'til they are twenty one. That doesn't make any sense. I mean you are an adult at eighteen right? Guys are old enough to be drafted into war but they aren't old enough to drink. It's a stupid law."

"But it is still against the law," she moaned.

"Well," I taunted, perturbed at her whining, "I guess you should have thought of that before you drank that beer. Hmmmm?"

I went over and plopped myself down. There was an older woman lying

75

over in the corner smelling of body odor and rotten booze. She was obviously sleeping off a drunk. Another woman just sat there popping her gum and staring at us, never saying a word. I thought about giving her a shot from the muff-dragon, but then I thought better of it. Gretta finally came over and sat beside me.

"I'm sorry," she said, "I guess I'm acting like a big baby. You're right. I need to grow up."

"Well, not too soon," I said. "You are going to grow up plenty fast when the baby comes. You're going to have to. Me, I'm going to hang on to as much of my life and my freedom as I possibly can for as long as I can. I may not ever have kids."

"You were always so adventurous," she smiled. "You remember first grade, standing outside the principal's office, you know, after we got in the fight? I couldn't believe that you were saying those nasty words out loud. It's like you have never been afraid of anything or anyone—and I don't think I've ever told you how much I admire you for that."

"For what?" I queried. "For being a jack-ass who doesn't give a shit?"

"That's not what you are, Lovella," she continued. "I don't believe you don't give a shit. I believe there's a lot you care about. I just think, in your family, you had to learn how to be tough early on."

"I'm not so tough," I said. "I'm scared, too."

"Really?" she said as she leaned back and looked at me. "What on earth could you possibly be scared of?"

"Goddamn! I wish I had a cigarette!" I exclaimed as I threw my face into my hands. "Why did they take my fucking cigarettes?" I took a deep breath and turned around to her so that we were sitting face-to-face on either end of the bunk. "I'm scared of a lot," I said. "As much as I hate Climax, I'm scared of leaving. I'm scared of going to college, of meeting people I haven't known all my life. I'm scared of trying to live my life without having my parents there to support me. I'm scared that my mother may finally go off the deep-end one day. And I'm scared that my daddy is going to die from all those years of soaking his liver in alcohol." I fiddled with the fabric of my clothing for a moment before I looked back up at her. "There you have it. I'm fucking scared." I turned my head to the side so she would not see the glimmer of a tear that had started to form.

"I think I was too stupid to be scared when I left home," she said. "All I knew was that I had fallen in love with Tommy and I wanted to spend the rest of my life with him. My parents didn't want me to drop out of school. They told me that if Tommy really loved me he would wait 'til I graduated. But I couldn't wait, and now—," she burst into tears, "I'm going to have a baaaaaabeeeeeeeeeee."

Confessions from the Pumpkin Patch

"Oh, honey," I said as I gathered her into my arms, "what a beautiful thing. What a beautiful thing that you are going to have a baby—and with the man you love."

"But I don't know how to be a mother," she sobbed. "I don't know how to do anything."

"Well, you'll learn," I said. "Nobody knows how to be a mother, really. I think it is something that we just kind of pull out of our ass when the time comes. At least some do. Could be worse. At least you are not going to be like my mother."

"Oh, god, Lovella," she returned, wiping tears from her eyes, "your mother is so weird."

"Oh, jeez, that's an understatement," I said. "Grandmother once told me a story that right after I was born mother went around knocking on the doors of people she didn't even know to show them her new baby. Grandmother said she carried me to about thirty houses before a policeman quietly suggested to her that perhaps she should go back home and show me off to her own family and friends. I guess someone must have called in a complaint about some crazy woman wandering around bragging about a newborn." I took a deep sigh, realizing the magnitude of what I had just said. "I think I was never any more than a prize to her, something to show off, and more like a pet than a child. I think it just kills her that I won't just play along and be the sweet little doll that she expects me to be."

"I could never do that to my baby," Gretta responded. "Don't get me wrong. I know that I'm going to be really proud and I'm going to want to show off my baby, but I'm not going to go looking for people. She never stopped doing that to you did she? It's like your whole life was supposed to be for her and you weren't supposed to have a life of your own."

"I guess that's one of the things that makes me a fighter," I smiled. "I've had to fight to have my own mind and my own choice my whole life. Otherwise, Mother would consume me; turn me to stone like Medusa. She does it to Daddy too, like everyone in the world is there to meet her expectations and she just doesn't get it that someone else could have feelings or desires of their own. Daddy deals with it by hiding from her, by drinking himself into a stupor whenever she'll let him."

"He must really love your mother to stay with her and let her control him like that," she spoke to comfort. "I know he really loves you and maybe he stayed because of you, 'cause he could never have taken you with him. I mean they hardly ever give the kid to the father when there is a divorce."

I looked back at her for a moment and then hugged her. "You are going

Karlyle Tomms

to make a wonderful mother, Gretta. I know you are. You care too much not to be a good mother."

About that time a police woman walked up to the bars and called, "Lovella Fucks."

"It's Fuuuuchs," I answered, "with a long 'u' and an 'h'."

"That's not what I heard," she snickered. "Come on Smokey Butt. Your parents are here."

"Are Gretta Smith's parents here?" I questioned.

"No," she said, "they are going to be a little delayed."

"Then I'm not going," I demanded. "I'll come out when Gretta's parents get here."

"Lovella, go on," chimed Gretta. "Your mom and dad are here. Go on."

"I'm not leaving you here by yourself," I snapped with one part of me in genuine concern for her and one part of me not wanting to have to face mother.

"Suit yourself," the officer said as she turned to leave, "but I think if you are married the state considers you to be emancipated. She may not need her parents to come."

"Wait a minute!" Gretta shouted to the officer as she took my arm. "I'm fine, really, Lovella. I'm all calmed down now. There is no reason why you shouldn't go on home. If my parents aren't here soon, Tommy's will be or Tommy will have things figured out." She turned back to the officer. "Have you heard anything from Tommy Smith's parents?" she asked.

"Oh you must be Mrs. Smith," said the officer sarcastically. "His parents are here. He's out at the check-out desk."

Gretta's face drained of color as she asked, "So, do I have to stay in here?"

"No," replied the officer. "His parents are bailing you out but I don't think they are too happy about it."

"Why didn't you tell me before that I was getting out?" snapped Gretta in a much more stern voice.

"You didn't ask," replied the officer now with the door unlocked. "Besides I'm not here for you." She turned to me and said, "Come on, Smokey Britches, I'll be back to get your friend in about five minutes."

The officer led me down a corridor into an area with a built-in, shoulder-height desk. Everything was dark and there was an area on one side that also had bars but the center gate was open. On the other side was a long bench against the wall. There sat Mother wearing sunglasses with a large scarf tied over her head like she was some well-known movie star going incognito. She was perched on the bench like she could fall off at any moment if she didn't grip her ass tightly to it. Her face was turned to

Confessions from the Pumpkin Patch

one side as she stared down the hall and away from the check-out area. One leg was bouncing up and down like a sewing machine. She never turned her head or changed her gaze even when she obviously knew that I had entered the room.

In the area with the desk, a couple of officers were standing over to one side of the room. I recognized one of them as the man who had arrested us. Daddy was standing at the desk signing papers, politely saying, "Yes, sir. Uh, huh, yes, sir," as though he was a disobedient school child being scolded by the teacher. The officer was casually explaining the process and the rules around setting bail. I heard him say that I would have to return for court on the fourteenth of July, and that, if I didn't show for court, a warrant would be issued for my arrest.

"Yes sir—yes sir," Daddy continued politely. "May we go now?"

"Hold on just a minute," the officer replied. "I'll need to have you sign for her things." The officer brought out my purse and the white shoes which were really the only things I had. They had each been placed in a large brown paper envelope and marked with my personal information. Daddy signed for my things and took the envelope. He turned to me and said, "Come on, Punkin' Patch, let's go."

I followed Daddy toward the hall where Mother was sitting. As we passed the officers, one of them said, "I'd walk a mile for a Camel," and the other officer immediately began trying to stifle a belly laugh. The advertising slogan for Camel Cigarettes implied, I suppose, how far he would go to see my muff-dragon puffing on one.

I just kept casually walking along behind Daddy, barefoot in my silver prom dress and as we neared the bars at the edge of the room I folded my arm up behind me and displayed the full length of my middle finger. I have no way of knowing if the officers saw it. Nothing else was said and I walked on.

When Mother saw Daddy approaching she stood up in a snit expressing her obvious displeasure and marched ahead of us to the door. When we got to the parking lot she reached in her purse and handed the car keys to Daddy. "You have to drive, John," she said. "I feel too faint to drive."

She stared at me and pointed to the front seat, then stood by the back door motioning for Daddy to come open the door for her. When he came around the car to open the door, she sat daintily down in the back and motioned for him to close the door. It was amazing on one hand that she would give up control enough to let Daddy drive much less take the back seat. But on the other hand, she had to demonstrate to me how wounded she was by my behavior. In the back she began slinking down as far as possible so that only the top of her scarf-adorned head was showing

79

through the window. I suppose it allowed her to feel a little more hidden from her imaginary critical public. I simply found it amusing.

"Interesting," I said, as I opened the door and slid into the front seat.

As Daddy was getting into the car he said, "Well, it sure has been an exciting night."

"Shut up, John!" Mother snapped and he dutifully became quiet.

We all sat in silence for a few moments. Then Daddy started the car and pulled out onto the street. Over the horizon, the first glimmers of morning were peeking above the Pennsylvania pines. Finally, Mother could stand it no longer. She took a deep breath and spit through clenched teeth, "I have never been so humiliated and embarrassed in all my life."

"Congratulations!" I spurted in a cheery voice. "Sorry it took you so long."

"Don't be flippant with me, Lovella!" she shouted as she stared straight ahead.

"Flippant, Mother?" I questioned in feigned confusion. "I merely thought I was stating the obvious."

"How dare you engage in such behavior!?" she snarled. "How dare you embarrass this family the way that you have?"

"Exactly what behavior are we talking about Mother?" I said. "The drinking under age or smoking cigarettes with my pussy?"

"You did what?" she shouted. "I knew there was a charge for indecent exposure, but oh my god! What did you do? What is that? How could you—you—ah—ah—ah—ah…"

She began panting in those familiar strains of an oncoming panic attack.

"I can smoke a cigarette with my pussy, Mother," I said calmly and scientifically. "It's one of my many talents. It's merely a matter of learning how to control the kegel muscles."

"Ah—ah—ah—ah, merciful god in heaven!" she huffed. "Eh—eh—in front of others? The police caught you doing that? Ah—ah—ah. This is more hor—hor—hor—hor—horrible than I could have imagined!"

"Now, Sissy—," Daddy began his usual attempt to appease.

Mother shouted, "Shut up, John!" At the same time I shouted, "Shut up, Daddy!" He then became quiet again having failed once more in his attempt to keep us from going at it.

"Personally," I said after a brief moment of silence, "I think it is quite a unique talent."

"I don't care what you think!" Mother screamed.

Her brief, little, fake, panic attack was over and her rage flared full throttle.

"It is horrible, disgusting, and perverted! It was bad enough when I

Confessions from the Pumpkin Patch

thought you had flashed your breasts or something, or that maybe you had gotten drunk and didn't quite keep yourself covered, but this is beyond any horrible disgusting embarrassment I could possibly have imagined!"

"Really, Mother?" I taunted. "Worse than the time I fucked a dog on the front porch after I had sold tickets to the neighbors for a dog show? Worse than that?"

"Heavenly father!" she started having believed me for just a moment—and then she realized that I was saying it just to get her reaction. She paused to compose herself. "Lovella," she said momentarily, "we will not discuss this again. We will make no mention of it to anyone. Is that understood?"

Daddy chimed in. "Well, you know they post the arrests in the paper?"

I started laughing. "Secret's out, Mother. Your little girl is a slut, a cunt, a fallen woman. She is tainted, damaged goods, nothing one would ever want to brag about."

"Do you just live to hurt me?" she wailed.

"Do you just live to try to control me?" I returned, "To make me some kind of ornament in your little bag of brags? Do you think that I live only to make you look good!?"

"Lovella, I have done nothing but try to give you a decent, wholesome, and successful life," she whined. "I have done nothing but encourage you and try to give you a happy life."

"You are so fucking dense," I said. "You don't even get it. You don't even see yourself, how everything you do for me is to make me look good for you. You try to make me into what you want me to be instead of letting me be who I am! You always have! Well it is my life, Mommy! God gave it to me! It is mine to do anything I want, including fucking it up if I am so inclined!"

"That is exactly what you are doing, Lovella," she droned. "You are—fu—fu—," She gathered her courage resisting her own law against never using such words. "You are fucking it up!"

I applauded dramatically. "Congratulations, Mother! You said a dirty word."

"Stop it, Lovella! Stop it! I've had enough!" she pleaded. "If you are not going to try to live a decent life for me, then at least try to live a decent life for yourself. Go on. Live your life any way you want to live it. Fu—," She caught herself, unwilling to use that word again. "Mess it up if that is what you want to do. I am through. I will never monitor your behavior again." About this time, Daddy was pulling into the driveway of our house.

"Excellent, Mother," I said as I opened the car door. "I would love to say that I believe you but I don't."

Karlyle Tomms

I got out of the car and walked to the front of the house where I waited for Daddy to unlock the door since he still had my purse and my keys. When he opened the door I marched in, straight to my room, and shut the door. A few moments later, I heard a clamor from the front room. Mother was wailing, "Oh dear lord! My child! My child! The devil has taken my child!" Daddy was attempting to comfort her fake sobs of remorse.

"Now Drucella, honey," he said, "It's going to be alright. It is just kids getting out and having a little fun, that's all. Kids make mistakes."

"It's going to be in the newspaper, John!" she snarled. "The paper is going to print that my daughter was arrested for underage drinking and indecent exposure! I will never be able to show my face in this town again! I'll be jeered out of church! My life is over!"

"Now, Sissy," he pleaded. "This will all blow over. People are going to forget about it in no time. There are other parents who have had this kind of thing happen to them."

"John!" she snapped, "she has publicly humiliated me!"

Finally, I could stand it no longer. I stormed from my room into the living room and screamed at Mother.

"You god-forsaken selfish bitch! You think this is about you? You are worried about your reputation, your appearance. Hell, you don't even acknowledge that I am Daddy's child, too! You say, *My* child. I will never be able to show *my* face. *My* life is over! Don't you think you should share some of that embarrassment with Daddy and me?"

"Lovella, go back to bed," she said. "Your father and I are having a discussion."

"No you are not!" I screamed. "You are having a big fucking pity party at my expense and as usual Daddy is trying to talk you out of it while you are gloating on the attention and the sympathy. You have to make every fucking thing that happens about you! Well here's a news flash, Mommy! The whole damn fucking world does not revolve around you! Every person in the world is not here to serve your needs! Your family has better things to do than to dance around like a couple of marionettes while you manipulate the strings! You may have Daddy fooled. Maybe you have him hoodwinked into this bullshit, but you don't have me fooled! Now shut up! Quit your whining and move on! I'm the one who is going to have to go to court, not you!"

Mother sat there for a moment with a dazed look on her face, speechless. She wadded up the handkerchief that she had been pouring her alligator tears into and shoved it into the pocket of her dress. "I think we are all very tired," she said finally. "Perhaps we should get some rest."

She rose gracefully from her position on the sofa, passed silently by me,

Confessions from the Pumpkin Patch

went to her bedroom, and closed the door.

Daddy stood there for a moment with a blank look on his face. Then he half smiled. He walked past me, kissed me on the cheek, and said, "Sleep tight, Punkin' Patch." He then followed her to their room.

I stood there silent for a while before retreating to my room. Having said what I had so long wanted to say, I felt a twinge of guilt.

Karlyle Tomms

Chapter 10

Graduation was a bore, a tedious, over-extended orgy of pontification about the future and our place in it. We were all, of course, going to save the world. I would rather have watched stones eroding in the desert. Mother, no surprise, did not attend. She had not yet spoken a word to me since my little outburst on the night of prom. Attending my graduation would have shown she actually cared, and even more would have shown she had forgiven me. Daddy made up for it. He took me to graduation and made over me like a mother hen. When I accepted my diploma, I half thought he would fall out of his seat he was applauding so hard.

The diploma to me was nothing more than a piece of paper to show that I had jumped through the hoop and could go on to the next level. High school meant nothing to me. For years, my attention had been on college, getting a degree and having something that would get me a permanent ticket out of Climax, a way to escape my crazy family—freedom.

For a time, life after graduation was even more boring, weeks of sitting around the house, waiting. I had already done my leg-work and got all the paperwork for Penn State finished early. I did a lot of reading that summer and fantasized about what kind of career I might have after school when I would become a respected, yet controversial, research specialist in human sexuality.

June was tortuously slow. Everything went along as usual. Daddy continued his Friday night drinking. Mother continued to attempt to manipulate him out of it, but she never said a word to me, and we repeated almost the same dinnertime ritual every evening. When I asked her to pass the bread at the dinner table, she handed the basket to Daddy and said, "John, why don't you ask your daughter if she wants some bread?"

Daddy dutifully held the basket over in my direction and said, "Punkin' Patch, would you like some bread?"

I genteelly replied in a fake southern belle voice, "Why, yes, Daddy. I would indeed enjoy some bread. Thank you ever so much for thinking of me." I then dramatically plucked my roll from the basket, held the basket in Mother's direction and said, "Mother, would you like some bread?"

She said nothing and ignored me as I held the basket across the table, smiling and staring at her. Finally, she said, "John, please tell your daughter to place the bread basket back on the table before her arm

84

Confessions from the Pumpkin Patch

becomes fatigued."

To this I said, "Oh, I'm fine, Mother. Would you like some bread?"

Mother stared off into the corner as she gingerly chewed her tiny little piece of meat. Finally, she asked, "John, would you please take the bread basket and set it back down on the table?"

I quickly darted a smile at Daddy and chirped, "Oh, that's alright Daddy, I enjoy holding the bread basket. Perhaps we should ask Mother if she would like another roll." I switched arms if one got tired but I continued to hold the basket in Mother's direction.

Daddy, quite in on the joke, said, "Sissy, would you like another roll?"

What Mother did not realize was that Daddy and I had taken bets before dinner as to how long it would take her to lose her patience. "Oh, for heaven's sake, John!" she snarled, "Take the basket out of her hand and set it back down on the table!"

"Poor Mother," I commented in my fake southern accent. "How difficult she must find it merely asking for a roll." I continued to hold the basket and smile until Mother finally took a roll and slapped it down on her plate. She refused to eat it, however, and the dog later enjoyed that roll.

When the time finally came for my court date Mother made absolutely sure that she attended the event. Far more important than seeing me graduate was her desire and hope to see me punished or humiliated for embarrassing her yet again. She was up early on July fourteenth, dressed in her finest, and ready to be at the courthouse in Kittanning. Despite dressing for the occasion, she still donned her headscarf and sunglasses.

Breakfast was not prepared that morning. Daddy and I had a quick fix of toast with peanut butter and jelly. Mother had nothing. Perhaps she expected to dine on my dignity later in the day.

We arrived at the courthouse several minutes before 8:00 AM and waited outside until the building was unlocked. We then had the privilege of sitting on hard, wooden benches in the hallway for another three hours before we were finally called into the courtroom itself. Daddy and I chatted and tried to make small talk as Mother sat in a trance-like state clutching her handbag on her lap.

In the courtroom the bailiff of course, not catching what he was about to say, mispronounced my name. "The State of Pennsylvania versus Lovella Fucks—huh? Lovella, what?" His face reddened in embarrassment as he realized the word he had just pronounced to the court.

I shouted out, "It's Fuchs! The 'u' is long and there is no 'k'."

To this the judge slammed down the gavel and said, "Young lady, speak only if you are spoken to." He then turned to the bailiff and said, "It's

85

Fuchs. The 'u' is long and there is no 'k'." To which the red-faced bailiff stated, "The State of Pennsylvania versus Lovella Fuuuuchs." The judge then took a look at the papers before him and stifled a snicker as he read the charges quietly to himself.

I sat in amusement watching the show. By this time, of course, I no longer had embarrassment about my name and delighted in observing the embarrassment of others when they inevitably got it wrong. Finally, the judge looked up at me and said, "Ms. Fuchs, you are charged with under-age drinking, minor in possession of alcohol, and indecent exposure. How do you plead?"

"Guilty, your honor," I said without missing a beat. "I am ready to accept whatever punishment you wish to provide."

"Oh, you are?" asked the judge.

"Yes, sir," I said. "I was drinking, though I am not yet twenty-one and I was definitely and deliberately exposing myself in front of my friends. I had considered it to be a private matter among friends and that we were technically not in public, but I am assuming that it became public when the policeman approached."

"You were in a public park," said the judge.

"Yes, sir. I am aware that it was a public park and I am therefore guilty of exposing myself in a public area although there was no one there but my friends until the policeman arrived."

"Are you arguing that you should not be charged with indecent exposure?" asked the judge.

"No, sir," I said. "I am pleading guilty to everything. I did it and I am prepared for my punishment."

It seemed as though the judge had expected an argument. He paused for a moment staring down at the papers and then said, "Very well, Miss Fuchs. I sentence you to a fine of fifty dollars and eighty hours of public service. For your public service you will come to the Kittanning courthouse beginning Monday, July twenty-sixth and you will assist in janitorial services, forty hours a week for two weeks. You will arrive promptly at 8:00 AM and leave at 4:30 PM. You will take breaks with the county employees and you will have a thirty-minute break for lunch. I suggest you bring your lunch as you will not have time to go out to eat. If you are late, either arriving for work or returning from break, or if you miss any day of work, this sentence will be converted to one week in county jail. Is that clear?"

"Yes, sir," I responded. "May I go ahead and opt for the week in county jail?" I assumed that I could spend my time reading and besides it would be a week that I wouldn't have to deal with Mother. In my naiveté I had

Confessions from the Pumpkin Patch

not considered what else I might have to deal with in there, or whether it might actually end up being significantly worse than having to deal with Mother.

"No you may not," replied the judge. "When you arrive on the twenty-sixth you will be in the charge of Mrs. Magus who is our janitorial services director. She will meet you in the downstairs hallway on that morning." He then smacked the gavel again and said, "Next case."

Mother had still said nothing. We left the courthouse with my papers and went back to the car. As we were getting into the car, Daddy said, "How about lunch? There's a nice little cafe around the corner." Mother said tritely, "How about we go home and I'll make sandwiches."

I simply got into the back seat of the car. I knew we would be doing what Mother wanted—back to her usual control. She got in on the driver's side and Daddy got in the passenger's seat. As Mother pulled the car away from the curb Daddy turned to me in the back seat and said, "Don't you worry about that fine, Punkin' Patch. I'll pay that for you."

"John Fuchs!" Mother snapped. "You will do no such thing!"

Daddy returned with an unusual vigor, "Well, how is she going to pay it? She doesn't have any money."

"She will earn the money," Mother hissed.

"Doing what?" asked Daddy.

"I don't care what she does," Mother continued. "She can get a job. She can pick up bottles by the roadside or she can sell her body on the street if she is so inclined. She is obviously well prepared to engage in the oldest profession. However, regardless of how she earns the money, she is going to pay that fine herself!"

"I will be happy to pay the fine myself, Mother," I said quietly but clearly. "I am the one who broke the law. I am the one who needs to take responsibility."

After a long period of silence Mother said, "Thank you, Lovella. I appreciate your willingness to be responsible for your actions." These were the first words she had spoken directly to me since prom night.

"You're welcome, Mother," I said. Then she continued to drive in silence.

July twenty-sixth was a little more than a week away. I spent the time boxing up my room. There were several things that I placed in a box to take to the local second-hand store to see if I could sell them. I had books dating back to my very early childhood and I had a sweet-sixteen necklace that Daddy had given me for my sixteenth birthday. I didn't want to part with it but I hoped that I might be able to pawn it for enough to pay for at least part of my fine. By the time it was over, I had come up with fifty-eight dollars and seventeen cents. I splurged with the remaining amount after paying my fine by inviting Mother out to lunch to say thank you because she would be driving me to Kittanning every day for the following two weeks. I wasn't sure if she would accept but she did. She was talking to me again although it appeared that our relationship had been permanently damaged—not that it had ever been much to begin with.

We all got up very early starting on the twenty-sixth. Mother would drop Daddy off at work at 7:30. She would then drive me to the Kittanning courthouse where we would wait on the steps 'til it was time for me to go in. She was not about to leave me fifteen minutes to myself for fear of what other trouble I might stir. She would pick me up at 4:30 and we then would drive to Daddy's factory to wait 'til he got off at 5:00. It was a tormenting two weeks.

Mrs. Magus was a very fat woman with a round nose. She had a few short stringy hairs growing out of her face between her nose and her lips. When she breathed she made a whizzing sound like air released from a balloon. Her two fat lips stuck out from her face as though they had been attached like the plastic lips on Mr. Potato Head and she smelled distinctly of Lysol. Her voice was coarse yet high-pitched. I thought she sounded remarkably like a cartoon character, but she was all business.

When I met her on the first morning, she was waiting for me at the door. As soon as she saw me she blurted out, "You are Ms. Fuchs?"—and there was absolutely no mispronunciation of my name. "Yes," I said.

Missing not a beat, she ejected, "Follow me." She turned and pranced military-like down the hall. She never did introduce herself to me. I guess she assumed I knew—and I guess that I did.

She led me to a room on the left side off the main hall. There were shelves of cleaners, an industrial sink, buckets, mops and brooms. In one corner a skinny black man in his fifties, wearing lose blue coveralls, sat on a bucket smoking a cigarette. He was flicking the ashes into the sink but he had to extend a long skinny arm about two feet to reach that sink.

"This is Donny," she said pointing at the black gentleman who nodded his head in my direction. "His name is Donnelle but we call him Donny for short. He will be working upstairs today."

She continued, taking no notice of him.

"You will work the main floor. If you have any questions, find Donny on the second floor or come to my office on the third floor. There are two bathrooms on this floor. You will check them every thirty minutes to be sure that they are clean and I do mean clean. I do not want to find so much as a drop of urine on the edge of the commode when I come to check them.

Confessions from the Pumpkin Patch

Beginning at 3:30, you will scrub the toilets, sinks, floors, and walls of those bathrooms again before you leave."

She grabbed a large plastic bottle from the shelf.

"You will place this in all the commodes to sit overnight. Read the instructions for the correct amount to use. Before noon, you will mop the main hall and all the offices on the first floor. Do not leave water on those floors," she emphasized as she looked at me sternly. "You can squeeze the mop out well enough that the floor will dry quickly. Use this in the mop water." She grabbed another bottle off the shelf and shoved it at me. "Any questions?"

"Yes," I said. "May I smoke?"

"You can smoke on your breaks only in this room," she said, "You get one ten-minute break at 10:00 AM and one at 2:30 PM. Do not smoke on the job and do not stand around the building on your break. Come to this room. This is the janitorial lounge, ain't it, Donny?"

She said this without even looking at him.

"Yes, ma'am," he said, as his long bony fingers pulled the cigarette to his lips for one last puff before he put it out.

"Get to work," she commanded and she marched out of the room.

As soon as she left the room Donny let out a contrived laugh. "Hee! Hee! I'm surprised her butt cheeks don't squeak from all that rubbin' together."

I could see that he had three or four front teeth missing. He got up from his bucket and walked over to the sink. "Them wasn't very good instructions was they?" he said as he smiled at me. "Lookey here. You're gonna use this bucket right here for your moppin'. See this hose here, clamps onto the sink faucet. Make sure it is up there good and tight so it don't leak. Pour a little of that in the bucket, then just hose your water on in there. Now for the bathrooms, you got these toilet cleanin' sticks up here. Don't pay no attention to instructions on that bottle. Just pour you a couple of capfuls into the toilet and scrub it out with the cleanin' stick. Now you can wash the walls and the counter tops with that too if you want to. Pour a couple of capfuls in a bucket with some water and grab one of these here sponges."

"Thanks, Donny," I said.

I had the feeling, at least for the next two weeks, that we were probably going to be buddies. I found myself liking him very much.

He gathered his equipment and before he stepped out the door he said, "You need anything, you just come on up the stairs and holler." Then he was gone.

It wasn't as though I had never cleaned anything before. I think the

Karlyle Tomms

judge must of thought that I was one of those pampered little princesses who had never done a dirty day's work in her life. He was wrong. While I liked to dress up as much as any girl, I didn't mind getting grubby.

I had actually finished everything on the list except for re-checking the bathrooms before the ten o'clock break came. Then I was bored. I meandered around the courthouse looking for any little speck of dirt that I might clean up. I met people in the offices and asked them if they would like to have their trash taken out. Most of them hadn't accumulated enough from the day before to make it worth taking out but they obliged me anyway even if there was nothing in the trash basket but a discarded envelope.

At ten, I met Donny back in the mop room where we both lit up a cigarette. I said, "Does Mrs. Magus come down here for breaks?"

He chuckled as he said, "Hell, she's on break all day up there in that office. You go up there, you're gonna' find her with her feet propped up on that desk while she's eatin' doughnuts. She ain't got enough to keep her busy. She just makes sure we stay busy."

"Does she just manage the courthouse?" I said.

"No," Donny continued. "She's over all the county buildings. I guess maybe over ten or twelve employees. She don't clean nothin' herself unless somebody don't show up for work. She used to be down here doin' this just like the rest of us."

"Must be nice to move up in the world," I said smiling.

He said, "Say, what kinda' crime did you commit to get you sentenced to do what I do for a livin'?"

"Well," I stammered for some odd reason feeling a little embarrassed, "I was caught drinking under-age and I was also charged with indecent exposure."

"Oh, now, he said. "Mmmmm. Mmmmm. Pretty young girl like you shouldn't be gettin' in trouble like that. You gonna ruin your reputation."

"What reputation?" I said. "The only reputation I have is a bad one."

"Now that's a shame," said Donny deliberately not asking the details. "Reputation is important, especially for a woman. Men start talkin' her down, she ain't gonna' get nowhere in life, but you know everybody makes mistakes."

"I don't think mine were mistakes, Donny," I said as I drew a long drag off my cigarette. "They were in fact quite deliberate."

"You mean you set out to get a bad reputation?" he queried.

"No, not exactly," I responded. "I didn't even think about a reputation but I did set out to explore life and I really didn't care about what rules I was supposed to follow. I don't mind obeying the rules when I can see a

Confessions from the Pumpkin Patch

good reason for them, but if I can't see why there is such a rule, why shouldn't I break it?"

"Well, cause—" he pondered, "cause there must have been a reason for it sometime."

"But you know, Donny," I said, "the world changes. It always has changed. Society changes. Nothing ever stays the same and the rule for one generation doesn't have to be the rule for the next. For example, there are people who would throw a fit if they knew I was in this room alone with you."

"Now, now, Ms. Lovella," he tweeted nervously and stamped out his cigarette. "Maybe we need to get off back to work now."

"It's okay, Donny." I said. "I'm not afraid if you're not. Nobody is doing anything wrong. Magus set us up to be here alone, and we are in the courthouse for Jesus sake. But it's just one more stupid rule that some people have but others don't. If Magus didn't think anything of us being in here for a break together, then I'm certainly not going to worry about it."

"Well, we do need to be gettin' on back to work," he said as he motioned for the door.

I put my cigarette out and gathered my tools.

That afternoon, I couldn't help thinking about how Mother would take it if she knew I was spending fifty minutes a day, breaks and lunch, in a room alone with an old black man. She would either assume that I was already lost so why bother, or she would throw a very public and dramatic fit in an attempt to blame Donny and somehow reclaim my virtue. I was going to make sure she never found out, not for my sake, but for his.

I did my work for that two weeks and had several, I thought, meaningful conversations with Donny. I never told the family anything more than there was an older black man who also worked there in janitorial services. By the second week of August I had paid my fine and done my public service.

On Sunday, August 15th at about 2:00 PM I got a call from Tommy. He was panting on the phone like he had just run a marathon. "Lovella! Ah, huh, we're at county hospital. Ah, huh, Gretta's having the baby. Can you come down?"

"Oh, Jesus, Tommy!" I screamed. "Mother is gone with the car to one of her church meetings."

"I'll come get you," he panted.

"No wait. I'll call a cab," I yelled nervously. "You stay with Gretta."

"Do you have money for a cab?" he questioned. "I'll pay for it when you get here."

Karlyle Tomms

"You don't need to pay for it!" I yelled. "You'll have a baby to take care of. Besides, I know where Mother keeps her stash."

"Jeez, Lovella!" he expelled. "She'll eat you alive."

"So, what's new?" I said. "Gotta hang up now so I can call a cab. I'll be there as soon as I can."

I hung up the phone and grabbed the phone book to frantically look up the number for cab service. I called and got the cab on the way. Then I pulled fifty dollars from Mother's stash— a lot more than I needed but what the hell. I wrote a quick note to the family letting them know what happened and not to worry. I included an I.O.U. to Mother for the missing money. I had completely forgotten that Daddy was working out in his shed. It didn't even occur to me to go ask him for cab money.

The cab was there in about twenty minutes and I was off to Armstrong County Memorial Hospital.

When we got there, I paid the cab driver and ran frantically into the lobby. Panting, I asked the receptionist for Labor and Delivery and then half-getting the instructions I ran in the semi-correct direction as the receptionist shouted after me, "Miss! Miss! Slow down. Don't be running in the hospital." I paid no heed to her and kept going. In short order I found the little waiting room outside Labor and Delivery and there was Tommy pacing the floor. As soon as he saw me he ran over and gave me a big hug.

"How is she?" I exclaimed out of breath.

"I don't know," he said. "They took her in over two hours ago."

"I'm sure everything is fine," I comforted. "These things take time." I then ushered him to a chair to sit down. "So," I continued. "Have you decided on a name?"

He nervously glanced toward the door. "Well," he stammered. "That is kind of supposed to be a surprise."

About this time, Tommy's parents walked in asking the same sort of questions I had been asking, and not five minutes after them Gretta's parent's came in. For both families this was going to be the first grandchild, so both sets of parents were as nervous as Tommy. I swear it was like watching a hive of bees with the chatter that went on between them. I just sat back in the chair next to Tommy, squeezed his hand to let him know I was there if he needed me. Then I got up and stepped to the side for a while.

It was only a very few minutes after that when the nurse came in and called for "Mr. Smith." How odd it seemed to me to hear him referred to as mister. He turned to the doorway where she entered and called back, "I'm Mr. Smith." That sounded even more odd. The nurse then responded.

92

Confessions from the Pumpkin Patch

"Mr. Smith, would you like to see your son?"

I saw Tommy's knees half buckle and his face flush red just as the grandparents let out a plethora of ooohs, aaahs, and other such gibberish that is common to such scenes. I was thinking to myself that if I ever had a child, I would prefer to do so in private without all the family ruckus.

"Yes! Yes." Tommy finally replied after he recovered from the shock that he had actually become a father. "A son!" he stammered excitedly turning attention back to family. "I have a son!"

Of course the whole of both families tried to rush the door as the nurse turned and said, "Just Mr. Smith at this time. I'll be back shortly to let you know when other visitors might be allowed."

She escorted Tommy through the doors and the disappointed families settled down into the uncomfortable industrial-designed chairs to wait.

After a while, Tommy's father, knowing in too much detail of my history with Tommy, said, "So, Lovella, what do you think of all this?"

I smiled politely as I responded. "I think that two people who I love very much have just had a beautiful blessing come into their lives and I am very happy for them."

"Yeah, yeah, it's a beautiful thing, a beautiful thing," he bantered, making small talk. "I tell you, I can't wait for the first time I take that boy fishing."

"That will be very nice, Mr. Smith," I said. "I'm sure you will make a wonderful grandfather. After all, it is my understanding that you have been a wonderful father."

"Well, thank you, Lovella. That is very sweet of you to say that." He grabbed Mrs. Smith's hand and gave it a squeeze. "Boy, this brings back memories, doesn't it sweetheart? I remember when you were having Tommy. I was pacing around the hospital lobby feeling like my heart was going to beat right out of my chest. I was so proud."

Just then, Daddy and Mother came in. "Well, there you are Punkin' Patch," Daddy said as he rushed over to me. "You had us worried."

He plopped down in the chair next to me. Mother said nothing but nodded politely to the other families. As soon as Daddy's ass hit the chair, I realized that something was terribly wrong and then I smelled the liquor on his breath. He was drunk. I didn't know what to think. I had smelled that smell before but I had never actually seen Daddy drunk. I had seen only the after-effects, and I had never known him to drink on a Sunday. It had always been Friday night when he had his love affair with alcohol. I then realized that Mother's silence was more embarrassment than anything else. I had suspected she would be pissed at me for getting into her money but it was shame more than anger that I was seeing on her face

Karlyle Tomms

that afternoon.

"Whoooh, I tell you what!" Daddy shouted toward the other families—and was far louder than he should have been. "This is an event! It sure is something watching your kids grow up and step out into lives of their own and have babies and stuff."

Mother snipped quietly, "John, there is no need to shout. I'm sure everyone can hear you."

I could not believe that she actually brought Daddy with her when he was so obviously intoxicated. I learned later that he had gotten into the car and refused to get out. She had a time convincing him that he was not going to drive. Any other time he would have sheepishly submitted but the alcohol had altered his usual pattern of behavior. I was surprised they had even come at all. Normally, Mother would never have allowed anyone to see Daddy in such a state if she could possibly help it.

"Oh, my goodness, Punkin' Patch," Daddy slurred as he patted my arm. "Little Gretta Tannenbaum is having a baby. Hell, you have been friends with that girl since you were in the first grade. You know that child is almost like another daughter to me. Hell, I wouldn't miss this for the world."

It was then that I realized Mother, in rare behavior, had given in to Daddy's demands to come down to the hospital. It wasn't necessary. They could have called. I could have gotten a ride back with one of the other families. I had this image in my mind of Daddy insisting that he had to come to the hospital, insisting that Gretta was like one of his own, and Mother finally giving in after the exhaustion of bickering with a drunk. I could see darting eyes and overheard the faint hint of whispers as the Tannenbaums and Smiths assessed the situation from across the room.

"Daddy," I pleaded, "they are probably not going to let anyone in today except for family. I only came down to be with Tommy because he called and he was nervous. I think we could probably go on back home now."

"Where is Tommy?" he shouted again, scanning the room and only that moment realizing that Tommy wasn't there.

"He has gone back to be with Gretta," I said. "The nurse called him back right after the baby was born."

"You mean the kid is already here? What was it boy or girl? Hey, let's go back and see the baby." He plowed the words out of his mouth, one sentence after another, and didn't give anyone a chance to answer the questions before he was up headed for the double doors.

"Daddy, no!" I shouted as I grabbed his arm. "We can't go back there yet."

"Well, why the hell not?" he said, as he pulled on my grip like an eager

94

Confessions from the Pumpkin Patch

dog on a leash.

"Because it is a private time for the parents to be with the baby," I said. "We need to wait."

"Oh, oh," Daddy softened to a whisper. "It's a private time, private—a private time. Oh, okay. I see. We need to just wait our turn."

"Daddy," I implored. "I really need to go home. Can we have Mother take us home?"

"But don't you want to see the baby?" He continued to whisper as he stood now obviously unsteady on his feet.

"I think I'm going to have to wait till tomorrow to see the baby," I said. "It's just immediate family today, and I really need to go home. Let's go home, Daddy, Okay?"

He looked at me in a brief stare, the love he had for me still shining through the haze of intoxication as he said, "Okay, my little Puh, Punkin' Patch, if you want to go home, then we need to go home."

I glanced at Mother and she gave me an acknowledging look as she moved over to Daddy's other side, took his arm, and began escorting him out.

"I'll be there in a moment," I said as I briefly let go of my grip on Daddy's arm and ran quickly over to the other families.

"Please tell Gretta and Tommy I'm sorry I couldn't be here. I'll try to come back for a visit tomorrow." I stared at them entreatingly, catching each one's sympathetic eyes as I scanned across the four of them. In a moment Gretta's mom said reassuringly, "Sure we will, sweetheart. You go on."

I then turned and followed Mother and Daddy out the door.

"What a waste" I thought to myself as I got into our car. Tommy needed me there for support but I wasn't even there that long before the baby was born and then this.

Daddy fell asleep on the way home. I sat in the back of the car thinking. In only a couple of weeks I would be going away to college. I would hardly see Gretta and Tommy after that. My life was going in an entirely different direction than theirs. They would be raising a family and settling into the day-to-day mundane life of Climax—and who knew where my life would lead me.

Mother didn't speak the whole trip back and neither did I. I guess we were both entrenched in thought. When we got home, we woke Daddy and he had sobered a little from the sleep. He half staggered into the house without our guiding, fell into bed with his clothes on, and continued to sleep.

Mother and I gathered back in the living room and sat down. After a while she said, "I'm sorry, Lovella. I tried to keep him at home."

"It's okay, Mother." I replied. "Who can handle a drunk if he doesn't want to be handled?"

Again, we sat silent for another long moment. Finally, I said, "I've never seen him drunk before, actually, and I've never known him to drink on a Sunday."

He's been drinking a lot more lately," Mother responded. "He has been pretty good about hiding it from you, at least until today. He hides in the shed and drinks."

"I don't understand why he would hide it from me," I said as I reached into my purse for a cigarette. If Mother continued to care about me smoking, she never let on.

Mother looked down at her hands, which were folded in her lap. She looked up at me with tears welling in her eyes and said, "It seems you are the only person in the world he can't stand to disappoint."

In that instant I realized how very disappointed she had been, perhaps not just in Daddy, but in me. I didn't know what to say. I didn't know if I should try to comfort her or even if she would allow it. I had not a clue what to do, and so I sat there dumbfounded in silence.

In a moment, Mother let out a huge sigh and said, "I think I would like a cup of hot chocolate, how about you?"

"Yes, that would be nice," I said as I followed her to the kitchen.

I sat at the table and watched as she prepared the hot chocolate from scratch. As she stood over the stove stirring the milk to warm I finally asked, "Mother, are you and Daddy going to be alright when I go to school?"

"I'm sure we will be fine, dear," she said, not looking up.

I fiddled with the handle of the cup Mother had set on the table. "This thing today just worries me, I guess."

"I've dealt with your father for a very long time," she said as she continued to stir. "I'm sure we will be okay—but—" She stopped mid-sentence, eyes gazing into the heating milk.

"But what, Mother?" I petitioned.

She turned the burner off under the hot chocolate, brought the pan to the table, and skillfully poured into my cup. "But, I'm going to miss you," she said, as she finished pouring her own cup

Again, I was dumbfounded. Part of me wanted to go ahead and reply, "I'm going to miss you too," but I resisted, knowing that I wouldn't mean it. On one hand, I wanted to slap her for waiting my whole life to even come close to letting me know I meant more to her than a showpiece. On the other hand, I wanted to affirm my mother. When I finally said, "I'll

Confessions from the Pumpkin Patch

miss you, too," I felt as though I was having to pull the words out with pliers. Within me, my empathy competed with the truth.

She put the pan back on the stove and then sat at the table first blowing across her hot chocolate before taking a sip. "I've decided to take a job," she said not even acknowledging my response. "I'm actually due to start at Martha's Dress Shoppe next Monday."

"That's nice." I said, stirring my chocolate. "Is this something you've wanted to do?"

"Truthfully," she sighed, "I don't know how much longer your father will be able to keep a job. He has already been reprimanded twice for drinking at work and it is probably only a short matter of time before he is fired. I have to do something."

I felt guilt rushing over me as though I was committing some terrible wrong for going to school and leaving them there to cope with the misery that was their marriage. There had always been a thought in the back of my mind, though never spoken, that I was supposed to have been the savior of their marriage. Have a baby and everything will be just fine. I felt as though the whole burden of their misery was mine to repair—and somehow I failed miserably.

As I sat there pondering what she had just said, I changed the subject. "Mother," I queried timidly, "why didn't you and Daddy have any more kids after me?"

She snorted, repressing laughter as though I had just told a joke, and when she saw the shock on my face she said, "I'm sorry, dear." Then she stammered a bit in her reply. "I, I guess I just didn't think your father and I could handle more than one." Then one finger came up and crossed her lips as though telling herself to be quiet, shush, don't tell, and she said, "No, I'm sorry. That is not true." She sighed and looked away, then back at me again. "The truth is your father came home very drunk one night shortly after you were born." She paused for a moment gathering courage, and then continued. "He forced himself on me. Well, he tried to force himself on me. It didn't work. I locked myself in the other room with you. He pounded on the door for a while and then went to bed. I didn't come out 'til morning. By that time, I had done a lot of thinking. Your father had sobered up, so I sat him down for a talk. I told him that if he ever tried to force himself on me again, I would leave, and that I expected him to control his drinking. He didn't. So, I decided that it would be difficult enough to raise one child in a home with a drunk. I wasn't going to do that to any more children. I'm sorry that I had to do it to you. I—" She paused as though having to pull her own words out with pliers. "I rewarded him with sex when his behavior was appropriate, but I insisted on protection.

Karlyle Tomms

After a while it seemed that his drinking was more important to him than sex, so I resorted to trying to manage him in other ways." Again, I saw the tears well in her eyes and watched as she stifled them. "At this point," she continued, "there is no managing him anymore."

For the third time that day, I was dumbfounded. I sat staring at her, trying to figure her out, trying to tell if this was acting and she was feeding me a load of bullshit, or if she actually believed her own reasoning. At last, I said, "Mother, did it ever occur to you that trying to manage everyone is not the way life works, that maybe the best most people can hope for is to be able to manage themselves?"

"Well, what was I supposed to do, Lovella?" she snapped.

Ah, there were the hornets.

"Let my marriage fall apart? Let my child grow up without a father? You adore your father and he adores you though for the life of me I cannot fathom what you see in each other."

Yes, there it was. There was the Mother I had always known. There was the anger and the sting, and there was no real answer to my questions. I had no way to confirm whether she was telling me the truth. My parent's lives were an inaccessible secret. I took the last few sips of my cocoa and then said, "Thank you for the cocoa, Mother." I rose and went to my room. I didn't read. I didn't sleep. I lay there on my bed staring at the wall thinking about so many things. I tried to dismiss worry about myself and about them. However, I was not entirely successful.

The next day I rode with my parents as Mother took Daddy to work just as she had done my entire life. She then dropped me off at the hospital while she ran errands. Gretta was asleep when I came in. After all, it was early. I had to sneak in as it was not during visiting hours. Tommy had taken the day off work and was slumped over in a chair near Gretta's hospital bed. When I came into the room, he roused.

"Oh, hi," he whined as he stretched sleep from his arms.

I walked around the bed and leaned over the rail just as Gretta opened her eyes. "Good morning, little momma," I said.

She smiled, and reached up to hug me. "Have you seen the baby?" she said.

"No, honey," I replied. "I wanted to see you first, and besides, it would just be peering through a window at a collection of newborns and trying to figure out which one was yours."

"Tommy," she motioned with her arm. "Go ask the nurse to bring the baby in."

He got up dutifully and walked out of the room.

Confessions from the Pumpkin Patch

"How are you feeling?" I queried.

She snickered as she snuggled down into the bed, "My coutchie hurts."

"I'm not surprised," I said, grinning. "It got a little bit of badgering didn't it?"

She nodded in agreement and said, "Oh, Lovella. He is so beautiful. I've never seen a more beautiful baby in my life."

"You think you might be a little prejudiced?" I questioned.

"Just a little maybe," she said, "but I'll bet you'll think he's beautiful, too."

In short order Tommy re-entered the room followed by a nurse holding the baby. She came to the bed and laid the child in Gretta's arms.

I felt goose bumps crawl over my arms as I saw her looking down at that baby. For the first time in my life, I realized what true adoration was.

"You're right," I said. "He is beautiful."

Tommy stood on the opposite side of the bed staring down adoringly at the two of them and stroking Gretta's hair.

"You want to know what we named him?" she asked.

"Yes, what?" I replied not realizing that I was about to get the shock of my life.

"We named him Derrick Lovel Smith." she said looking up at me. "Derrick, after Tommy's grandfather, and Lovel, after you."

"After me?" I exclaimed in shock. "Why in the world would you name the child after me?"

"If it had been a girl," she continued, ignoring my questions, "We were going to name it Jeanette Lovella Smith. Jeannette, for my grandmother, and Lovella, after you."

"You guys!" I exclaimed again. "I love you both. You know I do but I can't understand why you would want to name your child after me."

They started to speak at the same time. "Because—" They glanced at each other, caught themselves, and then Gretta continued. "Because if it hadn't been for you, Tommy and I might never have found each other. You brought us together, Lovella, and together we made Derrick Lovel and he is both of us together in one body for life."

I couldn't help myself, happy tears drifted over my cheeks. "You guys are so sweet," I said. "I don't know what to say. I'm just blown away."

"Would you like to hold him?" Gretta asked.

"Oh, hell, yes, I do!" I cried.

Then she handed the baby to me. I folded him into my arms and stood there cooing to this tiny little person who was waving his tiny little hands randomly and looking at me with the same big beautiful hazel eyes of his father. I looked up at the two of them and our eyes exchanged a moment of knowing, of feeling connected in a way that cannot be explained. There was a part of me which was green with envy, and a part of me that was so proud. I didn't know what to say at that moment and so I said nothing. I just kept rocking this beautiful little bundle in my arms, cooing to him. At some point, I knew I would have to hand him back, but I didn't have to make that decision because it was only a minute or two before his goo's became cries.

"Oh, no, no, no," I cooed, "What's wrong? Don't you like your Aunt Lovella?"

Gretta watched patiently as I tried to calm the baby and finally said, "Maybe I better take him."

I handed him over and within a few seconds the crying had stopped and he settled into her chest.

"I guess he already knows who the real mom is," I said as I watched her cuddle the baby. Then I reached across the bed and sat my hand over Tommy's. I put my other hand on Gretta's shoulder and said, "I'm going to miss you guys so much."

"Oh, jeez," said, Tommy, "we're going to miss you too."

"Oh, god, yeah!" Gretta exclaimed in a half whisper as the baby had closed his eyes.

"You know I leave for school next week." I wept and pulled back to wipe my eyes.

"But that's going to be so wonderful for you," said Tommy. "Wow! College! That's great!"

"I don't know that it is as great as having Derrick," I sighed.

"But your turn will come," Tommy replied. "You will probably meet some wonderful intellectual guy who will be just perfect for you."

"God knows it's going to be different," I said. "Mother is going to drive me up Monday after next. I have to register and sign up for classes. I already know which dorm I'll be staying in. My roommate is from Philadelphia. They have already sent our room assignments. I guess I'll meet her when I get there. Her name is Marcy Macintosh. Don't have a clue what she is like."

"So how often will you be home?" Gretta questioned.

"I don't know." I said, hesitantly.

After a pause, I said, "I have such mixed emotions about it all. All my life I've wanted to get out of Climax and god knows I've wanted to get away from Mother but now that it's actually here, I realize that it means leaving you guys, and it means having to adjust to a completely different way of life. It's kind of scary."

"You scared?" blurted Tommy, "That'll be the day. You may be a girl,

Confessions from the Pumpkin Patch

Lovella, but you got more balls than most of the men around here."

I laughed.

"Well, if I actually did have balls, I would certainly have to apply myself to learning how to use them."

"So how often will you be home?" asked Gretta, again.

"I guess at least during the holidays," I said. "If Mother has her way, I'll be home every weekend. She wouldn't miss a minute of torturing me, or making sure I don't do something—unseemly."

Tommy said, "She still hasn't figured out that you are going to do whatever you damn well please regardless of what anyone else thinks."

"No, she hasn't," I replied. "I doubt that she ever will."

About that time there was a little knock at the door as Mother stuck her head in and said, in a little sing-song voice, "May I come in?"

"Oh sure, Mrs. Fuchs," Tommy said as he stepped a little to the side.

"My, what an adorable child," Mother said stepping into the room. She made only a brief glance over at Gretta and the baby before turning to me.

"I'm done with my errands, dear," she said, all smiles and sweetness. "Are you ready to go home?"

"May I meet you in the lobby, Mother?" I replied. "I won't get a chance to see them before I go to school. I would like to say goodbye."

"Alright, dear," she said as she swished out of the room merely nodding to Gretta and Tommy when she reached the door.

Once Mother had passed through and the door was closed, Tommy said with a snicker, "Do you think she heard us?"

"What the hell difference does it make?" I responded. "I don't think she'll really ever hear anything more than her own beliefs rolling around in her head."

"Well, at least she was congenial," said, Gretta.

"Her congeniality is merely a thin veneer over her venom," I said, as I leaned over and kissed her on the cheek. "I hate it, you guys, but I've got to go. I'll miss you so much."

"You have our number," said Tommy as he rounded the bed to give me a hug.

"You are more likely to get a letter than a phone call," I said. "Long distance is expensive, but I most assuredly will write."

"We'll write, too," said, Gretta. "Be sure to send us all your contact information as soon as you get there."

"I will, honey." I said, opening the door to leave. "You'll get the first letter I write. Goodbye for now."

They both said, "Goodbye."

I walked down the hall and took the elevator to the lobby. Once inside, the number for the first floor punched, I leaned my head against the wall and thought anxiously to myself, "What the hell have I done?"

CHAPTER 11

September 13, 1966

Dear Gretta,
   Jeez this place is huge! The first day was hell. I don't have a clue how long I stood in line just to register for classes. All Mother could do was bitch about how much this is costing the family. I told her I'll get a fucking loan!
   The dorm is okay except we have to go down the hall and share a bathroom with every other girl on the floor and Marcy (you remember me telling you about my roommate Marcy?) is a twit! She was a cheerleader in high school and all she can fucking talk about are boys and ballgames. She is "sooooooo looking forward to trying out to be a Penn State Lion cheerleader." I'm hoping she breaks her fucking legs. She says that her major is psychology but I've come to the conclusion that her real major is husband-ology. Her father works as an executive for some company in Philadelphia. She obviously has been used to money. She spends it like I piss. Pretty girl—all blond and petite. Her head bobbles back and forth as she talks like she's some fucking spring-head doll. I have this image of her tiny little brain rolling around in it like a marble on a roulette wheel. Every now and then it falls into a slot and she seems to blink her eyes and go "ooh, what was that?" All I want is for her to shut the fuck up while I study.
   The campus is really pretty. It's kind of a valley here with mountains on both sides. The buildings are a blend of limestone and brick. I have to walk quite a way to my first class Monday, Wednesday, and Friday. We only meet three times a week but it's a two-hour class. The walk wouldn't be so bad except that the wind here is a real demon. It whips between the buildings almost like a storm every day. I dread when the weather gets colder. I know

Karlyle Tomms

the cold wind will chew on my cheeks as I'm walking to class.

"Old Main" is the administrative building. It is really beautiful. It reeks of antiquity and has a beautiful tower in the center rising high into the sky like a church steeple but somehow more tasteful and understated. The building is white limestone. I'm looking forward to seeing it after a nice snow. If I can, I'll send you a picture.

They wouldn't let me major in sexual biology. Apparently, there is no such major so I'm having to major in general biology. Maybe I can get a master's or doctorate degree later that will point me more in the direction of sexual research where I know I want to spend my career.

There are a lot of cute boys here and a lot of hippies too. I'm sorry. I just don't get the long hair, flower-child thing. Why a handsome boy would want to cover his face and head with all that hair is beyond me. The sexiest part of a man is his face and I want to see it. It doesn't matter how cute the boys are though. I just don't have time for it and I don't really care right now. I guess I did enough playing around in high school that it just doesn't hold the intrigue for me that it once did. Besides the academics are not as easy as high school either. I need to make the grades so I can stand a good chance of getting accepted into graduate school and from what I've seen in my classes so far, the grades are not going to be that easy to come by.

I hope you, Tommy, and little Derrick are doing very well. I love and miss you and I'll look forward to maybe seeing you at Thanksgiving. So far, to my surprise and gratitude, Mother has not been insisting that I come home every weekend. She has been working at the dress shop and even though she is bringing in a second salary she likes to remind me how she suffers for my future by supplying me with the money for books and tuition. Maybe I'll get a job and relieve her of the burden.

That's enough for now. If I keep bitching, I'm going to start sounding like Mother. Besides, I have to study. I'm off to the library to do a paper on Edgar Allen Poe for the damned English Literature class they require, like I

Confessions from the Pumpkin Patch

haven't had English classes before.
I will look forward to hearing from you.
Hugs and Kisses,
Lovella

As soon as I finished my letter to Gretta, I headed for the library and dropped it in a post box on the way. Libraries have always been like a second home to me although English literature has never been something I found interesting. "Never more," quoth the raven. Fuck off, Edgar Alan Poe. I would rather study the history of malaria in tropical countries. Nonetheless, I had to study on that day to see if I could learn a little bit more about Edgar Alan Poe. I found myself a table and collected a stack of books to browse through. I was looking for ideas on how to write a paper on something I found about as interesting as Marcy's banter on sports. As I was sitting there investigating one of the books, I happened to notice a boy at the next table who was staring at me. When I first noticed him, he smiled at me. That might have been intriguing except for the fact that he was a hippie and not a very attractive one at that. He was skinny and had a bony-looking face with a nose that was quite too large for it. His thin, straight, brown hair hung down over his chest and his large ears poked out between the strands, as it wasn't thick enough to cover them. He had a scraggly beard, a tie-dyed shirt, and beads around his neck. "Jeez!" I thought to myself as I buried my nose back in my book. "I would rather mate with a preying-mantis."

Even though I kept my gaze on my book and tried to comprehend some of the gibberish I had always considered poetry to be, I could feel his eyes on me, pulling at me to look up again. Although I resisted as long as I could not wanting to give him even the hint of an invitation, I finally could not help myself. I had no sooner glanced up to catch him in his unwavering stare when he gave me a tooth-filled grin and got up, moving in my direction. I could see then that he was not only skinny but quite tall. I stuck my nose back into the book as quickly as I could hoping to give him the idea that I did not want to talk to him but it was a useless gesture. I felt him slide into the chair next to mine and heard him say, "Hi."

"Go away," I said without looking up.

"You know," he continued. "You are a very pretty girl."

"And you are a very ugly boy," I replied. "Now, go away."

"I might not be the best looking dude around," he went on, "But I have certain talents."

"Scaring the farmer's crows," I said still not looking up.

"Oh, I've not tried that one," he replied now feeling that he had me

105

hooked on responding to him. "But I'm sure I would be quite good at it. No, you see, I'm a superb lover."

I snickered. I couldn't help myself. The idea of this scarecrow being a superb lover was as laughable as Edgar Allen Poe being an astronaut.

"You don't believe me?" he questioned. "You know I could prove it to you."

"You know," I said in a snarl as I snapped my book closed and looked at him, "If I wanted to get laid right now, which I don't, I think I could find a much better option than the one I'm looking at."

"Mmmmmm, fire," he said. "You know that makes the sex even better."

"Why the hell would you think I would be remotely interested in you?" I snapped trying not to get too loud. I realized that the quick close of my book had drawn some attention.

"Let me have your hand," he said as he reached his long fingers out to mine.

"Would you please stop it?" I said as I pulled away.

"Oh, hey, it's all cool," he continued. "I'm not going to hurt you. I just want to show you one little thing, and if you are not impressed, I'll go away and leave you alone."

I sat there staring at him wondering what planet this freak had descended from.

"Come on," he said. "It will only take a second."

He reached again for my hand and this time I let him take it. "What the hell!" I thought. "What have I got to lose? He's probably going to kiss it and pretend he is Casanova. I'll tell him that I'm not impressed and be done with him."

He gently took my hand with both of his hands, and to my surprise did not move it toward his lips but ever so tenderly moved it under the table to the inside of his leg where he had a huge erection angling toward his knee inside his jeans. When I say huge, I mean huge. It must have been at least ten inches long and a good inch and a half in width. As he moved my hand up and down the length of it he pumped it. He was looking at me, smiling, and said, "I told you I have other talents."

"That's not a talent." I responded. "That's a tool. Just because the carpenter has a big hammer doesn't mean he knows how to drive a nail."

I would like to say I drew my hand back in disgust, but I didn't. It certainly wasn't the first big tool I've ever had my hands on, but it was impressive, and I have to admit that I love the feel of a warm tool in my hands.

"You know," he cooed, "I can prove to you that I know how to drive a nail."

Confessions from the Pumpkin Patch

I pulled my hand back. "You undoubtedly think I'm easy."

"I don't know how easy you are," he continued to coo, "but I do know that you are a damn sexy girl. How about we continue to talk over a cup of coffee and a cinnamon roll? I know a great little diner that makes the best cinnamon rolls this side of the Atlantic."

As much as I hated it, I was intrigued by this tall, ugly boy. "How about you let me study," I said, "I've got a paper due tomorrow."

"How about I study with you," he smiled. "I've got a couple of chapters of my physics book I have to read because there will probably be a pop test tomorrow."

I looked him dead in the eye. "Are you going to study, or are you going to sit there and continue to pester me while I'm trying to study?"

"No, I'll study," he said. "I promise I won't say anything else to you 'til you are done and maybe later we could check out that cinnamon roll."

"Alright then," I said, "but not a word."

"Okay, deal," he said. "But one more thing first. What's your name?"

"Lovella," I said. "What's yours?"

"Lovella, hmmmmm, that's a pretty name," he teased. "My name is Earl. What's your last name?"

I took a deep breath before telling him. I was hesitant to tell him at all. Finally, I said, "Its Fuchs."

"Spell it," he said.

"What!?" I exclaimed.

"Spell it," he said, again. "I just want to make sure I've got it right."

"F. U. C. H. S." I spit out each letter with determination.

He looked at me and light filled his eyes. He grinned from ear to ear. "Great god almighty!" he said, "I've met my soul-mate. Wanna know what my last name is?"

"Sure," I said, puzzled.

"Titwallow," he replied. "T I T, as in breast, and W A L L O W, as in what I like to do to breasts."

I started laughing. I couldn't believe there was someone else out there with a derogatory name like mine. "You know," I said, "That's a really funny name."

"Yeah," he said, "just like Lovella Fuchs. You know they really should have replaced that 'h' with a 'k'."

"It wouldn't have made any difference," I laughed. "People still pronounce it 'Fucks' anyway."

By this time several people had started shushing us so we took the hint and began stifling our laughter. We each grabbed our books. He went back to his table and brought his bookcase over to mine. We then sat there side-by-side, noses in books. But for several minutes one of us would periodically snort or snicker triggering the other. We would then shush each other and turn our attention once again to our studies.

It was about 7:00 PM when I finally put the last line to my paper. Earl had finished his reading much earlier and had put his head down on the table for a nap. After I finished, I returned the books to the re-shelf bin and came back to the table. He was sound asleep. I thought about just walking out without saying anything but like I said I found this ugly boy quite intriguing. His head was lying sideways over his books with his arms wrapped around them. I sat down next to him thinking I could just walk away and he would likely not wake up or know the difference. Instead I touched his arm. His eyes opened. He looked straight at me and said, "Hello, beautiful. Where did you come from?"

"Climax, Pennsylvania," I said, "What about you?"

"Pittsburgh, PA," he said with a smile as he sat up.

"Oh," I said, "a city boy."

"You still up for that cinnamon roll?" he grinned.

"To tell you the truth, I'm a little hungry," I replied as I began gathering up my things. "A cinnamon roll might be dessert but I need a little more. It's probably too late for the cafeteria. You know where we can get a burger?"

"As a matter of fact I do," he said as he got up and picked up his bookcase. "It's the same place that makes the cinnamon rolls—and their burgers are even better than the rolls. Wanna go?"

"That sounds good," I said and we walked together toward the door.

"So are you a Physics major?" I questioned as we walked.

"No, I'm a business major," he replied. "I just like physics. It's kind of fascinating you know?"

"Well, if you think physics is so fascinating," I pried, "why are you majoring in business?"

"The business major is something I'm doing for the old man," he echoed. "Gotta keep the family happy."

"Don't I know it," I said. "You got a car or is this place within walking distance?"

"I've got a car," he returned. "Come on."

When we got to the parking lot he walked up to the strangest car I had ever seen. It looked like a dick and balls, a two-seater cab in the back and a front end that jutted out rounded and smooth like a dick. It was a teal green, sleek, new, and clean.

"What the hell is that thing?" I asked as he opened the passenger side door for me.

Confessions from the Pumpkin Patch

"It's a Ferrari 250 GT," he said. "It was my high school graduation gift from the family."

"Yeah, but what the hell is it?" I questioned again as I slipped into leather seats.

"It's an Italian sports car," he said as he got in on the driver's side.

"Looks expensive," I said.

"It is," he replied. Then he started the motor and I winced from the sound of it.

"Is your family rich?" I queried.

"A little."

He reached for the stick and pulled the car back from the curb. It sounded like a racecar and made me feel like I was in a rocket.

"Well, I have to say," I went on, "this is not what I expected."

"What did you expect?" he questioned as we sailed down local streets.

"Well, you have on all this hippie garb," I continued. "I expected you would be driving some beat-up old contraption, maybe a Volkswagen bus or something."

"I wouldn't mind a beat-up old contraption," he said, "but Dad wants me to live out the family image, not that he is old money or something. My dad owns a company that makes snacks. You know, potato chips, and crackers, and stuff like that."

"You mean like Frito-Lay?" I asked.

"No, it's not that big," he went on. "It is kind of local. We have distribution over most of Pennsylvania, and he is spreading over the border in a couple of the neighboring states. You've probably heard of it: 'Chum Snacks'."

"Yeah," I said, "I really like the cheddar and peanut butter crackers. "Wow! Your family owns that whole company?"

"Well, not the whole company," he replied. "Dad started it about 1947, and he still owns controlling stock, and he's the C. E. O. It probably brings him a couple of million or so a year in personal profit."

"That's really great," I said nervously, suddenly feeling very intimidated by my lower middle class roots.

"Yeah, it's great 'til you have to deal with the bullshit," he said. "Here we are." He crooked his neck around looking for a parking place as we pulled up to the restaurant.

The restaurant looked like a silver train car and there was a neon sign over the entry that said, "The Finer Diner" in a handwritten kind of scrawl.

He soon found a parking spot. I opened the car door, got out, and started to walk with him toward the diner.

"You're gonna love this place," he said as he reached back to take my

Karlyle Tomms

arm and placed his hand inside my elbow.

"Wow, this ugly hippie has manners," I thought.

The front inside wall of the diner was lined with booths. There was a counter parallel to and across from the front door and the booths. The counter was lined with round chrome stools that bellied up to it. Everything was chrome and orange-vinyl except for the tables and counter-tops which were black Formica with green and orange flecks. Behind the counter, a couple of fry-cooks were working the griddle. We took a seat at one of the tables.

In a moment, a forty-ish-looking waitress came by wearing a ruffled white apron over a robin's egg blue uniform. She had a little ruffled cloth tiara in her hair and a receipt pad in her hand. She handed us each a menu.

"Name's Sally," she said. "Be back to get your order in a sec." She then moved on to another customer without giving us a second glance.

I began looking at the menu when Earl said, "I really like the spice burger myself."

I glanced down to see a list of about ten different kinds of burgers. The spice burger was made with black pepper and melted Swiss cheese with sautéed mushrooms and onions, lettuce, tomato, and mayo.

"That looks interesting," I said. "I don't believe I've ever seen such a selection before. I always thought a burger was a burger. You know lettuce, pickle, tomato, and onion with a little yellow mustard."

"Hey," he said, "these folks think outside the box, even though they work in a box." He grinned. "I guess that's why I like this place so much."

The waitress then returned and gave a quick, trite, little question, "You folks ready to order?"

I looked at Earl then up at the waitress. "I think I'll have the spice burger," I said.

"Spice burger, right," she scribbled on the pad. "You want fries, onion rings, bell pepper rings or batter fried mushrooms with that?"

"Bell pepper rings?" I asked. "I've never heard of that."

"Yeah," she said, "it's just like onion rings, honey, except its sliced rings of bell pepper battered and fried."

"Oh—okay." I said. "I'll try the bell pepper rings."

"What you want to drink, honey?" she continued questioning.

"Coca Cola, I guess." I responded.

She immediately turned to Earl, "What about you, darlin', what'll you have?"

"I'll have the very same thing," he said.

"Double spice, double green rings," she yelled as she walked away.

Soon she was back with our drinks.

Confessions from the Pumpkin Patch

"So what about you, Lovella Fuchs," Earl said. "Tell me more about you."

"I'm afraid it's rather boring in comparison," I said.

"Who's comparing?" he asked. "Just fill in the blanks."

"Well, I was born and raised in Climax," I began with a sigh. "It's too small to be a real town, but New Bethlehem is nearby but it is not much bigger. My daddy works for a peanut butter factory and my mother has been a stay-at-home mom until she recently took a job in a ladies dress shop in New Bethlehem. I'm an only child, and that's about it.

"Oh no," he said leaning toward me over the table. "That's not even the tip of the tip of the iceberg. I could tell from the moment I first saw you that you are a deep and complicated person."

"Really?" I responded. "You could tell all that from a glance?"

"Really," he went on. "For one thing you are very intellectual. You like to learn. You are very sensual and passionate. You don't like your mother very much, and you think your father hung the moon."

I was in shock, not so much from the first part, which could have been concluded from the stack of books on my table at the library, or by the second part, which could have been a continuation of his attempts to bed me, but the third part about my parents threw me back in my seat.

"How on earth would you conclude that I don't like my mother and adore my father?" I questioned leaning back away from him.

"I could feel it," he said. "I feel things. I pick up on the vibe."

"I haven't even mentioned my parents except for that one sentence just now, and there was nothing in it to intimate your conclusions," I snapped.

"Hey, it's okay," he soothed. "I'm not judging. I just picked up on a little something in the tone of your voice when you were talking about your father working in a peanut butter factory and your mother being a stay-at-home mom. You want to try it? See if you can pick up on my vibe."

"Okay," I chirped. "You think your father's an asshole!"

"Bang on! Right you are, Lovella Fuchs," he said, "except for one part. I don't think he's an asshole. I know he's an asshole." He laughed. "See, you can read the vibe too."

"I wasn't reading your vibe," I said, "I was just trying to say something mean to you because I felt put off by your forwardness. Besides you already said something about having to deal with your dad's bullshit"

"It doesn't matter," he said. "You're right. My father is an asshole. So why don't you like your mother?"

"I never said I didn't like my mother!" I snapped again. "You did."

"I may have said it," he continued, "but you did not deny it."

"Okay! Okay!" I gave in. "My mother's a bitch. Now are you happy?"

Karlyle Tomms

"I was happy before you said it," he replied. "I'm always happy. Happiness is my thing, man. So why is your mother a bitch?"

"I don't know," I went on. "Maybe she doesn't get laid enough. Maybe grandmother pulled her off the tit too soon. She just is. She tries to control everyone's life—mine, Daddy's, the neighbors, you name it. If she is not manipulating something, she's bored."

"What about your dad?" he asked.

"Daddy loves me with every inch of his being," I said. "But he's a drunk. I never knew how bad a drunk 'til just before I left for school a few weeks ago. Mother has always contained it but this summer it got away from her."

"So you're a freshman," he said.

"Well, yes, mister-psychic-pick-up-on-the-vibe," I retorted sarcastically. "You didn't read that in my aura the first moment you set eyes on me?"

He continued to grin. He was always grinning. "Well, as a matter of fact I did," he covered. "I just wanted to make sure that you knew."

"You are so full of shit!" I laughed.

At that moment the waitress set our meals on the table.

"Two spice burgers with green rings," she said as she walked away.

The smell of grill-cooked meat wafted up from stoneware plates enticing consumption. We pulled the plates to ourselves and began to eat.

"So what are you?" I asked.

"I'm an alien from a distant planet on the other side of the Andromeda," he said.

"Yes, I know that," I said. "But what class level in school are you?"

"I'm a junior this year," he replied. "Can't wait to get it over with."

"Why?" I questioned. "I love school. I love to learn. Even the bullshit required classes that are a bore still give me knowledge I didn't have before. I like knowing things."

"Well for a start," he answered as he nibbled on a bell pepper ring. "I'm not really doing it for me. I'm doing it for the bastard old man. That's why I have a major in business instead of physics or psychology or art or something. He wants me to come back to take over his legacy and run the factory when he's gone. Never mind what I fucking want. You know, like what if I don't want to run a goddamn potato chip factory and live a bourgeois, fat-cat, fuck everybody else in the world, lifestyle?"

"Sounds like you would be set for life," I said.

"I don't care if I'm set for life," he went on, mouth full of burger meat, brown mushroom drizzle sticking to his scraggly beard. "Money isn't everything. I mean, what good is money when people are starving, man. You know, like there are places in this world where people don't have a

Confessions from the Pumpkin Patch

chance while fat-cats like my old man suck up more money than they can ever spend and do nothing of any true worth with it."

"Wow," I said. "I never thought about it like that."

"That's the problem, Lovella Fuchs," he went on. "We live in a society that teaches us to consume without any thought of what effect it might have on anyone else. Americans consume most of the world's resources while people starve around the world despite all these petty efforts like Peace Corps and shit."

"But your dad is not making money off of poor people," I said. "And what difference does it make if he has money. It's not like he is taking food out of the mouths of the needy."

"My dad makes money off everyone," he responded. "He makes money off anyone who has a quarter to buy a snack. The problem is not that he is taking food directly out of the mouths of the needy, but he is keeping money he doesn't need that could be used to help people. He is just not doing anything to help the needy and it's like he is addicted to getting more and more."

"Well, so he wants you to take over the company someday," I debated. "You would then be in control of all that money and you could set up foundations for the poor and do all those altruistic things that you want to do."

"Yeah, I guess you are right," he said. "I just don't have any interest in the business. Who the hell wants to sit there calculating inventories and overhead versus expenditures? It's just boring as hell."

I examined him carefully watching his expressions. I guess I was trying to pick up on his vibe. "Would you find it as boring if it wasn't something your father was pushing you into?"

"I don't know," he replied. "I was never given an opportunity to find out."

"You know you and I are a lot alike I think." I laid my burger down on the plate so I could emphasize the point. "Your dad pushes you into things you don't want and tries to control your life, and my mother pushes me into things and tries to control my life. I don't know. It seems like the difference is that I'm not here getting the degree that my mother wants me to get. She would prefer I meet a nice boy—by her standards—and settle down in Climax to raise grandchildren for her. I'm doing what I want and you are angry with your father for controlling you and pushing you, but you are still doing what he wants."

"You're right," he replied. "Regardless of how different I am from my old man, I still have this need to please him. I still crave a time when he might slap me on the back and tell me 'good job, son', so I do what he

113

Karlyle Tomms

wants. I work on a business degree so I'll know how to run the business when he is ready to retire." He looked up and grinned again. "However, he doesn't know that I have a second major in Physics."

"Why Physics?" I asked.

"I don't know," he said. "I just like it. It's fascinating. I don't have a clue what I would do with the degree once I have it. I don't want to teach and I can't see myself doing research in it. It's just this stuff is cool to know."

"So tell me something that is good to know about Physics?" I asked.

"Okay."

He thought for a moment. "Einstein's theory $E = mc^2$ means that the amount of energy contained in any object of mass is equal to the speed of light squared."

"So what the hell does that mean?" I laughed.

"It means that there is a whole hell of a lot of energy in everything," he replied. "Energy IS everything. Hey, you know when they exploded the first atomic bomb in the New Mexico desert they split the atom, right? Well, what came out of the atom when they split it? A whole fuck-load of energy, man. So, if you split any atom, what comes out of it is energy. So ultimately, everything is made of energy: you, me, this diner, the air, and the planets. There's space and there's different manifestations of energy and that's it. It's like the universe is energy given form by thought, like it is all one big dream that we dream together or something."

"You need to be on medication," I said. "How much time have you spent in institutions?"

"None so far, Lovella Fuchs," he replied. "I'm just living day by day."

He finished his burger before me, wolfing half of it down like a starving dog and only slowing down on the other half so he could talk. I pointed out to him that he needed to use his napkin as bits of the meal still clung to the hair around his mouth. I only ate about half of mine and that was plenty. I was full.

"Didn't you like it?" he asked, looking at the half-eaten burger on my plate.

"I loved it," I replied. "It's pretty big, a little too much food for me."

The waitress had set the check on the end of the table sometime while we were talking. I hadn't even noticed.

"You ready to go?" he asked reaching for the check.

"Yes, thank you," I said.

He slapped a tip onto the table and took the check to the register to pay. I stepped outside and lit up a cigarette. I couldn't believe I had gone so long without smoking. Of course smoking wasn't allowed in the dorm— for goodness sake we might start a fire. So every time I wanted a cigarette

Confessions from the Pumpkin Patch

I had to sneak it—and usually I just went outside somewhere. I was standing there enjoying my first cigarette in several hours when he stepped out of the diner.

"Oh, you smoke," he said as he walked toward me.

"You didn't realize that from the moment you saw me?" I asked just before taking a long deliberate drag on my Winston. "Didn't you even notice that my breath smells like a stale ashtray?"

"Nope, I missed that one," he said. "Let me know when you're done. I don't smoke."

I took one more drag, threw the cigarette down, and stamped it out on the sidewalk. "I'm ready," I said.

"So, where to?" he asked.

"Back to the dorm," I said, assuming that he also resided on campus.

"Well, I could take you back to your dorm or we could go to my apartment," he quizzed.

"Your apartment?!" I questioned.

"Yeah, I have a flat about ten blocks from campus," he said. "Wanna go?"

"Not tonight," I replied not believing what I was saying.

The truth was that I curiously found myself wanting to fuck him. I was intrigued by the ugly hippie. Not only was I fascinated by the cock I had my hand on earlier in the day, but I wanted to see if he was as much of a lover as he made himself out to be or if he would be another in a long line of boys I would teach how to screw.

"Oh, Lovella," he pleaded. "I'm disappointed. I thought you might be the adventurous type."

"My type is, for the time being, none of your business," I said. "Besides, I have an early class tomorrow. I have to turn in my paper and I don't function well without sufficient sleep."

"So you're telling me there's a chance we might get together again some other day?" He grinned. "Come on, I'll drive you back."

We walked to the car with his arm around my shoulder. I looked up at him in the streetlights. Somehow, the filtered darkness softened his looks and he didn't seem so ugly after all. His long arm felt comforting around my shoulder and I found myself wanting to lean my head into the side of his chest, but still I resisted the temptation.

"Just how tall are you?" I asked when we neared the car.

"Six foot five," he said, walking me around to the passenger's side. "Like it?"

"I don't know," I said. "I'll have to think about it."

I slid into the cool leather seats of his Ferrari and waited for him to enter the other side. I couldn't help feeling somehow special in that car, elegant, and pampered. When we got to my dorm, he walked me to the hall entrance.

"No boys allowed beyond this point," I said as I turned and gazed up into sultry eyes that I had previously somehow overlooked.

He smiled as he looked down at me, creating that distinctive grin of his. His warm eyes caressed me and I felt almost as though he was looking into my soul. "Well, I hope this boy is allowed to see you again," he said.

"Yes, I think so," I replied not believing the words coming out of my mouth and then I realized that this was the first actual real date I had ever been on. I didn't count the fiasco that Mother had arranged for the prom or times with Tommy which were just for sex. All the other times had just been me deciding who I wanted to fuck and then following through on my intentions. I couldn't believe I wasn't going to fuck Earl first time, right off the bat, especially after all the invitations he had given me. I don't know why it was different this time, but it was different.

"I'm going to kiss you now," he said, no question, no "May I?" just the identification of his intentions, a warning of what he was about to do. I felt a smile cross my face and a rush of energy through my breast. I felt like a child about to be bestowed with a birthday gift. I was gleaming with anticipation, not believing what I was observing in myself. "Yes," I replied as though he *had* asked—but also saying yes, to myself. Yes, he is going to kiss me. Yes, please kiss me.

He leaned down and cupped his hand gently behind my head, then his warm mouth covered mine and our lips danced together in a slow sensual chorus. Goose bumps ran down my arms. I felt a tingle of exhilaration unlike anything I had ever felt. I didn't actually feel horny so much as tender compassion. When he stopped, our lips parted slowly until the last bit of flesh separated. I felt myself sigh. "Jesus Christ!" I sighed! I felt a lightness in my chest like my heart had just floated up into the air. I had never felt anything like that before.

He reached into his pocket and took out a pen. He lifted my hand and then wrote his phone number across my palm. "Here is my number," he said. "Call me anytime." With that he gave me another quick peck on the lips and walked away.

I had images of telling Marcy and the two of us bouncing up and down with our knees on the mattress screaming: Oh, my god! Oh, my god! Yeah, like that was going to happen. Still, I felt like a giggly little school girl swooning over an ugly hippie.

When I got to my room, I copied the number down in my address book and went to bed. I fell asleep with fantasies of Earl making love to me.

Confessions from the Pumpkin Patch

The next morning I still had a faint trace of Earl's number inked on my hand. The rest of it came off in the shower as I prepared for my Tuesday morning classes. Marcy lay in her bed still snoring when I went out the door. Lucky bitch didn't have a Tuesday class till 1:00 PM.

I thought about Earl all day. I couldn't get over the fact that I didn't seem to care that he was kind of ugly. He was also kind of sweet and always smiling. I guess you could say that despite being an ugly hippie, he did have a pretty smile—and that kiss. Oh my god, that kiss! I had never had a boy kiss me that way. I didn't have to teach *him* how to kiss. He already knew. I began to think maybe he wasn't just bull-shitting me when he told me that he was a fabulous lover.

I finished my last class at 2:00 PM and headed for the library, this time it was just to have a quiet place to read the assigned chapters in my Physical and Life Sciences class. At least it applied to my major. I hoped I might see Earl there, but he didn't show. I kept peeking up from my book, and looking around the room, nothing. I had a hard time concentrating on the book. Finally, I finished my chapters and headed for the cafeteria for dinner.

I hate cafeterias but they are a necessary evil of dorm life. I had not yet made friends. It was too early I guess so I felt a little lonely. I damn sure was not interested in making friends with Marcy, but there she was in the cafeteria with her bubble-head pals. It sure didn't take *her* long to find friends. I suppose it is easy to make friends when you have the mentality of a lemur. All you have to do is squawk, hang by your tail from a tree limb, and here come all the other lemurs. I was trying to ignore her but about the time I got through the line she was waving and calling out, "Lovella, Lovella, over here. Come sit with us."

"Oh, Jesus!" I thought, "I don't want to sit at a table full of jock monkeys." But I was polite and carried my tray to their table.

"Hello, girls," I said as I sat down.

Marcy began immediately. "You guys! You guys! This is my roommate, Lovella. Lovella, this is Staa-seee, Nan-seee, and Pat-seeeeee."

"How do you do," I said politely, thinking to myself, my, my, a table full of seeeees. How interesting that Mar-seee said each name with a distinct little hiss on the last syllable. Good thing there is not a cat around. Someone might have been scratched.

"Lovella, guess what?" Marcy chirped. "Cheerleading tryouts are this week! We're all going to try out tomorrow. You should too."

"That's wonderful for you guys," I said, "but I have absolutely no interest in cheerleading. Besides, I have about as much bounce as a flat tire, and even if I could bounce the backlash from my tits would probably

Karlyle Tomms

knock me out." This comment gathered a round of giggles which I suppose was to be expected. The girls bantered on as I picked at my peas.

"Oh, but you look fit and it will be so much fun."

"I know, I know!" said one of them. I don't remember which seeeeee it was. "Let's tell her about all the cute guys she'll meet."

"Yes," said, one of the other seeees. "There are some very handsome men in sporrrrrrttts."

I knew that the nausea I was feeling could not be from the food so I kept eating. Downing a bite of chicken, I said, "I'm afraid it might be too much of a distraction from my academics."

"Oh, yes, you guys," Marcy twittered. "Lovella is a Biology major. She is soooo smart." She turned to me. "You're going to be a doctor or a scientist or something right?"

"I hope to be able to do research," I replied not wanting to get into the details with those who would spend more energy giggling over it than trying to understand the scientific value of my planned career. After that, thankfully, the conversation went to who was taking what class and how difficult it might be. It was a typical conversation, but I was happy to soon finish my meal and excuse myself. "I have to go now. I think I need to do a little more studying. You girls have a wonderful time."

"Oh we will. We will," they chattered. "You, too."

I was all too glad to excuse myself from the jock monkeys and go back to my room. In the dorm hall by the elevator was a bank of phones which dorm residents used. Everything went through the university operator except for local calls. When I got off the elevator I walked by them thinking that I wanted to call Earl but I dared not. I had only met him yesterday and it would be unseemly I thought to call so soon, and I didn't want him to think that I was desperate. Mind you, I had never had a problem with being forward before, but then all I wanted was sex and the power of knowing I could bring a boy to his knees to make him fetch and beg for his pleasure if I wanted to. This time was different. I saw more in Earl than sex. I felt something more than sex but I simply could not put my finger on what it was. I asked myself if it was his family's money that intrigued me about him and then concluded that I could care less about whether he had money. No, there was something different about this boy. It almost felt as though we had known each other before, more as though it had been a meeting of souls than a meeting of people. Despite the fact that I had avoided him initially, there was some kind of recognition there, like when a toddler encounters another toddler in a room full of adults.

Tuesday rolled into Wednesday and Wednesday rolled into Thursday. For three days, I fought the urge to call him. Finally, on Thursday, I

Confessions from the Pumpkin Patch

figured that I had waited long enough.

Thursday evening I went down the hall to the phone bank and dialed the number he had given me. After the phone had rung about six times, I was about to hang up when I heard a click and "Hello."

"Is this Earl?" I asked.

"Is this Lovella?" he asked.

"How did you know it was me?" I questioned.

"Well," he reasoned. "I don't exactly have a harem waiting around for my next command and I recognized your voice. It's good to hear from you. I was afraid you wouldn't call."

"No, I wanted to call," I said. "I've just been too busy." I had not been too busy to call. I had deliberately avoided it. The lie seemed sufficient as I waited for his reply.

"Well, how busy will you be tomorrow?" he asked.

"Are you asking me out again?" I teased.

"Could be," he teased back. "Are you interested in going out again?"

"I might be leveraged with the right crow-bar," I said.

"Well, you may recall," he teased on, "that I do have a nice, big crow-bar."

He could not see the smile that crossed my face from the other end of the line, but his tool, be it hammer or crow-bar, was not entirely what interested me. I searched my mind for the right response.

"Well, that does present some leverage," I finally responded.

"What time do you finish class tomorrow?" he asked.

"I'll be out by 4:00 PM," I replied. "I don't expect to be busy after that."

"So, if I pick you up in the dorm parking lot at 5:30, will that give you enough time?"

Then there was a moment of silence as he waited for my response. I gave it a moment on purpose and then said, "I think I could be ready by then. What will I be getting ready for?"

"How about dinner and a movie?" he inquired.

"That would be nice," I told him and I thought to myself, "Wow! A real, real date!"

He went on. "There is a Chinese place just around the corner from the Regal Theater. We could grab a quick bite there and then you have two choices: 'Who's Afraid of Virginia Wolf' with Liz Taylor and Richard Burton, or 'The Ghost and Mr. Chicken' with Don Knots. Your choice."

"They both sound good," I replied. "Which one would you prefer?"

I was actually just trying to be polite. I have never been a big fan of comedy. I had heard a lot of chatter about "Who's Afraid of Virginia Wolf," but I really didn't care. It was just something to do.

Karlyle Tomms

"Either one is fine with me," he said. "I want it to be something you would like."

Boom! It hit me! That was it! That was what separated him from every other boy I had ever known. He wanted to please me. It wasn't me teaching some boy how to please himself. It wasn't me fighting back some eager twit whose only interest was ejaculation and trying to get him to hold off long enough that I could get a little something out of it. Granted, I used them, took what I wanted, and did to them what they do to other girls. I fucked them and forgot them. But they still all wanted to please themselves and could have cared less what I got out of it. This was the only man I had ever met besides my father who wanted me to be happy.

"Still thinking?" he asked breaking my daze of thought.

"No," I said. "I think I've made up my mind. I love Liz Taylor and Richard Burton and 'Who's Afraid of Virginia Wolf' sounds both romantic and exciting."

"Great!" he said. "Do you like Chinese food?"

"I don't know," I returned. "I've only ever had it out of a can. There aren't any Chinese restaurants in Climax, or New Bethlehem, and Mother would never eat anything she considered to be foreign."

"Then you've never had Chinese food?" he said. "Are you up for that? There are other options if you don't think you would like it."

"No, Chinese food sounds wonderful!" I exclaimed. "Besides, I like adventure. It will be an adventure, a chance to try something new."

"Okay then," he said, sounding relieved. "Five-thirty. Dorm parking lot. Tomorrow. I'll see you then."

"Okay then," I parroted. "Bye."

I don't know why I said, "bye," much less saying it in a sing-song little girly voice. I didn't want to hang up. I wanted to keep talking, but the words just seemed to come out of my mouth.

"Bye," he said. "See you tomorrow."

I hung up the phone and walked back to my room, half of me disappointed that we didn't talk longer and the other half of me exhilarated that I was going to see him again. For the life of me the only thing I could understand about why this ugly hippie intrigued me so was the fact that he was kind and considerate.

The next afternoon I was standing in the parking lot only a few minutes when he drove up, leaned over and threw open the door for me. When I got in, the first thing he said was, "I want to kiss you."

I smiled and leaned toward him. He kissed my sensually for about ten seconds. He pulled back slowly and looked longingly into my eyes and

Confessions from the Pumpkin Patch

then reached for the gear shift. The next thing I knew the power under the hood of his Ferrari surged and zoom we were away.

We pulled up in front of a little place called "Happy Dragon." Earl turned to me and said, "They're open all night. Isn't that a hoot? It's not the finest, most elegant place you'll find, but its good food."

We walked up to a glass door in a little shopping center. Directly inside was a little podium with a Chinese lady standing there dressed in a black, silk blouse with a tight skirt around her tiny little ass.

"You have take out?" she asked as soon as she saw us. I realized from her chopped English that she had obviously not grown up in the U. S.

"No. Two for dinner," Earl replied.

"You come," she said, picking up two menus.

We followed her through what appeared to have been a converted old storefront.

Everything was in red and gold. Gold dragons crawled across the walls and little silk lanterns hung about the room with gold tassels drifting off their corners. She sat us at a small table, laid the menus before us and said, "Waiter be with you shortly." She then abruptly walked away. Earl grinned his trademark grin, picked up the menus, and handed one to me.

"I don't know what to order," I said. "I have no idea what any of this stuff is."

"Well, let me ask you a few questions," He said, "and then I'll see if I can direct you to something. Do you prefer, or are you in the mood for spicy, moderately spicy, or mild?"

"Spicy," I said

"Are there any vegetables you are opposed to?" he inquired.

"Only Brussels sprouts," I replied.

"Do you like a little sweetness in dishes or do you prefer completely savory?" he continued.

I pondered for a moment and realized that the only real time that I had anything with a meal that was a little sweet was either yams at Thanksgiving or Mother's cornbread which she made entirely too sweet. "I'm not really picky." I said.

"Okay," he continued. "Would you prefer beef, chicken, pork or seafood?"

"Seafood," I smiled loving the attention.

"Okay," he said again. "Shrimp, scallops? What kind of seafood?"

"I love shrimp," I said.

"All right then," he concluded. "How about Kung Pow Shrimp? You can tell the waiter just how spicy you want it to be. Personally, I like it very spicy."

"Somehow I knew that you would," I replied with a big grin across my own face.

The waiter brought a tea pot to the table and two little porcelain cups. "You like drink anything besides tea?" he asked.

Earl looked across at me. "Lovella, this is hot tea," he said. "Would you like something cold to drink as well?"

"Maybe just some ice water," I replied.

"You like to order?" said the waiter standing there posed like a little statue.

"Yes," said Earl. "She will have Kung Pao Shrimp and I will have Mongolian Pork."

"How spicy you like Kung Pao?" asked the waiter.

"Not so spicy that it makes me cry," I said, "but fairly close to that."

The waiter stared at me like I had just told him to cook it in a commode. Earl said, "Medium spicy."

The waiter nodded and left.

"So, Lovella Fuchs," Earl said leaning his elbows on the table and propping his chin onto long fingers. "I've been looking forward to this all week."

"Me too," I replied.

Then the conversation just fell into nothing as though neither of us knew anything to say or had any questions to ask. The silence went on until it was feeling uncomfortable and then Earl asked.

"So how often do you get home to see your parents?"

"As little as I can," I replied. "I think if I never saw Mother again it wouldn't bother me, and I love Daddy, but—"

Again the silence struck for a moment.

"But there's a problem," Earl said finally.

"Earl, my daddy is an alcoholic," I said feeling as though I had just confessed my sins to a priest and that I had betrayed my father by telling his secret.

"Join the club," he said. "Both my parents are alcoholics. You would never know it, and they would never admit it for fear of their appearance in the community. Everyone must be protected from the big secret, but, yeah, they both could drink a sailor under the table. Well, at least Mom used to. She has slowed way down."

"Do you worry about them?" I asked. "I worry so about Daddy. I didn't worry for a long time but just before I left for college I saw a side of him I had never seen before. It just seems like his drinking is getting worse and worse."

"My dad has been stopped by the cops a few times," Earl continued.

Confessions from the Pumpkin Patch

"But all he has to do is wave some money around and that takes care of that. Besides, a lot of the local cops know who he is and they'll stop him just for some extra cash that nobody talks about. He had a wreck a couple of years ago. He ran off the road. Said he was trying to keep from hitting a cat but the truth is he was smashed. Thank god neither he nor Mom got hurt too much and after that they have done almost all of their drinking at home. They will invite people over sometimes and let them be the ones who have to try to get home after having too much to drink."

"Local cops?" I said. "I thought you were from Pittsburgh. That's a pretty big town."

"Well, we actually live in Bradford Woods," he replied. "It's a little town just outside Pittsburgh, but people who aren't familiar with the area are rarely familiar with it. It's just easier to say you are from Pittsburgh. Besides we are so close to the Burgh you can barely tell where one ends and the other begins."

"Oh," I replied and then went back to the original subject. "I read about alcohol when I was little," I responded. "I tried to talk to Daddy about it because the dictionary says that it is a poison, but he assured me that it was okay."

"Maybe poison is determined by dosage," Earl continued. "You know, you take a couple of aspirin and your headache goes away, but if you take the whole bottle you get internal bleeding. You have a couple of drinks and you feel a little relaxed, but if you drink all night every night you kill your liver."

"Yeah," I said. "That makes a lot of sense. I just don't understand why Daddy doesn't have just a couple and quit. Mother does. I mean, I don't think I've ever seen her have more than two even at a party, and those are small. She is so controlled that she wouldn't dare let anything cause her to let her hair down, much less let anyone see her."

"Yeah, I know," Earl said. "Some people are just uptight that way. You would think there would be some happy medium somewhere."

"Maybe we are the happy medium," I said sipping at my tea. The waiter had brought my ice water but I hadn't really noticed.

"I hope we are," he said reaching across the table to cover my hand with his. I looked down as his long gangly fingers, but his hand was not skinny. His full, large, soft palm felt comforting, sensual, as it lay across the back of my hand.

The food arrived and was delicious. I couldn't believe how exotic and interesting it tasted. Earl let me taste his pork and it was wonderful too. We chatted over various things through dinner and almost lost track of the time.

Karlyle Tomms

"Goodness!" Earl exclaimed finally, looking down at his watch, "we better get over to the Regal or we will be late for the movie. He quickly paid and we went to the theater to see "Who is Afraid of Virginia Wolf."

I don't think either of us had any idea what we were in for. I didn't know how Earl felt about it 'til after the film, but it took me through a roller coaster of emotions that I had not expected. An alcoholic couple in middle age was entertaining a young couple in their home for the evening. There was a minefield of mind-games going on in the story, almost too many to keep up with. At the end of the movie, I didn't know if I wanted to cry, scream, run, or hit someone.

After the show, we both walked silently to the car. We got into the car, closed the doors, and just sat there. Earl didn't start the engine. He didn't say a word at first. He just stared forward. Finally he turned to me and said, "Are you okay?"

"I'm not sure," I replied. "I feel like an emotional rag that someone just twisted. Are you okay?"

There was a half sigh, half snicker with a twinge of a tear as he said, "No, I don't think I'm okay. Except for the fact that they are much more private than that, I feel like someone just took the parents of my childhood and put them into a film."

"Do your parents treat each other like that?" I asked.

"Well, not exactly like that, but they certainly have had their moments of mind games and bitterness," he replied. My mom is so much more relaxed now than when I was little. She has a lot less stress on her and her drinking is way down. The wealthier we get the more she seems to get back to normal and the more my dad goes off the deep end."

I took a long deep breath and let it out slowly. Looking down at my purse on my lap I said, "I don't think I saw my parents on screen because my daddy has much too sweet a spirit to be like that, but with the exception of the subject in the mind-games, I think I saw myself and my mother in this story."

"Jesus!" Earl said after a moment. "Do you think we should have gone to see 'The Ghost and Mr. Chicken'?"

I burst out laughing and he did too.

I said, "It's probably about a drunken ghost who is trying to make it with a chicken but the chicken's alcoholic rooster-husband keeps taunting the ghost that an ethereal cock won't do much for his frigid chicken wife!"

"And! And!" he can barely speak he is laughing so hard. "They invite a younger chicken couple for corn-mash, but it all turns into a complicated emotional drunken chicken brawl and the ghost gets so confused he gives up haunting."

Confessions from the Pumpkin Patch

We laughed off our anxiety for several minutes. When it all died down Earl said, "You know what I'm in the mood for? Icecream."

"You know what I'm in the mood for?" I asked.

"No, what, Lovella Fuchs?" he questioned.

"Sex," I said, reaching for his crotch.

He immediately kissed me with a passionate urgency. We might have consummated in the car except that we became potently aware we were in public when a young man walked by knocking on the window and gave a cat call. "Woooh Hooh! Go for it!"

Earl sat back in the seat and asked, "My place?"

"Your place," I replied immediately.

He could barely get to the ignition quick enough.

A few moments later we parked on the street in front of a row of brownstone houses. When we got out of the car he took my hand and led me up the steps of one of the brownstones just a few feet from where he parked. Inside was a central hall and stairs off to the right side of the hall. Everything was dark wood and a single light illuminated the entrance. Earl led me up the stairs to a dark wooden door just past the landing. He opened it and motioned me inside as he flipped on a light to the left of the door.

His apartment was simple. A bank of windows across the front overlooked the street. He had a nice console TV with bookshelves on either side. On the opposite wall was an old leather sofa with a Mexican-style throw over it and a floor lamp beside it. To the right near the back was a small kitchen and a little table with two chairs between the kitchen and the living room.

He took my coat and led me to the couch. "Can I get you anything to drink?" he said as he hung my coat neatly in a nearby closet.

"What do you have?" I questioned.

"What would you like?" he returned. "You can have anything from milk to wine."

"I'm a little scared to have anything with alcohol in it after seeing that movie," I said.

"So am I," he commented, "but I also think that if we attend to dosage a little something might relax us a bit.

"Okay," I said, "I'll have a glass of wine."

"What kind?" he inquired. "Red wine, white wine, dry, sweet, semi-sweet?"

"What the hell!" I said startled. "There are that many choices? I don't even know what dry means. How can it be dry when it's wet?"

"It means it has more tannin and has more of a savory flavor rather than a sweet flavor," he replied. "You haven't drunk much wine have you?"

"No, actually I haven't," I admitted. "I don't know what I like. I'll just have whatever you are having."

"Let's try this," he said grinning as he eyed a small wine rack near the kitchen. "You say only one of these two words: Red or white?"

I mulled the decision over in my head and finally I said, "White. It seems lighter and maybe more refreshing than red."

"White it is!" he proclaimed. Then he turned from his wine rack and went into the kitchen. I preoccupied myself with looking around his apartment. In a moment he returned with three bottles of wine and two glasses.

"You don't expect us to drink all that?" I questioned a little nervous.

"No," he said, "We're just going to taste."

He pulled a corkscrew from his pocket and opened one of the bottles. As he was pouring a little in the bottom of each glass he said, "First, we will start with a little sweet, but not too sweet. What we have here is a Riesling from Germany. Now, first, a lesson in wine tasting." He lifted the glass and stuck his large nose over the rim taking a big whiff. He pulled the glass from his nose and said, "You want to feel the aroma of the wine. Then you taste." He slurped a portion into his mouth and started swishing it around as though he had a mouth full of Listerine. I was laughing out loud as he turned to me, laughing himself after he swallowed, and said, "Now you try."

"You are so full of shit!" I said, giggling.

"No! Noooo! Try it!" he pleaded.

I pulled the glass to my nose and took a big whiff. It was kind of fruity, but not heavy like grape juice and the cold wine was cool in my nostrils. Then I slurped it just as I had seen him do and swished it in my mouth. As I did, the taste seemed to change a bit and there were layers of flavors that crossed moment by moment over my tongue. I looked at him astonished.

"You see! You see!" he smiled. "This is how the hoity toity do it. By the way, white wines are consumed cold and red wines are consumed at room temperature after allowing them to breathe of course. Now, for the Chardonnay."

I giggled and he continued to talk as he opened the bottle.

"The Chardonnay, as you might deduce from the name is from France. It is not quite as sweet as the Riesling and has a hint of dryness to it. But! But! But! In order to appreciate it without contamination, one must have a clean un-influenced glass." He darted to the kitchen and returned with 4 more glasses. He poured a bit of the Chardonnay into two of them and I imitated him this time at the same time he was doing it. He held the glass

Confessions from the Pumpkin Patch

into the air swirling the wine round in the bottom. I did the same. Then we both brought the glass to the nose, whiffed, slurped, and swished. Except this time just as he finished swishing he kicked his head back and gargled!

I laughed so hard I almost spilled what little wine was left in my glass.

"So, how did you like the Chardonnay?" he queried.

"I thought it was a bit more bitter than the Riesling," I said, in my best feigned British accent. "But, it has a fruity finish that is quite delightful."

"And now!" he announced. "Let's bring the Italians to the table! We will have our own little European summit right here in my room."

He began opening the bottle. "This, my dear, is Pinot Grigio, a dry Italian wine which is often served with fish."

He poured the wine, and we went through the rituals as before, but this time, I smacked my tongue against the roof of my mouth and stuck it out.

Laughing at me he said, "I take it that Pinot Grigio is not your cup of tea."

"It is not only not my cup of tea," I replied, "but I'm not sure it is not a chilled cup of piss."

"Oh, now, now," he comforted. "You must experience it under the right circumstances. Perhaps it is not the best sipping wine and would be better enjoyed with a meal."

"Well, you can turn me on to that some other time," I said. "How about a glass of the Riesling?"

He poured me a glass and we had only taken a few sips before he sat his glass on the floor. Leaning into me he began to kiss me. He took my glass and fumbled to set it down while he kissed me. When he was not able to reach the coffee table or floor he threw it across the room. His kiss was pressured but gentle, passionate, yet sweet and gently sensual. I began to feel the pulsing pressure of his phallus on my thigh as he pressed against me. Then he stood up, took my hand, and led me to his bedroom where he slowly and meticulously undressed me. After removing my blouse one careful button at a time, he reached around and unclasped my bra with surgical precision. His hand moved around my breast and his mouth covered my nipple. His tongue circled my nipple and the soft tingle of his long hair fell lightly between my breasts. He gently pushed me back onto the bed, ran his hands around the rim of my panties and slid them slowly down my legs. Then he stood there before me staring at me lying naked and vulnerable on the bed, undressing himself, softly and sensually flicking open the buttons of his shirt. When he pulled his pants to the floor and kicked them off, his giant cock popped up like a lever on a slot machine.

"My god!" I thought to myself, "That's the biggest damn cock I've ever seen."

Then he folded himself over me again and kissed me. He worked his lips gently from my mouth over my neck and down my body, his beard assisting in the tingling sensation of pleasure. I felt gorged with anticipation like I had never felt before. For once in my life a man was making love to me instead of me showing him every step, every scientific technique that he could use. A man who already knew what he was doing was just doing it. I wasn't having to stop him here or there to show him what to do or how to do it. He was just doing it. Yet he wasn't just doing it, he was enjoying the moment, enjoying the experience of pleasuring me.

When his mouth finally reached the muff-dragon, I lunged backward with a gasp of electric joy. He continued to thrill me while I alternated between grabbing fists-full of the sheets and his long thin hair in my hands. By the time he laid me back onto the pillow and was about to enter me, I was begging.

"Please—please," I heard myself whisper.

He reached down and guided his long shaft gently and slowly into me. At first, it was a little painful, a little too big almost, yet I thought I was going to explode with pleasure as he pushed himself deep into me. Then he drew back and pushed again, and again.

Suddenly I heard something that didn't quite fit with the moment. "Pabbbblllllllaaaaabbbbllllt!"

"What the hell!" I thought. "Did he just fart?"

Then I thought, "What the hell! Who cares! This is awesome!"

Then, there it was again. "Pabbbbbllllaaaabllllllttt!" And again. "Pabllat! Pabllaaatttt!"

Soon it was happening almost thrust by thrust, and there was no mistaking that he was farting almost every time he pushed into me and retreated his ass back up toward the ceiling. The distinctive smell of fecal gas filled the room. It became extremely difficult not to be distracted from the sexual pleasure by the smell of repeated flatulence. I held my breath.

When I could hold my breath no longer I released it with loud squealing gasp. Thinking I was nearing orgasm he worked harder rolling his ass around using his dick like a piston, round and round into me like the arm on the wheel of a steam train.

The farting slowed, but continued, so I took another breath and held it thinking it was better to smell the rotten atmosphere once in a while rather than repeatedly.

He pushed and pushed and the farts went, "Pabllllaaaattt! Pabllllaaaat! Pabllaaaat!"

Soon, despite everything else, I felt the explosion of an orgasm welling

Confessions from the Pumpkin Patch

within me. I blew like a nuclear bomb! The scream that came out of my mouth was primal and I pulled my fingernails across his back in unconscious surrender to the animal power! The muff-dragon spasmed like an epileptic in a grand-mal seizure. I knew that I was gasping in atomized shit, but somehow it didn't seem to matter. Not long after the first wave passed, then another followed and then another. I realized I was having one orgasm after another, after another. For the first time ever, a man pleasured me more than my own middle finger. The flatulence was a small price to pay for that exhilaration.

Shortly, I began to hear Earl's breath quicken. His moans became heavier, his thrusts more rapid and I knew he was about to finish, too. This brought me to yet another orgasm. Then we were both screaming in one big mind-blowing, banshee-flying, climax of sex.

After that, he fell silent and still on top of me panting like he had just run a marathon, but maybe he had. At last he rolled over on his side, pulled me to him and enfolded me in his arms.

"Oh, my god!" I said finally. "Where did you learn to do that?"

"I read the Kama Sutra when I was thirteen," he said. "Dad was too busy to tell me about sex and Mom was too embarrassed. I had to figure it out somehow."

I started laughing.

"What?" he questioned suddenly slightly embarrassed. "What? What are you laughing at?"

I grabbed his face with my one free hand and kissed him.

"I did the same thing," I said.

"You're kidding?" he asked.

"No. I'm not kidding," I replied. "I read the Kama Sutra when I was thirteen."

He began laughing too.

We laughed for a while. Then we fell asleep enfolded in one another's arms, me and the ugly, farting hippie.

CHAPTER 12

After that first night with Earl I was hooked. I couldn't get enough of him. Farts or no farts, Earl Titwallow had become my new obsession. As often as not, after that first night together, I stayed in Earl's flat rather than in the dorm. No more Mar-cee, Sta-cee, Tra-cee, or ooooh goody for me. At last, I was in the company of an adult. I suddenly felt domestic.

Mother had never taught me to cook. I think she found it frustrating and besides she wouldn't take a chance that I might have messed up her perfect little concoctions. I think she hoped that I would marry into money and forever have servants doing things like cooking and cleaning. Yet, even though I was in the company of someone who had grown up wealthy enough to have servants, I felt like cooking and cleaning.

When I wasn't studying or finding another excuse to have sex with Earl, I was checking out cookbooks from the library and watching episodes of "The French Chef" with Julia Child. Earl told me that I didn't have to cook that he could afford to take me out to eat or that he could have it catered in. Nonetheless, when he saw my interest in cooking, he bought me a copy of Julia Child's "Mastering the Art of French Cooking." I was in heaven. I plowed through the book as though I was being pulled by a farm tractor. I experimented with the recipes and destroyed most of them. Even though I put charred and unrecognizable reproductions of Julia's recipes in front of him Earl cooed over it as though it was a perfect delicacy cooked by Julia herself.

One night Marcy called and told me that Mother had called the dorm several times looking for me. I had not left a number for her. She managed to track me down by snooping with friends.

"Gosh," she said, "your mom seemed to be really worried about you."

"What did you tell her?" I asked.

"Welllllll—," Marcy dragged out the word, passive-aggressive little bitch that she was. "I told her that you were spending a lot of time at your new boyfriend's apartment. I hope that's okaaaaayyyyy."

"Marcy," I questioned. "Why would you tell my mother that I am living with my boyfriend?"

"Oh!" she gasped in feigned concern, "I would never tell her that you were living with him. I only told her that you were spending a lot of time at his apartment."

"How would you like it if I told your mother you were spending a lot of

Confessions from the Pumpkin Patch

time at your boyfriend's apartment?" I snapped.

"Oh that's silly," she snickered. "My boyfriend doesn't have an apartment. Besides, I'm dating two boys on the football team. It's hard to decide which one to spend most of my time with."

"How very monogamous of you," I quipped.

"What does that mean?" she asked in apparent shock that I must have just accused her of prostitution or something.

"It means I'm very happy for you," I replied gingerly hiding my disgust at her ignorance. "What did my mother say?"

"Oh, she said she wants you to call her right away."

"Thank you for calling, Marcy," I said in with a deliberate tone. "I will be sure to get hold of her."

"Oh, okay, good-bye now," she spouted in her usual cheery little tone.

I hung up the phone and stared for a moment at the wall. This was most assuredly going to be a call I would dread. It would be difficult enough trying to explain why I was not to be found in the dorm, but there was a nagging fear that something might be wrong. Perhaps Grandmother had died, or Daddy was ill.

At the time of Marcy's call, Earl had handed me the phone and then sat across the room reading a textbook and pretending not to hear.

"Earl." I said, after a moment of pause. "Do you mind if I call my mother? I will forward the charges."

"Don't worry about it," he replied. I can afford any phone bill. Call anyone you want."

"No, I have to forward the charges," I went on. "If I don't, mother will want to know how I'm paying for the phone call. I could pretend that I'm calling her from the dorm, but apparently she already knows better."

"Whatever you need to do is fine," he said.

I realized that I was merely stalling, not really wanting to make the call at all. Finally, I dialed the zero and when the operator came on line I said, "Yes, I would like to make a collect phone call please to Mrs. Drucella Fuchs at—."

After hearing the number the operator connected me. "I have a collect phone call for Mrs. Drucella Fuchs from Lovella Fuchs. Will you accept the charges?"

"Yes."

I heard Mother's terse voice on the other end of the line and then, "Hello, Lovella. It is good that you finally decided to call."

"I'm sorry, Mother." I apologized and then excused. "I've been quite busy."

"Do you have any idea how long I've been trying to get hold of you?"

she interrogated and then answered without giving me the opportunity of a guess. "Three weeks!"

"I'm sorry, Mother," I lied. "Marcy didn't tell me that you had been trying to call."

"You know, there were several girls who have answered the phone in the dorm over these three weeks. A couple of them said they had repeatedly left notes on your door."

"Perhaps they got the wrong door, or perhaps Marcy misplaced the notes. She is quite a ditz you know." I knew, even as I said, it, there would be no appeasing her.

"Lovella!" she shouted, "Do you take me for a fool? Marcy didn't even know how to get hold of you at first. How was I to know you hadn't been abducted or something!? Where have you been?"

"Well, it seems you and Marcy have been exchanging information," I replied in my own tense inflection. "Why don't you tell me where I've been?"

"That girl told me you are living with a man!" Mother snapped. "Should I believe her?"

"Mother, I think the question should be: Do you believe her?" I responded.

"Unfortunately, Lovella," she continued. "There is nothing that I would not put past you."

"Well, technically," I countered. "I'm not actually living with him. My address is still the University."

"Lovella Fuchs!" she screamed. "How dare you!?"

"How dare I what, Mother?" I questioned, "How dare I live my own life?"

"Don't be flippant with me!" she continued to bellow. "How dare you live with a man!? Not only is it unseemly and socially inappropriate, it's a sin!"

"Well, so is fucking a boy in the laundry room, Mother," I replied. "Sin is my forte. In case you haven't noticed, I do it well."

There was then a silence on the line. Finally, I said, "So did you call me to chew me out about living with my boyfriend or did you have something else on your agenda?"

"Tell me about this boy," she said finally.

"Oh, now he's a boy," I teased. "I thought I was living with a man."

"Well, whoever you are living with," she raged. "Explain yourself!"

"His name is Earl Titwallow," I began. "He is from Bradford Woods which, if you haven't heard of it, is outside Pittsburgh. He is two years ahead of me in school and he is studying business."

Confessions from the Pumpkin Patch

"What kind of character does this boy have?" she continued to interrogate. "What kind of family is he from?"

There it was Mother's ultimate question. Regardless of the fact that Daddy was a factory worker, and our family was at the bottom end of middle class, Mother's aspiration was that we only associate with the most refined. I hesitated to tell her about Earl's background. It would mean that I had finally landed the kind of man that she always wanted me to land. I would rather have told her that he came from a family of Kentucky sharecroppers who had used their last pennies to send their toothless boy to college, and listen to her squirm on the other end of the line. However, despite whatever is going on in my life, I usually tell the truth about it, even to Mother. I seldom saw the need for deception. Finally, I said it, taking a deep breath to compose myself and feeling as though I was confessing to a priest. Just one sentence would satisfy her, and for that, all else would be overlooked. "His father owns the Chum Snacks Company."

She literally gasped. I imagined her swooning with glee, and then her tone changed completely, just as I had anticipated.

"Oh, well," she said and then paused. I could almost hear the gears in her head turning as she began to justify for herself why her daughter was living with someone out of wedlock. All in all, it was simply a different form of prostitution that Mother happened to endorse, and she would indeed find a way now to endorse it. "Well," she said again after her pause. "I'm sure he must be a very nice young man." He could have been a serial killer for all she knew, but the instant I told her that he was from a wealthy family all was forgiven. It actually didn't matter to her what kind of man he was. It only mattered that he was rich.

"Yes, Mother," I acknowledged. "I have to say that I am quite fond of him."

"Well, um," she stuttered. "I had originally called to make plans for Thanksgiving. Your Grandmother Claudella would like for the family to come to her house, and she said that she would like to see you."

I had completely forgotten about the nearing holidays. I literally had not even thought about Thanksgiving or Christmas. I had been so caught up in just being with Earl that I had forgotten to make my regular calls home much less anything else. "That's very nice, Mother." I said, "I've been so busy that I had not even thought about the holidays."

"Yes, I know you must be working very hard," she went on. "How are your studies?"

She could have cared less about my fucking studies at that point. I had, in her mind, already accomplished what she hoped I would accomplish in college. Regardless of my major, or my desires for a career, she lumped me into the same category as Marcy and her inane little friends. Regardless of what I claimed as my major, Mother had secretly hoped I would be getting a degree in husbandology.

"I'm doing quite well with my studies as always," I replied. "However, I have been spending a lot of time with Earl, and I plan to continue doing so as long as it is something he also continues to desire."

She then asked something she would never have asked without the knowing that Earl was wealthy. "Would you like to spend Thanksgiving with Earl's family this year?"

I stifled the impulse to tear into her about her hypocrisy. Instead, I said, "We haven't discussed it Mother. I don't know."

"Well, why don't you talk to him about it dear and call me back," she happily enticed. "By the way, did you tell me this boy's name?"

"Yes, Mother. I told you his name is Earl Titwallow." As I said it, my mind saw the image of her writing it down to be sure to remember it, then gallivanting around the neighborhood knocking on doors and telling everyone, "Oh yes—my daughter is dating a wealthy socialite. His name is—" I found myself becoming embarrassed that she might actually do it before she even hung up the phone.

"Well, dear," she chirped. "Discuss it with Earl and call me back. If need be, I'll explain to Grandmother. I'm sure she will understand."

I hung up the phone and buried my face in my hands.

"Are you alright?" Earl asked looking up from his book.

"My fucking Mother is a gold-digging cunt!" I said without removing my face from my hands.

"What's up?" he questioned.

"Earl," I began, "are we officially dating? Are we a couple?" Then I looked up to see his response.

"Hmmm," he pondered. "We have never really discussed that have we? I don't know about you, but I just assumed that we are a couple."

"That's what I assumed, too," I said, "but I've never brought it up and I probably wouldn't be bringing it up now except for my mother. If it wasn't for family, I think I would be content to just let our relationship naturally evolve into whatever form it wishes to take."

"It seems to me," he reflected, "that it has been taking shape, and I don't know that we need to allow family to cause us to worry about that."

"Okay."

I spoke finally after building my resolve. "Here is the deal. My Mother was a furious bitch with me about living with a man out of wedlock 'til I told her that your dad owns the Chum Snacks Company. Then—and I know her well enough to know that she would do this—then she wanted to

Confessions from the Pumpkin Patch

know if I would like to spend Thanksgiving with your family. However, she had called to tell me that my Grandmother wants to see me over the holidays."

"Jeez," he responded, "Thanksgiving is next week isn't it? I've been so caught up with everything that I hadn't even thought about that."

"I know," I replied, "Neither have I but Mother has brought it to the doorstep."

"Well, what would you like to do?" he said.

"I would love to meet your family Earl," I replied, "but do they even know about me?"

"Well, actually, no, they don't," he contemplated, "but there is no reason why they shouldn't, and there would be no problem with having you spend the holiday with us."

"See, that's just the deal."

I got up, paced the room a bit and then turned back to him. "You don't know my mother. You don't know how she is."

"I've heard you talk about her," he cut in.

"No," I popped back. "It's not the same. You don't understand. She will try to manipulate everything that happens to me and to one end. To see me married into a quote, respectable family, end quote. The only reason she offered for me to spend Thanksgiving with your family is that she now knows you come from wealth. A moment before I told her who your father is, she was bitching me out for living with someone."

"Well, actually, I don't come from wealth," Earl related. "My dad has built this company from the ground up and it has taken most of my life to do it. We have only been on the opulent end of profits for about the last eight or ten years. I know what it is like, or at least I think I do, to struggle a little bit."

"No, honey, you are missing the point," I pleaded. "Since I reached puberty, and probably before, Mother has tried to match me up with the kind of boys she thinks are appropriate for me. She set me up on a blind prom date, without my permission, with this doctor's son who was a jerk. But Mother wanted to push him on me. She has pushed those kinds of boys on me for years, and as hard as she has pushed, I've resisted. By dating you, I'm dating exactly the kind of person she wants me to date. She will even overlook the scruffy hippie exterior if she thinks there might be wealth on the interior. She is going to push, Earl. She is going to push our relationship because she is a gold-digging cunt. She won't let us just be together. She will try to MAKE us be together, and the one and only reason she will do that is because of your family's wealth."

"Lovella," he pleaded as he rose from his chair and came to hug me. "I

135

want to be with you. I enjoy being with you. So what difference will it make if your mother pushes us together?"

"It's the chocolate cake principle," I said. "I love chocolate cake. It is one of my very favorite deserts and given the chance I will sit and savor it, enjoying every moment of it, but I don't want it shoved in my face. That completely changes the experience. I don't want Mother shoving me in your face, and I don't want her shoving you in my face, but I know, as sure as I'm breathing, that is what she will do."

He paused, cupped my face in his hands, and kissed me gently.

"You know," he said, "I think if someone did shove chocolate cake in my face, it might be kind of fun to try to lick it from my lips."

I started to giggle a little. "You're a freak," I said.

He laughed, too. "You know you like that freaky stuff. So what do you want to do?"

"I don't know," I whined. "I would love to meet your parents, but I know at some point Mother is going to insist on meeting you, and——. Are we at that point? We have only been seeing each other a few weeks. Are we already at the point where we divide up the holidays between in-laws like a married couple?"

"We have been seeing each other since September," he said. "That is longer than a few weeks. We have the option of going, each of us, to our own families over the holidays, or we have the option of trading off. You said your grandmother wanted to see you? I say we go to your family for Thanksgiving if they are willing to have me as a guest. Besides I would love to meet your family."

"Oh my god, Earl," I pleaded. "My family is a bunch of lower-class lunatics, inbred freaks and drunks. I think one of the reasons Mother tries to palm herself off as highbrow is because she is ashamed of the whole damned lot. As much as I love Daddy, he is a drunk. His drinking is getting worse, and I have no idea what he might do over Thanksgiving. Mother will give us no peace. Grandmother is a fat, frumpy, little woman who wears strange clothes, has fat lips, smokes cigars, and picks at Mother like an ill-tempered Chihuahua. I don't know who will be there. My Grandpa Fuchs is dead, but Grandma Fuchs might be there, and she will be quoting the Bible sweetly but persistently. I don't know——. I just don't know. I can barely tolerate them myself."

"Hey, you said I am a freak," he smiled. "I should fit right in."

"If you want to spend Thanksgiving with my family," I said as I walked over and plopped myself on the sofa, "then you are a freak."

He came and sat beside me. "Look," he said as he put his arm around me. "My family is no piece of cake. My Dad will give me no peace. He

Confessions from the Pumpkin Patch

will be pushing the company down my throat the whole time we are there. There is usually some point when I want to throw him out the window. Now that he has made millions, he thinks that somehow makes him better than other people, so he will be critical and judgmental of—you name it. He may even direct some strategically placed put-downs to you. Long before he made the money, he seemed to think the world should revolve around him, and as far as Mom is concerned, it has. My mom is a quiet, reserved doormat, who has always done whatever he wanted her to do because she thinks her job as a wife is to please him at whatever cost. When I was small, she worked two part-time jobs in addition to taking care of the family so Dad could spend a jillion hours a day trying to build his company. She drank and resented him for not being there. He drank and resented her for not being more than she was."

He sighed deeply, stared at the floor for a moment and went on.

"When I was very small, I didn't see either of them much and my Grandmother Shaw took care of me most of the time. My grandma was wonderful but she was killed in a car wreck when I was fourteen. I would tell you about my Grandpa Shaw, but he is more a story in the family than anything else. He abandoned my mom's family when Mom was in her early teens. If Grandpa and Grandma Titwallow happen to be there, it will be because Dad has sent a car for them. He does that more to impress my Grandpa Titwallow more than any other reason. Grandpa insists on driving because he refuses to be impressed, and Dad insists that he send a car for them. It is a battle every holiday often with a Mexican standoff. If Grandpa comes, it will only be for the sadistic pleasure of torturing my Dad in much the same way that my Dad tortures me. My Grandpa Titwallow, even though he doesn't have the financial success, is basically just like my Dad. He thinks the whole fucking world owes him something, and that they should just kowtow and give it to him. Although Dad keeps trying, there will never come a time when he will win Grandpa's approval. Grandma Titwallow gets through it all by cracking jokes—constantly. Honestly, I think if my Dad, her own son, were to drop dead at her feet, she would crack a joke about it."

Earl gave me a quick squeeze around the shoulders and continued to tell his story.

"You've heard me talk about my little sister. She is okay, I guess. I kind of looked after her when we were little kids but she never went through the brunt of it, the hard years, when Dad was building the company. I went through that alone. She has grown up used to having things, and I guess she kind of takes it for granted. My Dad favors her and gives her everything. Instead of his time, he gives her money and things. She only

137

has to think she wants something and there it is. I don't want to say that she is spoiled, but there is an expectation that she will always be taken care of and she will never have to put forth the effort herself. She says she wants to be a nurse. Yeah, man, I can see that happening. The first time she has to empty a bed pan, it's over."

"My family is worse," I said.

"Wanna bet?" he quipped. "I say we tell them all to go fuck themselves while you and I spend Thanksgiving together, just the two of us. Hell, if you want, we can drive down to the Keys."

"I can't, Earl," I said. "Either way, if I don't spend Thanksgiving with my family or yours, I'll never hear the end of it. Mother will torture me with it, and if I spend Thanksgiving with your family she is going to insist that you come for Christmas."

"Whatever," he said. "Wanna flip a coin? Heads, we spend Thanksgiving with your family. Tails, we spend it with mine."

He reached in his pocket for a quarter.

"I suppose it is as good a way to make a decision as any other," I sighed. "Why not?"

He flipped the coin into the air, caught it and slapped it on the back of his hand. Then he teased, barely lifting his hand off the results and closing it back. "Are you sure you want to see?" he grinned.

I punched him playfully in the arm. "Show me the goddamn quarter!" I said.

He gradually lifted his hand up, and there it was lying on the back of his opposite hand—heads!

"I guess we go see your folks this first holiday," he smiled.

"You don't know what you are getting yourself into," I quipped.

"Well," he chided throwing back his shoulders in a mock display of strength, "Daniel survived the lion's den. Surely Earl can survive Thanksgiving with the Fuchs."

Confessions from the Pumpkin Patch

CHAPTER 13

November 14, 1966

Dear Gretta and Tommy,
Wanted to let you know that I will be home for Thanksgiving break and would love to see you. I have a boyfriend now. His name is Earl Titwallow and he is from Pittsburgh, PA area. He is two years ahead of me in school, and although he is not anything like I ever thought I would pick for a man, he is very nice, and I am quite fond of him. Earl will be coming with me and I hope for you to meet him. Mother wanted me to spend Thanksgiving with Earl's family, but we tossed a coin and decided to spend it in Climax instead, although I have to say that I am quite embarrassed over the idea of Earl meeting my family. You know how they are.

Mother will not hear of Earl staying with us. She could not tolerate for the community to know that she let her unmarried daughter and her boyfriend sleep in the same house, much less the same bed. Yet she is quite aware that we are fucking. Earl will therefore be staying at a hotel and will meet us for family dinner. We will arrive Wednesday evening the 23rd and spend the evening with Mother and Daddy. Thursday belongs to Grandmother Donner who insisted that she wants to see me over the holiday. I'll explain the discrepancy between that and Mother's wish when I get there. I thought, therefore, if you guys are not also busy with family on Friday after Thanksgiving, we could perhaps spend some time together. Call me at Mother's next Wednesday evening after 7:00 PM, please.
    Much Love,
    Lovella.

The whole week after Mother's call, I was a nervous wreck. I usually would have cared less about whether a boy liked my family or not, but this was different. Earl was different and he was wonderful that whole week constantly reassuring me that everything would be fine, that he didn't mind staying in a hotel, and he repeatedly affirmed that he was sure he would love my family.

Mother and Daddy did not have a guest room in our little two bedroom bungalow. Earl could have stayed with Grandmother Donner but I could see a complete disaster brewing in that arrangement and Mother would have found a million excuses why he couldn't stay with Grandmother Fuchs.

Truthfully, I had little to do with either grandmother when I was growing up. I think Mother somehow wanted to shield me from them for fear I might pick up their lowbrow ways. There was none of the normal sleepovers at grandmother's house like so many other children enjoy. As with so many things, Mother insisted—I just accepted. It really wasn't that important to me anyway. I would rather have my face in a book.

Earl and I arrived in Climax in time for dinner on Wednesday evening. When he pulled the Ferrari up in front of our house I let out a big sigh. He reached over and took my hand.

"Are you alright?" he asked.

I smiled as I looked over at him. "I'm fine," I said. "I just never want to deal with Mother, especially when she is in one of her little gloat fests and I know there will be so many questions."

He patted my hand and then got out of the car to get my bags. Earl dutifully carried them to the porch. Rather than walking through the front door as I normally would, I knocked on the door like a stranger. Mother came to the door and looked at me startled. "Oh, for heaven's sake, Lovella, you have a key. Why didn't you just come on in?"

"I suppose I was just feeling somewhat formal," I replied as I walked across the threshold. I turned, motioned to Earl and said, "This is my boyfriend, Earl Titwallow."

Mother scanned him like an X-Ray machine trying to pick up on every tiny perceived abnormality. She thrust her hand out to him forcing him to put the luggage down and shake it. "How do you do, Earl," she twittered with her trademark three fingers laid daintily across his palm. "So nice to meet you. I'm Drucella Fuchs, Lovella's mother."

"How nice to meet you Mrs. Fuchs," Earl said with perfect etiquette.

"What a sweet boy, Lovella. What nice manners." She gleamed toward me, overlooking the long hair and hippie clothing as she glanced back and

Confessions from the Pumpkin Patch

forth between me and the doorway where she could see the Ferrari parked in front of the house. She then gleamed back at Earl. "Come in! Come in!" she stammered on. "Lovella, would you show Earl and your luggage to your room please."

"Yes, Mother," I replied as I presented my best behavior.

Daddy was nowhere to be found, and I wasn't sure if I wanted to ask.

I led Earl to my room and he set the luggage beside my bed. He hugged me close after putting the luggage down and then he kissed me. After the kiss, I asked, "Are you ready for this?"

He said, "I'm fine. It's you we should be worried about. It seems like you are the one who is nervous."

"I've gotten through eighteen years with this family," I said, "I'm sure I can make it till the weekend. Let's go."

I took him by the hand and led him back out into the living room. There was no one there or in the kitchen, but it soon became obvious that Mother had headed out the back door to the shed to fetch Daddy. As recent years had progressed, he had spent more of his time in the shed drinking rather than in the house dealing with Mother. I'm sure that my leaving for school didn't help that situation. I saw her through the back window lecturing him. She appeared to be commanding him to come into the house. When I saw this, I motioned Earl back into the living room where we took a seat on the sofa. I didn't want him to see any more than I could possibly prevent. I knew, for certain, that he would see enough. Finally, Daddy staggered into the living room with Mother behind him.

"Well, look there!" he shouted in a voice far too loud and far too enthusiastic. "It's my little Punkin' Patch." He made a staggered move to hug me and hit his shin on the coffee table. "Oh, goddamn, ouch!" he exclaimed and then practically fell into me as I was getting up. When he hugged me, the stench of stale alcohol filled my nostrils and I had a feeling of horror in my heart as I realized that Daddy's drinking was progressing to a point beyond control. "Hi there young man," he slurred as he reached his hand for Earl's.

Earl had stood up when I did. He politely shook Daddy's hand and said, "Pleased to meet you, sir. Earl Titwallow is the name."

"Titwallow," Daddy snickered. "Now that's a funny name. Not like Fuchs, eh Punkin'?" Laughing, he poked me in the shoulder and said, "Sit down. Make yourself comfortable." He motioned Earl to sit back down on the sofa and then Daddy plopped down right beside him and pulled on my arm for me to sit. Daddy ended up sitting between us. Across the room, Mother had watched this spectacle with a failed attempt to disguise her disgust.

141

"I think I will finish dinner," she said irritably as she turned back toward the kitchen. She had warned me about bringing Earl to Climax for Thanksgiving. I found myself wishing I had tried harder to convince Earl that we should either spend the holiday separately or go to his parent's.

"So, tell me, Earl," Daddy exclaimed as he slapped Earl on the leg. "What do you do for a living?"

"Well, sir," Earl responded politely. "Right now I'm a student at Penn State with Lovella. We met in the college library."

"Oh, yeah! Yeah!" Daddy went on. "My daughter's going to college up there. She's going to be a doctor. Did you know my daughter is going to be a doctor?"

I saw Earl visibly wince from the odor on Daddy's breath, as Daddy got much too close to his face in the conversation.

"Earl is studying business," I said cutting in on the conversation and hoping to pull Daddy back in my direction.

"Hey, Punkin Patch'," you know what?" Daddy turned and slapped me on the knee. The stench of his gullet intruded toward me. "Why don't you go see if your mother needs some help in the kitchen so me and Earl can have some man-time?"

I had no idea what Daddy meant and I barely knew what to do for I had never seen him behave that way. I knew his drinking was getting worse, but his entire personality seemed to have changed. I looked at Earl questioningly and he motioned his eyes toward the kitchen. I did not want to leave Earl alone with Daddy. Still, I got up and left the room with intense hesitation. I had no idea what would ensue if I left them alone, but I also trusted Earl to manage a situation if it were to arise.

In the kitchen, Mother was preparing brown and serve rolls to go into the oven. She looked up at me briefly and I could swear I caught a hint of shame in her eyes.

"Dinner will be ready in a few minutes," she said. "We are having roast beef. I'm going to make a pumpkin pie after dinner to take with us tomorrow."

"That sounds very nice, Mother," I responded quietly. "Is there anything I can do to help?"

"No, of course not, dear," she smiled faintly. "Sit down. I'll get you some tea."

I sat at the dining table and in brief, she set a glass of tea in front of me. She saw me glancing back toward the living room and seemed to guess what I was thinking.

"He has been getting terribly worse over the last year, Lovella." She spoke staring momentarily toward the living room. "I was successful in

Confessions from the Pumpkin Patch

hiding it from you for most of that time, but you recall how he behaved at the hospital after Gretta had her baby. That was mild compared to the last few months."

"Mother, shouldn't we be getting him some help?" I queried. "Doesn't he need to see a psychiatrist or something?"

"He won't go to the doctor," she said as she slipped the rolls into the oven. "He won't admit that there is anything wrong. He keeps saying it's perfectly natural for a man to drink."

"Maybe we could get Dr. Whitmire to make a house call," I suggested.

"Maybe," she said. "I don't know what else to do. I've tried pouring out his liquor when I can find it, but he just finds another place to hide it or he steals money out of my purse to go buy more."

"Why would he steal money out of your purse, Mother?" I inquired. "He works. He has money."

"No, he doesn't," she sighed as she leaned against the counter. "He got fired last month for coming into work drunk. It wasn't the first time and there had also been times he had gone straight to the bars instead of going to work at all. Right now I'm supporting us on my income."

"Oh my god," I exclaimed quietly. "Will that be enough?"

"Well, the house and the car are paid for, thank god," she reasoned. "As long as we have no more than utilities, food and taxes, I think I can handle it, and I have a little savings."

"I'm so sorry, Mother," I said with genuine empathy.

"Honey," she said in uncharacteristic concern. "Your father and I will be fine. We will all play the cards that life has dealt us."

I couldn't believe what I was hearing. Where was the control? Where was the manipulation? Was my mother growing a heart?

She checked the oven to see that the rolls were browned. The table had already been set. She had plucked the roasting pan from the oven just prior to putting in the rolls to give the meat time to rest before serving. If I had never read those cook books, I might not have realized what she was doing. I had never really cared before, but now cooking skills that I had never paid attention to were making sense. She had timed the meal perfectly. She opened the roasting pan and lifted the beef onto a serving plate. She then surrounded it with the vegetables that had roasted along with it, potatoes, carrots, celery, and onions seasoned with no more than salt, black pepper and the juices of the roast, but perfectly delicious.

"Go and get the men," she said as she prepped the table for dinner.

Daddy actually seemed to sober up a bit over dinner. There was no huge fiasco, and nothing was mentioned about his job. I worried some about what he and Earl had been discussing in the living room.

143

Karlyle Tomms

After dinner, Mother served ice cream and cookies for dessert. We ate it in the living room in front of the TV. This too, I thought was uncharacteristic of Mother. I was surprised we didn't have dessert and coffee at the table which was something she would have considered to be formally correct. I enjoyed the more relaxed atmosphere and appreciated being able to let go of a little of my stress. I was just finishing my ice cream when the phone rang. Mother answered it, and I heard her say, "Yes, dear. She is right here." She motioned me to the phone.

Gretta was on the other end of the line. As soon as I said, "Hello," she said, "Oh my god it is so good to hear your voice!"

"It's wonderful to talk to you too, sweetie," I said. "How is everyone?"

"Oh, little Derrick Lovel is so perfect and precious," she exclaimed. "Tommy and I are both doing great! Oh, I can't wait to see you and meet this new boyfriend of yours!"

"So is Friday open?" I asked.

"You bet it is!" she bubbled on. "What would you guys like to do? Tommy's mom can keep the baby if you would like to go out, or we could have dinner here—whatever?"

"Well, Earl and I were hoping to go back early Saturday morning," I replied. "So I wouldn't want to be out too late Friday night. I have a paper due next week and I really need to get back and do some research on it this weekend."

"Oh, don't you sound like the scholarly type?" she laughed.

"Well, I guess we are growing up," I commented. "So what does Friday noon-to-afternoon look like for you guys?"

Gretta said, "That would be fine. Do you want to come hang out here at the house?"

"That sounds wonderful," I replied knowing that Earl had already said to make whatever plans I wanted to make. "Shall we bring something, box lunches, cookies or something?"

"Just bring yourselves," she said. "I'll nail the lunch thing. So, about noon on Friday?"

"Yes," I said, "That sounds wonderful. We will see you then."

I said my goodbyes and looked over at Earl as I hung up the phone. "Lunch with Gretta and Tommy on Friday, okay with you?"

"Sounds wonderful," he said. "I'm looking forward to meeting them."

After the call I couldn't shake the feeling that there was something not quite right underlying Gretta's enthusiasm. I had known her since the first grade and as far as I was concerned, she was as close to me as a sister. Like a sister, I felt things. I shook it off and went on with my evening but it continued to nag subtly at the back of my mind.

144

Confessions from the Pumpkin Patch

Not long after that, Earl left for the hotel. Mother went to the kitchen to make pie. Daddy fell asleep on the sofa and I went on to bed. It was uncharacteristic of me, but I felt tired early.

The next morning Earl arrived back at the house in time for breakfast as Mother had insisted. He had brought books to read and swore that he was not bored staying at the hotel alone.

Time flew by. After breakfast, Mother threw together a squash casserole to go with the pumpkin pie that she had made the night before. She loaded her goodies into the car and insisted on driving, as always. I had suggested that Earl and I could ride separately in his car. I had hoped I might pick his brain about what he and Daddy had been discussing the night before, but Mother would not hear of it. So Earl squeezed his long legs into the back seat of Mother's car. I rode in the back with Earl, and Daddy, who was obviously hung over, rode in the front with Mother. The drive was far too long for me to have to listen to inane and worthless conversation over nothing.

"Oh look the Johnson's painted their house," Mother noted as she drove.

Daddy grunted recognition and I avoided the intense urge to shout, "Who the fuck cares!?"

Earl commented, "Climax seems to be a very nice little town."

Grandmother and Grandfather Donner lived about twenty miles out of town on a few acres they had purchased when they first moved to Pennsylvania. I explained to Earl on the trip that they had originally come from southern Kentucky and had settled in Pennsylvania when Mother was a little girl.

When, at last we got there, Earl helped Mother by carrying her casserole to the door. I was about to knock on the front door when it suddenly opened as though Grandmother Donner had been peeking out and waiting for us to step onto the stoop. There she stood in all her bizarre glory. Her fat little jowls hung on either side of her tiny little round chin. She had beady little brown eyes and a big nose. I was not at all disappointed in her presentation. I knew it would be grand. She had a half-smoked, unlit cigar sticking out of her round little mouth. She was wearing a lemon yellow-and-white flower print dress that clung to her rolls of fat like it had been painted on. On top of her head was a pink, baby blue and white home knitted toboggan cap with a little blue knit ball bouncing around on top. She had no shoes on at all. She had no sooner opened the door when she exclaimed, "Weeeelllll, if it ain't my prim and proper daughter, Drucella, and the Fuchs clan come to see me on Thanksgiving! Get your asses in here. I gotta go check my sweet

145

potatoes." Without saying another word, she turned and waddled off to the kitchen.

We stepped through the door and stood there a moment. Grandpa Donner sat in his recliner in the front corner of the living room beside the door. He was facing the opposite wall where the television was playing the Macy's Thanksgiving Day Parade. He was wearing nothing but overalls and white crew neck T-shirt. His feet were propped up and he had on white tube socks with his big toe poking through the fabric on the right one. The toe, with nail long overdue for a trim, was fully exposed.

"Hello, father," Mother said politely.

He grunted back in song: "Here I am at Camp Granada. It is very entertaining. It might even be fun if it stopped raining." He bellowed in laughter and waved us further into the room.

Mother was not amused. She said nothing back to Grandfather but turned to Earl and said, "Earl, if you will, please accompany me into the kitchen with the casserole, then you may return to enjoy the parade show with the others."

I had seen her around Grandma and Grandpa Donner before. She had always been defiant of their ways, determined to present herself as something more. I suppose there had always been a little bit of anxiety there, but I had never seen her as nervous as she was on that day. Earl followed her to the kitchen. Daddy and I sat down near Grandfather Donner and stared at the TV. Nothing was said.

In a moment Earl returned, leaving Mother in the kitchen with Grandmother. He sat beside me and also stared at the television. After a brief moment, realizing that he was not going to be introduced, he stood up and offered his hand to Grandfather Donner.

"How do you do, sir," he greeted. "I'm Earl Titwallow, Lovella's friend."

Grandfather didn't offer to get up and barely offered his hand back to Earl to be shaken.

"Hell! I know who you are," he said. "Drucella has told me about you. Now sit down and enjoy some television."

Earl sat back down and the ominous silence continued. After a while he said, "Not a bad day to get together with family is it?"

To this Grandfather exclaimed, "Shut the hell up and watch the damn television."

When Earl looked startled, Grandfather chuckled, a sinister little chuckle, as he pointed toward the TV. "Hey! That's an awful good marching band wouldn't you say?"

"Come on, Earl," I said as I took his hand. "Let's see what kind of

Confessions from the Pumpkin Patch

conversation we can get into in the kitchen."

As we left the room, Grandfather and Daddy sat silently staring at the television. Grandfather didn't want to talk and Daddy was obviously too hung-over to put in much of an effort to talk. In the afternoon, they would do the same with the football games. Grandfather had long been addicted to the television. I think in some ways it was his refuge from having to talk because Grandmother scarcely ever shut up.

As we neared the kitchen, I heard Grandmother shouting. "I don't give a damn what the recipe calls for. This is the way I make it." "Very well Mother!" I heard my own mother say tritely. "Make it however you wish."

Insight began to come to me in those moments as I found myself realizing that Mother had probably become her perfect stuck-up self in rebellion against Grandmother Donner just as I had become the independent, liberal minded, intellectual in rebellion against Mother. We had in common that we were both bucking control.

"Anyone else coming today?" I questioned as Earl and I entered the kitchen.

"Oh, hey there!" exclaimed Grandmother as she looked up from the counter. "Come here and give your Grandma a hug!"

As I neared, I could smell the smoke from the cigar she had obviously re-lit. I dreaded it, but realized that there was no escaping Grandmother's standard greeting. She pulled the cigar out of her mouth between her thumb and two fingers, wrapped her arms around me in a vice grip smashing me into her huge soft tits, and then swung me from side to side. She ended this with a sloppy wet kiss to my cheek that I dared not wipe off even though it felt wetter than a dog lick. If I had given into the intense temptation to wipe my cheek on my sleeve, the action would have been met, as it always had, with accusations that I must not truly love her if I had to wipe off her kisses. She had no sooner finished with me than she turned on Earl.

"Now who is this fellow you have here?" she questioned.

"Grandmother," I said with the formality always required by Mother.

"Grandma!" she snapped back. "Call me, Grandma! You don't have to put up with all that bullshit et-e-quetttttte that your momma insists on when you're in my house. Now start over."

My eyes darted toward Mother. She simply looked away.

"Grandma," I continued hesitantly. "This is my boyfriend, Earl Titwallow."

Grandmother waddled over to him, held out her hand palm down, fingers pointing toward the floor in lady like fashion, and curtsied! "Pleased to meet you Earl of Titwallow," she gurgled in a very poor

British accent.

Earl took her hand and softly kissed the back of it. "The pleasure is all mine, Madam Donner."

I heard Mother whisper under her breath, "I think I'm going to vomit."

Grandmother rose back up from her bow and smiled. She then placed a hand on her hip and exclaimed, "You know you are probably a damn good-looking man, but I don't know if I can tell for sure, 'cause I can't see through all that nasty hair all over your head."

Earl grinned, un-phased by this show. "It helps to keep me warm in winter," he responded.

Grandmother glared him up and down. "You know, I heard you are a rich man and yet you are wearing clothes that look like flea market discards."

"Oh, but I was certain that you would be a fan of interesting clothing," he said in feigned disappointment.

"You're alright!" she laughed. "Sit down and stay out of the way now, we got some cooking to do."

Earl and I sat at the little side table in Grandmother's kitchen.

"Drucella!" she snapped, "get that pot off the stove and mash those potatoes."

Mother moved the pot of boiled potatoes to the sink to drain off the cooking water. She gathered butter and milk and began to quietly do as she was told.

"Is anyone else coming?" I asked.

"Well, your Aunt Cloella and her bunch are supposed to come," Grandmother explained without looking up from her work. "But if I know them, they will either show up at the last damn minute or they'll call at the last damn minute to say they ain't coming. Johnella and her bunch are going over to Frank's parents for Thanksgiving."

"How are Aunt Johnella and Uncle Frank?" I asked trying to make polite conversation. "I haven't seen them in a long time."

"You ain't missing nothing," Grandmother forged on. "They're stupid as usual. Frank has gotten them into another one of his stupid get rich quick schemes. Something called Shamway or Claimway or some dumb-ass thing like that. It's bad enough they have had to file bankruptcy twice already. He is going to keep on 'til they have to live under a damn bridge and skin stray cats for meat."

"Pity," I responded. "So how are Aunt Cloella and Uncle Joe?"

"Well, I guess you can ask them yourself if they show up."

She waddled across the kitchen and nearly bumped into Mother who was standing at the counter doing as she was told—mashing potatoes.

Confessions from the Pumpkin Patch

Grandmother exclaimed, "Stay out of the damn way."

Mother said nothing but continued to dutifully carry out her orders.

"I think what I want to know," Grandmother went on, "is how the hell are you doing, Dumpling?" She turned a quick glance in my direction with the question, then immediately went back to her work.

"Well, I'm learning a lot," I replied. "College is really not exactly what I imagined it would be. I'm enjoying my studies, and, of course, I've met Earl."

"Yeah, what about that meeting Earl stuff?" she interrogated. "What is going on with that?"

"I'm not sure what you mean Grandmother—I mean Grandma," I queried.

"Are you two getting serious?" she questioned as she diddled back and forth between the stove and the sink.

"Well, we have only been dating since September," I replied.

She popped back. "Your Grandpa and I got married after four dates. I knew he was what I wanted. He knew I was what he wanted. What more do you need to know? If you are going to get with a boy, you are going to get with a boy."

Mother turned to her then looking up from the mashed potatoes which she had been nervously decimating. "Mother, please don't encourage the child into wickedness," she said.

"What the hell!" Grandmother turned toward her in a snap. "Drucella! You better go back to church with all those holier-than-thou-dip-shits who think they have got all the damn answers. I'm not encouraging this child to do nothing but follow her heart. Now shut the hell up!"

Mother said nothing but began furiously pounding the potatoes with the masher.

"Grandma," I said quietly and politely, "Earl and I do want to take our time and make sure we really get to know each other before we make any kind of big decision."

Mother couldn't help herself at that point. She turned to me and shouted, "So is that why you waited so long to move in with him? What was it a week? Two weeks?"

Grandmother burst out laughing. "Holy hell!" she exclaimed. "Are you living with this boy?"

"Well, not exactly," I stammered. "I am still technically living in the dorm, but I do spend a lot of time at Earl's apartment."

Grandmother snickered. "By spending time, you mean spending the night, right?"

"Yes," I said sheepishly. "I do spend the night there some."

149

Grandmother was laughing again. "Well ain't that the shits!" she exclaimed. "My perfectly prim and proper daughter has got herself a little sinner child."

Mother had hidden a lot of my exploits from Grandmother, but it was not as though she did not already know that I was a bit of a sinner.

About that time, the phone rang and without missing a beat Grandmother yelled, "Sid! Get the damn phone."

Grandfather shouted back from the living room, "Get it your damn self. Me and John are watching the parade."

"Whatever the hell you are doing," Grandmother shouted, "ain't as important as getting your damn food on the table! Now answer that damn phone!"

The ringing stopped as we heard Grandfather say, "Hello."

Grandmother turned back to me. "You know little girl, it is just as easy to fall in love with a rich man as it is to fall in love with a jackass like your Daddy. You might as well be getting some action with Earl as anyone else."

"Grandmother," I said ignoring her demand about what I should call her, "first of all, I don't appreciate those kinds of comments about Daddy. Regardless of whatever faults you think he might have, he is my Daddy and I love him dearly. Second of all, I'm eighteen years old. Regardless of the fact that you may still see me as a child, I am an adult. I may have a lot to learn about life, but it is my life, and I will decide for myself how I will live it. I am very fond of Earl, but I am not going to act like a gold-digger or try to push him into anything, much less something as serious as marriage. I am also not going to be pushed. I appreciate your concern and your advice, but I would prefer that from this point on you only offer advice when I have requested it."

I saw a smile come across Mother's face as she realized that I had just given Grandmother the kind of lecture she had always hoped to give her but never tried.

Grandmother propped both hands on her hips and glared at me. "Well, first of all," she imitated me mockingly, "you are not an adult. You may think you are an adult but it don't really count until you turn twenty-one. However, it is your life and you are old enough to make your own decisions so do whatever the hell you want with it."

She then popped her face toward the kitchen door and shouted. "Sid! Who the hell was on the phone?"

"It was Cloella," he shouted back. "Says they can't make it."

"Goddamn it! I knew it!" Grandmother declared. "We got enough damn food to feed a Navy fleet and they are not coming."

Confessions from the Pumpkin Patch

She looked around the kitchen, sizing up the efforts and said. "Well, hell! I say we start getting all this crap on the table and enjoy some Thanksgiving!" She then turned to me. "Lovella, you go set the dining table. Drucella, ain't it about damn time you had some mercy on those potatoes and got them in a bowl?"

We all stepped to our assignments and soon the table was set for a feast. Grandmother finally sat down after double-checking the kitchen and announced, "Let's all say what we are thankful for. Sid, why don't you start?"

Grandfather snarled back, "Oh don't start with that stupid shit! Let's all be thankful! Bullshit, let's eat!"

Grandmother demanded. "This is Thanksgiving. It is a holiday specifically for being thankful and we are all going to talk about what we have to be thankful for, now you start!"

"Why the hell do I have to start?" Grandfather blurted back.

"'Cause I said so, damn it!" Grandmother retorted. "Now say something you are thankful for or I'll come across this table and gouge your eyes with this fork!" She pointed her fork at him ominously and glared with beady eyes and pursed lips.

Grandfather laughed. Then he rubbed his chin and said, "Let me see— I'm thankful for my loving wife cause she treats me with such respect and that bitch can damn sure cook!"

Everyone laughed except for Mother who stewed in the embarrassment that she must have felt all her life. Daddy sat right next to Grandfather who turned to him as if to say you're next.

Daddy began nervously. "I'm also thankful for my loving wife." Tears began to well in his eyes as he looked at Mother, "'cause I don't know if you realize it or not Drucella, but you have been my Rock of Gibraltar. You have propped me up and kept me going when I didn't think I could go any more, and you have been a fine mother to our little girl." He turned to me then. "I'm thankful for you too my little Punkin' Patch. You have been the light of my life ever since you were born. You have grown up to be such a beautiful and intelligent young woman, and I am so proud of you for going off to college and making something out of your life."

"Stop, Daddy," I said. "You're going to make me cry too."

"Your turn, Drucella," Grandmother spouted carelessly, completely ignoring the intimacy of that moment.

Mother hesitated and looked down at her plate as though she had something to say but she couldn't seem to make herself say it. As I watched her, I wasn't sure if I would trust anything she had to say. How would I know if she was telling the truth or making something up just to

151

Karlyle Tomms

placate the situation? Finally, she said, "I, too, am thankful for my child, and like John, I'm thankful that she is in college, and that she has a bright future."

For a moment, she looked as though she wanted to bolt from the table. Instead, she fiddled with her fork, and waited for the ordeal to be over.

"You're next, hippie boy," Grandmother said as she pointed her fork at Earl.

Earl said, "I am thankful to have the opportunity to be here, to meet Lovella's family. I am so glad I met Lovella, such a brilliant, beautiful, and intriguing girl, and I am thankful for the Penn State library for giving me an opportunity to meet her."

"Okay, kid," Grandmother said as she glared at me. "Give it to us. What are you thankful for?"

I looked around the table and caught everyone's eyes, one person at a time. Then I said, "I'm thankful for all of you. I'm thankful for my family, and I'm thankful that I met Earl because whether our relationship takes us to a lifetime together or a break-up next week it has been an experience worth having. I'm thankful for all my experiences and for the future adventures of Lovella whatever they may be." I then looked back across the table. "Now your turn, Grandma."

Grandmother never missed a beat. "Hell!" she said. "I'm just thankful we got all this shit done and on the table! Now let's eat!

The rest of the day was more of the same. Grandmother would not let Grandfather get away with telling people to shut up when we were all back in the living room in front of the TV.

"Sid!" she exclaimed. "You shut the hell up! We have all got just as much right to be in this room as you do, and besides you might look up from the damn idiot box once in a while and try to have a little conversation with your family."

Grandfather grinned, looked around the room and said, "Hello family." He then put his gaze immediately back to the afternoon football game.

We finally headed home about 5:00 PM. Grandmother made sure we were loaded with leftovers so there was plenty to snack on for dinner. Earl and Daddy continued their conversations here and there throughout the evening and seemed to always want me to be somewhere else when that was going on. It made me more and more curious and just a little nervous as I watched it progress.

Earl went back to the hotel about 9:00 PM and was back to pick me up the next morning to go see Gretta, Tommy, and the baby.

The visit was congenial and discussions were as usual. Little Derrick Lovel was growing and healthy. Tommy and Gretta were professing to

Confessions from the Pumpkin Patch

still be deeply in love and I was so happy to see them. I told them stories about college: Marcy and her inane friends, and about meeting Earl, and how he was different from any other boy I had ever met. Gretta and Tommy told stories about the baby; and how he is growing so fast. Earl went along with the whole process, answering questions and interjecting periodically, appearing to be completely comfortable with my family and my friends.

Everything seemed to be perfectly normal, but I had a nagging feeling that something was wrong. There were little tell-tale signs in glances and little momentary expressions that ran across their faces for maybe a second and then were gone. I didn't know if I should ask out-right or just let it pass, but the more we visited the more I felt a knot tightening in my stomach. Gretta had never kept secrets from me, none that I ever knew of, and I had no idea why she might be keeping a secret now. I just knew that something wasn't as it appeared to be on the surface. Finally, I just blurted it out.

"Okay—something is going on here," I exclaimed. "Something is not right. I've known you both a very long time and whether you might like it or not, I can also read you both like a book. What's wrong? Stop pretending and fess up."

Gretta immediately began to tremble and a tear rolled down her cheek. She glanced over to Tommy and then back at me. I could see the struggle in her eyes as she struggled over what to say.

Finally, Tommy announced, "I've joined the Marines."

"You what?" I blurted, both with astonishment and anger.

"I didn't want to tell you," he said. "I knew how you would react."

"Well, did you not think this might be something I would figure out after a while?" I questioned. "No wonder she's upset." I pointed back to Gretta. "You have a child who is less than a year old and you are going to go away and leave her here to care for that baby by herself!"

"It doesn't necessarily work that way," he said, "We can live on base and I can be there with them just like any other job."

"Unless you get deployed to Vietnam!" I demanded. "Tommy! Did you stop to think what this would do to your family? I mean it's not like you have to worry about being drafted. They are not drafting married men, especially married men with children."

"But that's exactly it," Tommy responded. "Johnson changed the law last August. They can draft married men now. So I have thought about my family. With a military career, I can do more for my family than I ever would be able to do at that damn feed store. They will have benefits I can't provide now and if something was to happen to me, they would be taken care of."

"You have bought the bullshit, haven't you?" I scolded. "They would not have drafted you when you have a baby."

Earl sat silent allowing me to have this conversation with my friends. I had an idea what he thought about it all, but he didn't interfere.

Gretta spoke as tears lightly rolled across her cheeks. It was not as though she was actually crying, but it was also not as though she wasn't. "Yeah, it will be great," she lied. "Only thing is we will have to move out of town and live on a base somewhere, eventually, maybe." She shot a nervous look back at Tommy.

"Did you even bother to discuss this with her?" I scolded Tommy again.

"We talked it over," he said. "I didn't just rush into it. We agree it is going to mean a better life for us."

"A better life?" I summoned. "You are going to go to Vietnam, leave your beautiful wife and your beautiful baby, and maybe get killed or comeback in pieces and that is going to give you a better life?"

"Well, now," Tommy argued "Only a small percentage of troops go to Vietnam and only a small percentage of those go into combat. I know it's a gamble but I think it's a gamble worth taking."

"Too late now—ugh," I replied.

Tommy looked down at his feet and then over to Gretta and the baby. "Yeah," he said. "I guess so. I've signed the papers. I leave for boot camp in two weeks."

"Oh Jesus, Tommy," I pleaded. "I love you, and I know you think you are doing the right thing. I just pray that everything is going to be okay."

"It will be fine, Lovella," he assured. "You will see. We will prosper from this. I can retire from the military before I'm fifty and maybe even go to officer's training. I know it's going to be stressful, but we've thought it through. It's gonna work out fine."

I knew I was defeated before I even started the argument. The decision had been made. "Do you have any idea where you are going to be stationed?" I asked.

"Not yet." Tommy reached over and patted Gretta's arm, "But we're kind of hoping for Germany. Isn't that right sweetheart?"

Gretta nodded and smiled through her obvious grief. Her head bobbed up and down in affirmation as she pulled the sleeve of her free arm across her tear-soaked cheek.

"You are really not into this are you?" I questioned her.

"No, yes—no, I'm in," she bantered quickly. "Germany would be great. It is just going to be a big adjustment and it's going to mean leaving friends and family. It's not exactly like Grandma will be able to baby sit."

Confessions from the Pumpkin Patch

"We will hire some sweet old German lady to babysit," Tommy assured as he patted her knee.

"Well," I sighed, "I just hope you both know what you are doing." I looked over at Earl with a pleading look on my face that silently said, "Save me."

He got the message and said, "Probably about time for me to get back to the hotel."

"Yeah," I tentatively affirmed. "I guess we better get going."

Normally, they both would have begged us to stay a little while longer, but I think they were as weary of where the conversation had taken us as I was. They both walked us to the door. Tommy shook Earl's hand and affirmed how glad he was to meet him and Gretta nodded the same affirmation with her attention divided between goodbyes and a distracted baby. Before I walked out, I hugged Tommy first and then Gretta. I took Derrick's face in my hands and planted a big wet kiss on his fat round little cheeks. "I love you little man," I exclaimed. After goodbyes, I placed my hand firmly on Gretta's shoulder and gazed at her.

"Honey," I admonished. "If you need anything, or if, god forbid, anything should go wrong, I am to be the first person you call after your mom and dad. Got that?"

"Got that," she replied with a brief nervous laugh.

The next morning Earl picked me up early. Suitcases went back in the car and we headed back to his apartment. I hugged Mother and Daddy goodbye and so did Earl. I couldn't help noticing that there had been some kind of bond forming between him and Daddy. When, in conclusion, we got in the car and pulled away, I asked him, "So what was it I saw going on with you and Daddy these last few days?"

"Well, despite the drunken greeting," he replied, "I think I've developed an appreciation for your father."

"What is that?" I questioned.

"I just realize that he is a man who loves very honestly and very deeply," he said. "I appreciate that."

"You see something more in Daddy than just an alcoholic factory worker?" I questioned.

He glanced over at me, then back at the road, both hands firmly gripping the steering wheel. "Of course I see more in him than that," he responded firmly. "Despite his flaws, your father is a man who looks out for his family, maybe in ways that you and your mother have never fully realized."

I stared at him for a moment, pondering, taking in what he had just said.

Karlyle Tomms

Then I settled back comfortably into those leather seats and watched the small town that had produced me flow gradually out of sight. There was a warmth in my heart then. I can't really explain how it felt. Up until that morning, I was indeed very fond of him, but I think it was then, right there in that brief passing of time that I fell in love with Earl Titwallow.

Chapter 14

I don't want to sugar coat it. The 1960s was a tumultuous time. I know I haven't talked much about it, but to tell you the truth, before I met Earl, I never thought much about it. My family, even Mother, always avoided politics. I guess we thought that as long as we were comfortable, why worry about it. However, the fact is the Vietnam War was going on all through the 60s. There were the Kennedy and Martin Luther King assasinations, too. Difficult as it was to avoid the conversation, I tried always to find a way to change the subject, an excuse to leave, or a way simply not to listen.

Earl, on the other hand was passionate about the fate of people. I'm surprised he didn't want to study social work instead of physics. I don't know how much of his attitude had to do with trying, in many ways, to be the opposite of his father, but his attitude certainly was one of a socialist nature. He also could not stand the fact that the Vietnam War seemed to get worse, with no clear objective and no end in sight.

In October of 1966, Senator William Fulbright published "The Arrogance of Power." It happened to be one of the books that Earl began to absorb in his hotel room over Thanksgiving with my family. When we got back home, he continued to plow through it. He didn't just read it. He underlined statements and went back over them. He became absorbed with the evening news, and managed to bring up criticisms of the war in many of his conversations. I doubted that his ideas would set well with his father.

I did my best to ignore it but that couldn't happen. I was trying to settle into a life of domicile comfort with him, a retreat from the boring dorm room and the inane ranting of Mar-cee. Most of the time when the evening news was on, I was in the kitchen preparing dinner and trying to play housewife. I had a long way to go considering that Mother had taught me little or nothing about cooking. Still, with cooking shows, experiments, and quality cookbooks, I was beginning to get the hang of it. I learned to prepare a few complicated dishes, but as often as not I cooked fried burgers with a side of something like boxed macaroni and cheese.

Earl didn't seem to mind what I prepared. When I first started staying with him, we would often eat in the tiny dining room with candles and glasses of wine, but as time went on, and he became more and more preoccupied with Vietnam, our meals tended to take place in front of the

Karlyle Tomms

television. I would eat quietly as he cursed the TV, half spitting his food, and trying to retain it in his mouth between exclamations of "Goddamn it!" and "Those lousy war-mongering bastards!"

I understood that war was bad. I understood that boys were dying but I didn't want to know. I would rather have stuck my head in the sand and pretend it wasn't happening and considering the gruesome scenes of war often shown on the evening news, I certainly didn't want to eat my dinner while watching the news.

One evening as I was sitting beside Earl on the sofa, I began gagging at the scenes. I slapped my fork back down on my plate and said, "I can't stand this." I got up and went to the kitchen. I threw my half-eaten plate into the sink and began to cry. The next thing I knew, I felt Earl's large gentle hand on my shoulder.

"Honey, what's the matter?" he said, calmly and patiently.

I turned to him and wiped tears from my cheek with the back of my hand. "I can't stand this anymore," I said, glancing back toward the living room. "Every night we sit there in front of the TV and watch that horror unfold. I don't want to see it! I don't want to know about it, and I damn sure don't want to be trying to have my dinner while that is going on. I feel like I'm eating the war. I feel like I'm consuming all that anguish and devastation! I mean, how soon 'til I see some boy I went to high school with on a medic stretcher with his guts falling off the side? Earl, I can't stand it."

He took a long deep sigh and then hugged me. "I'm so sorry," he said. "I guess I got so caught up in my anger about it that I didn't think about how it might be affecting you."

"I know it's important to you," I returned without lifting my head from his comforting chest. "I don't want to deter you from it, but maybe we could have dinner later in the evening or something. I can study while you watch the news."

"No," he responded. "From now on, the rule is TV off during dinner. Whatever I need to know about the war, I'll get from the newspapers."

I found myself saying, "I just wish there was something we could do." And as soon as the words came out of my mouth, I wished that I had not said them. What I really hoped was that we could just live our lives in a little cocoon of denial, playing house, and loving each other, but life was not going to allow that.

"Well," he explained softly, "there is something we can do. This weekend there is going to be a meeting of a group called 'The Students for A Democratic Society'. I learned about the group through a friend of mine and I think we should go and see what it's about."

158

Confessions from the Pumpkin Patch

Jesus! If there was anything I didn't want to do it was to become involved in anything to do with the war, pro or con. I was torn between wanting to please him and wanting to run terrified into the street. I looked up into his eyes and realized they were filled with genuine commitment. He wanted the war to end. He wanted a resolution. I knew that he loved me, but I also knew that he cared a great deal about what was happening in our country. "Sure," I said. "Sure, we can go to that. Maybe there is something we can do."

I had no idea what this 'Students for a Democratic Society' thing was all about. I had no idea what I might be getting myself into. I knew that it was somehow anti-war, but I didn't know anything else.

He held me close and stoked my hair. "I love you," he said, quietly.

When Sunday afternoon came and it was time to go to this meeting I found myself playing a role for him. Never in my life had I ever pretended to be something that I was not. Never in my life had I ever hesitated to say what I was really thinking, but for Earl I was pretending that I really did want to do something about the war, and maybe there was a small part of me that did. However, for the most part, I just wanted it all to go away.

Later that afternoon we pulled up in front of an old house near downtown. We were met at the front door by Earl's friend Jake. He appeared to be a little older than us. Had it not been for his hippie persona, he would have looked to be a very average man in his twenties. However, his brown hair fell down his back like a waterfall, a bit wavy. His mustache drooled down to his chin in a horseshoe shape on either side of his lips. His chin itself was shaved clean like the rest of his face. A pair of small orange lens glasses sat low on his nose, and a peace sign necklace lay across the ample hair of his chest which was exposed by an open collar, tie-dyed, pilgrim's shirt.

"Come in! Come in!" Jake motioned as he turned and left us standing at the door to follow.

Inside there was a living room to the right with a beautiful old Victorian fireplace that had an ornate walnut mantle. The walls had been hand painted with flowers, peace signs and slogans. There was no furniture on the floor; instead, there was a circle of large pillows where several people sat. On some pillows, young men sat with a girl curled up between their legs. All the girls were either wearing blue jeans and assorted tops or some long, frilly, crinkled, cotton skirt that went to their ankles. The whole place smelled of patchouli.

I instantly felt out of place. I had dressed like I was going to church and my outfit was more befitting the traditional middle-class girl of the early

1960s. I was wearing a tight knee length baby-blue skirt and a white satin blouse. I had placed my hair up over my head in a bun with matching plastic clips. I felt like one of those little puzzles one finds in the Sunday papers: "One of these things does not fit with the other. Can you tell which one?"

A thin, young, barefoot woman glided down a hallway from the back of the house to the front room. Her hair looked almost identical to Jake's but her eyes were a brilliant blue. She wore a reddish-brown, flowing, cotton dress, and her smile was magnetic.

"Hey!" Jake said, as though the woman's presence came as a complete surprise. "This is my old lady, Tonya."

"Greetings," she replied smiling as she extended her hand to each of us in turn. "Welcome. Welcome. Welcome," she continued as though one welcome would not have been enough. "May I get you something to drink? Beer? Wine? Soda? Milk?"

"Nothing for me," I said, politely.

"I'll have a beer," Earl blurted out cheerfully.

"All right, okay," Tonya responded in a sing-song tone. "Have a seat. Be right back."

Earl and I found an unclaimed pillow on the floor and proceeded to descend together. Unfortunately, I had made the mistake of wearing that tight skirt which made the whole process rather difficult to accomplish even for someone so young. I twisted around uncomfortably for a while wondering how I was going to manage sitting on the floor without shooting someone a shot of the muff-dragon's outline through my panties. Then finally, I told myself, "What the hell! Since when have I ever really been worried about anyone seeing my pussy, much less my panties?" I stopped trying to hide the inevitable, went to my knees, then to the floor, and sat in whatever position I could find that was comfortable. Unfortunately, the discomfort of that skirt on the floor required frequent repositioning. At last, I found a reasonably comfortable position where I could lean against Earl as Tonya returned from the kitchen with his beer. She handed it to him without fanfare or a word spoken then turned on her heel and left the room.

A scraggly boy sitting next to us exclaimed, "Hey, man. Ronnie's the name." He extended his hand.

"I'm Earl and this is Lovella," Earl said, shaking the boy's hand.

Upon completing the handshake with Earl, Ronnie exclaimed, "Peace!" He then shot two fingers in a V toward the ceiling and nodded in my direction.

"Yes," I said, having no real clue what the appropriate response might

Confessions from the Pumpkin Patch

have been.

A moment later Jake was shouting, "Okay, okay everybody. Let's get this meeting started. Let's get started." He stood by the fireplace mantle with papers in his hand. Tonya had come in from the kitchen and was standing beside him.

Everyone ceased their individual conversations and careened their bodies in his direction. Some of them had to twist around to keep from having their backs to him. I was thankful that Earl and I had gotten a position opposite the fireplace. I couldn't help wondering why the pillows were in a circle if he was going to stand at one end of the room. It didn't seem like very good planning, but it was what it was.

"All right. All right," Jake began, leaving me to wonder if the couple's last name was Redundancy. "You all know this war sucks!"

"Yeah!" shouted the young man next to us.

Jake continued, "I don't know if everybody realizes just how serious this shit is, but here is some information you ought to know. First of all, the number of draftee's for the fucking Vietnam War is getting close to a million. Think about it man. A million or more men are being forced into slavery by the government to fight a war that only serves the fucking military industrial complex. Man, it was Eisenhower who said, 'Beware the Military Industrial Complex.' Why? Because he knew, man. He knew that war had changed. He knew it was about to stop being about a fight for right, but a fight for the rich. He knew that war was about to become an economic decision based on the development of the war industry. These fucking fat cats are making millions off the manufacture of weapons! They don't want to stop the war. They would fucking lose money, if they stopped the war. Seventy five percent of the soldiers in Vietnam are from middle-class or working-class and poor families. You don't fucking see the rich sending their kids to war. They send their boys to fancy schools like Harvard and Yale where they get a fucking college deferment."

I found myself wondering if he realized the irony of what he was saying, given that this was a group called "The Students for a Democratic Society." I figured that everyone in the room was likely a student and that each one of them had been given the college deferment as well. The irony was not lost on me, but I just continued to listen.

"Man, that is ten percent of our generation, culled out, and massacred!" Jake continued to preach. "There are ten-thousand boys a year dying in Vietnam who get drafted out of high school without a chance to choose their own future! They can't even fucking vote, man! They can't even fucking vote! At eighteen years old, you are old enough to be drafted to go get slaughtered in jungles of Vietnam, but you can't even vote against the

161

Karlyle Tomms

fucking politicians who put you there? You are old enough to fight in a rich man's war but you can't buy a fucking beer? What is wrong with this picture, man? What is wrong with this picture?"

It had never occurred to me to even think about that before. I heard myself saying out loud, "That's not fair!" I found myself becoming swayed, not by Jake's speech, but by the facts he had just stated. I knew that was true. I had just never taken the time to think about it.

Jake went on. "The war is costing the American taxpayer sixty-six million dollars a day. Man! Fucking imagine that! Sixty-six million dollars a fucking day! Man, Johnson used the Gulf of Tonkin Resolution in 1964 as an excuse to escalate the war and send even more troops and the bastard hasn't stopped. He is not going to stop. I mean Kennedy was probably fucking assassinated because he would have tried to stop this damn war! This fucking insanity is not going to stop 'til the American people start shouting enough is enough! We need to shout it from the streets, man. We need to shout it from the mountain tops. We need to shout it everywhere. Enough is enough! No more war! Make love not war!"

Shouts of, "Yeah! Yeah! Peace! No more war! Right on man!" scattered throughout the group as Jake continued talking.

"We need to take a lesson from David Miller," Jake continued, spurred on by the shouts. "He was sentenced to two years in prison last year for burning his draft card. I say we need to get every man in this country to burn his fucking draft card. We need to stand in front of the fucking White House, ten million strong and burn all of our goddamn draft cards. They can't send us all to prison!"

All through Jake's speech the shouts of affirmation continued. Except for the periodic profanity it could have been a Pentecostal worship service, or a black, Baptist church. I half-way expected someone to stand up and shout: "Praise, Jesus!" but that one never happened.

After Jake finally finished, he and Tonya came down and joined the circle. Then they began planning how to get protesters together, where they were going to protest next, how they were going to get the word out to the whole country. They knew that media coverage was going to be important, and they knew that the more organized they were the more likely they were to get results. They were taking lessons from the free speech protests at Berkeley in 1964, and there was a commitment to pacifism. If war was violent, they were going to be the opposite. Passive resistance was the strategy. Most of them had read about and took lessons from Mahatma Gandhi's resistance to British rule in India. If the police came to move them, they would just go limp and it would then have to

Confessions from the Pumpkin Patch

take several police just to haul them away. The idea was to overwhelm the police so that they could not stop the protest. I began to realize why this was important to Earl and I began to wonder if it shouldn't be important to me too.

We came home with options to participate in a protest called the "Human Be-in" that would take place in San Francisco in January or one in April in New York starting in Central Park and marching to the U. N. The one in New York seemed to be the one most likely for us to be able to attend. There was a part of me afraid to be involved in this. What if the government put me on some kind of blacklist so that I would never be able to work except for menial jobs? What if I got arrested or sent to prison? Then what was I going to do with an arrest record? I could see my own family shunning me. I could see my career plans being destroyed. I could see most of the people in Climax thinking of me as a low-life and a criminal. All this was a risk the others seemed to accept, but my heart was not so fully committed.

We had determined after Thanksgiving that I would go with Earl to spend Christmas with his parents in Bradford Woods. I wondered if he was going to tell his father about protesting against the war and suspected that it was likely to be at the forefront of his mind as the one Christmas gift he most wanted to give his father. Perhaps it was a gift that he wanted to give to himself just to see the old man react in disgust that he was not applying himself to learning business but was instead applying his energies to breaking down the very institution in which his father most believed.

When we got back home that evening, I hung our coats in the closet and went to the kitchen.

"Earl, how does a cold cut sandwich sound for dinner?" I asked.

"That sounds great," he said as he plopped himself on the sofa and picked up an old newspaper, one I suspect that he had already read.

I proceeded to make the sandwiches and found a few potato chips in the cupboard. After throwing some lettuce and mayo on the bread, I added a couple of slices of bologna, cut them in half, and carried a plate to Earl.

"What would you like to drink?" I asked as I headed back toward the kitchen.

"Coke will be fine," he said.

I poured him a coke and then joined him on the sofa with my sandwich and coke.

"So what did you think?" he quizzed as he bit into his sandwich.

I didn't really want to tell him what I thought. I hesitated long enough for him to say, "Well?"

163

Karlyle Tomms

With a few bites out of my sandwich, I laid it back down on my plate. "I'm not sure what I think." I said.

"Jake can really stir it up can't he?" Earl proceeded, seeming to not take note of what I had just told him.

"Yeah, he got it going there," I replied.

"So you are not sure what you think?" he questioned again.

I sighed long and deep. "I have a mix of feelings, Earl."

"So, what's in the mix?" he asked.

I mustered my courage to tell him my real feelings. "I know the war is bad," I said. "I disagree with making boys go fight when they can't even vote and don't have any say in the matter, but—"

"But?" he pressed.

"But it all scares me," I stated at last. "I'm scared of violence, of getting arrested. I'm scared of getting put on a black list or something. I'm even scared to go meet your family. I mean, it's like you and your father are on two opposite ends of the pole where the war is concerned. You are the rich kid that Jake was talking about in his speech."

"Yes, I am," he returned.

"I mean, do you think it's fair that you don't get drafted?" I asked.

"Hell, no, I don't think it's fair," he flared in his argument, "But I don't want to go fight a war I don't believe in either. Does that make me a hypocrite?"

"No," I responded. "I didn't mean it that way."

"If you want to see a hypocrite wait 'til you meet my dad," he went on. "My dad actually has some investments in the military complex. He will fucking make money off making weapons to kill innocent people and send other people's kids off to war, but he has plans for me."

"Still your father must be thinking about what he hopes is best for you," I mumbled through a bite of my sandwich.

"Yeah, he's just like the government," Earl replied. "He is happy to decide for me but give me absolutely no say in what I want for my own life. That is exactly what the government is doing to these draftees. I mean it is one thing if you want to be a soldier, but if you didn't ask for it, it is just another form of slavery. We abolished slavery after the Civil War, didn't we?"

"You're right," I said softly. "I agree. We did abolish slavery and I think it's wrong to force people into the military too. It's just—."

"Just what?" he questioned. "Tell me."

"Earl, I've never been afraid of conflict, or at least I never thought I was afraid of conflict." I sat my mostly empty plate over on the coffee table and took a sip of my Coke. "When I was growing up," I went on, "I didn't

Confessions from the Pumpkin Patch

mind letting anyone know what I thought. I've gone toe-to-toe with Mother ever since I was little but this is different. I've never gone toe-to-toe with the United States government. It scares me. The government is big and powerful and I'm not."

"It is a government of the people, for the people, and by the people," he returned. "It is not supposed to be some overlord like a dictatorship. It is not supposed to tell the people what to do. The people are supposed to tell it what to do and right now it is not listening."

"Do you think all this will get the government to listen?" I questioned in honest interest.

"I think if we don't organize and make our voices known the government is not going to listen," he replied. "But, I don't want you to feel obligated to do any of this. It is a freedom movement, and that means your freedom too. I'm not going to think any less of you if you tell me that this is not something you want."

"Can I have time to think about it?" I petitioned.

"Absolutely you can have time to think about it."

He smiled, sat his plate down, and pulled me to him.

"Besides, over the next couple of weeks, I think what we really need to be thinking about is finals."

"Yuck." I said, laying my head on his chest.

"Yuck indeed," he echoed.

I nuzzled my head into his chest, comforted by his embrace.

Karlyle Tomms

Chapter 15

The time between Thanksgiving and Christmas went fast. With college, I felt particularly rushed. Higher education was indeed higher. It was nothing like high school. It was a lot more demanding, especially coming up on semester finals. I was determined, however, that I was going to do a few things to get ready for Christmas.

I bought a few gifts for family and Earl drove me home so I could deliver them to Mother the week before Christmas. It was only a two-hour drive home and a fairly easy day trip if one was not planning to spend time with family. I bought a cute little baby outfit for Derrick and a Christmas ornament for Tommy and Gretta. Mother promised me that she would get the gifts to them. I bought Daddy a bottle of Chardonnay. Yes, I know he didn't need it. He shouldn't have had it, but maybe if he could learn to drink the fine stuff he might stay off the rot gut. My reasoning was incredibly flawed, immature and naive. I bought Mother a new purse, and for Grandmother and Grandfather Donner, one of those packaged cheese things. Their greatest pleasure seemed to be eating anyway.

I had no idea what I might get for Earl's parents having never met them. They were so rich, I couldn't think of anything that they could possibly need or want. Earl told me not to worry about it and just enjoy the season, but I felt I had to do something. Finally, I decided that I would make a Reine de Saba avec Glaqage au Chocolat cake from "Mastering the Art of French Cooking." I figured that even rich people like to eat, especially chocolate.

I went to a bakery shop and got a cake box. I then proceeded to make the cake just before we left for Bradford Woods. I followed the recipe to the last fraction and to my surprise I didn't fuck it up. It was beautiful, so luscious looking, I had a hard time not giving in to the temptation to go ahead and have a slice. I simply put a bow on the box, along with their name—to and from.

When we left for Bradford Woods, I carried the cake box on my lap the whole way. I wanted to be sure that it would not be jostled around too much. The last thing I wanted to do was have them open the box and have it look like an elephant sat on it. Earl, knowing this was important to me, was very careful about his driving.

We arrived in Bradford Woods on Christmas Eve, 1966. I had known

Confessions from the Pumpkin Patch

that college was going to mean new adventures for me but my god I had no idea! The neighborhood where Earl's family lived was opulent to say the least, but when we pulled though a gate to his home, huge brick columns flanked either side. The paved driveway led to a house like nothing I had ever seen except perhaps in magazines or the movies. It was brick with huge white Greek columns across the front that rose all the way to the second floor. The round white columns lined the entire front of the house like they were standing guard at an ancient temple. There was a circular drive leading up to the front door, and though it was winter, the lawn was immaculate. Like a leading man whose Hollywood hair had just been clipped by the finest barber, nothing on the lawn was the least bit scraggly or out of place.

As soon as Earl stopped the car at the crest of the drive by the front walk a man appeared, it seemed, from out of nowhere. He threw open the door on the passenger's side of the car and I was a bit startled. I heard Earl say gently, "It's okay."

I got out of the car with my cake box in hand. The man smiled sweetly and nodded then went around to Earl's side of the car where Earl had already exited from the vehicle.

"Hello John," Earl said as he greeted the man with a handshake.

"Welcome home, son." The man replied in a fatherly tone, but I knew from description and photos that he certainly was not Earl's father. Besides, there was a distinct air of servitude.

Earl rounded the car and took my arm. "Come on," he said as he led me up the short walk to the house. "John will take care of the car and bring in our luggage."

As we stepped up onto the veranda, the columns loomed over us. I looked up, near dizzy from the enormity and commented, "My god, Earl! This damn place is bigger than my high school gymnasium."

He laughed. "It's just bricks and mortar," he said as he reached for the door with his key. He had no sooner slipped his key into the lock than the door opened as though from some magic.

A short woman in her forties opened the door. She was wearing a black and white uniform and had a little doily white lace cap on top of her head. Her hair was short and curled perfectly, and her large bosoms hid behind the top ruffle of a white apron. With an accent that was clearly British she said, "Earl, so good to see you my boy!"

"Good to see you too, Nora," he replied.

We stepped into the foyer. The walls around us were a dark paneled wood, mahogany or walnut or something similar. A glistening chandelier, three or four foot in diameter, lit the space with tiny twinkles of light.

167

Karlyle Tomms

White Italian marble floors spread around us like so many blocks of ice. I felt as though I should have brought my skates. Directly in front of us was a grand staircase with wide fluted rails inviting up to the second floor. To the left was a formal living room which looked to have more square footage than the house I had grown up in. I could see that the walls were a very pale yellow and the furniture was tufted in a subtle white and gold floral pattern on a cream background. In the far corner was a Christmas tree like nothing I had ever seen before. For one thing, it was at least ten feet tall and it seemed to have been placed there as part of the overall décor. It matched the living room like it had been created by the original designer, not like the scraggly little tree that might be found at home, or at grandmother's house which was half decorated with construction paper ornaments I or my cousins had made when we were small. I doubted seriously that there would have been any primitive ornaments on the tree that might have been made by Earl or his sister when they were small. To the right was a dining room with an ornate chandelier cascading from the ceiling. It was centered over a sleek dark glistening and finely polished wood dining table that would have seated at least a dozen people. The walls of the dining room were also dark, though not as dark as the wood paneling of the foyer. They were more the color of slightly creamed coffee. On the walls I could see huge oil paintings that were lit from above with little individual lights protruding from the ceiling and installed specifically for the purpose. The windows which went floor to ceiling, lined the outside walls. Cream colored drapes flowed down the edge of the windows from cornice boxes that crowned the top of the windows. Beyond the sidewall was a view through the window to a small lake framed by tall pines. I could see white painted benches on the edge of the lake. I had never been so uncomfortable in my entire life.

"May I take your coat, Miss?" Nora said to me politely smiling.

"I'm sorry," I said, holding out the cake box in front of me and suddenly feeling that it would be considered insignificant to everything else in their lives. "This is for Mr. and Mrs. Titwallow."

"Oh, how sweet, dear," she said as she took the box and trotted it to the dining table and then returned to me.

"Now your coat, dear," she said as she popped back up in front of me. Earl had already taken his coat off and had it lying on his arm. She helped me out of my coat and then took both our coats to some unknown place out of the way.

As soon as she left with our coats, Earl took my hand and led me to the living room. There sat his whole family nestled around the huge fireplace. They must have known that we had arrived, but they sat patiently waiting

168

Confessions from the Pumpkin Patch

instead of getting up and coming out to greet us. Mother might have been comfortable with such formality, but there is no way that any such thing would ever have happened in our family. The personal greeting was one of the most important parts of a visit. Never in a million years would anyone in my family ever have allowed the door to be opened without standing there to greet their guests themselves. Never would they have sat waiting when a guest arrived instead of getting up and going to the door to greet them in person. It all seemed rather cold to me, but I accepted that it must be the custom.

When we entered the living room, Earl's father stood. I immediately knew who he was. He was huge, not quite as tall as Earl, but almost, and the facial resemblance was uncanny. Soon after he stood, Earl's mother and sixteen-year-old sister, Anna, also rose.

"Well hello there stranger," Earl's father said gleefully as he approached Earl and gave him a hug. His huge potbelly was outlined by the suspenders that held up his pin-stripe dress pants. His suit coat and tie could not have hidden that belly though they appeared to try. It seemed to me that he was dressed more appropriately for a funeral than a family gathering. Earl's mother stood by. She was tiny but very pretty. She could not have been more than five-and-a-half-feet tall. Her dress was an elegant dark burgundy velour, and it clung to her figure as though it was hanging on a manikin in a storefront window. Her blond dyed hair came down from her head in wave flips on either side and in the back also, as though it had been molded by a machine and planted atop her head. She waited her turn and as soon as Earl was finished hugging his father, he bent his frame to the task of embracing her. I saw a sweetness there and a reverence for his mother as he held her gently as though she might break like a fragile porcelain doll.

"I'm so glad you're home, son," she said in a raspy little voice.

Earl's sister Anna had stood up more as though it was expected of her than as though it was a courtesy she actually wished to extend. In some respects, she looked like an average sixteen-year-old girl, but she, too, was wearing a formal dress of forest green chiffon. I felt as though I wanted to run from the room. My simple little department store dress suddenly felt like a traitor in the war of fashion. I felt humbled and insecure.

After the hugs, Earl said, "Mom, Dad, Anna, this is Lovella."

He reached for my hand and pointed it toward them like a letter he was expected to deliver. His mother reached out and clasped my hand between both of hers and said, "Hello, Lovella. It is so good to meet you. My name is Clarese. This is my husband Daniel, and our daughter Anna." She nodded to each of them as she spoke their names. Earl's father stepped forward and shook my hand. "So glad to have you visit with us young lady," he grunted as the grip of his handshake practically broke the bones in my hand. Even though they were nouveau riche, they had obviously adopted the formality of old wealth. Afterward, the two of them parted like the gate at the edge of their property to reveal Anna standing coyly behind. "Hi," she said, reaching her hand out and barely touching mine with the tips of her fingers. How like Mother's handshake, I thought when her little fingers crossed my palm. I realized as soon as she opened her mouth that she was wearing braces, and that she was embarrassed by it despite the fact her upbringing made mine look as though I had been raised in a chimp cage. Still it was comforting to know that she felt a little uncomfortable too.

"Won't you sit down, dear," Clarese said and motioned to a chair.

"I think Lovella would probably like to sit next to me on one of the sofas if you don't mind Mom," Earl said politely guiding me to the seat.

"Oh that's fine, honey," she responded. "Do sit down."

When I sat next to Earl, the others seated themselves as well, his mother in one grand chair to the right of the marble faced fireplace and his father in a matching chair to the left.

Nora entered with a silver plate full of hors d'oeuvres. She came straight to me first and held the tray before me. There was a collection of options, none of which I recognized, so I simply picked one that looked interesting and said, "Thank you."

"So, Lovella, tell us about yourself," Earl's father inquired as he picked from the hors d'oeuvres tray.

Nora passed it around the room and then set the tray with the remaining treats on the circular coffee table in the middle of the room.

"Excuse me a moment, Mr. Daniel," she said, interrupting him. She looked straight at me. "What might I get you to drink, dear?"

My eyes darted back and forth between her and Earl hoping that he would answer the question for me. He didn't. Then I asked nervously, "Do you have Coke?"

"Yes ma'am, we do," she smiled sweetly,

"And you, sir?" she queried switching her gaze to Earl.

"I'll have a glass of Merlot, Nora. Thank you," he said.

She then turned on her heal and trotted from the room. I looked around to see that the others already had a drink of some sort sitting nearby.

When she left, I turned my attention back to Mr. Titwallow. "Sir," I began with much greater formality than I was used to extending and feeling as though I had been asked for a resume. "I grew up in Climax. My father worked for a peanut butter factory. Mother stayed at home until

Confessions from the Pumpkin Patch

I graduated high school and she recently took a job in a downtown dress shop. I am an only child, and I entered college—" I hesitated to say the real reason. Had it been anyone else, I might have blurted out my interest in the study of sex, but I simply could not do it there. Instead I told the falsehood that Mother chose to believe. After a short pause I finished, "to study medicine, and hopefully become an M. D., perhaps do medical research."

"Well, that is a grand pursuit, young lady," Earl's father gloated his approval. "That is a fine choice of career indeed. Which peanut company does your father work for?" he interrogated further.

In my entire life, I had never had anyone ask me that question. It was a given that everyone in the area knew that it was the Nutty Boy Company. For a moment, I was almost taken aback, but I answered, "Nutty Boy."

"Oh, yes, yes," he half mumbled. "We don't use that brand, but it's a good company." He continued, "I'm sure that Earl has told you about our family's company and his plans to take over after completing a degree in business."

I felt Earl's grip on my hand tighten slightly. I didn't know if it was a stifled angry response to his father's assumption, an under the table message to me that I should not tell, or a simple gesture of reassurance. "Yes," I replied shortly. "He has told me that you started Chum Snacks. I think it is wonderful that you have worked so hard to achieve so much."

"Well now," his father cleared his throat in false modesty. "It has been quite successful, but we have a long way to go. We now have distribution in five states and in time I am certain that we can go national."

"That would be wonderful, sir." I said, finally taking a bite of the little cracker I had been holding in my left hand. I had been unsure because I didn't recognize the tiny gelatinous balls that rested on top of the cracker. The flavor of decayed brine-fish filled my mouth, and my expression was a combination of surprise, horror, and congeniality, as I attempted to cover the first two initial reactions.

"Beluga!" Mr. Titwallow exclaimed.

I chewed quickly and tried to down the muck as soon as possible.

"I beg your pardon, sir?" I questioned after swallowing.

"Beluga Caviar," he said. "Finest in the world. Delicious, isn't it?"

I was not used to lying. I may have kept some secrets in my life but I had never been afraid to say what I thought. I realized in a moment of clarity that I would not be able to be so honest in this setting. Here the rules had changed. If I told the truth, I took the chance of insulting Earl's family, and despite my rebellion and independence, I now wanted desperately for them to approve of me.

Karlyle Tomms

"Oh, yes sir," I said with an obvious grimace on my face. I reached for my coke which Nora had placed on a coaster beside me.

Earl's mother must have seen the hint of disgust on my face for she quickly came to the rescue. "Well, you know," she said, in her little whisper of a voice, "I think there is something to be said, for good old-fashioned down-to-earth food instead of all this fancy stuff, don't you, Earl?"

"Yes, Mom, I do," he chimed right in. "I'm really not a fan of caviar myself."

Mrs. Titwallow immediately twisted in her chair and called for Nora who arrived in about ten seconds flat.

"Yes, Mum," Nora said, as she stood somewhat at attention on the edge of the room.

"Nora, I have a craving," Mrs. Titwallow enticed. "You have made wonderful hors d'oeuvres, dear. I don't mean to complain, but I just happen to be peckish for something like good old-fashioned peanut butter and crackers or cheese and crackers. Do you think you could throw together another tray with a bit of that on it?"

"I will get right on it, Mum," Nora said, and then trotted cheerfully from the room. She was gone only briefly before returning with something a bit more palatable. I noticed that Anna didn't hesitate to dig into the new tray as well.

In the meantime, Mrs. Titwallow changed the subject. She talked about having worked in a dress shop herself when the business was first starting and when the children were young. I began to feel more comfortable and more at home. I also began to realize that, just as Earl had told me, his father was all about the show, a pretense of wealth, the nouveau riche of the twentieth century. In Earl's eyes, and perhaps in truth, he was trying to be something that he was not.

Earl's mother, however, seemed to have held on to her simple roots. I didn't know if it was the wealth that had made her gracious of if she had been that way all along and the wealth merely served to compliment it. She seemed to know intuitively how to make me feel more comfortable.

While we were chatting around the fire, Nora had been busy setting the dining table. When all was complete, she appeared and announced, "Dinner is served," then, we all rose and migrated across the foyer to the dining room.

The table was set with fine gold-rimmed china and crystal stemware. The table settings were at the end nearest the foyer so that whoever sat at the head of the table had a view across the grounds to the pine-rimmed lake. I assumed that was Mr. Titwallow's place.

Confessions from the Pumpkin Patch

Earl pulled a chair out for me on the inside wall of the dining room so that I would have a view to the opposite window across the front grounds. He then seated himself as his father pulled the chairs out on the opposite side for his mother and sister.

As we were being seated Mrs. Titwallow said, "I hope you don't mind salmon, Lovella. We are having braised salmon with fennel for dinner. Tomorrow for Christmas, we will have a traditional roast goose, English style, for Christmas dinner."

Roast goose, English style, had certainly never been traditional in my home, nor was salmon unless it was out of a can and fried into croquettes. I was sure that Mother and Daddy must surely be having Christmas Eve dinner with Grandmother Fuchs. They were probably sitting down to turkey and dressing, and tomorrow at Grandmother and Grandfather Donner's they were likely to have ham. I caught myself thinking grandmother and grandfather formally as Mother taught me and asked myself why I couldn't just think grandma and grandpa.

"I love salmon," I replied. "Thank you." Little did I know that the salmon I was about to be served was nothing like anything I had ever eaten before.

I discovered over dinner that the cook was Nora's husband, Ralph, a professional chef, and that Mr. Titwallow had shipped them over from England to work for the family. There was a little two bedroom house to the back corner of the property that he had actually built for them so that they would be nearby and on call. I suppose having a maid and cook from Europe was part of the mystique of wealth that he was trying to create.

Nora soon began to circle the table bringing in shallow bowls of soup first. A white wine was poured into the stemware, even for Anna, and water was poured into the other glasses. I learned the soup was leek and celeriac cream. Whatever it was, the flavor delighted me. I had never tasted anything like it and I was hooked from the first spoonful.

I tried to be as gracious and mannerly as possible but the truth is, I felt like a cow loose in Macy's. "The soup is wonderful," I muttered after my first dip into it.

"I'm so glad you like it," Mrs. Titwallow replied. "Ralph has quite a talent in the kitchen."

"I would love to learn to cook like this," I stammered. "Mother never taught me to cook, so I've been trying to teach myself by watching Julia Child and experimenting with recipes from her cook book."

"Lovella has developed quite a talent herself," Earl said, as he smiled gingerly in my direction.

"Cooking is wonderful when it is something you do as a special treat

173

for yourself," Mrs. Titwallow commented. "However, I am personally quite glad to be freed from the drudgery of the kitchen. It is quite another thing when you are having to cook for a family. It is not nearly so much fun when it has become a regular chore."

"How long have Ralph and Nora worked for you?" I questioned as I sipped carefully at my soup.

"About three years now," Mr. Titwallow entered. "Best investment I ever made. They have been wonderful, and I think they really enjoy living here as well."

"Have you lived here long?" I continued to question.

"Well we finished building the house when Earl was about thirteen, so we have been here about seven or eight years."

Mr. Titwallow poked his finger into his napkin and touched the corner of his lips. I noticed that Earl wadded his napkin up and smeared it across his lips, which drew a stern look from his father.

When we had just barely started on the soup, Mr. Titwallow had already downed his glass of wine and had motioned for Nora to bring another.

"So, Lovella," Mr. Titwallow continued after taking his attention back to his food, "How long have you known that you wanted to go into medicine?"

"Yes Lovella, tell us about that," Earl looked at me grinning, taunting me to tell the real story.

I didn't know what to do at that moment, blurt it out—Ever since I learned that I like to fuck—or give the affable answer that was expected. I went with the affable.

"I have always been curious," I began as I reached for another spoonful of that delectable soup, "and I've always been a bookworm. So, I had this curiosity about my own body as I watched myself develop, and that led me to doing some research at the library where I began to discover medical books." The implication was clear that a developing young girl might want to know more about what was happening to her own body, but it was not overtly stated. I was very proud of my answer.

"So!" Earl snickered. "You needed to figure out why you were growing breasts."

I almost snickered myself but quickly darted my eyes toward my soup bowl because I knew that if my eyes met his I was sure to burst out laughing.

"Earl, don't be rude!" Mr. Titwallow commanded.

"Yes sir," Earl replied in mock conformity. "It's just that I am very curious about Lovella's breasts myself, and I find them very interesting."

At this point Anna snorted outright, and I fought hard to keep from

Confessions from the Pumpkin Patch

laughing.

"I actually started to study the books long before that development," I said, in an effort to quench the brewing conflict.

"Your parents must be very proud of you, Lovella," Mrs. Titwallow interjected seemingly un-phased by the interaction between Earl and his father.

"I know that Daddy worships the ground I walk on," I replied, glad to have a way out of the fray. "And Mother constantly brags about me becoming a doctor."

"I'm sure when you have set up your own practice one day they will be extremely proud," Mrs. Titwallow complimented.

"Actually, I hope more to go into research rather than have a practice," I said as I lay my spoon into my empty soup bowl.

At this point Nora was circling the table picking up the soup bowls and refilling glasses. I have to say that I had begun to feel a little tipsy from the wine by that time. It had not escaped my observation that Mr. Titwallow had consumed a little over four glasses of wine during the appetizer and Mrs. Titwallow had consumed two. Neither of them seemed as tipsy as I felt.

"Medical research?" Mr. Titwallow exclaimed in a half questioning tone. "Well, there is a noble profession for you."

"Yes, Lovella is planning to study human sexuality," Earl taunted unable to resist the urge to pick at his father.

"Oh, I see," said Mr. Titwallow. "Like how to prevent venereal diseases and that sort of thing."

"More like how to make getting it on a lot more fun," Earl retorted with a grin.

"Young man!" Mr. Titwallow shouted. "There will be no more of that! If you cannot sit at this table and behave like a civil human being then you can get up and leave the rest of us to enjoy our dinner in peace."

"You know what?" Earl shouted back.

Sensing that he was about to blow, I quickly reached over and placed my hand on his arm. He turned to me instantly as if he was about to attack, but as soon as his eyes met mine, I saw the anger melt. He relaxed back down into his chair.

"You know what?" he said again in a much softer tone. "You are right. I apologize. I have been rude to Lovella and she deserves much better than that. Mom, Dad, Anna, I apologize to you as well."

"Thank you, son," Mrs. Titwallow responded. His father said nothing and continued to glare at him.

By this time, Nora was serving the salmon. I had never seen salmon like this before. There it was looking more like a pink steak sitting atop a bed of fennel. Bits of fresh dill were sprinkled over the top. I felt as though I was dining in a five star restaurant. I had never eaten fennel before, and had never eaten salmon this way before. The taste was exquisite. The fish was tender and perfectly seasoned and the fennel, which had some interesting herb blend, seemed to melt in my mouth. I thought quietly to myself, "I could get used to this."

The conversation continued in a much more civil tone. Mrs. Titwallow told funny stories about Earl as a small boy being tall and gangly and towering over the other children in the first grade. We laughed at the funny stories and I told a few myself. As we were finishing the entree, Nora came back into the room and posed a question.

Mr. and Mrs. Titwallow," she explained. "Ralph had made strawberry tarts for desert. However, Ms. Lovella brought a cake for you and it is indeed a beauty. I thought, perhaps if you would like, we can serve Ms. Lovella's cake for desert this evening, and Ralph can rework the tarts for something tomorrow."

"Oh, really?" Mrs. Titwallow questioned gleefully, "What kind of cake is it, Lovella?"

"I'm not even sure if I can pronounce it correctly," I answered. "It is called Reine de Saba avec Glaqage au Chocolat. I got the recipe from *Mastering the Art of French Cooking*."

"It sounds delightful," Mrs. Titwallow said cheerfully. "Nora, we will have the cake. Thank you."

Nora soon returned with desert dishes on which my cake was neatly carved and artfully placed. Ralph had put some kind of cream glaze around the plates before placing the cake on them. I was both filled with pride at the beauty of the dish and terror that it would taste horrible.

Mrs. Titwallow was the first to take a bite. "Oh, Lovella, this is mouth-watering delicious," she exclaimed. "You have outdone yourself."

"I wanted to give you something for Christmas," I said, "But I had no idea what I would possibly be able to give you on a student's allowance." I did not expose that Earl had actually paid for the ingredients.

"Well, this is perfect, Lovella," Mrs. Titwallow affirmed. "We would not have expected you to bring anything, but it is very sweet that you did. Thank you."

"Yes, indeed," Mr. Titwallow echoed. "Thank you, Lovella, this is extremely good cake."

Earl turned to me and leaned in to give me a little peck on the lips. "You are so wonderful," he said. "Thank you."

"Thank you all for letting me share Christmas with you," I said. "This

Confessions from the Pumpkin Patch

will be a treasured memory for me."

After dinner, we had coffee in the living room and chatted more by the fireside. Mr. Titwallow, who had consumed at least eight glasses of wine with dinner continued to drink by having Nora add liquor of some sort to his coffee. Despite the obvious tension between Earl and his father, I soon began to feel very comfortable and welcomed.

Along about ten o'clock Nora came to lead me to my room. She led me to a six paneled door with brass fixtures. When the door opened, the room was like a scene from a fairy tale. A cherry wood four-poster bed sat on the back wall of the room between two slender windows draped in a shimmering cream colored fabric. The bed was elevated on a platform, which was about a foot high and it looked as though the hardwood floor merely elevated itself seamlessly at that point. Beside the bed were matching night stands and there was a beautiful dresser on the side wall beside another door. The wallpaper was a kind of plum and cream with accents of silver.

Nora led me to the side door. "This is your bath, Mum," she said, holding the door open for me.

The bath was similar in décor to the bedroom. There was a walk-in shower on one side of the room across from a marble topped vanity. At the end was a large claw foot white porcelain tub and there was a little closet door. I thought it strange that they would put a little closet in the bathroom and assumed it must be for linens until I realized there was no commode.

"Nora, there's no toilet," I proclaimed. "Should I use a different bathroom for that?"

"No Mum!" she giggled. "It's right here." She opened the little closet door to reveal a little separate room just for the toilet. It even had a vent fan and light that came on automatically when the door was opened. Our house had only one toilet for the whole family and there certainly was no separate little room just for the toilet much less a vent fan. I never knew that people could live in such opulence. I had never really given it any thought, but there I was being treated like a princess in a castle with servants and everything.

Shortly after Nora left, there was a little knock at the door. When I opened the door, there stood Earl with a little box in his hand and a big tooth-filled smile on his face.

"Merry Christmas," he said as he handed me the box.

"Oh, Earl," I started to say but I never quite got the words out of my mouth before he kissed me. I melted every time he kissed me and I was never able to explain why each kiss was like the first kiss, but every time it happened, I felt that same delightful tingle that I felt standing outside the dorm that very first night. When our lips parted, I said, "Wait, I got you something too. I didn't know if I should give it to you with the family or if maybe we might exchange gifts privately. I ran to my suitcase and pulled out my own slightly larger box. Mine was wrapped in traditional paper with a tacky little green bow on top that had been crushed in the luggage. His was in what appeared to be a black velvet case with no other adornment. I handed my gift to him and said, "You first."

He leaned against the door jam and offered no protest. He carefully unwrapped the package to see the product box under the paper. It was a Norelco electric razor. I couldn't think of anything else to give him, and besides I thought it might entice him to shave some of the fur from his face, maybe to get the hint that he might at least trim it.

"Oh, an electric razor," he grinned and kissed me again, this time a little quicker. "That's really sweet honey. Now you."

There was no unwrapping to be done. I fiddled a bit with being able to open the box until he showed me a clasp on one side. I opened it to see an incredibly beautiful bracelet. The smooth pink, green, and cream-colored stones lined up all the way around it, each one held by tiny gold clips. It took my breath away and I gasped. "Oh, my god!"

"They're opals," he said.

"Real opals?" I questioned.

"Of course they're real," he chided. "There is nothing fake about you and I would never give you anything fake."

"Oh Earl, it's too much," I pleaded. "I only got you a crappy little electric razor that was more of a hint than a gift. I didn't expect anything like this."

"Put it on," he pleaded. "It's a beautiful gift for a beautiful girl. It's precious stones for my precious sweetheart."

Tears welled in my eyes and rolled down my cheeks.

"Now, don't cry," he said pulling me to his chest.

"But it's so beautiful and it's so sweet," I blubbered, "and all I got you was a stupid electric razor and you don't even shave."

"I will. I will shave," he comforted. "I'm looking forward to using my razor. It's a wonderful gift, really." Then he held my face back and wiped the tears from my cheeks with his thumbs. He gazed into my eyes and said, "I just wanted you to know how wonderful you are to me. I'm falling in love with you, Lovella. Right now, I can't see anything but you."

"I love you, too," I blubbered.

He took my hand, led me to the bed and sat with me on the edge. He then took the box from my hand, lifted the bracelet out and wrapped it around my left wrist.

Confessions from the Pumpkin Patch

"This is yours forever," he whispered. "This is yours no matter what happens. If for any reason we might not make it, it is still yours. I want you to have it. I want you to know that no matter what else happens, you are the most wonderful person I have ever known in my life, and if our time together lasts only a few months or a lifetime. I will always be grateful."

The tears came again and I fell into his embrace.

The moment was broken by his father's call from the door, "Is everything alright in here?"

"Yes, we're fine," Earl responded as he kept his embrace.

"Well, don't you get to thinking that you are going to sleep in here, young man!" his father lectured. "You have got your own room and you need to be getting to it. Time for lights out."

"I'll be there in a minute, Dad," Earl replied. His father knew that we had been living together and had to have assumed that we had sex. It just wasn't going to be permitted, wasn't proper, under his roof.

"Well, all right," his father continued, "but don't you get to thinking you're going to sneak in here or anything. I'm going to be checking on you."

"Jesus, Dad! We live together," Earl shouted.

"Well, you don't live together in my house!" his father shouted back. "Now get your ass to bed."

"All right! All right! Give me a moment," Earl pleaded. "I'll be right there."

"You better be!" his father snarled as he went on down the hall. I was amazed at how clear and non-slurring his father's voice was considering how much alcohol I had watched him consume over the evening.

Earl let out a huge sigh. "He fucking has to ruin everything in my life!" he growled.

I sat up. "He didn't ruin anything," I said. "You said everything I could ever wish to hear before he ever came to the door. It's okay. We'll have lots of moments together. This is not going to be the only one."

"You're right," he said as he hugged me again. He stood up, cupped my face in his hands and kissed me again as I sat on the bed. Then he started for the door.

"Earl—," I called after him.

He turned.

"Thank you for loving me," I said.

"Thank you for loving me," he replied as he gently closed the door behind him.

After a hot bath I fell into bed like a zombie.

179

Karlyle Tomms

I didn't realize anything until I heard a faint tapping at the bedroom door the next morning. It didn't really even occur to me 'til then that I had not had a cigarette all evening. The craving hit me shortly after I heard Nora outside my bedroom door calling a tender little, "Yoo Hooo—Miss Lovella—time to get up, dear."

I pulled the covers back and staggered to the door. I opened it still feeling more asleep than awake and there stood Nora in her cheerful glory.

"Good morning, dear," she sang delightfully. "Would you be having breakfast with the family?"

"Yeah, uh, yes mam," I drooled out. "I would love to have breakfast with the family."

I had no idea what time it was, but it was still early enough, the sun was still sleeping behind the horizon.

"Well then dear, we shall be meeting you in thirty minutes in the kitchen," she explained. "It is down the front stairs and through the dining room to the left. I would give you directions down the back stairs but it is too confusing for this time of the morning. Will you be having coffee, dear?" she queried.

"Yes, mam," I replied hoping that the door would support me and I wouldn't fall into a sleepy lump on the floor."

"Cream? Sugar?" she quested on in her singsong voice.

"Yes, both, please," I said, not used to such a routine in the morning.

"We are having Eggs Benedict, dear," she sang on. "I hope you like it."

"Yes, I love it," I said being familiar with the dish. It was something that Mother used to make for me as a special breakfast treat. Although Mother's version was quite good, I was sure that Ralph's would be superior.

"Wonderful, dear, I'll see you downstairs." She then trotted on down the hall.

I called after her, "Miss Nora."

"Yes dear." She turned on her heels.

"I hate to ask, but is there any where I could smoke a cigarette?" I asked sheepishly.

"Oh, dear, you have the habit." She came back to my door. "I hate to say it, but I do too." She looked up and down the hall as though to make sure no one shared our little secret. She said, "Why don't you smoke in the toilet dear. Flick the ashes into the water. Then put the cigarette out, wrap it in a napkin and bring it to me when you're done."

She then cheerfully trotted on down the hall and tapped on another door. As I closed my door, I heard her sing, "Yoo Hoo, Master Earl. Time to get

180

Confessions from the Pumpkin Patch

up, dear."

I didn't wait to see Earl come to the door, but retreated back into the bathroom to do as she had instructed. When I got dressed, I didn't know if Earl had gotten ready before me and had gone down or not, so I went on to the kitchen. Nora met me in the dining room to take care of the little package of my carefully wrapped cigarette butt. I then entered through the double doors from the dining room to the kitchen to find a large expanse with beige tile floors and a room that was at least half again more than the square footage of my childhood home. Along one wall was a bank of cabinets. There were at least two built in ovens, and a cook-top that had six burners. It looked to me to be more like a restaurant kitchen than a home kitchen. An average looking man in his forties wearing a chef's hat was standing before the stove. I assumed this was Ralph. He didn't look up from his work when I entered and seemed not to even notice me.

Opposite the bank of cabinets was a long island with marble counter tops. The refrigerator that stood on the wall closest to the dining room looked like it could hold a year's worth of food without so much as a belch. On the far corner from the dining room door was a white round table with six chairs. A sleek sage green tile ran up the wall behind it. Slightly higher than chair-rail height, the tile circled the entire room. There was one set of windows behind the dining table, and sunlight had begun its first creep into the room. The soft morning light filtered across the dining table and then the floor. Above the tile, the rest of the room was painted with a darker sage green, and even the ceiling was green.

At the table, Mr. Titwallow sat in his pajamas and robe with a coffee cup in front of him. His nose was buried in a newspaper. Mrs. Titwallow sat beside him also wearing a robe and she was reading what appeared to be a paperback novel. As soon as she saw me, she called out "Lovella, come sit down."

I crossed the room to sit at the table. "Good morning," I said as I pulled myself up to the table beside Mrs. Titwallow. A hairy male hand came from out of nowhere to sit a cup of coffee on the table before me. I didn't even think Ralph had noticed me, but the coffee was there on the table as if by magic and then he immediately returned to his work without muttering a word. It was creamed and sugared just as I had requested.

Mr. Titwallow grunted a good morning from behind his paper without ever peeking out.

Mrs. Titwallow laid a gentle hand across my arm and asked, "Did you sleep well?"

"Like a rock," I replied as I sipped the warm sweet caffeine nectar from my cup. I had no sooner answered the question than Earl entered the room

Karlyle Tomms

from a door adjacent to the dining table.

"Good morning," he chirped cheerfully as he took the chair beside me.

I stared at him in astonishment but before I could get a word out of my startled mouth, I heard his mother say, "My goodness, Earl. You shaved."

His father instantly popped his paper down to his lap to see if his vision would match what he had just heard. It seemed as though some miracle had happened. We all glared at him like spiritual pilgrims at the foot of Fatima. Not only had Earl shaved his entire face clean, but he had pulled his long hair behind him into a pony tail and he was wearing a white oxford button down shirt! I found myself thinking that my ugly hippie wasn't so ugly after all. Behind all that scraggle was a chiseled and classic face.

"Son, what in the world prompted you to do that?" his father goaded with a hint of sarcasm. "You look good for a change!"

"Well, last night Lovella and I exchanged Christmas gifts," he explained. "She got me an electric razor. I just felt that I had to—um—couldn't wait to use it."

"You look very nice," Mrs. Titwallow said softly and sincerely.

In that moment, my right hand went instantly to my left wrist. For a moment, I had forgotten whether I had put the bracelet back on after my bath, but there it was around my wrist.

"Well, Lovella," Mr. Titwallow spouted. "You managed to accomplish in one night what I have not been able to accomplish for the last three or four years. Congratulations, and thank you."

I didn't know what to say. "Well, I just thought it would be a nice gift," I said after a moment of hesitation. "I was just trying to figure out what I could get him for Christmas. I wasn't sure what to get him."

Mr. Titwallow noticing that I was fidgeting with my left wrist commented, "That's a very nice bracelet, Lovella."

"Thank you," I said, embarrassed. "This was my Christmas gift from Earl."

"You're spending quite a lot of money on this young lady, Earl," said Mr. Titwallow with that now familiar tone of sarcasm underlying his voice. "You must really like her."

"Stop it!" Mrs. Titwallow swatted at him. "That's rude."

"I do more than like her," Earl said, as he reached over and took my hand. "I love her."

"Is that so?" piped Mr. Titwallow. "Well, good luck with that, Lovella. You're going to need it."

"Daniel, please," Mrs. Titwallow whispered under her breath to him.

A cup of coffee showed up in front of Earl. Nora had entered the room

Confessions from the Pumpkin Patch

and was beginning to transport food to the table from the island where Ralph had assembled it.

Mr. Titwallow folded his paper and sat it in the chair beside him. "I hope you like Eggs Benedict, Lovella. Ralph makes the best I've ever had." He then adjusted himself to the table and began unfolding his napkin.

"Anna won't be joining us," Mrs. Titwallow said sweetly. "She likes to sleep in. She works so hard at school. We usually let her have this little indulgence when she is on vacation."

"I can't blame her," I said. "I'm rather fond of sleep myself."

"Oh, I hope we didn't get you up too early," Mrs. Titwallow said apologetically.

"No, this is wonderful!" I soothed. "This is something I've never experienced before. I wouldn't want to miss it by sleeping."

You have never had family breakfast before?" Mrs. Titwallow questioned.

"Oh, of course," I replied suddenly nervous. "I have just never had breakfast like this. Just like last night I had never had dinner served to me anywhere outside a restaurant."

"Well, I hope you enjoy it very much," Mrs. Titwallow commented.

We began to dig into breakfast, and Mr. Titwallow was right. Ralph's Eggs Benedict was the best I had ever eaten. Toward the end of the meal, Mr. Titwallow threw his napkin on the table and pushed his chair back. "If you will excuse me," he said. "I have to go pick up my parents for Christmas dinner. I have offered repeatedly to send a limousine but my father just won't hear of it. So I have to go pick them up myself."

"Grandpa doesn't really enjoy the pomp and circumstance," Earl whispered as he leaned toward me.

"What about your parents, Mrs. Titwallow?" I said, as I was finishing my last bite. "Will they be here for dinner as well?"

Her face turned pale and there was a slight lift to one side of her lip. "No," she said, quietly. "My parents aren't with us anymore."

"Oh, I am so sorry," I said feeling intensely embarrassed. "I was just blurting out questions and not thinking." For some reason it had slipped my mind that Earl told me about her losing her parents.

"It's alright, dear," she said politely. "You could not have known." She then pulled her chair back from the table and said, "I think I will go get dressed as well, and accompany Daniel to pick up his parents."

After she and Mr. Titwallow had left the room, Earl must have realized my embarrassment. He put his arm around my shoulder and squeezed me a little. "It's alright," he crooned. "I'll tell you more about it later. Come on, let's get our coats and go for a walk."

183

Karlyle Tomms

As we were leaving, I stopped by the cook's side of the room where Ralph was obviously already working hard on dinner. "You must be Ralph," I said.

He looked up from his preparations. "Yes Mum. May I get you something?" he said, in a thick British accent.

"No," I replied. "I just wanted to meet you and to tell you how wonderful everything has been. I really appreciate all the hard work that you and Nora put in."

"It's what we get paid for, Mum," he responded only half looking up from his work. "It's just like any other job."

"Well, thank you," I said as I started to walk away.

"Thank you, Mum," he replied.

Earl took my hand and led me up the back stairs to our rooms. We each grabbed our coats and went back down and out a door behind the kitchen. It was partly cloudy and there was an occasional flurry of snow. More often than not, the sun peeked through but it did little to warm my cold face from the twenty-degree chill. Earl walked with his arm around my shoulder.

Not far from the house was a garage that had six doors. "You guys have that many cars?" I questioned.

"Well, Mom has a car. Dad has a car. I have a car. Anna just got a car, since she got her driver's license in September." He counted off the doors with one finger as though trying to remember for sure. "And Dad has a couple of antique cars that he likes to piddle with now and then."

We walked past the garage and to a little knoll in the middle of the property. We stopped there a moment in the open. I estimated that the property must be about fifteen or twenty acres. There were carefully planted trees around the rolling lawn. Around the edge of the property there was a bank of mature trees and through the bare winter limbs, I could see other houses, but I could make out only two. I figured that in the summer the other homes would not be visible at all. Off to the left, I could see the little cottage that Mr. Titwallow had built for Ralph and Nora.

"It's beautiful," I commented, turning this way and that to look at the expanse.

"Yeah, there is a lot that money can buy you," Earl said, his eyes scanning the property as well.

We stood atop the knoll holding gloved hands and feeling the crisp winter chill on our faces.

"I felt like I had hurt your mother's feelings at breakfast," I said.

"Don't worry about it," he comforted. "It is just something my mom has never quite been able to accept."

Confessions from the Pumpkin Patch

I stood there looking at him, wondering if I should ask, but knowing that it was absolutely none of my business. He must have read the curiosity on my face.

"When mom's father abandoned the family, she was a little girl," he began to clarify. "I think she adored her father and it really hit her when he just left one day. He packed up some clothes while Grandma and the kids were at church and just left. I don't even think he left a note. They never knew what happened to him and my Mom has never heard from her father since then."

"How old was she?" I asked.

"I think she was maybe ten or twelve," he replied. "She had two little brothers. One was about eight years old and one was six years old when my grandfather left. I think it devastated the whole family. Grandma never remarried, never had anything to do with any man after that. She worked at whatever job she could find to support herself and her kids. Lots of times she had to work more than one job, and she left Mom to take care of her little brothers. I guess that's where my mom gets her work ethic and her loyalty."

His eyes moved from mine to the sky as the snow flurries seemed to thicken a bit. Then he continued his story. The pale gray light of winter filtered across his face. "My Uncle David was killed in World War II before I was born. My Uncle Tim followed in my grandfather's footsteps and just left one day. I think I was about six years old when that happened. He had never married. There was some talk that maybe he preferred men to women and that maybe he was not being treated very well in the community because of that. I don't know. He just left. At least he went to the trouble of paying his last month's rent before he took off and he left a note to Mother telling her that he loved her, but asking her not to try to find him."

"Oh, wow," I said, feeling empathy moving through my heart. "Your mother has had a hard life. What about your grandmother?"

I heard the crackle of grief in his voice as he explained. "Grandmother died in a car crash when I was about fourteen."

"Oh, my god, Earl," I said. "I remember that you mentioned something about losing your grandmother." I hugged him. "I've never experienced anything like that. I feel like such a brat for all the complaints I've had about my mother and growing up in Climax. I've had it so easy and didn't even realize." Then it struck me why his mother might have had a hard time with my question at breakfast. "So your mom doesn't have any family but this one," I said. "Everyone from her childhood is gone."

"Except for a couple of aunts and uncles who don't have much to do

185

Karlyle Tomms

with her," he said. "Yes, they're gone."

"I am so selfish and spoiled," I whined.

He took my shoulders in his hands and pulled me out away from him so he could look me in the face. His eyes scanned mine and then centered in my soul.

"No, you are not selfish," he scolded. "You've done so much for me already. I had no idea that day in the library what a wonderful person you are. I just wanted to get laid. If I had continued to pursue just that alone, I never would have realized what a treasure I had found in you."

"Well, I need to apologize to your mom," I said.

"No you don't," he admonished. "You didn't do anything wrong. You just asked a question, an understandable question. Believe me. Mom is all right."

He then put his arm around my shoulders and pointed me toward the pine grove that surrounded the lake on the south side of their property. For much of that morning, we just walked without speaking. We just enjoyed being with each other.

"So, what about your dad's family," I said, after a while. "Your grandpa doesn't like the pomp and circumstance?"

"Oh, just wait 'til you meet Grandpa Titwallow," he laughed. "I love him. For one thing, he puts Dad in his place. He won't let Dad get away with anything, including pestering me."

"Sounds like it is going to be a fun evening," I acknowledged.

"I hope so," said, Earl. "Our Christmases can get a bit—." He hesitated for a word. "Tense at times. They may be a bit better behaved with you here."

We walked into the hidden sanctuary of the pines. Light brown pine needles and fallen pinecones crunched beneath our feet. Earl stopped beneath the canopy, turned to me, and kissed me. There it was again, that feeling I treasured, that tingling in my body down to my toes. Of all the boys I had ever been with, he was the only one who could do that to me. I desired him like no other man in my life. I wanted to have him right there in the cold. I wanted to lay our coats on the pine needles and make love, but we both knew that it was far too chilly to undertake such a thing outdoors at least on that particular day. We kissed, warm lips contrasting cold cheeks and then he held me for a while. We stood there, a warm island in the cold pines, and then he said, "You know what? My nose is a little cold. Want to go back to the house and see what's going on?"

"Sure," I replied and we walked through the pines, around the lake, and back to the house.

By that time it was around 10:30 in the morning. I asked Earl if I could

186

Confessions from the Pumpkin Patch

use the phone to call Mother and Daddy to wish them Merry Christmas. "I'll call collect," I said, not wanting to impose.

"Oh, nonsense," he chided. "My family could afford thousands of such phone calls. Just call them and don't worry about it."

He led me to a room adjacent to the formal living room. The décor was entirely different. There were large leather sofas and the walls were paneled in what appeared to be oak. Low windows looked out over a covered porch to the opposite side of the property from the dining room. There was another fireplace that probably backed up to the one in the living room but this one was stone and had a thick rustic oak mantle. A color console TV sat in one corner of the room. On the opposite corner, near the fireplace, was another Christmas tree. This one looked more like what I had been used to. This one had the handmade ornaments that Earl and his sister had made while growing up. It had an assortment of ornaments and didn't look like someone had done it just to match the room. This Christmas tree also had presents beneath it. It occurred to me in that moment that I hadn't even given thought to the fact that the tree in the formal living room had no presents beneath it at all. It was just for show.

"You have two living rooms?" I questioned.

"No, this is the den," he replied. "This is the hang-out room. The other room is for formal guests. Sometimes Dad has business associates over for dinner and they sit in the formal living room pontificating about business."

He led me to a sofa with a black phone sitting on the table beside it. I picked it up and dialed direct. Daddy answered the phone and I heard the slur in his voice. As soon as he said, "Hello," I knew he was drunk.

"Daddy, this is Lovella," I said wondering how Mother was dealing with this.

"Oh, hey, my, my leeetle Pun-kin—Pa Patch." He was so drunk that speaking took effort.

I heard Mother in the background shout, "John! I told you not to answer the phone! Let me get it."

"It's—Lo—vell—Lo—vell—ah," he shouted back.

Then I heard her closer by, "Oh, for goodness sakes, John, give me the phone!"

There were sounds in the background and in my mind I could see her wrestling the receiver out of his hand. Then I heard her say, "John! Go sit down." He mumbled something in the background and then she came on the line.

"Hello." She sounded frazzled.

"Hello Mother" I said. "How are you?"

187

Karlyle Tomms

"I've seen better days," she said. "How are you? Are you enjoying your Christmas?"

"Yes, it's wonderful," I replied. "Earl has a wonderful family and a very nice home."

"That's good, honey," she said, her tone softening. "I'm glad you are having a good time."

"I just called to wish you Merry Christmas," I said. "I wanted to catch you before you headed over to Grandmother and Grandfather's house."

"We're not going," she said. "I'm not going to expose anyone to your father in this condition."

"Yeah." I felt sad for both of them, and I wasn't sure what to say. "He sounds like he is drunk."

"He has been drunk, Lovella," she pleaded, a tone of sadness and grief in her voice. It was something I wasn't used to hearing. "He gets drunk more often and drunker than he ever used to get. I don't know what I'm going to do with him."

What was I going to say? There was nothing I could do. I began to feel sorry for Mother. The inevitable had finally happened after all the years she had spent trying to keep him sober. I felt afraid for Daddy. I was no longer the naive little girl who could make herself believe with his reassurance that his drinking wasn't really a big deal. I knew better. I had read about cirrhosis and many of the other things that could go wrong as a result of chronic drinking. I was scared for both of them.

"I'm sorry, Mother," I said after a brief silence.

"I'm sorry too, honey," she said.

I could imagine that she was not only saying that she was sorry for herself and for what they were going through but that she was saying she was sorry for the way she had raised me, for all the control she had attempted to wage over my life.

"Is there anything I can do?" I pleaded hoping that there might actually be something. But I could see the writing on the wall. I could see that this wasn't going to end well.

"No, honey, of course not," she comforted. "There appears to be nothing that any of us can do. I can't keep him from drinking. God knows I've tried. I can't. He always finds a way. Anyway, I just try to keep him out of trouble, but I've long since given up the delusion that I could prevent him from embarrassing me. I wish there was something that someone could do. I pray about it. More praying is the only thing I know to do."

I felt a tear roll across my cheek, almost out of nowhere, stealth crying. I rolled my lower lip under my teeth and said, "I will pray, too, Mother."

Confessions from the Pumpkin Patch

"Thank you, honey," she said. "Now go enjoy your Christmas and don't worry about anything here. I've got it under control for now."

This was not my Mother. This was not the cold, controlling bitch I had grown up with. That man who had been on the phone was not my father. He was not the hard-working family man who adored me. He had deteriorated into a kind of human mush.

I hung up the phone and starred dazed into a blur before my eyes. Earl sat down beside me having overheard the conversation. He put his arm around me and pulled me to his chest and I cried.

I felt so guilty about having gotten Daddy that bottle of Chardonnay. I should have realized that the last thing he needed was more alcohol. Mother had not even mentioned it, a kindness that was unlike her. A year or two earlier and she would not have missed the opportunity to thrust the knife of guilt into my heart and twist. She would have made sure that I realized what a horrible thing I had done. She didn't have to. I realized it myself.

We sat there on the sofa for a while and Earl just held me, no questions, just comfort. He seemed to have some intuition about me, when to speak and when not, and if he messed up he was quick to correct it.

Only a few moments later we heard a shout from the front of the house, a man's voice, clear, yet with an undertone of gravel being swirled in an empty glass. "Hey! Hey! What is going on in the big house?"

Earl put a large comforting hand to the side of my head. "Grandma and Grandpa are here," he said. "Are you ready for this?"

Never having been one to linger too long in the morbid, even my own pain, I sat up straight and said, "I think so. How do I look?"

I know that there must have been evidence of sadness on my face. At the very least mascara must have cut roads across the pits of my eyes. I seldom wore much make up in those days, maybe a little lipstick, a thin line of eye liner, and a touch of rouge at the most. However, on that day I had tried to pretty myself a bit more for his family. At that moment, I regretted it.

"You always look beautiful," he said, "But maybe you might need a little touch up." He rose and crossed the room to a tissue box, returned, and wiped the black worm lines from beneath my eyes. When he finished, he smiled and said, "Now, you look stunning."

I snickered a bit at his comment, "It is so good to have adoring fans," I commented.

"Ready?" was his next question.

"Sure," was my quick reply. Then we rose and ambulated to the formal living room.

189

By the time we had gotten there, Nora had already taken the coats and his grandparents were being seated in the living room.

His grandfather was a white-haired man of average height, build, and looks. He was moving toward a chair by the fireplace, cane in his right hand keeping rhythm with his movements like a third leg. Seeing the way he used it, I doubted that he actually needed it. His cane seemed more like an accessory to his persona than a medical necessity. He wore pin-stripe slacks with black suspenders over a white dress shirt, but no tie and no suit coat.

Earl's grandmother was at least four or five inches taller than his grandfather and I saw then where Earl had inherited his height. She had salt and pepper hair kept in a style reminiscent of the 1930's with a horseshoe roll circling her head. There was the faint hint of an osteoporosis hump crossing over her shoulders. Her head jutted out in front of her shoulders arriving at any destination at least a second before the rest of her body. When she walked it seemed as though each foot was thrust out in front of her to keep her from falling face-forward. Surprising to me, she wore a tan pant suit with a little waist jacket that fell just to the top of her broad hips. A white blouse with cascading ruffles rippled between the flaps of her jacket.

As soon as we entered the room Earl's grandfather spotted us, stopped directly, and waved his left hand in the air and then to his hip making a broad half-moon circle to the side of his body.

"Hey, Earl, my boy!" he exclaimed. "Who's that beautiful doll you got hanging on your arm."

Earl led me across the room. "Grandpa, this is Lovella Fuchs, my girlfriend."

"Pleased to meet ya, young lady!" he half shouted. "Hope these folks have been treating ya right."

Earl said, "Lovella, this is my grandpa, Frank Titwallow." He then motioned to the tall woman standing just behind him, "And this is my grandma, Sarah Titwallow."

"I'm very pleased to meet you both," I said, trying to be as affable as possible.

"Good to meet you, too," spewed his grandfather.

His grandmother in her half-stumbling walk crossed around behind the sofa where we were standing, held a huge hand out to me, and said, "How do you do. I'm Sarah Titwallow." She acted as though she had not just been introduced.

"I'm very pleased to meet you, Mrs. Titwallow." I said.

She then waved her hand at me, put a funny little snarl across her lips

Confessions from the Pumpkin Patch

and said, "Awah! Call me Sarah. Besides, I wouldn't know if you were talking to me or my daughter in law with all that Mrs. stuff."

"Yeah, call me Frank," Earl's grandfather echoed as he placed himself in front of the chair and then fell into it as though his ass had suddenly turned into a sack of potatoes.

Sarah crossed back around the sofa, talking as she went. "Come on, sit down, take a load off. Put your feet up."

Earl and I followed her around into the seating area. She plopped down on the sofa adjacent to Frank's chair where I had sat the night before, patted her hand on the cushion, and said, "Right here, sweetie, I wanna talk to ya."

I didn't know if she was talking to Earl or to me, but we crossed around and sat on the sofa next to her.

Apparently Mr. and Mrs. Titwallow had taken the car around the house to the garage in back. They came in the back through the den so that they entered the room behind us.

"Is everyone comfortable?" I heard Mrs. Titwallow say as she rounded the sofa to stand in front of us.

"As comfortable as I can be in a fancy house," Frank exclaimed.

Mr. Titwallow followed close behind Earl's mom and asked, "Dad, Mom, would you like a drink?"

"Are you gonna get it?" Frank teased.

"No, I'll have Nora get it," Mr. Titwallow explained. "You know I'm not much of a bartender."

Nora had just entered from the dining room side, almost as if on cue and asked, "What shall I get everyone?"

"I'll have a gin and tonic," Frank responded, "and I assume Sarah will have her usual."

Nora looked directly at Frank's grandmother and said, "A Bloody Mary then, Mrs. Sarah."

"Yes, please," Sarah responded and then started to get up. "Here, I'll help you with that."

"Nonsense, Mother," Earl's father exclaimed. "That's why Nora gets paid. Sit down."

Nora took the orders for the rest of us and then left for the kitchen.

After seating herself, Mrs. Titwallow asked, "Lovella, did you have a pleasant morning?"

Mr. Titwallow took the throne of his chair like a king surveying his court, both hands lying over the ends of the chair arms.

"Yes," I said, feeling scrutinized. "Earl showed me the grounds and we walked around the lake."

Karlyle Tomms

Sarah slapped a large bejeweled hand on my leg and announced, "Clarese has been telling us about you, Lovella," she said. "You are studying to be a doctor. How wonderful!"

"Well, I'm actually studying to be a research scientist in a medical field," I replied and saw a scorned look come across Mr. Titwallow's face. I realized in an instant that he had no desire to repeat the conversation of the night before. So I quickly changed the subject.

"Earl tells me that your family has lived in Pittsburgh for several generations." I smiled, and crooked my head to the side to get a glance at her expression.

"Oh, yes, yes," she laughed, "both sides of the family have been in Pennsylvania about as long as there has been a Pennsylvania"

"Really?" I questioned. "I don't think I even know that much about my family. I'm afraid I don't actually know any further back than my own grandparents. I do know that my mother's family came from southern Kentucky near the Tennessee border." It had never occurred to me before that moment how little I knew about my family tree.

The conversation ensued and I learned more about Earl's family than I ever dreamed of knowing about my own. His grandmother's family had been some of the original settlers soon after the Revolutionary War. They were German. I had never even realized that there had been German settlers in Pennsylvania. Honestly, I hadn't paid that much attention in State History class. For the most part history had bored me. Although I had no problem making the grade, I soon forgot it after the test had passed. So, German settlers. Okay.

Earl's grandfather's family had been both Dutch and English. This much I expected. There was also a story about a great great grandmother who had come from the South after the Civil War and married into the Titwallow clan. It was fascinating to me that they could sit there and discuss family stories that went back several generations. That sort of thing just never happened in our family. It was not as though Mother wouldn't have loved to be able to account for some heritage. I think she always hoped for and dreamed of having a heritage but feared any research might turn up some horrible secret that she would rather not have known.

We had drinks and talked for some time and then Nora came in and called us to dinner. Apparently a couple of people had been hired to help with serving dinner for a larger group of people. There were two young men dressed in black tuxedoes who were also assisting with serving. Nora rolled the goose in on a serving cart and carved it beside the table. The young men brought each plate to her. She laid the goose meat daintily

Confessions from the Pumpkin Patch

across each plate with knife and fork. The meal was huge. There were roast potatoes, Brussels sprouts wrapped in bacon and apparently a baked medley of root vegetables. There was some kind of dressing that tasted lightly of ginger and an herb. I couldn't quite make it out. Earl told me that it was a chestnut dressing but I was unable to discern what herb I was tasting. There were several sauces and bread rolls that were so tender and flavorful it was almost like eating air. I had never seen cranberry sauce with whole cranberries in it. I learned that Ralph had made the cranberry sauce from scratch. Although Mother would mash it up and grate orange peel over it, her cranberry sauce actually always came from a can.

Dinner culminated in a flame of brandy. I learned that it was a traditional English pudding and that setting it ablaze was all part of the presentation, but the alcohol also enhanced the flavor. Like everything else, it was totally wonderful. I felt like royalty.

This was all so amazing to me that it was almost overwhelming. I would have felt so totally out of my element if I had not known that Earl's family had come from earthy roots themselves. I knew that his mother had struggled and that she was probably where she was, not just by marriage, but by her commitment and hard work in that marriage. I knew that his father had not always been rich, and that he had scraped himself up from the lower end of middle class to being the creator and CEO of his own company. On one hand, I felt so proud of them. On the other hand, I felt out of place. I felt ashamed of my own family. There were so many thoughts going through my mind, I could scarcely contain them all. I tried not to do it, but I had a hard time listening to the discussions about family history, and family accomplishments without judging myself and my own family. My father, after all, was a drunk. As much as I had loved him and adored him as a child, I had begun to realize how much he had wasted his life and his own opportunities in life. As much as I resented Mother's control of him, I began to realize that she had a reason for pushing him and that it was not entirely for selfish reasons. She also wanted our family to be more.

After dinner we retired to the den to open Christmas gifts. I sat nervously watching as gifts were handed out, family member to family member. Both Earl's parents and his grandparents had gotten me gifts.

"I'm so embarrassed," I said as the gifts were placed on my lap. "I didn't really get anything for any of you."

"Oh, that's not true," Mrs. Titwallow retorted and turned to Earl's grandparents. "Lovella made us a lovely cake. What was that called dear?" She turned back to me with the question.

"I don't even know if I can pronounce it correctly," I said feeling the

Karlyle Tomms

heat of embarrassment flood my face. "But I think it is de Saba avec Glaqage au Chocolat"

Sarah hooted, "It's French and its chocolate. That's all I need to know."

"It was delicious," Mrs. Titwallow followed. "We had it for desert last night—wonderful! I think there are left-overs so I'll have Nora pack some up for you tomorrow. You can take it home and share in Lovella's gift."

Earl put his arm around me and grinned, "Now, Lovella, shut up and open your presents," he teased.

I looked down at the first box in my lap and realized that it was probably the most beautiful wrapping I had ever seen. "It's too pretty to unwrap," I said. Nonetheless, I began carefully pulling the paper away. Inside was a white box, and when I opened it and pulled back the tissue there was a log shaped leather purse, brown with gold emblems on it and hand-flaps of a softer tan-colored leather. "I've never seen anything like it," I said as I pulled the purse up to examine it.

Earl's mother said, "It was designed by Henri Vuitton. It's called 'The Papillion.' Isn't it beautiful? I love the classic and elegant lines."

"Yes," I said, not quite knowing what I was going to do with it and feeling as though it was too expensive and beautiful to actually use. "It is very beautiful. Thank you so much."

Sarah then squawked, "Well, the gift we got you is not going to be quite as fancy as Mr. and Mrs. Moneybags over here, but we hope you like it."

I smiled nervously as I opened the package to find a Maybelline Cosmetics Kit including tweezers, eyeliner pencils, eyelash curler, and a collection of other things. It was packaged in a nice little box and was something I was far more comfortable receiving.

"Oh, I love Maybelline," I smiled. "It was so nice of you to get me something. Next year, I'll have to make sure to include you on my list."

Following gift opening, we settled back into a comfortable evening of continued conversation. Having heard Earl talk about his father, I was amazed and thankful that they didn't get into some big spat. I thought perhaps they were both trying to be on their best behavior with me present. More and more I was feeling cozy and contented with Earl's family. For all his complaints about his father, his family still seemed to be the kind of family I would have been grateful to have had. His father might have been a little controlling, but there was none of the drama I had grown so accustomed to in my own family. Even though his father and mother seemed to drink a little heavy, they never seemed to be drunk and I never saw them out of control like Daddy.

Later we settled into our rooms for the night. Earl came by my room to wish me goodnight. He stepped through the door of my room, kicked the

Confessions from the Pumpkin Patch

door closed behind him, lifted me into his arms and kissed me. I loved it when he did things like that. I loved knowing that he not only loved me but he desired me. When he finished his long warm kiss he said, "So, what did you think?"

"I think you are a very lucky person," I said. I reached a hand up and stoked his now smooth cheek. "I love your family. They are so welcoming and affirming."

"Well, you haven't seen the rough stuff yet," he said.

"Compared to my family, they look like saints." I took his hand and pulled him over to the bed to sit down. "So, we leave tomorrow morning?" I questioned.

"Yep," he replied. "About 9:00 A.M. Sound all right to you?"

"Fine," I replied. "I don't know how I can ever thank them, or you," I went on. "This is the best Christmas I've ever had and just being here without the wonderful gifts still would have been the best Christmas gift I've ever had."

"Just having you with me makes this the best Christmas I've ever had and it's more than thanks enough for the gifts," he said. "Besides, in time you'll understand that it's just stuff."

"It seems like pretty damn special stuff," I said.

"No," he replied, squeezing my hand. "It's just stuff. There may be more of it. It may be fancier than what you are used to, but honestly it means nothing by itself."

"I'll take your word for it," I said.

He then kissed me, said goodnight and walked to the door. He turned just before opening the door to leave and said, "Nora will wake you for breakfast just like today."

"Okay," I replied.

After he left I got ready for bed and fell asleep quickly even though my mind was full of the day and all the experiences I had.

Breakfast the next morning was similar to the first morning. Earl and I packed after breakfast. Our bags were taken out and John brought Earl's car around to the front. We said our goodbyes and waved as we drove away. I settled back into the cool leather seats of Earl's Ferrari and couldn't help feeling that something in me had changed, that I would never really be the same again. I couldn't put my finger on it. It was some lingering secret in my subconscious yet to be revealed, not a bad thing like a revelation in therapy, but a shift in the way I thought and the way I viewed the world. I had seen both sides on the coin of life. Despite the multiple opposing factions of perception and intent, life seemed more whole to me after that. In some way, I felt more complete.

Earl reached over and took my hand. His long, warm, fingers lay like a blanket of comfort over mine. I watched the Pennsylvania landscape flow by my window, and I realized I would go with him whenever he wanted, wherever he wanted. Regardless of what I had ever planned for my life before he found me, from that point on I would follow him.

Confessions from the Pumpkin Patch

Chapter 16

The winter of 1967 dragged on cold and slow as winters are prone to do. I settled back into my routine with Earl, spending enough time in the dorm to keep my status there and stay off the radar of any university official who might consider it unseemly that I was living with a man off-campus. Most of my time was spent with Earl. He continued his activities with The Students for a Democratic Society and it became evident to me that if I was going to be with this man it meant a change of wardrobe, a Louis Vuitton purse designed by Henri Vuitton not-withstanding.

It was a fact that I didn't own a pair of jeans. Mother considered them to be un-lady-like and for all my rebellion against Mother, I didn't rebel much as far as fashion was concerned. I liked looking like a woman. I enjoyed hair styles and pretty dresses but if I was going to be a hippie things had to change. For Earl, I would be a hippie. If I could have been a chameleon able to morph into anything he wanted, I would have done it.

On a mid-January morning, I had gotten ready for class wearing a double-buttoned, long-sleeve, hip-length blouse of thick cotton and a matching knee skirt. As we were walking out the door I asked Earl, "How do I look in this?"

"You always look beautiful," he said.

"No, I mean honestly, Earl, how do I look?"

He eyed me up and down confused about what I was trying to determine and said, "You look like a fashionable, modern woman."

"But you're a hippie," I replied.

"So?" He looked puzzled.

"So," I said, "I don't look like a hippie. Shouldn't I look like a hippie if I'm going to be dating a hippie?"

He gave me a quick kiss on the forehead as we were walking to the car.

"You should look any way you want to look," he said. "It doesn't matter. Besides, you look like you fit right in with my family."

"Yes," I went on. "But do you remember the first time we went to a Student's for a Democratic Society meeting?"

"Yes. What?" He strolled beside me with his hand dangling off my shoulder.

"You remember what a hard time I had getting down on the floor in my

197

Karlyle Tomms

knee length skirt?"

"Yeah, so?" A slight grin crossed his face.

"Well, I think I need to have some more comfortable clothes if we are going to participate in the anti-war movement. My wardrobe does not appear to be conducive to the activities we might encounter with that group."

"Yeah. So we'll get you some more comfortable clothes." He opened the car door for me and I slipped into the seat like a lady. Then he stepped off the curb, rounded the car, and entered the driver's side. "We'll go shopping after class this afternoon," he said.

"Do you mind buying me a few new outfits?" I questioned.

"I don't mind buying you anything you want," he said as he was pulling away from the curb. "We'll go shopping."

By 1967 there were quite a few hippie boutiques showing up in American cities. State College, PA, was no exception. Earl knew right where they were. In addition, there were second-hand stores where one could buy old sailor's pants with the stripe down the side and bell bottoms. A little tie-dye set to the pants turned them into an entirely different garment.

I finished my last class at 2:00 P M. Earl was done by noon but he would usually go to the library and study while he waited for my class to end. He met me like always right outside my classroom and we walked half-linked to each other in the cold crisp winter air. The sun was shining and there was not a cloud in the jewel blue sky. The outlines of gray tree limbs carved cracks into the blue sky overhead.

Later, Earl pulled up in front of an old building, a store front of years past. The brick had been painted a bright yellow and the windows had painted outlines of peace signs around the edges. Maniquins stood in the windows draped in the latest of hippie garb. As we walked through the door jingle bells chimed and I realized they had been tied to the bar of the glass door on the inside to announce the arrival of customers. Clink, they went against the glass as the door closed behind us. There was a smell of incense and speakers mounted to the ceiling were playing The Doors', "Come on Baby Light My Fire."

A man with hair just past his ears came walking toward us. His thin face was strewn with hair and his brown cotton shirt hung from his shoulders like he was one of the maniquins in the window. The brown shirt was open, and beneath, a red t-shirt bore the face of Che Guevara.

"Peace, man," he said with a toothy smile. "Get you folks something?"

"My girlfriend is looking for some comfortable clothes," Earl said.

The store attendant then eyed me up and down. "Groovy. Follow me."

Confessions from the Pumpkin Patch

He led me to a wall of blouses and t-shirts and pointed out slacks and jeans behind me. I picked out a couple of paisley blouses with flared sleeves, a t-shirt with a Volkswagen bug showing a peace sign in place of the VW hood ornament, a tie-dye shirt and a shirt showing the face of Jimi Hendrix. However, I have to admit at the time I really had no idea who Jimi Hendrix was. I got a couple of bell bottom slacks and two pairs of jeans in addition to several blouses and t-shirts. Earl paid for it without batting an eye. As we were leaving the store Earl commented, "There now. You are officially a hippie chick."

The first time I got to wear one of my hippie outfits was to a meeting of The Students for a Democratic Society. I had no problem getting down on the floor at Jake and Tonya's house this time and I felt more like one of the crowd. I even began to feel myself getting into the anti-war movement, not just going along with it because it was important to Earl. I began to realize that it was something important that had to be done and it was becoming important to me too.

Plans were being made to get as many people as possible to go to New York on April 15th and it looked as though we were going to have quite a few going to the march. I was impressed that Martin Luther King Jr. was going to be there leading the march from Central Park to the U.N. This was going to be an adventure for sure. I had never been to New York. I had never been in a march of any kind and the possibility of seeing Martin Luther King Jr. was something I found to be exhilarating.

Winter eventually passed into spring. Tulips and Jonquils began to lift through the ground and spread color around campus and around our building. The march in New York would take place on a Saturday and would coincide with spring break so that students could attend without disrupting classes. Earl and I had gotten hotel accommodations near Central Park in February, so we were ready to go and ready to be a part of it all.

We went up to New York a few days early. Earl took me to see the Statue of Liberty and the Empire State Building. It was quite a sight for a little girl who had barely been out of Climax, Pennsylvania her whole life, but it was nothing compared to what I was going to see on April 15, 1967.

We got up very early, and thanks to Earl's planning, we had only a few blocks to walk to Central Park. By the time we got there the park was already full of people. There were people of every color, style, and age. I saw Lakota Indians in full Native American regalia. There were hippies, black people, and even grandmothers, although the crowd was mostly young people. There were people with painted faces and people wearing outlandish costumes. I had never seen so many people in one place at one time in my life. Afterward, we heard estimates that over a hundred thousand people were there.

The tone was one of happiness and celebration. Here and there a joint was being passed around. That was the first time I ever smoked pot. I didn't quite know what to do with it when it was handed to me. Earl gave me instructions. "Keep your lips open a little and draw some air in with it so that it doesn't burn your throat too much. Suck it deep into your lungs just like your cigarettes and then hold your breath for a little while so you'll get the maximum effect."

After a joint had passed by me several times I began to notice that the sounds of the crowd became crisp. Here and there bits of music tinkled in my ears becoming ever so enhanced and beautiful. The colors around me became vibrant and people's faces seemed to be more animated. However, I found myself having a bit of difficulty thinking clearly, and I was having problems following conversations, although I found that a single person at a time could become enchantingly fascinating.

I met a woman in her fifties, at least my mother's age or older. She had a wide-brimmed hat with a huge bow and she had stuffed the band of her hat with a couple of Forsythia blossoms. She had layers and layers of beads around her neck and bright red lipstick. Her gray hair hung off her shoulders like that of a young girl and she was filled with life and vitality.

"Hello, darling," she said, to me. "You look—stoned." She then laughed in a great cackle. Never had I dreamed that anyone in Mother's generation could ever have acted like that.

"I think, indeed, I am stoned," I replied.

She cackled again. "Isn't it wonderful, darling? So am I."

She then disappeared into the crowd as instantly as she had appeared.

Behind me, Earl was having a detailed conversation about the war, the power elite, the military industrial complex, and I don't know what else. I heard bits and pieces of his conversation with a young man about his own age, a tubby boy dressed in loose-fitting clothing, a white pilgrim's shirt and baggy flare-legged jeans. There was so much going on around me that the intensity of the experience was almost overwhelming.

Word came around that Martin Luther King Jr. was about to speak. Listening as hard as I could, I could still only make out little bits and pieces of the overall speech. The one thing I did hear, the one thing that stuck in my mind the most was, "There comes a time when silence is betrayal." I thought deeply about those words. I thought about my avoidance of politics in a time when so much was happening. I thought about how my silence and my avoidance had become a betrayal to the

Confessions from the Pumpkin Patch

men and women of my generation. I had stood silently by while boys my age were being slaughtered in the jungles of Vietnam for no good or worthy reason. I heard him say something to the effect that social change comes through non-violent action. He had taken a lesson from Gandhi who, by non-violent resistance, had been able to overthrow the British rule of India, the only time in history that the British had ever given over ruling authority without being forced out by war. I thought about the power of nothing, not doing nothing about a problem but the act of nothingness, no action, as an act of solving a problem. Sometimes the opposite of action is the action that is needed and when applied appropriately can be very effective.

There was an action taking place on that day but it was an action of nothingness. It was an action of non-violent resistance and expression of concern. There were people there who were in opposition of what we were doing and they were shouting at us. There were a few very heated arguments, but the action as a whole was an action of nothingness, an action of simply being in a place at a particular time and letting that being speak for itself that we were against the war, that we wanted no more violence, that we longed for the gentle nothingness of peace.

Shortly after the speeches were over we marched. I had no idea where the U.N. building was. I simply followed the crowd and walked by Earl's side. As we marched there were television cameras about, recording the event— and reporters were periodically interviewing people. We were going to the U.N. to ask them to put pressure on the United States to stop the bombing in Vietnam.

Somehow I was ignorant on that day. I was ignorant that I was part of making history. That this would be one of the most famous war protests in history. I was ignorant that there would be any personal fallout from the simple experience of listening to speeches and walking from Central Park to the U.N. Yet it was going to mean more than I ever dreamed that it would.

When we got back to Earl's apartment late on the following Sunday evening his father's car was parked in front of the building.

"Hmmm," Earl said, "Wonder what the old man is doing here. Hope everything is okay."

His father had a key to Earl's apartment and had let himself in. When we walked in with our luggage, Mr. Titwallow was sitting on the sofa reading some materials we had picked up at the Students for a Democratic America meeting.

"Hey," Earl said, "What are you doing here?"

Karlyle Tomms

His father tossed the literature back onto the coffee table where he had found it. "I think the more important question is where have you been?" He glared at Earl.

"We've been to New York," Earl replied with a look of confusion.

Both of us were wondering what Mr. Titwallow was doing there and why he was acting so strangely and being so intimidating.

"Yes, I know you have been to New York," Mr. Titwallow responded. "I happened to see your face on the evening news last night."

"Hey, honey," Earl poked me lightly with his elbow. "We made the news."

"What the hell do you think you were doing going to that goddamn antiwar protest!?" his father exploded in anger. The fury on his face frightened me and I wondered if he was going to become violent.

"Well, sir." Earl replied calmly. "I was exercising my right as a citizen of the United States of America to engage in free speech and peaceful protest."

His father stood up and poked a rigid finger in our direction. "Did you ever stop to think for one goddamn moment what an embarrassment this would be to your family?"

Earl set our luggage down, pried mine from my nervous hand and set it on the floor. "I don't see why it should have been an embarrassment to anyone," he said.

"You know goddamn good and well that you have a reputation to uphold," his father continued to shout. "What the hell do you think it is going to do to the business of my company if word gets around that my son is a traitor to the United States Government?"

Earl continued to remain calm. "First of all, Dad, I am not a traitor to the government. I am merely protesting actions of the government with which I disagree. I am well within my constitutional rights to do so. Second of all," he continued, "it is highly unlikely that anyone other than close family or friends are going to even recognize my face on TV much less say to themselves, 'Oh, that's Daniel Titwallow's son. He's acting like a traitor. Let's boycott the company'."

"Don't you smart mouth me!" his father snarled.

For the first time I realized what Earl was talking about when he said he resented his father's control. It was almost like Mother's hornet nest of anger for anything I did contrary to her wishes. The difference was that I think Earl's father had more control over him than Mother had over me.

"Dad," Earl went on, still in a calm tone of voice, "don't you think we could sit down and talk about this like civil human beings?"

"Don't you dare accuse me!" his father retorted. "I've been as civil with

Confessions from the Pumpkin Patch

you as I'm ever going to be. I've raised you up to be a man and act like a man. I sent you to this goddamn college so you could make something of yourself, not so you could go behind my back and act like some goddamn anarchist! You would be fighting in that war yourself if it wasn't for me!"

Earl turned to me and said in a reassuring tone, "Lovella, why don't you go in the kitchen and make us some coffee. I'm sure Dad would like a cup of coffee."

I did as instructed, happy to get distance from the animosity. I busied myself in the kitchen, but I could still hear the conversation that was going on.

Earl sat in the chair adjacent to the sofa. "Why don't you sit down, Dad? It seems as though this conversation could take a while, too long to be on our feet."

His father did not sit down immediately. "I am sick and tired of your defiance, boy!" he snarled. "I have worked my ass off to make a good life for you and your sister. I have done everything to try to get you to understand that this company will give you, your children, and your grandchildren more of a life than they will ever need. I'm trying to give you a life where you don't have to bust your ass like I did, where you don't have to scrape for pennies to get by, and all you do is fight me and defy me every damn step of the way."

"Sit down, Dad, please," Earl pleaded.

Finally his father sat reluctantly back down on the sofa.

From the adjacent chair, Earl went on. "I know you have worked hard. I know you think that running the company is the best thing for me. The problem is that you have never asked me what I think, or what I want."

"I know what you want," his father continued with bitterness. "You want to run around acting like a jackass, taking no responsibility for yourself, and thinking nothing about how your actions might affect other people."

"Anything that I do," Earl responded slowly with bitterness welling in his own voice, "which you do not prescribe for me to do, you consider to be acting like a jackass."

"You have a reputation to uphold for this family!" his father yelled.

"And what is a reputation?" Earl queried. "What is it? A reputation is what you try to get other people to think of you. It has nothing to do with your character. It has nothing to do with what you really stand for. It is a facade for the world to see. You don't care who I am. You don't care what I believe in or what I want for myself. All you care about is your fucking company and your fucking reputation."

"I built that company for my family!" his father screamed, veins popping in his neck.

"Thank you," Earl said, retreating back to his calm tone. "Thank you for building that company for us, Dad. Thank you for a wonderful beautiful home, for all the money we could ever want. Thank you for making sure we have luxury and opulence available at our every whim. Thank you for servants who do everything for us short of wiping our asses. Thank you for trips to Europe, fine cars, and elegant dining. Thank you. But you know, there is one problem, one very big problem. You never asked us if we wanted all that. You never asked any of us if we wanted that much. In my entire life, you have never asked me what I wanted because the truth is, no matter how much you give us, no matter how much money you make, or how much opulence you can afford, it is never enough. It will never be enough. So, if I say, that's enough. No, Dad. I'm good. Thanks. I have enough. I don't need any more. You don't listen because you want me to be just like you. You want me to never be satisfied, to never look around and think I'm grateful for what I have. You want me to take over the company and run it the way you have, like an obsessed madman who is crazy for wealth. You want me to take the baton and run with it so you can realize your dream of going national, of being the biggest, best, snack company in the world. But you know what? It won't matter. You could be the richest man in the world and it wouldn't be enough. It's never going to be enough, Dad. I realized that a long time ago."

"So you just want to fart around and act like a goddamn bum? Is that it?"

His father spoke as though nothing Earl had said meant anything to him. He didn't get it. He didn't hear.

"You don't care about the family business. You don't care about trying to leave something meaningful to your children so they don't have to work as hard as you did."

Earl leaned in toward his father. "Dad, I'm here because you want me here. I am studying business because you want me to study business. I am doing what you want me to do so that I can take over the family business someday and keep your legacy going because that is what you want me to do. You are getting your way. I'm suspending my own desires so that I can fulfill yours, but I am not going to stop being who I am because you don't like who I am. I am not going to stop believing what I believe because you don't like what I believe. I am not going to stop fighting for what I believe because you disagree with it. I'm holding out one small morsel of my life for me."

I carried a tray with cups, percolator, sugar and cream on it into the

Confessions from the Pumpkin Patch

living room and set it on the coffee table. I poured the steaming coffee from the percolator into each cup and let them decide for themselves what additions they might want to make.

His father turned to me, "So, are you influencing my boy to think like this?"

"GIVE ME A FUCKING BREAK, DAD!" Earl yelled for the first time. "You know better and how dare you attack Lovella or try to drag her into this? She didn't even dress this way or know anything about this stuff till she met me. If anyone is influencing, it's me influencing her."

"Mr. Titwallow," I said as I grabbed a text book from the floor at the end of the couch. "I think I'm going to go in the other room to study while you and Earl work this out on your own."

I then retreated quickly for the bedroom. However, I couldn't study. My mind wouldn't take in the words written on the page. I picked the book up briefly, but soon threw it on the bed. I lay there worried about what was happening in the living room. I could no longer hear the exact conversation, but I could hear their yelling. After what seemed like forever, I heard Earl's father scream, "Fine! You want it your way! You can have it your way! I'll cut you off support and you can see what it is like to have to struggle to get by!" After that I heard the door slam and there was silence. Earl eventually meandered into the bedroom and lay down beside me.

"Hello, beautiful," he said, as he rolled over and looked into my eyes.

"Hello, lover," I responded softly. "Is everything okay?"

"Everything is always okay," he said.

"So, your Dad is going to cut you off. No more money?"

"We'll see." He smiled as his warm hand glided across my face. "This is not the first time we have had screaming matches like this, but it is the first time that I've ever told him what I really think."

"So what are you going to do if he cuts you off?" I asked.

"Get a job maybe. He's not going to cut off school tuition. He wants too much for me to graduate and do what he could never do. As long as he thinks I'm willing to study business, he'll probably keep paying the tab."

"So you are going to keep doing what he wants you to do," I said, as a statement, not a question.

He rolled over on his back and sighed. "You know," he said a moment later, "I've never had the courage to do what I wanted to do. Not really. I've piddled with things that I wanted to do while still doing enough to keep the old man happy, but I've never really done anything totally my way."

"What would doing it your way mean?" I questioned.

"You know the hell of it is that I don't really know for sure." He glanced

205

Karlyle Tomms

at me questioningly as though I might know. "I've lived so much of my life for him that I don't really know what it would be like to live my life for me."

"How would you find out?" I pondered.

"I don't know," he said. "It might be extreme."

I then rolled over on my back beside him and together we stared at the ceiling. "You know," I said, "I learned something about myself when we went to visit your family at Christmas."

"Really, what did you learn?" he said without removing his gaze from the ceiling.

"Well, I learned for one thing that I like having nice things and great food. I learned that I could get used to all of that very easily but I learned something else that is much more important."

"What's that?" he wondered, still not wavering in his glare.

"I learned that I love you, that I'll do anything you want me to." His eyes left the ceiling and met mine as I turned toward him. "I learned that I will follow you wherever you want to go and do whatever you want to do."

"If I asked that of you, how would that be any different from what my Dad is doing to me?"

He propped himself up on his elbow inspecting me.

"Lovella, I don't want you to live your life for me. I want you to do what makes you happy. You came to Penn State to get a degree in medical science. That is what you need to do because it is what you want to do."

"No, it isn't," I said.

"It isn't?" A puzzled look crossed his face.

"No," I responded. "I just went to college to get away from Climax. I didn't really know anything about college or what I really wanted to do. My interest in sexual research is a product of my own lust and an inherent desire to piss Mother off. I don't really care if I study anything or not, unless it's something that really interests me."

"Well, what do you want to do with your life?" he asked.

"I want to love you and be with you," I said. "Anything else is just icing on the cake. If I happened to finish my degree and got a job in medical research that would be wonderful, but I don't care. I don't care if I'm a cleaning lady as long as I'm with you."

He sighed. "Lovella, I don't want you to ever feel like you have given up what you want from life for what I want."

"Well, since I don't really want anything, it doesn't matter does it?" I stuck my tongue out at him in mock defiance.

He smiled.

Confessions from the Pumpkin Patch

"So, Mr. Earl Titwallow," I said after a brief silence. "If you could do anything in the world that you wanted to do and do it just for you and nobody else, what would you do?"

He lay back down on his back, put his arm around me, and pulled my head to his chest. "I don't know," he said. "I'll have to think about it."

After that, we lay there in silence. A short time later, I heard the quiet little snore that told me he had fallen asleep. With my eyes closed, my head snuggled in the warm comfort of his chest, I soon followed.

Karlyle Tomms

Chapter 17

In late May the Penn State campus had turned into a green blanket of perfectly manicured lawns. Here and there mulched flower beds sprouted petunias and geraniums amid the monkey grass. Annual varieties of flowers morphed into a colorful quilt of flora as the season progressed. An entire crew of gardeners kept the campus pristine.

Earl and I had both finished our classes. Finals were over and summer vacation was about to begin. Earl's father still was not speaking to him. He had already paid for the semester's tuition and rent through May on Earl's apartment before they had their big fight. Getting through the rest of the semester was therefore no problem. His mother tried to mediate between them but too little avail. Earl's father was a stubborn man, and Earl was determined to figure himself out. He was determined, for once in his life, to do what he wanted to do and not what his father had insisted he must do.

I was expecting that I would probably go home and spend the summer in Climax with Mother and Daddy. I certainly had made no other plans. I had packed up my things and had made plans for Mother to come pick me up. She would arrive on campus just before Memorial Day weekend. I would go home for the summer and hope that I could see Earl as often as possible during the time before the next school year. The day before Mother was to come get me Earl popped into the living room with excitement radiating from his face. "Lovella, come look!" he said.

"What?" I questioned.

"No, you know what? I want it to be a surprise!" He ran into the bedroom and grabbed one of my scarves. He returned just as I was about to follow him. "Turn around," he commanded.

"Okay?" I turned my back to him with curiosity looming as he tied the scarf over my eyes.

"Now, come on," he commanded, leading me blindfolded from the apartment and maneuvering me around the steps and obstacles to the street. He aimed me toward the street and said, "Now keep your eyes closed even after I take off the blindfold and I'll tell you when to open them." He then lifted the scarf from my head and said, "Okay, open your eyes."

I opened my eyes to find myself staring at a pink Volkswagen bus. The sides had been painted with huge flowers and peace signs and I immediately thought to myself, "This looks familiar."

208

Confessions from the Pumpkin Patch

"So, what do you think?" he questioned.

"I think it's—," I measured for a moment what I was going to say as I wondered what he wanted me to say. "A Volkswagen bus," I said finally not being able to think of what might be a welcomed response.

"Isn't it cool?" he queried with his ongoing excitement.

"It looks familiar," I said.

"Yeah," he said. "It belonged to Jake and Tonya and now it belongs to us."

"Ooooooh."

I dragged out the exclamation fearing that my acting would not be good enough to convince him of genuine excitement. The truth was I had no interest in a broken-down old VW bus. "Where is your Ferrari?" I asked as I formed a fake smile.

"I sold it," he replied. "I got enough money to buy the bus off Jake and Tonya and then have enough left over for us to go on an adventure."

"An adventure?" I questioned. "Where are we going?"

"To San Francisco, man!"

He declared this as he made a fist of each hand and punched the sky like he was in a boxing match with heaven. He kicked in the air and hooted. "It's gonna be awesome!"

"Okay—," I hesitated. "Why are we going to San Francisco?"

"Because that's where it's happening!" he ejected again. "The Haight district. Hippies, Be-ins, Love-ins. We have got to go, Lovella. We have got to be in on this!"

"Okay," I said, with a slight edge of trepidation welling within me. "Let's plan a trip."

"No, no, no, no, no," he said, his eyes gleaming like a mad man. "There's no planning. We just go."

"Now?" I questioned.

"Right, fucking, now!" he exclaimed grabbing my shoulders and giving me a quick hug. He pulled away from me, still gripping my shoulders and scanned my face for reaction.

"Earl, Mother is supposed to come pick me up tomorrow and take me home for the summer."

"So call her and tell her you have other plans," he gleamed. "Let's do this, Lovella! You said you would go anywhere with me. Here is a chance to test it out: a trial run over the summer to see if that is really going to work for you."

I grinned at him and stepped out of the 'responsible young lady me' then back into the 'don't give a fuck me'. "I did say that. Didn't I?" I ran to him, threw my arms around him and shouted, "Let's do it! Let's go!"

209

Karlyle Tomms

"How soon can you be ready?" he asked.

"I'm already packed to go home," I responded with sudden ne'er-do-well attitude. "I only need to change a few things, so then as soon as you pack." He grabbed my hand and we ran into his flat.

I had almost everything packed for the trip home the following morning, but for this trip, I would not be needing those neat little dresses. Mother had never seen me in my hippie outfit, so I had not really planned to take my hippie cloths home. I quickly hung the girly things back in the closet. I wasn't sure if Earl would keep the apartment over the summer or if they would still be hanging there when we returned in the fall and if they weren't, fuck it. I opened my suit case and began exchanging out clothing. Earl threw open his suitcase and began shoving things into it in wads.

"Fold them," I said. "You are not going to get much to fit in the suit case if you don't fold them."

"I could fucking care less," he exclaimed laughing. "I don't fucking care if I go naked."

I looked at him sternly and he got the message.

"You're right," he said, "I need to fold them." He proceeded to pull them back out of the suit case and fold them, sort of, and put them back in.

We were both grabbing things like mad. Finally we looked around and realized that there was nothing else we could think of to pack. We ran out of the house, threw the luggage in the bus, and headed out of State College, west toward Pittsburgh.

We had driven for almost two hours when I exclaimed, "Oh my god. I forgot to call Mother."

It's okay," he said. "When we get to Pittsburgh we'll stop at a pay phone."

"Since we are going to be in the area," I questioned, "do you want to stop and see your parents?"

"What for?" he quipped. "The old man is only going to tell me what a fool I am and Mom will likely just cry."

"Okay."

I understood. I really didn't want to call Mother and might not have if she wasn't about to make an unnecessary trip to pick me up.

We arrived in Pittsburgh a little after 7:00 PM and Earl pulled into a grocery store parking lot where we had seen a pay phone. I dialed the operator and told her I needed to make a collect call. The phone rang a few times. Then Mother answered and accepted the charges.

"Hello, Mother," I began.

"Where are you, Lovella?" she demanded. "I hear traffic in the background."

Confessions from the Pumpkin Patch

"I'm at a pay phone in Pittsburgh, Mother," I responded as though it wouldn't make any difference to her at all.

"Lovella Fuchs!" she shouted. "What are you doing in Pittsburgh at this hour of the night!? I am supposed to pick you up at State College tomorrow morning."

"I know, Mother," I attempted to soothe. "But we have had a change of plans."

"You what? Is something wrong with someone in Earl's family?" She sounded genuinely concerned for a moment.

"No, Mother, everyone is fine. We have just had a change of plans. That's all." I knew she would not take the news well but I continued. "Earl and I are going to San Francisco for the summer."

"You absolutely will do no such thing!" she demanded. "Your father and I need you here. Besides, you don't have the money to go to San Francisco."

"No, I don't, Mother, but Earl does."

"Lovella, I took a day off work!" she yelled "I'm missing a day of pay tomorrow so I could come pick you up. Now you better turn your butt around and go back to State College! I'm picking you up tomorrow morning!"

"No." I said, simply and completely.

"What?!" she badgered.

"I said, no, Mother. I'm not going to be there so you might as well not come. Take the day off and enjoy yourself. I know you need a break. Enjoy it. I'm going to San Francisco with Earl and that's that."

There was silence on the other end of the phone. She knew that there was nothing she could do. She knew there was nothing she could threaten me with but there was something she could guilt me with. She then said, rather mournfully, "Lovella, your father is not well. The doctor said that he is dying of cirrhosis and he doesn't have long to live. You know he will want to have some time with you before he goes."

"Oh, that's good, Mother," I retorted sarcastically. "That's one of the best guilt trips you have ever pulled on me."

"I'm telling you the truth, Lovella!" she snarled back at me.

"Even if Daddy was dying," I lectured, "he would want me to do what would make me happy. He would never try to guilt me into doing something and he would never demand anything of me or try to manipulate me like you do."

"Lovella, the doctor has only given him a few months to live," she pleaded.

"Is Daddy there, Mother?"

I would confront her guilt trip with the facts from Daddy. I knew he wouldn't lie to me. However, if he was drunk I would have very mixed feelings.

"Yes," she responded hesitantly.

"Well, put him on the phone."

"He's sleeping," she said and I thought even more that she was creating one of her deceptions to trick me into doing what she wanted. I had seen her do it to Daddy far too many times.

"Oh, how convenient," I quipped with a snide tone. "Wake him up. I want to talk to him."

She fell silent just a moment and said, "He needs his rest, Lovella. He is not well."

"Get this, Mother!" I shouted. "I think you are a lying, conniving bitch and this is just another one of your stupid tricks. If Daddy tells me himself that he is sick, then I will come home, but if I don't hear it from him, fuck you!"

I heard the phone drop and pop as it fell against the table. She went to the sofa where one could almost always find Daddy as long as I can remember. I heard her faintly in the background. "John. John, get up. Lovella wants to speak to you."

"What? Huh?"

His groggy words could be faintly heard. Then in a moment I heard him come on the phone. He was sober. I could tell from his voice that he hadn't been drinking.

"Hello, Punkin'."

"Hi, Daddy," I said. "How are you?"

"Oh, I'm fine. How are you?"

"I'm good, Daddy. Earl and I are going to San Francisco for the summer."

I heard Mother in the back ground. "Tell her what Dr. Lewis told you."

He ignored her. "Oh that's wonderful sweetheart. I hope you have lots of fun."

"Tell her, John!" Mother insisted again.

"Daddy," I cut in. "What's this Mother has been telling me about you having cirrhosis?

"What?" he declared. "She told you that?"

"Yes, Daddy," I went on. "Is it true?"

"Oh, no, no, no. I'm fine Punkin' Patch. Dr. Lewis just says my liver enzymes are a little elevated, that's all. He said I need to quit drinking, so I've been taking his advice and trying to be a good boy for your mother. I haven't had a drop in over two weeks."

Confessions from the Pumpkin Patch

In the background again I heard Mother exclaim, "Oh for Goodness sakes, John! Tell her the truth!"

There was a part of me at that moment that wondered which one of them was lying and which was telling me the truth but I had always trusted Daddy.

"There is nothing wrong that a month or two without drinking won't fix and I think I might just quit altogether," he said. "You go on with Earl and have a good time. Your mother and I will be fine."

Mother grabbed the phone from his hand. She came on the line and said, "Lovella! Don't believe him. He's dying. He might not even live 'til the fall. He has continued to drink despite the doctor warning him to stop."

"Well, that's a problem for you then isn't it, Mother?" I said coldly. "I do believe him."

She was silent.

Finally: "Alright then," she fell silent for another prolonged and dramatic pause. "Call me when you get there and let me know you are safe."

"I will," I said.

A mix of feelings washed over me. I did feel guilty, and I questioned myself over the decision to go. Then I realized I would be spending a wonderful exciting summer with the man I loved and with no distractions of school or either family. In my heart I convinced myself that Daddy was okay.

"Bye now," I said, making a nervous effort to sound reassuring.

She gave a chilly goodbye and hung up the phone.

I jumped back into the bus where Earl had patiently waited.

"Let's go!" I blurted. "Let's go to San Francisco!"

He sensed something. "You okay?"

I quickly hid my trepidation behind a fake laugh.

"I am fucking awesome!" I shouted. "Let's go!"

He steered the bus away from the parking lot. We grabbed a burger for dinner at a truck stop and we drove 'til past midnight. He found a gravel side road just east of Toledo, Ohio, pulled off the main highway out of sight, and parked the bus over to the side of the road.

"What are we doing?" I asked as he pulled off the road.

"We're spending the night," he said. "Hotel VW."

"You're kidding?" I probed.

"Nope, not kidding," he said.

"But I thought we would stay in a hotel?" I pleaded.

"The less we waste on a hotel, the more we have for a good time," he replied. "Remember Dad cut me off if I didn't do what he wanted? All we

Karlyle Tomms

have is the extra money I got out of the Ferrari and that has to last us all summer."

"How much is that?" I asked.

"About eight hundred," he said, "should be plenty."

"Wait a minute," I said. "You sold your Ferrari which should have brought ten or fifteen thousand dollars even used. You bought this bus, which is used and old and probably should not have cost more than a couple of hundred at the absolute most, but you only have eight hundred dollars left?"

"Okay, you got me," he said. "Dad and I had another big fight. He took the car to get back at me. I guess he thinks if I have nothing left, I have to turn to him and beg. I happened to have about a thousand left in my bank account that I got to before he did. I closed it out and took the cash. I paid Jake and Tonya a hundred fifty for the bus, bought a few things for the trip and eight hundred is what I have left."

"A hundred fifty is probably more than this is worth," I said.

"Earl, why didn't you tell me the truth?"

"I was embarrassed."

He ran his long fingers nervously around the steering wheel.

"What on earth did you have to be embarrassed about?" I asked.

"I don't know," he said. "I'm about to turn twenty one years old and my Dad can still take the car away from me like I'm a sixteen year old who got a speeding ticket. It's pathetic. The car wasn't even in my name. It was my high school graduation gift, but I still didn't have the title. He was not about to let go of one inch of power over me unless I totally broke it."

"It doesn't matter," I comforted. "You will make your own way. You are an intelligent and talented man. We will make our own way."

"I'm sorry I lied to you," he said.

"Just don't do it again," I responded. "There is no need to lie to me, Earl. I'm not your Dad. I'm not going to come down on you like that. We need to be honest with each other. Trust is the mortar that holds a relationship together. Now, explain something to me."

"Yeah, what?"

He finally stopped running his fingers around the steering wheel and took my hand.

"How are we going to sleep in this bus?"

"Sleeping bags," he said. "Camping gear, I bought camping gear before we left."

"Earl, there are seats back there." I reasoned.

"Yeah. They come out," he said teasingly.

He got out of the bus, opened the side doors and fiddled with the back

Confessions from the Pumpkin Patch

seats till they came off. He then lifted them out and sat them beside the bus on the gravel road. I don't know if the bus had been designed for the seats to come out or if it had been something that Jake and Tonya had rigged, but they came out to my amazement. In those days, that was something you just didn't see. After he had removed the seats there was a fairly smooth surface left. He rolled out sleeping bags on the floor of the bus.

"So, now what?" I questioned.

"So, now we sleep," he said. "It's late."

I walked around the bus smoking a cigarette and he continued to fiddle with the set up for a while before we crawled into the bus and each snuggled into our own bag.

"I would really like to brush my teeth," I said wishing that one bag had been big enough for both of us.

"Sorry," he responded.

The floor of the bus was hard but I was tired. We snuggled our bags up close to each other and in a short time, I was asleep.

I woke the next morning with the first glimmerings of light coming through the windows of the bus, and, yes, there was one other thing that woke me. Earl was zipping down the side of my sleeping bag and crawling already naked in beside me. Kissing and caressing all the way, he moved down and began to open my jeans. He pulled my shirt up over my breasts and moved back up to caress and lick my nipples. The only thing I had taken off the night before was my bra and my shoes. Soon we were making love, the bus rocking in motion to his thrusts. His now routine love making flatulence filled the bus with an aroma I had long since come to accept. I still held my breath, not because I couldn't take the smell any more, but because I learned during that first love making with him that it seemed to substantially increase the power of my orgasm.

Earl was about to complete his orgasm when we heard the sound of a car engine revving as though picking up speed. Earl pulled back, got up and looked out the window. Suddenly he exclaimed, "Goddamn it! Goddamn! NO!"

Earl scurried to get out of the bus and went running naked up the gravel road after the old green truck that had just sped away. I leaned over out of the side doors with my sleeping blanket pulled up around me.

"Earl, what is it? What's the matter?"

"They fucking stole our stuff!" he screamed. "Goddamn it!"

"You mean the bus seats?" I inquired.

"The fucking bus seats and our luggage, damn it! I fucking left the luggage sitting outside the bus last night."

Karlyle Tomms

"Okay," I said, not being overly concerned. "We'll find a flea market or something and buy a few cloths to get us through."

"No, you don't understand!" he ejected. "Damn it! Goddamn it! I was so fucking stupid to leave that stuff out! Lovella, our money was in my suitcase!"

"Oh shit!" I exclaimed.

"Oh shit is right!" he returned. "Jesus! Now what are we going to fucking do?"

"I guess we could see if our parents will wire us some money," I said.

"No way!" he exclaimed. "No fucking way. I am not going to go begging to my Dad and have him rub it in my face and gloat about being right. No fucking way! Besides he would probably just come, pick us up, and take us back instead of fronting me any money."

"Maybe the police could help us get it back," I suggested.

"I don't think we have much other option," he responded. "Let's get dressed."

We put on the clothes we had worn the night before. I had kept my shoes in the bus, but Earl unfortunately had left his outside with the luggage. They had not been stolen but in the ruckus were jostled around and we could only find one. He had to go barefoot. We drove back up the road and found a store were we learned that we were in Seneca County and the county seat was Tiffin. The store clerk gave us directions to Tiffin and we were finally able to locate the sheriff's office.

There was a stark, tiled lobby with a window and a speak-through in the back. Earl walked up to the window and was greeted by a woman in a tan police uniform.

"We would like to speak to the sheriff," he said through the metallic hole.

She eyed him with disgust as though she had just encountered week old road kill fuming with stench.

"And what may I say this is about?" she questioned with a terse sound in her voice.

"Our money was stolen," he said. "Well, my bag was stolen and it had our money in it."

"How do you know it was stolen?" she asked.

"I saw him throw it in the bed of his truck and take off. Then I went running down the road screaming, that's my stuff," he replied becoming obviously perturbed at her attitude. "Is that enough for me to know that it was stolen?"

"Sir, you do not have to take that tone with me," she replied.

216

Confessions from the Pumpkin Patch

"Ma'am," he said in fake congeniality the words dripping off his tongue like poisoned honey, "I am only responding to the tone you took with me. Now may we please get some help?"

She slapped some papers and a pen underneath the window slot and said, "You can fill out a report."

Earl took the papers and pen. "Is that it?" he asked. "I fill out some paper work? And then what?"

"And then we will examine the paper work," she responded, "and if you can work on that attitude, I might even allow you to speak to a deputy about it."

Earl sat in one of a row of hard, plastic chairs that were shoved up against a concrete block wall and began to fill out the report. I sat beside him and said nothing. I knew he was as upset with himself as he was with the thief and he was worried.

When he finished filling out the papers he took them back to the window. She perused them briefly and then made eye contact with him for the first time. "Have a seat Mr. Titwallow. I'll have a deputy come speak with you about this."

He sat back down beside me, leaned his head back into the wall, and took a huge breath. I reached over and took his hand.

In a moment we heard the lock click on the solid steal door which was next to the reception window. A very handsome man in his mid-thirties popped his head out the door. His jaw was square, hair brown, and there was a faint hint of stubble across his face. He had a thick brown mustache and grey blue eyes. His face was perfect. He spoke to Earl but looked at me. My eyes met his and there was instant attraction. I felt both guilty and tantalized at the same time.

"Mr. Titwallow, would you follow me please?" he questioned politely.

"Is it okay if my girlfriend comes?" Earl inquired while rising.

"Sure, no problem," he said as he reached his hand out to shake Earl's. "I'm Deputy Reynolds."

He then extended his hand to me. I shook his hand and felt the huge, soft, warm muscles around his fingers bulge gently as he squeezed. I could almost have had a climax from that handshake. I felt the thrill pulse through me like sensual electricity.

When we followed him up the hall, I could see his khaki slacks wrapped tightly around his perfectly round ass. I tingled in his presence and yet felt as though I was betraying Earl to have such feelings. I also noticed the wedding band on his left hand and wondered to myself if he thrilled his wife as much as he wished he could thrill me.

Deputy Reynolds led us to a small room with no windows. There was a

Karlyle Tomms

Formica desk-top bolted to the block walls, a seat at the desk, and two more of those plastic chairs with metal legs. He seated us and then proceeded to go over the report between glances at me.

In the rush that morning, I had failed to put my bra back on, so my large firm tits and erect nipples were perfectly outlined beneath the thin T-shirt I was wearing. Officer Reynolds seemed to be having a very difficult time keeping his eyes off them. On one hand, he was perfectly professional. On the other hand, I was fairly certain that if we had been in the room alone, in no time I could have had him pushing himself into me as I lay back on that desk-top with my legs spread. In fact, the fantasies of that often kept me from paying attention to the process at hand.

"So," Deputy Reynolds started, "You say your bags and the back seat to your van were sitting on the edge of the road and you saw an older model green truck driving off with your possessions in the flat bed."

"Yes, sir. That's correct," returned Earl.

"Were you able to get a look at the person driving the truck?"

"Yes, sir. He was an older man, probably in his sixties or seventies. He had gray hair, of course, and he was skinny, and he might have been tall."

Earl fidgeted with his long fingers as he answered the questions.

"Did you happen to get a license plate number?" Deputy Reynolds continued.

"No, sir, I didn't," Earl responded. "In fact, I'm not quite sure, but I think there might not have even been a license plate."

"Can you tell me what kind of truck it was?" Deputy Reynolds met my eyes as I caught him staring at my tits first and then up to my face to see if I was noticing. I was.

"It was an older model Ford, maybe ten or fifteen years old," Earl said, becoming exasperated. "I don't know. Actually I don't really know much about vehicle models and types."

Deputy Reynolds grinned. "I think I might know who took your belongings. Would the two of you like to take a ride with me out to meet this fellow and see if we can get your stuff back?"

"Sure," Earl responded looking over at me.

He caught me staring rather longingly at Deputy Reynolds. Embarrassed, I popped my eyes quickly to meet his and said, "Sure, yeah. We want to find this guy."

Officer Reynolds led us to the back of the station where his patrol car was parked. "You can either both sit in the back or one of you can sit up front with me."

"I'll sit in the back," I said wanting a little distance from the obvious sexual tension that was going on.

218

Confessions from the Pumpkin Patch

"No, I'll sit in the back," Earl said. "Lovella, you go ahead and sit up front with Officer Reynolds."

Although that response from Earl made me nervous on one hand, it enticed me on the other. Of course I loved Earl and I would have loved to sit next to him in the back seat, but I was also tantalized by Deputy Reynolds and I very much wanted to sit in a position where I could catch my eye-candy-glances of him.

We got into the patrol car and Deputy Reynolds headed out of town. I sat sideways in the seat with one leg bent beneath me where I could have a view of Deputy Reynolds and be able to carry on a conversation with Earl in the back as well.

"So, what brings you kids to Tiffin?" Deputy Reynolds inquired having seen on the crime report that our address was in Pennsylvania.

"We were hoping to spend the summer in San Francisco," Earl replied. "I don't know how we are going to accomplish that without any money. We sure didn't get very far. This was our first night on the road."

"I'm sure everything will be fine," I interjected between the scans of my eyes up and down Deputy Reynolds's all-too-enticing body.

"So, what's in San Francisco?" Deputy Reynolds continued.

"Well, we just heard that there were some really cool goings-on there," Earl replied. "You know like people who are really cool and accepting— loving, peaceful kind of folks."

"Shame you should have to go to the other side of the country to find people who are cool and accepting." Deputy Reynolds said this as he darted his eyes up and down my body, making absolutely no effort to hide the fact that he was eating my tits with his eyes.

"Yeah, it is a shame isn't it?"

I smiled at him the way I would smile at a piece of cheesecake that I was about to devour

"You might find that people around here are pretty cool and accepting if you gave us a chance," he said.

"Oh, I'm not saying that people around here or anywhere aren't cool," said Earl. "We just heard that San Fran really has it going on and we wanted to maybe check it out. You know a little summer adventure before we have to go back to class next fall."

Deputy Reynolds had turned onto the same dirt road where we had parked to sleep the night before. About two or three miles up that road he turned into a drive through the woods that was little more than a couple of tire tracks between the trees. This path curved around between the standing oaks until we came, after a long while, to a clearing in the woods where there were piles of junk everywhere."

219

Karlyle Tomms

"Hey, that's the truck!" Earl exclaimed leaning forward in his seat and pointing to an old green truck which was parked next to a dilapidated trailer house.

"Hey, and there are the seats to my bus!" he exclaimed again noticing the seats unloaded and sitting near a pile of junk.

"Hang on," Deputy Reynolds said in a reassuring voice. "Just stay calm and let me talk to him."

As the patrol car came to a stop in front of the trailer a tall elderly man came out of the front door. He had on a pair of soiled and worn gray pants and a tank top shirt that looked like it had its share of greasy hands smeared across it. Deputy Reynolds had admonished us to stay in the car and when he got out. The old man grinned wide showing only two or three tobacco stained teeth inside an otherwise empty and nasty mouth.

"Weeeeelll, hey there, Jimmy," he proclaimed, jutting out his hand to shake with Deputy Reynolds. "What brings you to these parts?"

"Come on, Fred," Deputy Reynolds said shaking the old man's hand. "You really know why I'm here, don't you? Now why is it that I always show up around here?"

"Cause you are always accusing me of something I didn't do," the old man responded. "I just don't know why you do that. I am a legitimate business man just trying to make a living."

"You know I catch you red-handed in almost all of those things you say you didn't do."

"Well, now, maybe you do, maybe you don't."

The old man cackled with laughter.

"Just 'cause you say you got proof don't mean nothing, but I try to be fair and give a little, you know. I try to keep the peace. Lord knows I don't want you riled up at me."

"Alright," Deputy Reynolds continued as he pointed back to the car. "Now these two young folks over here say that they saw you driving off this morning with their bus seats and their luggage, and this young man has not only described you and your truck he has already pointed out that those bus seats over there belong to him."

"Sheeee, eeeeht!" the old man squealed. "I don't know where he would have gotten some kind of idea like that 'cause I didn't even get out of bed 'til about thirty minutes ago and I picked up those seats at an auction last week. I was gonna sell 'em for twenty dollars but hell, if it will make that young man feel better, he can have 'em."

"Yeah," Deputy Reynolds went on. "I think it would probably make him feel better to get those back. Now, what about the luggage?"

"I don't have any idea what you are talking about," the old man pleaded.

220

Confessions from the Pumpkin Patch

"I don't even deal with luggage most of the time. Don't seem to have much of a re-sale value."

"Come on, Fred," Deputy Reynolds chided. "You know who you are talking to here and this is not a road we haven't been down before. What happened to these kids' luggage?"

"You know, I don't know what might have happened to it," the old man continued to lie. "I haven't ever seen them kids before. Sure is a shame they lost their luggage though."

"How about I have a look inside your trailer?" Deputy Reynolds inquired.

"Oh, now," the old man protested. "I haven't even washed the breakfast dishes yet or made the beds. I just wouldn't want you to see it in that kind of a mess."

Deputy Reynolds laughed. "Come on Fred. You are not exactly Suzy Homemaker. Let's have a look."

"Now, now," the old man continued to protest. "I just sprayed for fleas. I was on my way out of the house for a few hours when you folks pulled up."

"You know," Deputy Reynolds negotiated as he rubbed his chin. "If I have to call into town and get Judge Thomas to issue a search warrant, it is probably going to be much more likely that this will result in you spending a few days in county jail, but if you were to cooperate, I think we might be able to keep you from getting in a lot of trouble."

"Oh, hell. All right!" the old man blurted. "But don't blame me if you get sick from flea poison."

"I'll take my chances," Deputy Reynolds said as he entered the trailer.

He came back in a few moments with Earl's empty bag. He motioned for us to get out of the car but had to come unlock the back for Earl since that was set up for prisoner transport.

"Is this your bag?" he questioned Earl.

"Yeah," Earl replied. "But it wasn't empty when he took it."

"Well, let's go see if we can find what was in it," Deputy Reynolds said as he turned to the old man. "Fred, you don't mind if these young folks have a look at your beautiful home decor do you?"

"Oh, hell, no." The old man spit tobacco to the ground. "The more the fuckin' merrier."

We entered the trailer to find nasty, tattered, old furniture. There was a 1940's-age radio standing off to one corner and a really old 1950's TV against one wall under a window. Earl's clothes were thrown about the room haphazardly as though they had been dug out of the luggage and thrown in whatever direction was handy at the moment. My suitcase sat

Karlyle Tomms

over in one corner, opened a little. At first glance it seemed essentially undisturbed.

"Are these your clothes?" Deputy Reynolds inquired.

"Yes they are," Earl replied, "but what about my money? I had $800 cash in my luggage."

"I didn't see any money," Deputy Reynolds replied. "Go ahead and pick up your clothes. Here is your bag if you want to put them in it. While you do that, I'll go have a talk with Fred."

We picked up Earl's things, what we could find, while the deputy went back outside. When we came back out with Earl's bag re-packed, the deputy walked up to Earl and handed him three hundred dollars in cash.

"Look," he said, "this is probably the best I'm going to be able to do. I got him to give up this much but the fact is whether there was any money at all in that luggage is basically your word against his."

"I had eight hundred fucking dollars in that bag!" Earl exclaimed.

"I believe you," Deputy Reynolds responded, "but think about this. Is a judge going to believe you? How are you going to prove how much money you had in the bag? How would you prove that you didn't have that money hidden somewhere else and you were just saying it was in your bag? If you press this, then it is going to mean waiting around for a court date, going before a judge, and then you still might not win on the money. You could prove he stole your seats and your bag maybe, but there is no way to prove how much money you may or may not have had in that bag. My advice would be to take the three hundred dollars and go on down the road."

"Let's search the old bastard!" Earl spouted, his anger building. "How much fucking money does he have in his pockets this afternoon? Where did he get it? Doesn't look to me like he is exactly wealthy."

"Well, let's say he has eight hundred in cash on him," the deputy continued with a calm voice. "Can you prove that it is your money? How do you know he didn't sell that much at an auction last night?"

"I could call the bank and see if they could match the serial numbers on the bills," Earl exclaimed.

"How long is that going to take you?" Deputy Reynolds continued. "Let's say you can find the money around here and you can match up the serial numbers on the bills. More than likely, by the time all the legal proceedings are done and the lawyers get their cut, you are not going to have much more than three hundred left anyway and it will likely take you all summer to get that. Now you might enjoy spending the summer around here. We do have some pretty nice people here in Tiffin but I heard you say you were looking to meet some of those nice folks out in San

222

Confessions from the Pumpkin Patch

Francisco."

"Shit!" Earl proclaimed. Then he stood there silent for a moment as I watched quietly.

"Alright, fine," he finally said in a subdued tone. "But how are we going to get my bus seats back to my bus."

"Fred is going to load it up and follow us back into town." Deputy Reynolds was sympathetic. "I'm sorry. That's the best I can do."

Earl put the money in his pocket and turned silently to walk back to the car with his bag. Deputy Reynolds walked over to the old man and motioned to him. They loaded the bus seats on the bed of the old man's truck. The old man got in his truck and started it up. The deputy came back and opened the back of the car. Earl got in with his bag and mine but didn't say a word. He was sullen, disappointed. Deputy Reynolds opened the front passenger door for me.

"Thank you," I said, as I slid into the front seat. "Thank you for everything."

He smiled. Then he walked around to the driver's side and got in.

We backed up and headed back down the rut road. The old man did indeed follow us all the way back to the police station. After Earl had installed the seats back into the bus and stored the luggage, he turned to the deputy and asked, "Isn't he even going to go to jail for this?"

"Not this time," Deputy Reynolds responded. "But he is getting close and he knows it. He's been there before. He even spent a couple of years in prison but it doesn't do any good. You can't keep him in there forever and most of the time his crimes are petty and fixable."

"This one wasn't exactly fixed," Earl demanded lightly.

"I'm sorry," Deputy Reynolds returned. "I wish there had been some way to prove that the money was actually there and it was your money, but at least you got some back without too much hassle, and you got your things back."

"Yeah just a percentage of what we had," Earl proclaimed. He took a long slow breath then reached out to shake the deputy's hand. "Thank you," he said.

I shook the deputy's hand one more time and told him thank you as well. The sexual arousal seemed to have faded. He was still very beautiful to look at but my little fantasy was over and it had become mixed with the sadness for Earl's disappointment.

I followed Earl to the VW and we drove away.

"Do you still want to go to San Francisco," I questioned, "or would you rather just go back home?"

"Fuck, no. I don't want to go back home!" he snapped. "We are going to

223

San Francisco one goddamn way or another!"

"Okay," I said quietly. "I'm sorry."

He reached over and took my hand.

"I'm sorry," he said. "I shouldn't have snapped at you. I'm just so pissed off about this."

"I know," I told him. "I understand."

He sighed. "At least we have enough money to get there. We are just going to have to figure out how we are going to live once we're there."

"We have enough to live on a month or so," I responded.

"I guess," he said softly.

We headed back out onto the highway toward the west. After a long silence Earl said, "You wanted him didn't you."

"What?" I questioned as though I didn't know what he was talking about. I had not realized how much he had noticed.

"Deputy Reynolds," he went on. "You wanted to fuck him didn't you?"

I was quiet for a moment, not really knowing what I should say or how but knowing I had to be honest. "Yeah," I said, finally. "I thought he was really sexy."

"Looked like he wanted you too," Earl said.

"Yeah, I caught that," I said.

"You want to go back and try him out?" he questioned.

"What do you mean by that?" I responded.

"If you would like to fuck him we can go back," he said. "I'll give you time with him if you want."

I couldn't believe what I was hearing. I was trying to listen for any variance in his voice that would tip me off to whether he was being honest or just testing me. I couldn't tell. Part of me wanted to tell him to turn around and take me back so I could experience what my lust had pushed me to try, but instead I said, "No thanks. I'm with the man I want. Besides, fantasies are most often best left as fantasies, and I've already been with more men than most women will ever be with in a life time."

He smiled and drove on down the highway. If it was a test, I must have passed it. Some men would have screamed at me for even having thoughts about another man but not Earl. He was not threatened by my thoughts. He might have been threatened if I had chosen to act on those thoughts, but that was not going to happen, not this time anyway.

"I love you," he said.

"I love you, too." I replied—and we drove west toward the Summer of Love.

Confessions from the Pumpkin Patch

CHAPTER 18

Three hundred dollars was a lot less than eight hundred. With the original amount at start we would have had little trouble making it through the summer without working. In those days that amount could easily have taken us quite comfortably through three months. However, things had changed. It worried me. We spent the next night parked at a truck stop in Iowa. We ate greasy truck stop food and loved it, but for every penny we spent there was a worry in me that I couldn't shake.

That night Earl was careful to make sure that our luggage was piled in the front seats and that the doors to the bus were locked. If we lost the back seats it was not nearly as big a deal. In fact, he decided the following morning that he didn't want to spend the trip putting them in and taking them out every day so we drove off and left them sitting in the parking lot of the truck stop. Maybe we should have just let that old man back in Tiffin have them.

"Earl," I said as I gazed off down the flat Iowa highway lined on each side by the unending fields of foot-high, spring corn, "I was thinking that it might be a good idea to stop at a grocery and maybe get a bunch of canned food instead of eating at restaurants. It might make our money stretch a bit further."

"I'm not worried," he said glancing a reassuring look in my direction.

"Don't we have to make it through the entire summer on what we have got?"

"We'll be fine," he replied. "We have got enough to get us there and once we get there we will get jobs or something. If need be we can sleep in the bus all summer. All we have to do is move it around from one park to the other. We don't even have to rent a place if we don't want to."

"It is not exactly the lifestyle I'm used to." I fiddled with the fringe of my blouse. "I know it is certainly not the lifestyle that you are used to."

"What is lifestyle?" he blurted with a hint of irritation in his tone. "I mean what the hell is it anyway, and what do we actually need? My family has millions more than they actually need while others scrape to get by on less than what we will be spending the summer on. What do we need? Food in our bellies? If we have to we will go to soup kitchens. A roof over our heads? We have the VW. Clothes on our backs? We brought that with us."

Karlyle Tomms

"I'm sorry," I responded. "I guess I just have really never had to wonder about whether things would be taken care of. I mean as poor as we were, getting by on Daddy's little factory salary, we still had a nice little house, a car, and really everything we needed. I never worried about it. If Mother and Daddy ever worried about money, they didn't discuss it with me, so I guess I grew up in a kind of illusion of protection."

"We're Americans, Lovella," he went on. "Almost all of us grow up in an illusion of protection. Most never realize how protected we are. Compared to most of the people in the rest of the world, your little house in Climax is a mansion. We are also about the most paranoid country in the world. You have never been to a foreign country before have you?"

"No," I replied.

"I have," he continued. "I've been to Mexico and South America. I've been to Africa. Dad could afford it and he got off on thinking that his kids could do things that others would never have the opportunity to do, so during our summer vacations, when we were old enough, we got to choose a country we wanted to visit. Then Mother would usually accompany us to those countries for a two week visit while Dad stayed home with his first love—making money. Anna would choose which country she wanted to visit. Mom would take her and then when they came back, Mom would take me to the country of my choosing. Anna always picked places like France, England, or Sweden. I picked places like the Belgian Congo. I mean, hell, even visiting a place like Mexico is an experience. Our next door neighbor is a third world country. When you drive through villages where people are begging in the street and living in dirt floor huts you begin to think. Our poor are not poor. Compared to almost anywhere else in the world, our poor are not poor, but they are all too poor as far as I am concerned. Right now, this moment, you and I are rich. Compared to the majority of the people in the world, we are rich. We have almost three hundred dollars left and we own our home outright, a VW bus. We are fucking rich!" He reached over and took my hand. "We are going to be fine, Honey. Don't worry about it."

We spent the next evening in Nebraska right on the Wyoming border and the next in Utah. It seemed like no time before we were crossing over Nevada into California and then to San Francisco. By the time we got there, we still had about two hundred sixty dollars left. I couldn't believe it. I had in my head that it would take all the money just to get there if we didn't run out before we got there. However, the gas prices were cheap and so was the food. We could buy gas for twenty-five to thirty cents a gallon and since we slept in the bus, we didn't have to pay for a hotel. We found showers in some of the parks, and there were times we bathed in little road

Confessions from the Pumpkin Patch

side creeks.

At a campsite in Utah, Earl taught me the proper way to roast a marshmallow. We cooked hot dogs on sticks held over the fire and had marshmallows for desert. Then we made love on the bare ground beside the camp fire. I had momentary fantasies that the flames from the campfire might ignite his flatulence into a stream of fire from his ass, but no such tragedy occurred. I committed myself to one day asking him why sex gave him gas. However, I never did. I just accepted that little quirk.

After we arrived in San Francisco we wandered through the streets until we finally came upon the intersection of Haight and Ashbury. It was a sight to see. Hippies everywhere. People walked along the street arm-in-arm throwing us peace signs, two fingers jutted in the air like rabbit ears. I thought to myself they only have to drop the index finger to make it an entirely different sign.

Earl found a place to park the bus and said, "Let's just get out and experience this."

I had thought that our painted VW would stand out like a sore thumb, but the truth is it was a bit tame compared to some of the vehicles I saw there.

We locked up the VW and got out to just walk up and down the streets. Most of the men had long hair. I remember coming up behind this person on the street who was wearing pink and white striped hip-hugger flared jeans and what appeared to be a yellow and pink halter top. Tattooed just above the ass crack was a heart shaped garland of flowers, the heart becoming an arrow pointing down to the crack surrounding the words: Feels like pussy.

"Well," I thought to myself as we approached from behind, "she must be into some kinky shit." Then I giggled to myself that I had made a pun on ass-fucking and kinky shit. As we passed by this person, I glanced back at her to see that she had a goatee beard, heavy eyebrows, and quite a bulge in the front of those bell bottoms.

"Holy crap!" I thought to myself as I also noticed the two rather large pink hoop earrings dangling from under the hair. "Oh my god!" I whispered to Earl. "Did you see that guy back there?"

"Which guy?" he questioned.

"The guy that had feels like pussy tattooed over his ass crack, the guy in the pink hip-huggers with the big pink hoop earrings."

"Yeah, what about it?" he quipped.

"Jesus, it's like a freak show at the circus," I said to him under my breath.

"No it's not," he returned. "They are just people expressing themselves.

That guy back there is probably a homosexual."

"Well—yeah—I figured that," I told him.

I had read about homosexuals since I was in my early teens, but I had never actually laid eyes on one, at least not one who admitted it, and definitely not one who flaunted it. Part of me wanted to be open and accepting and another part of me had small town sensibilities that were shocked by the experience. At least once on every block that we walked, there was something that fascinated or surprised me.

"Let's find a place and get something to eat," Earl said as he put his arm around my shoulder and pulled me to him.

We walked arm in arm, his arm on my shoulder and mine around his waist. I realized that we really looked like everyone else around there. When I had adopted the look, I stopped putting my hair up so that it flowed around my shoulders like most everyone else. From the time Earl had first introduced me to the anti-war movement, I had been letting my hair grow and I had not put a perm in it for months. I had stopped wearing the skin tight knee skirts and wore blue jeans and T's as often as not. I hadn't really gotten into hippie beads and maybe I looked a little odd because I retained some of my more traditional jewelry to wear with my casuals.

Soon we came upon a little store front with the smells of food wafting out into the street. The windows were painted with vegetables in addition to the flowers, and wind chimes clinked in the breeze outside the door. The sign over the door said: "Simone's." There were about four little street-side tables with seats for two, and inside I could hear the music of "Jefferson Airplane" playing rather lightly in the background.

We entered and found a table. A girl with long pig tails brought us menus printed on lime green paper and took our orders for drinks.

I scanned the menu. Each dish had some odd sounding name like "Peas on Earth" or "Good Will Goulash." I hunted for something like a burger or a chicken sandwich, but it was nowhere to be found. In a moment, I looked up and asked, "Earl, what is tofu?"

He smiled. "It's soybean curd."

"And what the hell is that?" I returned.

"Well, soybeans are beans often grown in Asian countries and many of those Asian countries take the whey, I guess you could say that, 'cause I can't think of a better word to describe it, from those beans and press it into blocks that slice kind of like cheese. The 'Temple of Tofu' sounds good doesn't it?" he questioned without missing a beat. "Deep fried tofu over brown rice with steamed broccoli, kale, and zucchini with a teriyaki sauce."

228

Confessions from the Pumpkin Patch

"I don't see any meat on this menu," I commented without looking up from the page.

"That's because it is a vegetarian restaurant," he said.

"I never knew there was such a thing," I declared in innocent honesty as I looked up from the page. As well read as I was I still had an amazing number of little pockets of ignorance in my brain.

"There is probably a lot you haven't known about before now, Honey," he comforted. "It's okay. Just pick something."

"I don't know that I've ever had a meal without meat," I said. "I have no clue what any of this will taste like."

"I'm sure it will be good," he went on. "Come on, be adventurous."

By this time the pig-tail waitress had returned to take our order. Earl ordered the "Temple of Tofu" and I ordered something called "Southern Sunshine". At least it contained two things I was familiar with, beans and cornbread. When the meals arrived, there was a lot of food on the plates. The cornbread was a big yellow block with the crust barely toasted. It was a bit dry, but it moistened well with the soup in the beans.

"Try some of my tofu," Earl enticed handing me a bite of this gelatinous stuff with a brown crust around the edge. The taste wasn't bad except for the middle that appeared to have no taste at all. The texture was a little disconcerting, but the sauce had a nice flavor.

"Yes, it's good," I said, after chewing a bit. It was okay, but I figured I would have to develop a taste for it rather than liking it on first bite.

While we sat there eating, I noticed a fairly handsome black man sitting at a table by a window. He was thin and only a little muscular. His hair was about ten inches long in a full-teased-out Afro. He wore a tie-dyed tank top and blue jeans with the cuffs frayed into blue and white strings. When he caught my eye, he tossed his chin back in acknowledgment as though I was someone he knew personally.

"Earl," I whispered leaning forward across the table. "That black guy at that table over there, is he someone you know?"

Earl glanced over and when the man saw him he again tilted his head back as though acknowledging recognition.

"No," Earl said turning back to me. "I've never seen him before."

The next thing we knew this man had carried his chair and a cup of tea across the room to our table. He turned the chair around backwards and straddled it. He sat his tea on the table. He extended a big muscular hand first to Earl and then to me. "The name's Screech," he said. "How you folks doing?"

I caught a hint of southern accent in his speech.

"We're fine," I said, a bit nervous at his forwardness.

Karlyle Tomms

"Cool," he went on. "Well, the name is not really Screech. That's just what they call me. My birth name is Jimmy Miller. They just call me Screech 'cause that is what I do. I have a band called Blue Horizon. I'm lead singer. Got that James Brown screech you know." He then made a noise that sounded like a cross between fingernails down a chalkboard and a musical note and followed it by a brief little almost jazz-style scat.

"Very nice," I said, glancing up at Earl nervously hoping that he would send this strange man on his way.

"Yeah, very nice," Earl said. "My name is Earl and this is Lovella."

"Sweeeeeet," Screech continued. "Ya'll look like sweet people. I like sweet people. The world needs more sweet people. Peace!" He jutted a peace sign into the air.

"Peace," Earl and I both responded. Earl tossed his peace sign straight up in Screech's direction. I barely lifted mine six inches off the table. I felt as though I must have missed something. There was some social code that I didn't understand, some secret hippie code of conduct that seemed completely foreign to me. I wanted this strange man to just go away. I didn't want to talk to him. I didn't want to learn the art of hippie socializing, at least not at that moment.

"You folks been in town long?" Screech questioned.

"No, just rolled in," Earl responded.

"Hey, cool," Screech expressed in an exuberant voice. "Where are you folks from?"

"Pennsylvania," Earl replied. "Lovella just finished her first year at Penn State."

"Oh hey, that's cool!" Screech almost sang as he nodded his head in my direction. "I dropped out of school about the tenth grade. I figured what's the use. The Man ain't gonna give the Black Man much of a chance anyway, and besides I've got this talent, you know. I can screech." His head was bobbing like spring-loaded doll in the back window of a Buick.

"Wow," Earl said. "We would love to hear your band play sometime."

"Hey, it's your lucky day," Screech announced. "We have got a gig at this club up the street called 'Aquarius'. My band plays there every Friday and Saturday night. We've been courting a record deal. Got to build up the fan base, you know?"

"And tomorrow is Friday," Earl responded. "Maybe we can make it up there. What time do you go on?"

"We usually kick it about 10 PM," Screech replied. "Say, where you folks staying? You got digs yet?"

"Well, we got a VW bus," Earl explained. "We figured we could sleep in that and catch a shower wherever."

Confessions from the Pumpkin Patch

"Hey, I got a little apartment upstairs across the street," Screech said. "You are welcome to crash man. Sure beats a bus for sleeping comfort and there is a nice old bath tub."

He reached over and patted my arm. I resisted the intense urge to jerk back from a stranger touching me as he said, "Lady might like to have a nice sensual bubble bath, you know."

By this time I am looking at Earl with *NO* written all over my face but to my horror he said, "Oh, yeah man, that would be cool. We would love to hang out with you, man."

"Yeah, well, as soon as you finish your meal, I'll take you up to see my pad."

Screech gleamed like a beacon. His head continued to bob and he smiled a smile full of clean, white, perfectly aligned, teeth. He was an attractive man and he seemed nice, but I couldn't bring myself to feel comfortable with meeting a stranger who just invited himself to my table and then to live with him that same afternoon.

"We're about done," Earl replied. "You about done, Lovella?"

I really didn't feel much like eating anymore anyway.

"Yeah, I'm done," I said as I dropped my fork on my plate. I was too nervous to eat another bite.

"All riiiiiight," Screech said, head bobbing a perpetual yes.

Earl called the waitress over and paid our check. We followed Screech across the street and up four flights of stairs in a dark stairwell. A few times I tugged on Earl's shirt tail as a sign that I really didn't want to do this, but he either didn't seem to notice, didn't get it, or he ignored it.

The old, brown, wooden door to Screech's apartment was in the back of the building. The living room had no other door. A sheet hung over what I assumed was one other doorway. There were a couple of twin mattresses in the middle of the living room floor covered in colorful blankets. Posters of Jimi Hendrix and James Brown were haphazardly tacked to the walls. There was also a poster of a brightly colored peace sign with a black background. The walls were a dingy plaster the color of mud, more stained from years of cigarettes than actually painted that way. There were hints here and there that they had probably once been an off white. Plastic beads hung almost to the floor from the overhead light around the metal edge where a globe cover had once been. Instead there was a single bare bulb that caused the beads on the upper end to gleam with color. Screech flipped on the light when we came in. I couldn't see a single lamp or any furniture other than the mattresses on the floor. Screech had made some shelves of concrete blocks and what appeared to be old, worn, boards that might have been taken off the side of someone's house. There was a pile

Karlyle Tomms

of clothes in one corner and there were some clothes folded on those shelves. Then I noticed that there was really only the living room. Near the back was a kitchenette, apartment-size stove, a single sink, and a counter top about six feet long covered with a dark red linoleum. There were cabinets painted the same color as the wall and beneath the counter top were only shelves where the plumbing to the sink was readily visible. There was one small window above the sink overlooking an alley. The only door leading off the living room stood open to reveal a pedestal sink behind which was an old claw foot bath tub. The walls of that room were lined with white and black subway tile and there was a tiny glazed window over the tub. I doubted that anyone could have seen anything through that window even if it had not been glazed.

"So, what do you think?" questioned Screech, grin spread wide to reveal those perfect teeth. His head was still bobbing and I began to amuse myself that he might have Parkinson's.

I bit my tongue. I fought the urge to tell him that the place looked like a badger den with color.

Earl tactfully said, "Yeah—cool."

"Have a seat. Have a seat," Screech invited, repeating himself. "Yeah, have a seat."

We both plopped down on one of the mattresses. Screech busied himself in the corner opposite the shelves where I had failed to notice a stereo system sitting atop a rickety old table with several albums leaning against the wall. The next thing I knew Jimi Hendrix music was blaring so loud that we had to shout to be heard over it. Screech returned to the middle of the room where we were sitting and shouted, "You folks toke."

I looked at him in puzzlement and Earl said, "Yeah, all right," and gave him a thumbs-up.

I leaned over and shouted in Earl's ear, "What does he mean, toke?"

Earl put thumb and finger to this lips and sucked in air, "You know, pot, weed, marijuana," he shouted back.

"I don't want to smoke marijuana," I shouted.

"That's cool," Earl replied. "You don't have to. Do you mind if we do?"

Actually, I did mind, but I told him no. Even though I had smoked it at the march in New York back in April, I didn't feel as safe with Screech as I had in the crowd. I knew marijuana was an illegal drug, and the stories I heard said that it caused psychosis, reefer madness, or something like that. Paranoia kicked in and I worried about being there with them while they smoked it. I wondered if they might suddenly go crazy and do something horrible. Nothing like that had happened at the march to me or anyone else I knew of, but I found myself worried.

232

Confessions from the Pumpkin Patch

Screech returned to the middle of the room with a box. He opened it and pulled out a cigarette paper. He then began to sprinkle green leaves along the middle of the paper with his large, long, fingers. Then he rolled it, licked one side, pressed it down, and twisted the ends. He popped one end of the joint in his mouth, lit it, puffed, and held his breath momentarily before releasing the smoke out his nose. While he was doing this Jimi Hendrix music continued to blare in the background and I realized that the music was not helping my anxiety, and, in fact, was tending to agitate it.

"Screech, I shouted, "Can we please turn the music down a little?"

"Oh, yeah, sure—sure," he said as he handed the joint to Earl. He went back to the stereo and brought the volume down to a reasonable level then returned. "I was just wanting you to get the full effect of the music, you know, feel the beat, get the vibe. You know, *GET* Hendrix, the greatest guitarist who ever lived man."

"I hope that I can get enough of the vibe without having to shout over the music," I said as I watched Earl inhale, hold his breath, and half cough.

Earl handed the joint toward me. I looked at him and shook my head so he handed it back to Screech. I found myself sitting there thinking that Mother would absolutely freak if she knew where I was and what I was doing. There would be a hornet's rage buzzing around that damn beehive hair of hers while her eyes glared and her tongue was ready to sting. I kind of grinned to myself thinking about it, and then I relaxed a little. I finally got the courage to ask, "So what does marijuana do for you?"

Screech replied, "Oh, it mellows you out, man. It's smooth."

"Yeah," Earl echoed. "It's a gentle high."

"What about reefer madness?" I questioned in all sincerity.

They both began to laugh, not just any laugh but more like uncontrollable giggles.

"Fuck!" I shouted. "I'm just asking. I don't know. I've never seen the damn movie, but I've heard about it a lot."

"Did they show you anti-drug films in high school?" Earl asked.

"Actually, no," I replied. "Daddy told me about it. He told me drugs are very bad and that they can cause you to lose your mind." It had never occurred to me to be so paranoid at the New York march.

"And yet your dad is a drunk," replied Earl.

"Fuck you, Earl Titwallow!" I shouted as I stood to my feet.

I don't think he had ever seen that side of me. He certainly had never really had my anger turned on him. The truth is I could make Mother's rage look like child's play if I was angry enough and saying anything bad about my Daddy was enough.

233

Karlyle Tomms

"Wow, honey, I'm sorry," he pleaded. "Please sit down."

"You don't talk about Daddy like that!" I scolded as I slung a pointed finger at him.

"I know. I know. I'm sorry," he said. "Please sit down."

I sat back down but continued to sulk. Earl reached over and squeezed my hand gently and reassuringly. "I'm just saying that alcohol is a drug too, and probably a lot more dangerous in the long run than pot is. No, pot doesn't cause reefer madness. Look at me and Screech. Do we look like we are losing it?"

"No," I said, and then continued to sit quietly.

He continued. "Reefer Madness is the name of an old film from the 1920s that was put out as propaganda to squelch the use of marijuana more because hemp was becoming a competitor to the American cotton and paper industries than because smoking pot was really causing any problems. There was also the prejudice involved since migrant workers and people of color tended to use it. Your dad had probably seen the film or something, and probably really doesn't know anything about marijuana other than what the film had to say, and that film is pure misleading propaganda. Besides, didn't you take a few hits when we were at the peace march back in April?"

"Yes," I said, sheepishly. I felt extremely naive especially since I had always been so well-read. I hated not knowing things. I despised feeling ignorant.

"Well," he said, smiling reassuringly.

"Hemp?" I questioned.

"Marijuana is in the hemp family of plants. Most of them do not cause a high, and the fibers can be used to make everything from paper to clothes," Earl replied.

All this time Screech had been sitting there watching silently in apparent fascination. He had not taken another toke on the joint. I looked from one of them to the other and then said to Screech, "Hand me that."

He passed the joint to me. I held it between my fingers and asked, "What do I do?"

"Don't you remember how you were taught to do it back in New York?" Earl asked. "Smoke it like you would a cigarette except pull a little outside air in and hold the smoke in your lungs for a little longer before you release it."

"I forgot," I lied. The truth is I was just feeling a lot more anxious there than I had in New York. I put the joint to my mouth and inhaled deeply but just as I was about to hold my breath I went into a fit of coughing. My throat felt like it was on fire. I had not really had that problem in New

234

Confessions from the Pumpkin Patch

York and I was aghast since I had smoked cigarettes for almost half my life. It was like I was starting over, like being that little girl in the culvert with Gretta, smoking for the first time. I would have thought my throat would be used to smoke.

"That shit is harsh!" I exclaimed.

"Yeah, yeah," Earl commented. "You kind of have to get used to it. Hold your mouth open a bit and pull a little air in with it to cool it. You want to try it again?"

I put the joint to my mouth again and this time I was able to hold the smoke in my lungs a little longer. Then I passed it on to Earl. Eventually the three of us had smoked it down to the very tip. I figured that we would just put it out like a cigarette, but Screech brought out a pair of tweezers and began to pull off the last little portion of half an inch left on the joint. I watched this happening as though I was watching the most fascinating film ever created. The fire on the end of the joint and the smoke rising from it seemed as beautiful as any sunset I had ever seen. I watched Screech's lips gently fold over the tip of the joint like a child's fingers picking a flower. I just watched in fascination not really realizing yet that I was high. The music now seemed to twinkle on my ears like some sort of audio fairy dust with magical properties to enhance the experience. Screech snuffed out the roach on a glass jar lid using the tips of the tweezers. He then leaned back on one arm and began to sing along to the lyrics of "All Along the Watch Tower." Until that day, I had never really paid much attention to Jimi Hendrix, but now the type of music that I had dismissed and labeled as too disjointed suddenly seemed ingenious.

"This is really nice," I said, and then seemed to fade into a moment of eternity in which time ceased to exist.

Screech replied after what seemed like a near-indefinite pause. "Yeah, man. Hendrix is awesome."

I found myself hearing him and then searching my mind like a file drawer for what I was going to say in return. Eventually I said, "No, I mean the high."

"Oh yeah, yeah," Screech replied, an echo on a distant island.

Earl seemed to drift off into some fantasy. He was lying over on one side just smiling. They seemed content to just listen to the music but I felt as though I should talk, not because I wanted to talk, and not because I didn't want to also drift off into the music, but because I had the idea that conversation was the socially appropriate thing to do with a man we had only met an hour or two earlier.

"I never really realized before how much depth Hendrix has," I said, as my own mind drifted off into the music.

235

Karlyle Tomms

"When the power of love overcomes the love of power, then the world will know peace," Screech replied. "Jimi Hendrix said that."

"Wow," I said as one song on the album became silent and then another began.

For a very long time we just sat there, listening and drifting off into the time-warping cannabis high. When the Hendrix album finished the first side, the needle drifted to the center of the vinyl and became music itself. Shhhh, click. Shhhh, click. Shhhh, click. Shhhh, click. We all sat there listening to it as though it was a Siren song. Finally Screech got up to flip it to the other side.

I think we must have just laid around the entire afternoon listening to one album after another. Screech had quite a variety of music from Jimi Hendrix to The Beatles, from old New Orleans blues and black gospel to Hank Williams and Patsy Cline. They all seemed to be infinitely more fascinating when stoned.

Late in the afternoon, a loud knock at the door startled me out of my meditative daze. I jumped and let out a short little chirp in my startled response.

"It's alright. It's alright," Screech said as he motioned his flat hand down toward the floor as though to say calm down. He got up and went to the door. When he opened the door, a tall dark-headed hippie with crinkly, shoulder-length hair and a short, skinny girl with cheek bones that looked like craters, stood in the hall.

"Hey, man," Screech proclaimed.

"What's up?" the hippie responded.

"Come in."

Screech stood back and motioned them into the room.

"Hey this is my friend Earl and ah, ah."

He looked at me and snapped his fingers as though trying to remember my name.

"Lovella," Earl said.

"Yeah, Lovella," Screech echoed.

"This is Dave and his old lady, Lorenda," Screech said as he motioned back to the couple. "Dave is the lead guitarist in our band."

"Hey, Lovella and Lorenda," Dave said. "The names sound so much alike we might have trouble telling them apart."

I thought to myself as he spoke, "If you can't tell me from that mousy-looking, skinny, bitch you are damn fool blind." But I simply said, "Hello."

Earl repeated my hello. Neither of us made any effort to get to our feet or shake hands. We were probably both still too stoned to motivate toward

236

Confessions from the Pumpkin Patch

any social ritual.

"Hey, if you don't mind," Screech said, "we have got rehearsal tonight for our gig tomorrow. You are welcome to just hang out here or you can come to the rehearsal if you want."

"What would you like to do, Lovella?" Earl questioned as he turned to me.

"Watching the rehearsal would be fine," I said, "but what about dinner?"

"We all usually bring a little something with us and share," Screech replied. "We can get something to go over at Simone's and take that."

I didn't relish the idea of another all-vegetable meal. I said, "I'm sure vegetables are very good for you but I was kind of hoping to maybe have some kind of meat with dinner."

"Oh, well, that's cool," said Dave. "Lorenda made a pot roast. You are welcome to join us."

"A pot roast sounds fantastic," I said.

Earl and I got to our feet and followed them out the door. We did stop at Simone's across the street and Screech ordered a box of potatoes and onions that had apparently been baked with black pepper and some type of herbs. I could not discern the herbs, although it did have a bit of an Italian food smell.

Dave and Lorenda patiently waited for our order to come, then we walked for what seemed like an eternity before we came upon what appeared to be an abandoned storefront. The windows on the street were covered in paper tacked up from the inside. Screech and his friends led us down an alley alongside the building. From an upstairs window there were several extension cords dangling off the side of the building and going under a side door that led to the alley.

We entered to find a large, dark, open space that was lit more by stage lighting than anything else. The band instruments were set up on the opposite side of the room. The lights had been plugged into the extension cords as were the instruments. There were a couple of lamps perpendicular to where the band was set up. They were at either end of a large fold-up table which was lined with food. A couple of women flitted around the table checking everything as though to make sure it was all there. In front of the band area there were several different types of chairs, mostly metal fold-up chairs. Some people were sitting at the chairs eating with their drinks sitting on the floor beside them.

Screech set the potatoes on the table and said to us, "Go on, help yourselves. I don't eat before I sing."

There was already a muscular young man sitting at the drums popping

Karlyle Tomms

out noises. There would be a few seconds of rhythm. Then he would stop, bang around on this or that, and start again. I couldn't help noticing that he was the only man in the room who didn't have long hair. In fact, his hair was fairly well groomed, almost business like. He wore a white tank top and a pair of gray and black pin striped slacks. Somehow he seemed out of place. Screech caught me staring at him and must have read my mind.

"That's Denny," he said. "He works the counter at a department store. They won't let him grow out his hair. Wouldn't fit their image. He comes straight from work to rehearsal."

"Come on, Hon," Earl tugged at my arm. "Let's go get something to eat. I'm starving"

It had not even occurred to us to pick anything up when we were at Simone's. I felt a little guilty, but we went to the table and Screech went to the microphone. He began to warm up vocally while the drummer continued to play drum rifts that clashed with Screech's vocalizations. We got our food, introduced ourselves to several of the folks around the table and made trite little comments like, "Oh that looks good." And, "Hmmm, I didn't know you could do that with deviled eggs." We then went to sit in the chairs facing the band, and ate while we watched the band assemble.

Screech seemed to lead the process. "Let's start with 'Tripped Out'. Dave, we need to tighten up the guitar solo on that and I've got to work on reaching those higher notes in the bridge." Eventually he shouted, "One and a two and a." The band began to play very loud, a song that I think I could have gone my entire life without hearing with no regrets.

Screech was indeed screeching the lyrics in the chorus, "Tripped out— didn't want to be here. Tripped out—what am I supposed to do? Tripped out—someone call my Mother. Tripped out—you know there is no other way that I can say I love you unless I'm—tripped out."

The band broke down at Dave's guitar solo. Everything came to a halt. There were discussions about what went wrong and where, then they picked it back up two or three times before Dave managed to flow through the solo easily.

There were a lot of stops and starts and by the time rehearsal was over about 10:30 PM I felt like I had worked all day. I was exhausted and looking forward to sleep. Still, we had to wait 'til all the instruments were broken down and equipment packed before we could leave. I don't think we could have found our way back to the bus anyway without one of them to lead us.

I helped the women pack up the remaining food and fold up the table to put away. Screech and Earl were talking while I helped with the food. I kept looking back over my shoulder hoping that this would all be over

Confessions from the Pumpkin Patch

soon and we could just go crash.

Earl came and got me. We said our goodbyes to the people we had met. Screech was waiting just outside the door.

As we walked back toward his place Screech said, "So what do you think, Lovella? Damn good music?"

"Yeah," I said half-heartedly. "Damn good." I didn't have the heart to say that I really thought it was all total garbage, and there was not a snowball's chance in hell they were ever going to get a record deal. I had not heard a single song that evening that had made me want to tap my feet, sing along, or had lyrics that touched me in any special way. I hated it all.

"Dave has a cousin who works for Columbia Records," Screech went on. "She's a secretary, but I mean she is around all the producers and executives, you know. Dave says maybe she can get one of them to listen to our demo."

"Yeah that would be great," I said, again lying and wondering what chance a secretary has to get any executive to listen to anything.

"Hey, what did you think of 'Tripped out'?" he continued.

I was hoping he would just stop asking about the band, and why me? Why wasn't he asking Earl what he thought? Did he sense somehow that I really didn't like the music and was he trying to trip me up on my fake enthusiasm?

"Oh, yeah, that's an interesting song," I said, knowing that *interesting* was the most truthful thing I could say without sounding negative. Then I took the opportunity to change the subject. "You know, after driving all morning to get here, and being out late, I'm pretty tired."

"Hey, well, you are welcome to crash at my place. The door is always open. I love to have company."

Screech was walking on the opposite side of me from Earl. Earl had his arm around my shoulder. When he said this, he moved over, put his arm across me, and his hand up on Earl's back. We walked like this for several more yards. I felt like a piece of meat in a sandwich, squeezed on both sides and not very comfortable. I didn't want to offend the person who might be giving us a place to sleep, but something didn't feel right. Finally, I came up with the solution to pull out of the hug and take both their hands, instead of being a walking sandwich. I took Screech's hand more to keep him at a distance than as an act of affection. Eventually we reached Screech's building and drudged up the long flight of stairs to his apartment. He had not locked the door when we left. I found out later that he never locked the door. Earl went back down to get our bags while Screech poured me a cold glass of water.

Screech sat down across from me on the opposite mattress and said,

Karlyle Tomms

"You know you are truly a very beautiful woman," he said. "You are not what they call a classic beauty. You are maybe bigger than most women, and taller, but still there is an essence about you that is—I don't know—enticing."

I thought to myself, "Shit! What the hell! He waits for my boyfriend to leave the room and then makes a pass at me?"

I said, "Thank you," rather tritely and took a sip from my glass of water.

"No really," Screech continued. "I could see you in the movies or something. I think you would be like one of those Hollywood beauties who has a strange beauty, you know, like Betty Davis. She is both beautiful and ordinary at the same time, but also really sexy—you know?"

"Well, no, I don't know. I don't think that I've ever thought of Betty Davis that way before," I said. "She looks rather ugly to me." I found myself somewhat offended by his left-handed complement.

"But she's not," Screech went on. "She is anything but ugly. She has a presence that calls to you. You know, you have a presence, Lovella. You don't realize it. I watched you today. People are fascinated with you and you don't even seem to realize how fascinated they are."

"No, I don't realize that," I responded. "I've never thought of myself as fascinating."

"When you walk into a room it's like people feel it before they even realize that they are feeling it. They sense your presence and they are drawn to it," he said as he stood and began unbuttoning his shirt.

"Jesus Christ!" I thought. "He's stripping! Is he going to try to fuck me while Earl is down getting the luggage?" For a moment I pondered whether there was any indication that he was thinking of raping me.

He then turned and walked over to the pile of clothes in the floor where he dug until he found what appeared to be an extra-long T-shirt. He dropped the shirt he had been wearing into the pile, pulled the long T over his head and then took his pants off under it never revealing anything. He then returned to the mattress. He laid down and pulled the blanket up over him. He then propped himself up on an elbow and continued. I felt relieved.

"You should develop your senses, Lovella. You should be more aware of your surroundings, recognize what other people sense about you, realize how special you are."

Earl came through the door with our bags. I got up to meet him.

"Thank you, Screech," I said over my shoulder as I walked to the door.

Earl handed my bag to me. I took it to the bathroom and changed into a nightgown. It was maybe a little revealing, but not intended to be sexy, just functional. I brushed my teeth, and then when I came out, I folded my

240

Confessions from the Pumpkin Patch

arms over my tits as though I could hide my body. I needn't have bothered. Screech was already asleep, and I certainly didn't care if Earl saw me. When I saw that Screech was sleeping, I relaxed.

Earl kissed me as he walked by on his way to the bathroom. I snuggled beneath the blankets on the mattress opposite to Screech, and Earl soon joined me. I was happy to be on a real mattress even if it was a twin size and not the best. We could barely both fit on it but at least it somewhat resembled a real bed instead of a sleeping bag on the hard floor of the VW. Earl folded his arms around me. "I love you," he whispered in my ear.

"I love you too," I replied and drifted almost immediately off to sleep.

Chapter 19

I awoke the next morning to the sound of clinking in the kitchenette area and Screech humming one of the tunes of his band. Beside me Earl was lightly snoring. When I moved to get up, he also woke and stretched long in the bed.

"Good morning, beautiful," he said as he leaned over and kissed me on the cheek. He then examined the room as though he had never seen it before looking around at every corner. I half expected him to ask, "Where are we?" but he didn't. I kissed him back and got up.

When I stood up and headed for the bathroom Screech spotted me.

"Oh, hey, good morning," he said with his perfect white teeth.

"Good morning, Screech," I said as I stumbled toward the bathroom.

Screech had scrambled a few eggs and had made toast and coffee. When I came back from the bathroom he delivered a plate and a cup of coffee to me on the mattress, then to Earl, and then he joined us sitting opposite.

"It is really nice of you to make breakfast for us," I said. "You didn't have to do that."

"Hey, I make breakfast every morning," he replied. "It don't take nothin' to add a few extra eggs."

"Well, you have been more than gracious," Earl said as he bit into his toast.

"So, Screech," I opened a new topic. "You asked us about ourselves and how we got to San Francisco. How about you? How did you get here? Are you from here?"

"No. Hell, no," he said. "I'm from Alabama. Grew up a few miles outside of Birmingham. My daddy was a sharecropper and Momma worked the fields right along with him. Clevus and Nannette Miller broke their backs for nothin' their whole lives."

"So why did you come out here?" I went on.

"You got any idea what it is like for a black man in the deep-south?" he questioned. "I mean it's not like we get spit on in the streets or nothin', well, least not all the time. I heard that folks out here were free-loving and gentle people. I wanted to see if I could get in on a little of that."

"It seems to me," I said, "that a lot of colored—I'm sorry—black people have been getting involved in the civil rights movement and working with

Confessions from the Pumpkin Patch

Dr. Martin Luther King."

"Yeah, yeah," he pondered. "I don't know what I think about that. I don't know that the South is ever going to change. There might be other parts of the country that might be more open to black folk, but the South—?" He stared off into space for a moment. "The South ain't ever going to give colored people a chance."

"Don't you think that Dr. King has been making some progress?" Earl entered. "We were in New York in April for the march on the U. N."

"Yeah, that was more about protesting the war than civil rights," Screech returned.

"I think it was about both," I said. "Did you participate in the protests out here?"

"You know," Screech continued as he wolfed down a bite of scrambled eggs, "I figure the best way for me to have peace is not to put myself into a situation where somebody is going to be challenging my peace. I don't consider it to be very conducive to my peace to have some cop beating me over the head with a night stick."

"Don't you think we have an obligation to our fellow countrymen and women to fight for causes that contribute to everyone's freedom?" Earl pressed, staring directly at Screech.

"No, I don't!" Screech returned, obviously upset. He got up and carried his plate back to the kitchenette and tossed it in the sink. "I am just trying to live my life as peacefully and as comfortably as I can while staying out of 'The Man's' way."

"That's cool. That's cool," Earl spoke gently trying to comfort.

"I'm going to go take a bath," I said, leaving the two of them to talk.

As I gathered my things and headed for the bathroom, I saw Earl join Screech in the kitchen. He put that big comforting hand of his between Screech's shoulder blades. Then the two of them turned around, leaned against the counter and began to talk.

After I came out of the bathroom, Screech offered for Earl to have access to the bathroom, but Earl told him to go ahead.

I put my things away and then sat down next to Earl on the mattress and brushed my wet hair. It was beginning to get out to hippie length and I had begun to enjoy t-shirts and jeans. It felt so good to have a real bath and I felt more refreshed than I had in a week.

"Screech has offered for us to live with him if we want," Earl spoke. "What do you think about that?"

"I guess I'm okay with that," I said, "but I don't think that it is fair to him if we don't contribute more than we have so far."

"I know," said Earl. "I talked with him about that. He said as crappy as

243

this place looks it is not cheap. He said you can't find cheap in San Francisco unless you are about ready to live on the streets, and that is an option. I mean, we do have the bus, but we could maybe give him about seventy dollars a month in rent and stay here."

"That would give us about two months with a little less than forty dollars left for spending money," I said.

"I know," Earl went on. "I would probably have to get a job or figure some way of making a little more money while we are out here. I don't think we'll need much."

"I don't mind getting a job." I said.

"No, I'll do it," Earl replied. "I want you to enjoy your time here as much as possible and I don't want you having to worry about bringing in money."

I grinned at him. "You sound like your father, Earl. Besides, how much do you think I'm going to enjoy just sitting around this apartment day-in and day-out. Work would give me something to do with my time."

"Okay," he said. "Cool. If you want to try to find a job, that's cool."

We certainly were not the average hippie. Most of the kids who came to Haight-Ashbury that summer most definitely did not work. Many of them lived on the streets, and most of them did drugs. The "Summer of Love" turned out, in the long run, to have a lot less to do about love and a lot more to do with kids who were running away from some desperate or horrible situation at home. To most of them the streets were preferable to living in abusive homes. Some of them prostituted. Some dealt drugs. Almost all of them were emotionally wounded in some way. On one hand it was very sad and on the other hand, I was so glad that I wasn't one of those kids. My family had its problems but I never had a father who raped me or a mother who was violent. I met kids out there who had been through hell and unfortunately that hell was their own home.

I learned a lot that summer. I learned eventually that Screech had run away from a situation in which his father had sexually and physically abused him since he was about school age, and had done the same with all Screech's brothers and sisters. He had two sisters, twins, Maggie and Molly. They were two years younger than Screech. His oldest brother, Leon, was eight years his senior and had abused Screech just as his father had. Leon was spending twenty years in prison for armed robbery. Screech was close to his next oldest brother, Delvar, but he drowned when Screech was about twelve years old. He had little to do with his other brother, Simon, who generally avoided everyone. His mother, who was also abused by his father, was passively compliant with the abuse of her

Confessions from the Pumpkin Patch

children. I learned that despite my conflicts with Mother and with Daddy's alcoholism, compared to many others, my life was a fucking piece of cake.

Earl had a hard time finding a job. In a week or two, I hired on as a waitress across the street at Simone's. I learned a lot about work, vegetarian food, and the restaurant business that summer. It was technically my first job. I brought in enough to pay half the rent on Screech's place and a little extra for food and spending money. I bought a few things to fix the place up a little, and give it a bit of a feminine touch, being sure to ask Screech for permission, and being sure that the touches he had brought remained in place. I was not about to touch his Jimi Hendrix posters.

Jimi Hendrix played that summer at the Monterey Pop Festival. Even though it was only two hours away and Screech was dying to go, he had to fulfill his own commitments to play his own gigs.

Earl spent a lot of time with Screech, often accompanying him to band rehearsals which I had long since decided I could live without. Besides there were often times that I worked evenings at the restaurant. In late July the two of them came home one evening when I was off work. They were both grinning from ear to ear.

"Well don't you two look like you swallowed the Cheshire cat," I commented.

"We scored some Acid," Earl said, half giggling. "I've never done Acid before. I want to try it."

"I heard that it causes chromosome damage," I cautioned.

"I heard that it doesn't cause any more chromosome damage than taking aspirin," Earl replied.

The truth is that neither of us knew for sure.

"Chromosome. Chromosome. Where for art thou, Chromosome?" Screech interjected and they both began to giggle uncontrollably.

It was at that point that I realized they had both already been smoking pot.

"Looks like you guys have already been enjoying a little high," I said.

"Yeah, but we haven't taken the Acid," Earl replied. "We want to share it with you, Lovella. I want to share it with you. Don't you think it would be so cool to trip out together?"

"Honestly," I went on. "That stuff scares me. Who knows what it will do."

"I've done it several times," Screech cut in. "It's not really a big deal."

"But I've heard about people having bad trips and stuff," I continued.

"Well, that's usually because they have some bad vibe going on to start with," said Screech. "As long as you keep your mind positive and you feel

Karlyle Tomms

safe enough, you'll be fine."

"That's the problem," I pleaded. "I don't know that I feel safe about taking that stuff at all."

"Hey, it's cool," Screech negotiated. "We're cool. We all get along. We all trust each other, and I can create a nice relaxing environment. How about some classical music to calm the nerves? I even have some Chopin over there in my collection. We'll lock the door. It will just be the three of us."

"Come on, Lovella," Earl practically begged. "I think this could be a great experience, and I really do want to share it with you. I'm so curious to experience tripping."

"Didn't we have some wine in here the other day?" I questioned as I got up and headed for the kitchenette. "If I'm going to do this, I'm going to need a little wine to calm my nerves first."

"All riiiight! Cool!" Screech exclaimed. "That's the spirit. I'll just make us a little nest here to trip in and get the music started."

He pushed the two twin mattresses on the floor together and threw the blankets over them. Then he spent what seemed like a very long time digging through his albums for Chopin. He placed the gentle piano music on the stereo and returned to the mattresses in the floor. Earl joined him and they lit another joint. I returned from the kitchen with my glass of wine and a lit cigarette. The three of us sat cross legged on the mattresses facing each other in a triangle. I half-gulped my wine as they passed the joint to me. I put out my cigarette and took a long, slow, drag on the joint. Soon, I began to feel the relaxing effects of the alcohol combined with the mild hallucinatory effects of the cannabis.

Earl removed an envelope from his pocket, opened it, and brought out what appeared to be some kind of elaborately decorated postage stamp. He handed one to Screech and then one to me.

"Just place it on your tongue," Screech said, "like this." He stuck out his tongue and laid the stamp across it and closed his mouth over it.

Earl followed suit. I sat and stared at mine lying in the palm of my hand and hesitated.

"It's okay," Earl said.

I looked up at him, stared for a moment, and placed the Acid on my tongue. Then I waited.

At first, I don't know that I noticed any difference. I went back to the kitchenette and got myself another glass of wine. When I returned, the mattresses were empty. Screech and Earl had vanished. I stood there at the edge of the mattresses looking down—looking around the room. I didn't see them anywhere. I thought, "What the fuck! What kind of bullshit is

246

Confessions from the Pumpkin Patch

this? They give me a fucking hit of Acid and then just leave me to go through this shit by myself!" My anger was about to turn to sadness and fear when I heard Earl say, "What's wrong, honey?" I looked in the direction of the mattresses and there they were both lying there as though they had been there the whole time but I had seen nothing but an empty space.

"Come here," he said gently.

I sat down beside him, took a sip from my wine and set it on the floor. He placed a reassuring hand on my leg and rubbed gently. To my surprise it felt like bugs crawling up and down my leg.

"I need a cigarette," I said.

I reached for my purse which was lying on the floor nearby, took out a cigarette and lit it. When I took the first drag, I felt as though I was being blown up like a balloon. Warm air filled me, and I felt my body expand. I looked and it seemed as though my arms and legs were swelling with air.

"What the fuck!" I exclaimed and snuffed the cigarette out in a plate I used for an ashtray, pressing to be sure that every ember was extinguished. Still each little orange glowing ember at the tip of the cigarette seemed to sparkle and sparkle and wouldn't go out. Finally, I smashed it hard into the plate. Then it turned black and stopped glowing. When I turned back around Earl said, "I'm hot. I think I'm going to get a little more comfortable." He then rose and began to disrobe. Screech said, "Me too." Then he also began to take off his clothes. When they were both totally naked, they sat back down on the mattress. Earl leaned toward me and placed his hand on my breast, caressing it gently. "Aren't you warm, honey? Do you want to get more comfortable?"

To that point in my life, there were very few times I had ever felt self-conscious about my nakedness but this time I didn't want to take off my clothes. "No." I said feeling somehow subtly violated.

"Are you sure?" he said, as he leaned in and began to kiss me.

His mouth felt wet. His face seemed to trickle with water, like rain falling across a window pane. My emotions were surprising me. At the same time, I felt the sexual arousal that I had so much enjoyed, but I also felt like crying. Then I realized I was crying and the rain falling was my own tears. As Earl pulled back from the kiss, I watched the tears fall from my face and splash in slow motion into a pool of water. It was as though the mattresses had become a pool in which we were all swimming.

"I certainly can't go swimming with my clothes on," I said and I began to disrobe. As I pulled off my clothes, I felt as though I was sensually peeling off my own skin, emerging from within like a snake pulling free from last year's growth. The skin clothes fell dead and useless, no longer

247

Karlyle Tomms

needed. I felt a sense of freedom and renewal as the sensual touch of the fabric fell softly around me.

By the time I had disrobed, we were no longer in a pool. We were instead sitting in soft green grass under a canopy of trees. The sunlight flickered through the leaves overhead. I looked over to see Earl and Screech sitting together, touching one another. Their penises seemed to be two snakes, a black one and a white one and they began to intertwine encircling each other rising up together toward the canopy. Then I saw Earl and Screech kissing. I looked in fascination with a blend of emotions from sexual arousal to jealousy. I asked myself, "Who am I jealous of, Earl or Screech, or maybe both?"

It seemed as though the piano music of Chopin became bird songs in a jungle and it seemed as though my spirit and my body flowed with that music from crescendo to the subtle gentle little tinkling of notes. Then I noticed two leopards mating across from me, a spotted leopard and a black leopard. The spotted leopard was mounting the black leopard, pushing itself into the black leopard, and I saw the spotted leopard lift its head and roar. It frightened me. I screamed and slunk back away from it. Then the spotted leopard rolled off the black leopard and lay back on the grass. As it did, it became a man, and I saw that it was Earl. He appeared to be dead. I shouted out, "Earl!" I was so scared that he was dead. He lifted his head from the grass and put a finger to his lips as though to say be quiet. When he went "shuuuuuuush," I felt a wind sweep by me blowing my hair back. Then the black leopard stood on its hind legs and changed forms. It morphed into a jungle witchdoctor with feathers and native regalia, and I realized that I was in a village in Africa. The witchdoctor moved in jerky little movements toward me. He had a rattle in each hand and he was shaking them, holding them out away from his body as he approached me. Then as he came closer, he knelt down in front of me and the rattles disappeared. Instead, I heard a rhythm of "shhs, shhs, shhs, shhs, shhs," coming rhythmically from his lips. He wrapped his arms around me. Then I felt warm and safe. He held me close and I could feel his feathered head dress against my cheek. He pulled back away from me so that I could see in his eyes. I saw that the witch doctor was Screech. His eyes were like dark brown pools, like a window into the universe. Looking into them was like looking into the night sky, and in the distance of his eyes I could see tiny stars glimmering. He kissed me. Lips like soft pillows enfolded mine. I felt his tongue on my tongue as he gently lay me down onto a mat by a grass hut. I looked over to see Earl watching as he sat in a meditation position, legs crossed, thumb and forefinger encircled on each knee like a Buddha. Then he began to fade into the distance. I reached out for him,

Confessions from the Pumpkin Patch

and the witchdoctor kissed me again. He pushed me down on the mat and lay on top of me. I felt tremendous arousal. I felt his erect penis slide slowly into me as though it must have been three feet long. It seemed to slide extremely deep into me, sliding, sliding, sliding, and then it would withdraw just as slowly, tantalizing, teasing. I felt my hands upon his naked back. I ran my hands down his body and felt the smooth warm muscular contour of his back and his ass.

It seemed as though he fucked me for days with the sun setting and the moon rising over his back. I looked up into the sky and watched the days pass as he fucked me, and fucked me, and fucked me. I felt my body shiver in climax, convulse, explode and relax, then, again and again. Then Earl sat beside us. He was big like a giant looking down from the sky with one hand caressing the witch doctor's back and his ass and the other caressing my face. Then the witch doctor began to chant incantations in a language I had never heard before. Slowly at first he chanted and then louder and faster until he screamed as though stabbed. He pushed up from me and thrust his hips into me. I saw his head tilt back as the scream came from his mouth. Then I began to feel trickles of fluid falling out of my vagina as though I was bleeding. At first I thought I was bleeding, and then I realized that it was the witchdoctor filling me with a magic potion. He poured this potion through his penis like the spout of a pitcher. It filled me so much I could not contain it and it trickled out onto the grass mat beneath us. I felt a tingle run through my body as the potion began to take effect. I felt myself turn into a bird, as did the witchdoctor, and I felt us rise and fly over the village. I was a dove and he was an eagle. We flew through the sky looking down on the African land filled with herding animals, rivers and grasslands. Then we began to fall. I was frightened as we fell. I began frantically trying to flap my wings so I could stay aloft. I looked as the witch doctor who had folded his wings back behind him into a dive. Then we hit the ground with a thud together. We were back on the grass mat. We were back in human form and the witchdoctor had fallen on top of me. He lay there and panted as though he had just run a marathon. Then he rolled over to my left side, reached out his hand and caressed my cheek. I looked in his direction. I saw Screech looking longingly and lovingly at me.

When I awoke late the next afternoon the three of us were lying naked, side by side on the mattresses. Screech was between me and Earl. I wasn't sure if I was still tripping but then everything began to have the familiar and remembered appearance of reality. I lay there for a very long time trying to make sense of what had happened the night before. I rolled over

Karlyle Tomms

on my back, stared at the ceiling and thought. Had I really seen Earl having sex with Screech or was it just a hallucination that the drug had created. Did Screech really have sex with me or had it all been part of the acid trip. After all, I imagined that I was a dove flying over the African grasslands. I knew that couldn't be real so the other things I thought I had experienced might not be real either, but we were all lying there together on the mattresses naked. I felt like I had awakened from an elaborate dream.

After a while, I got up and went to the bathroom. When I came back, the two of them had roused up and were sitting on the edge of the mattresses. I came back across the room, not concerning myself about my nudity. Until that point, Earl and I had only made love when Screech was out of the apartment. Screech had never seen me naked before. I figured since I knew that he was attracted to me, that it wouldn't be fair to him for me to prance around half clothed, or unclothed. I didn't want to lead him on and I was being monogamous with Earl. However, after waking up nude next to him, I saw no further use in worrying about my clothes. I came and sat down on the mattress next to Earl. When I did, Screech got up and headed for the bathroom without saying a word.

After Screech left the room, Earl and I sat there silent. "We need to talk," I finally said.

"About what?" he said.

"Well, there is a lot about last night and that whole experience that I need to try to wrap my head around," I said. "Things have changed here. It's not just the acid trip. Relationships have changed. We have crossed over into something we didn't start out with, and I don't know that we can ever go back."

He buried his face in his hands. "Yes," he said.

"Yes, what?" I questioned.

"Yes, I've been having sex with Screech," he replied. "I'm sorry. I didn't mean to hurt you or deceive you. It's just that—."

I took a huge breath and sat silent for a moment trying to take it all in. On one hand I felt hurt and betrayed, but I also felt curious and intrigued.

"Are you homosexual?" I questioned.

"No," he replied. "I mean, not really. I guess I just like sex. I don't know. It felt good to explore."

"Are you in love with Screech?" I continued.

"No—well—not like I'm in love with you," he began to explain. "I love Screech, but I think more than anything, I just like having sex with him sometimes. I don't know. This is all so bizarre. I've never felt this way before. I've never had sex with a man before other than maybe a little

Confessions from the Pumpkin Patch

curious playing around when I was just hitting puberty, but that wasn't real sex. I had never climaxed with a man until Screech, and I had never done anything with males since I hit puberty. I thought I was straight. I thought, because I'm in love with you, that I wanted only you. I don't know how this happened, Lovella." He began to cry.

"Is Screech a homosexual?" I asked.

"No," he responded. "I don't know how he feels sexually. He has girlfriends and he sleeps around with quite a few women. I don't know if he sleeps with other men, but you should know, shouldn't you? I mean, he fucked you last night didn't he? At least I think he fucked you. It looked to me like he did. I don't think I was just tripping."

I sighed deep and slow.

"It seems to me that one of the effects of drugs is that they diminish your judgment. You do things you would not normally do, or you do things you might have fantasized about doing, but wouldn't do otherwise. Either way, they cause you to make choices you maybe shouldn't make."

"Yeah," he said. "I guess we can blame it on the drugs. Still, it must have been something inside of us that made us do it. Regardless, it is still a choice that we made."

"You're right—it is," I said. "But would we have made those choices if we weren't high? Until you confirmed it just now, I wasn't sure if Screech had fucked me. In my hallucination, it was a witchdoctor who fucked me. He sometimes looked like Screech. Sometimes he didn't. I had all kinds of other dream-like things that happened too, like flying, so I questioned if it had really happened or not."

"I think it did," Earl replied, "and before that I fucked Screech in the ass right there on that mattress in front of you." He sobbed. "Lovella, I feel so ashamed."

"Shame is not going to fix anything," I said. "Human sexuality is a strange thing. It is amazing to me how it can manifest. I've read about things like this. I've just never experienced anything like it before." I placed a hand on his shoulder and looked away. "Is Screech in love with you?" I asked.

"I don't think so," he responded. "I think it was just doing something that felt good because it felt good. I think that's all it was. I love Screech as a friend and I think he loves me, but I don't think either of us wants to set up housekeeping together."

I turned back to him. "Then, Earl," I said, "I want to go home."

He lifted his head up, tears still streaming down his face. He reached over, took my hand and squeezed. "Me, too," he said. "I want to go home too."

251

Screech was not at all happy to hear that we were going back to Pennsylvania. Maybe he really was in love with Earl. Maybe he just didn't want to lose the steady income I brought in from working at Simone's. I had done fairly well that summer. I had paid the rent, bought food, saved money and had plenty left for us to make the trip home. I learned that men give very good tips to big-busted, flirty waitresses even at vegetarian restaurants, and I wasn't above shaking my junk for a little extra green on the table. There had even been one odd-looking little man who had left a hundred dollar bill under his plate with a note on a paper napkin saying, "Thanks for the fun." All I had done was lean over the table when I served him to give him a good long look at my cleavage.

We waited a couple of days after our acid trip to tell Screech that we were leaving. We wanted to get everything arranged and ready to go so that we wouldn't be having to run around trying to tie up loose ends at the last minute. We got up early one morning and packed the bus while Screech was still asleep. He had been out very late with his band so he slept so hard he didn't notice what we were doing. After we were finished loading the bus, we came back upstairs and woke Screech to tell him that we were going. I realize it was kind of underhanded to do it that way, but Earl suspected that he would be upset, and we didn't want to have to be picking through our stuff and moving things in the middle of an angry scene.

When we told him, I realized that screech was not just something he did when he sang. It was something he did when he was angry. The angrier he became the more the pitch of his voice heightened and he began to stretch his words like rubber bands and snap them back between quick spurts of syllables.

"WHAT THE HEEEELLLL DO YOU MEEEEEEEEEEAN YOU ARE GOING BACK TO PENNSYLVANIA? SO YOU ARE GOING TO JUST UP AND FUCKIIIIIIING WALK OUT WITH NO NOTICE, NO TIIIIIIMME FOR ME TO PREPARE FOR SHIIIIIT!? YOU ARE DOING THE SAAAAAAAAAAAME DAMN SHIIIIIT TO ME THAT EEEEEEEEVERYBODY DOES! JUST LEEEEEEAAAVE OLD SCREEEEEEEECH HANGING. NOBODY FUCKIIIIIIINNNG CARES!"

"Screech, man," Earl responded. "We don't mean to leave you hanging. Lovella is going to give you fifty dollars toward next month's rent."

"FIFTEEEEEEEEE DOLLARS!?" Screech screamed back. "WEEEEELLL, BIG FUCKIIIIIING WHOOOPTEEEEEEE DAMN DO! I MIGHT GO OUT AND BUY MYSELF A FUCKIIIIIIING YACHT!"

Confessions from the Pumpkin Patch

"Screech, you know we love you," I interjected. "But we have got to keep enough to get back home on."

"Yeah you love me." He began to lower his tone to the level of being somber but sarcastic. "You reeeeeeeealy love me. What have you known me for—two months? Yeah that's plenty of time to really fall in love, ain't it? Oh, yeah, Lovella, I know you got my back." He turned to Earl and continued. "What is this, Earl? Did the bitch here talk you into going home? Is she a little jealous of us spending time together? She don't want you fucking my ass? I thought we was tight man."

"We are tight," Earl replied. "This doesn't have to mean that we will never see each other again. We'll be in touch. We are just tired of the scene out here. We need to go home, and Lovella's not a bitch. Come on, man. That's not fair. She didn't talk me into anything. We just think it's time to go home."

A tear fell from Screech's eye and he began to tremble. He turned away. "No, it means you're gone. The two of you are gonna go back and get married, make babies, have a family. You are going back, back to the nine-to-five. You will go back and work at your daddy's potato chip factory and the last damn thing you are going to want to associate with is a—." There was a very long pause before he was able to choke out the remaining phrase, "po nigger from the south."

Earl fell silent. His shoulders slumped. The muscle tone drained out of his face like water from a plastic bag. It was then when I realized that not only was Screech in love with him, but he obviously had very deep feelings for Screech. He looked at me and I nodded with understanding. I didn't understand, but I wanted to. He walked over to put a caring arm around Screech's shoulder. Screech threw his arm off and said, "Get the fuck away from me." Earl did not try to touch him again. He stood back away from Screech and said softly, "I thought you knew me better than that. I thought you knew both of us better than that."

"It don't matter," Screech replied without looking up. "It don't fucking matter what kind of good intentions you got, and that's all it fucking is man, good intentions. You still don't get it. I know how it is. I've been a fool to even let this happen. I should have kept my heart in my chest, instead of letting it go walking around with you."

"I do love you, Screech." Earl pleaded. "Honest I do."

"It don't matter!" Screech shouted. "Cause you know the only fucking thing in the world that is worse than a nigger?" He looked up at Earl, his eyes pleading. "A faggot nigger!"

"Oh, god, man don't—please don't." Tears began to drift slowly across Earl's cheeks.

Karlyle Tomms

"I come out here thinking maybe things might be different," Screech explained. "You know faggots and niggers neither one ain't too popular around Alabama. Sleeping with girls, I can do that, but maybe it's just to cover up the fact that I suck cock. I like girls, but—." His eyes drifted off to the other side of the room. "I thought maybe I could get in on the start of the Aquarius Age; you know, peace and love and all that shit. I thought people would see *ME* instead of seeing their judgment of me, but it don't matter." He walked to the opposite side of the room and turned his back to Earl. "So you have had your little adventure, rich boy. You got to go slummin'. You got to have a little taste of this fruit that wasn't as forbidden as you thought. You got to pretend for a while that you ain't part of the establishment, but you are. You got no idea how much you are."

"This was not some kind of game!" Earl shouted. "I didn't fall in love with you because I wanted to see what chocolate tastes like! I fell in love with who you are, man."

I sat down at this point and buried my face in my hands. My mind was reeling with so many fears even though I was trying to keep it all level in my head. I decided that I would just stay out of it, let it go wherever it was going to go, and then pick up the pieces from there.

"Goddamn it!" Earl shouted. "I don't care what color your skin is!"

"Yes, you do," Screech replied. "Even if you don't think you do—you do. You might try, but you can't look at me without seeing somebody different from the 'supposed to be' somebody who is maybe not quite as good as you are. Oh, you tell yourself that you're cool, that you are different from the rest. You tell yourself that you ain't prejudiced, but deep down, nagging at the back of your mind is the truth—and someday it is gonna bite you in the ass when you least expect it. It will pop out of your mouth and it will tell everybody around you what you really think. You grew up that way. You can't think no other way."

"I disagree with you, man," Earl replied. "But even if you're right, at least I'm trying to think different."

"Well, tell you what," said Screech. "How bout I go back east with you guys and come prancing into your daddy's house. What the hell do you think is gonna happen? You think your rich, fat cat daddy is gonna like you any better? You think he is gonna sit me down and have the maid bring me a drink?" Screech took both fists up and slammed them down on the air as though he was beating them against a table. "FUCK IT MAN! FUCK IT! FUCK IT! FUCK IT! FUCK IT! FUCK IT! I CAN'T HAVE YOU! I CAN'T EVER HAVE YOU AND YOU CAN'T HAVE ME! We can't be together. It wouldn't make a fucking bit of difference how much we love each other. It's all pretend man. It can't be real. They won't let it

Confessions from the Pumpkin Patch

be real. Even if I was white, the world ain't ready for two men to be together. Probably won't ever be. There sits who you love man." He pointed at me as I sat there helpless with my arms clinched around my knees. Screech walked to the back and leaned over the sink facing the back wall. "You and your old lady better go," he said without turning around.

Earl started to say his name, still desperately seeking some resolution, but he didn't get the words out of his mouth before Screech shouted, "JUST FUCKIIIIIIIING GO!"

Earl turned back toward me silent, sad, looking very much like a little boy whose dog had just died. I got up, crossed the room, took his hand and tilted my head toward the door. There was a hesitation, a brief moment when I thought he was going to tell me that he wanted to stay, but then he moved with me toward the door. When we stepped outside the apartment and pulled the door closed we heard Screech scream into sobs a moment after the click of the latch. Earl started to turn back, but when I touched his arm, he stopped.

Descending those stairs for the last time felt like a sinner's shame on the descent to hell. Both of us wanted to go back. Both of us wanted to make it okay. Both of us cared enough about Screech to want to make it right, but we couldn't have done that, even if we had gone back. I wanted to be cool about it but I couldn't help that my heart was wounded because Earl had a homosexual affair. If he had any affair it would have hurt me, but the fact that he had been with a man left doubts in my mind. It made me wonder if he could ever commit himself fully to me, if deep down he might really be homosexual. I knew that he loved me. I knew that he had not done this to hurt me. Still my heart ached and whimpered like a beaten puppy.

When we had both gotten back to the VW bus, Earl planted himself in the driver's seat, placed both hands firmly on the steering wheel and said without moving his gaze from the windshield, "So, which way home?"

I reached for our maps even though I had already plotted the course. Gazing intently at the squiggles that represented San Francisco I said, "Head east toward Divisadero Street."

He started the bus and turned east. Except for occasional references to the map, we were both silent for a very long time.

Chapter 20

We stopped at a little roadside cafe in Reno, Nevada. I found a pay phone and called Mother. I knew she would be angry. I hadn't bothered to call her except to let her know that we had arrived safely in San Francisco back at the end of May. The phone rang an inordinate number of times and I was about to hang up thinking that she wasn't home when I heard her voice come onto the line.

"Yes, what is it?" she said in a rather impatient tone. It was completely out of character for her to answer the phone this way. What happened to the normal?

"Hello, Mother," I spoke into the scratchy line.

"Oh, for goodness sakes, Lovella!" she yelled. "It is about time you called. I was frantic with worry. I had no idea how to get hold of you, or what might have happened to you. You have got to come home now. I'm telling you that you have got to come home!"

"I'm on my way home, Mother," I replied calmly ignoring her angst. "What's the rush?"

"I was headed out the door to go back to the hospital when the phone rang. John is in intensive care and they are saying he may only have a few days to live."

"John, who?" I said, thinking I had no idea who she was talking about. Maybe I didn't want to know.

"Lovella!" she screamed into the line. "This is no time for your nonsense!"

"I'm sorry, Mother," I replied. "I'm not trying to be funny. I don't know anyone named John."

"YES YOU DO!" she screamed. "IT'S YOUR FATHER! YOU KNOW IT'S YOUR FATHER! THAT'S HIS NAME! HE IS IN INTENSIVE CARE DYING WHILE YOU ARE BEING YOUR USUAL TEASING, LITTLE BITCH, SELF! DO YOU EVEN CARE THAT YOUR FATHER IS DYING?!"

"Oh, my god!" I said. "Daddy's in the hospital? Why didn't you say it was Daddy? What happened?"

"I told you before you left he was dying! I told you he had cirrhosis!" she snarled on. "I told you and you wouldn't believe me! You had to go on some childish, selfish, little adventure instead of spending the last few

Confessions from the Pumpkin Patch

months of your father's life with him!"

"He told me he was fine!" I shouted back.

"Well, he lied!" Mother snapped. "He has lied to you more than you will ever know."

"DON'T YOU SAY THAT!" I screamed. "HE HASN'T LIED TO ME A TENTH AS MUCH AS YOU HAVE! At least he must have been trying to protect my feelings."

"Yes, that's what he does, Lovella," she quipped back. "He protects you. You protect him, and meanwhile the real world is falling apart."

"Oh, my god," I said contemplating the implications of this. "We are still at least two days away."

"Where are you?" she questioned.

"We are in Reno, Nevada," I said. "We started back this morning, but even if we drove straight through and didn't stop to sleep, it is still going to be about two days before I can get there. Is Daddy alert? Can he talk? I could call him."

"You missed your chance on that one," she said in a glib manner. "He has been unconscious for several days now."

A wave of grief swept over me like a tsunami. I began to have trouble breathing. I sucked tears back into my soul and tried desperately to keep her from knowing my pain. Yet I felt as though I couldn't get my breath, as though I could faint at any moment.

"I'll talk to Earl about it," I said. "We will get there as fast as we can. I'll try to call periodically to check in."

"Fine," she said, sounding very cold. "I will see you when you get here."

"Where is he, Mother? What hospital?" I said, thinking of it at the last minute.

"He is in Armstrong Hospital," she replied. "I have to go now."

I didn't get goodbye out of my mouth fast enough. She had already hung up.

Earl had found a booth in the cafe and ordered coffee while he waited for me. When I walked in it was all too obvious to him that something was wrong. He scooted over in the booth and patted the seat for me to sit next to him.

"Baby, you look terrible," he said. "What's wrong? Your mother being mean to you again?"

I sat down next to him and buried my face in my hands as I leaned over the table.

"When I called her in May to tell her we were headed for California she told me Daddy was dying. I didn't believe her. I told her to put Daddy on

257

Karlyle Tomms

the phone and he said that everything was fine. I believed him. I never felt I ever had a reason not to believe Daddy." I turned to make eye contact. "But he lied to me, Earl. He's dying."

I burst into tears. Earl pulled me to his chest and held me. He didn't say anything. He just let me cry. When I had finally collected myself, I went on.

"Mother says he has cirrhosis and that he has been unconscious for several days. He is in intensive care at Armstrong Memorial and they are saying that he has only a few days to live."

"Then we have to get home," he said without missing a beat.

"What am I going to find there?" I asked. "I can't talk to him. I can't tell him that I love him."

"Of course you can tell him you love him," Earl comforted. "I read somewhere that even though people are unconscious they still know when someone they love is in the room. Their mind can still comprehend even if their body can't move."

The tears came and went. The waitress avoided us calculating correctly that this would not be the time to take an order.

"We have to go," Earl pleaded. "We have got to get you back so you can be with him.

"It will take us two days to get back there at least," I said. "What if he dies before we get there?"

"He's not going to die before you get there," Earl consoled. "He will wait for you. You know he will. We'll drive all night. We'll get there."

I nodded my head. Then Earl called the waitress over and ordered a couple of burgers and fries to go. We got back in the bus, and he headed east on Lincoln Highway. He woofed down his burger and then the rest of mine after I only took a couple of bites. We had been on the road since about 9:00 A.M. and it was about 2:00 PM when we got back on it after lunch.

"Earl, please keep it at the speed limit," I requested. "Getting stopped might be more of a delay than going slower."

"Sure, no problem," he returned and let up off the gas.

Earl just drove. We had little bits of small talk here and there, a few bitches about detours and road construction, but that was about it. It was about 10:00 PM when we got to Salt Lake City. Earl noticed that I had been nodding in my seat. He reached over, gently touched my arm and said, "Go in the back and lay down. Get some sleep."

"But, what about you?" I reasoned. "Don't I need to stay up and help keep you awake?"

"I'll be fine," he said, "Go lay down."

Confessions from the Pumpkin Patch

I dutifully climbed over into the back, pulled a sleeping bag across the floor and lay down on top of it. I don't know how long I was asleep, but I awoke with a faint, dull, gray light coming through the windows of the bus. I sat up and looked around and then climbed back into the passenger's seat.

"Where are we?" I asked.

"We are about an hour past Cheyenne, Wyoming, headed across Nebraska," he replied.

"My god," I exclaimed. "Haven't you slept?"

"I've been drinking coffee all night," he explained. "I have stopped at a few truck stops and roadside dives so I could refuel the bus and refuel myself on caffeine."

"Still, you have to be exhausted!" I exclaimed. "Why don't we pull over so you can sleep a while, or I'll drive while you sleep?"

"You don't have a driver's license," he responded. "Being pulled over might delay us more than me doing the driving." He tossed my own logic back at me.

I felt a twinge of anger at Mother just then. Never getting my driver's license was one more of her ways of controlling everything. She had every excuse under the sun and as a result I had never learned to drive.

I fumbled in my purse for a cigarette, dug frantically, and finally said, "Shit!"

"What's up?" Earl questioned.

"I don't have any fucking cigarettes," I exclaimed. "I'm a nervous fucking wreck and I don't have any cigarettes."

"We'll get you some at the next gas station," he said. "I need to get gas pretty soon anyway."

About twenty minutes later he stopped to fill up the tank. I went in to get a couple of packs of cigarettes while the tank was being filled. After that, he drove while I puffed one cigarette after another and then flipped the butt out the window. We were getting near Lincoln, Nebraska when I noticed his head beginning to bob.

"EARL!" I shouted jolting him awake. He had a brief little swerve and then corrected back into the lane.

"What, hummm," he said. "I'm alright."

"No you're not," I pleaded. "Pull over and take a nap at least."

"No, Honey. We've got to get there," he continued.

"We may not get there if you fall asleep and run us off the road—now pull over."

"Okay," he said, "when I find a place."

I began pointing out one place after another where he could pull over to

259

Karlyle Tomms

nap, a grocery store parking lot, a side road, the underpass of a bridge. He bypassed them all.

I was getting more and more angry hearing one excuse after another why he couldn't pull over to rest. Finally, I began telling him that I had to pee really badly. I did have to go a little bit, but not that bad. I didn't let him know that. I just complained about by bladder being about to rupture if we didn't find someplace soon. Eventually he pulled into a gas station and let me out. When I came back, he was slumped over the steering wheel sound asleep. I was torn between letting him sleep like that knowing that he would probably be sore when he woke up, and going ahead and waking him so he could sleep in the back where it would be more comfortable. I stood there for several minutes thinking about it and then finally came up with a plan. I reached in carefully and took the keys from the ignition and placed them in my jeans pocket. Then I nudged him several times before he woke up. He lifted his head and looked at me, his eyes glazed and bloodshot.

"Oh," he mumbled. "You ready to go?"

"No, I'm not," I replied. "I'm ready for you to get in the back of the van, lie down and sleep for a while."

"Honey, I can't," he coaxed. "We have got to get you home to your Daddy."

"I can live with a couple of extra hours, Earl," I responded. "Now, go lie down."

"No, we got to go," he reached for the keys. "Hey where are the keys?"

"I have them."

"Well give them here and let's go," he begged.

"I'll give them back to you when you have had some time to sleep," I protested.

He knew that he needed the sleep, so he complied and snuggled up on a sleeping bag in the back of the bus. "You wake me in thirty minutes," he commanded.

"Sure," I said. It was only a few seconds after that when I heard him snore.

By that time it was about 2:00 PM. We had left San Francisco at about 9:00 on the previous morning. As far as I was concerned, we were making good time.

I let Earl sleep until 6:00 PM. I didn't wake him. At various times in the afternoon, I took a magazine, folded back, to fan him in the back of that hot bus. At other times, I read the magazine. Most of the time, I just waited and a time or two, I took little cat naps myself. I contemplated starting the bus and heading on down the road, but since I had never been

260

Confessions from the Pumpkin Patch

trained to drive, I feared that only previous observations of the skill would not be sufficient to allow me to do it smoothly. I could see myself bouncing the van around or choking it out because I didn't have the feel for the clutch. Then I could see Earl waking up and being mad at me that I was trying to drive when I didn't know how. I decided that I would simply let him sleep.

He finally roused a little bit and looked around. Then he looked startled as though he didn't know where he was.

"Did you have a good nap?" I asked, and this seemed to orient him a bit.

"Where am I?" he responded not answering my question.

"You are in the back of your Volkswagen bus in the parking lot of a gas station somewhere in Iowa, about an hour and a half east of Lincoln, Nebraska."

"Oh, jeez. Jeez. What time is it?" he questioned.

"It's about 6:30 PM," I replied.

The summer sun was still hanging in the sky, although low on the horizon. Even though we parked in the shade and left the windows open, he was still drenched in sweat from sleeping in the hot bus.

"Oh shit!" he exclaimed. "We've got to go."

He scrambled to get to the driver's seat and reached for invisible keys. "Where are the keys?" he asked, obviously having forgotten the conversation we had earlier in the day.

I took the keys from my pocket and handed them to him. He started the bus, but before he backed out of the parking space, he reached over, put his hand behind my head and kissed me. "Don't ever forget that I love you," he said. "No matter what happens, no matter what mistakes I make. Please don't ever forget that I love you." Then he steered the bus clear of the space and we were on our way again.

It was midnight when we got to Davenport, Iowa. I began pleading with him again to pull over and take a nap but he wouldn't do it. About 2:00 AM I went to the back of the bus to sleep again. About 9:00 AM I woke again and asked, "Where are we?"

"We are about forty-five minutes, maybe an hour, from Kittanning," he replied.

He had driven straight through and he was not about to stop at this point for any longer than it took to take a piss, eat, or gas up the bus.

Finally, he pulled up in front of Armstrong Memorial Hospital about 10:20 AM. He reached over and took my hand. "Go ahead," he said, quietly. "I'll park the bus and meet you in there."

My emotions were like a cut power line sizzling with power one second and waning to absolute fatigue the next. I pulled the rear view mirror

261

Karlyle Tomms

around to take a look at my face. "Jesus! I look like a hobo," I said trying to straighten my hair.

Earl squeezed my hand. "It doesn't matter," he said, "Go on."

I got out of the bus feeling like a lost and forlorn little girl. I didn't know whether to bravely push through those hospital doors or run away as fast as I could. I didn't want to face this. I didn't want it to be real. I didn't want to see Daddy lying on a death bed, and I didn't want to have to deal with Mother's bullshit. I had no idea what I was in for. As Earl pulled the bus away, I turned, put on my brave face and pushed through the double glass doors.

Inside the lobby there were several chairs with a few people sitting around here and there. I looked around and saw a squat little woman sitting behind a reception glass. I walked over to the window, watched her as she seemed to be more interested in a crossword puzzle than in attending to me. Finally I tapped on the window. She looked up and said, "Yes, may I help you?"

"I am Lovella Fuchs," I replied. "I understand that my father John Fuchs is in intensive care."

"Yes," she said, "but his wife is in with him now and rules only allow one person at a time in the intensive care room."

I fought the urge to ram my fist through that window. "You don't understand," I said, tersely. "I haven't seen my father. I just drove in from San Francisco."

"Oh, well, that is a very long drive. You must be exhausted. Why don't you have a seat and rest for a while till Mrs. Fuchs comes out." She actually tilted her head back down to her cross word puzzle.

I slammed my fist down on the Formica counter in front of the window. "I HAVE TO SEE MY FATHER NOW!" I screamed.

"Young lady!" she said aghast. "You will curb that behavior or I'll call security!"

"I DON'T FUCKING CARE!" I screamed. "I just need to see my Daddy."

About that time a matronly looking nurse with her dainty little white nurse cap stepped up from behind the receptionist. "Linda," she said, sweetly. "Is there a problem?"

"MY DADDY IS DYING! I HAVE TO SEE HIM!" I shouted to the nurse not even giving the receptionist an opportunity to answer her.

"Oh, I'm sorry, dear," the nurse replied to me. "Who is your father?"

"My Daddy is John Fuchs," I said with angry tears running down my cheeks. "He is in intensive care. I haven't seen him in two months and now he's in a coma.

Confessions from the Pumpkin Patch

Linda cut in. "I explained to the young lady that Mrs. Fuchs is still in the room and rules only allow one person at a time."

The nurse still smiling as though it was permanently painted on her face said, "I'm sure we could make an exception in this case, don't you think? Please buzz her though, Linda. I'll meet her in the hall."

She motioned me toward a steel door that was opposite the main entrance. I walked over and stood for a second in front of the door. I heard it buzz and click, so I pushed it open to the hall. The matronly nurse was standing on the other side of the door still smiling. She put her arm around my shoulder and said, "You must be devastated, dear. Let me walk you up to your father's room."

I felt a mix of anger, relief, revulsion, and tenderness as she placed that arm around my shoulder. We walked together to the elevator. She pushed the call button and we waited for a few eternal seconds before the door finally opened. She motioned me to get on the gurney-length elevator, and then followed behind me. We went up to the third floor of the hospital which I think was the top floor. We walked around another hall to yet another steel door where she pushed a button on the intercom. A voice came back with a, "May I help you?"

"This is Sheila Simpson," the nurse replied to the box, "Please buzz us in."

"Certainly, Mrs. Simpson," the box replied and then there was another buzz and click at this door.

As we walked together through the door I said, "Jeez, is this a hospital or Fort Knox?"

Still smiling, she said, "It's both, dear. We do have to keep a tight security in some areas. Emotions often run high when loved ones are ill."

As we walked around the nurse's station for intensive care, I noticed employees subtly coming to attention, perking up as though the general had arrived. They all stopped just short of a salute. I learned later that Mrs. Simpson was the Director of Nurses. She led me to Daddy's room, opened the door for me and said, "Here you are, dear. If you should happen to need anything, please let me know."

Mother was sitting in an uncomfortable looking chair beside the bed. She looked up in acknowledgment, but didn't say a word. Daddy already looked like a corpse, gaunt and frail, his skin the color of a carrot. He had tubes in every orifice and an IV dripping into his arm from beside the bed. The stench in the room was like nothing I had ever smelled before—sweet like some kind of spoiled candy, salty and rotten.

I barely had time to take it in. I burst into tears, threw my purse on the floor and ran to Daddy's side. "Oh, my god! Oh, my god!" I cried. "Daddy,

263

Karlyle Tomms

can you hear me?"

"Of course he can't hear you Lovella." Mother spoke as though her words were intended to cut. "He's in a coma."

I gripped Daddy's hand tightly and pulled it up off the bed.

"How long has he been like this?" I questioned, as tears fell off my cheek and onto Daddy's hand.

"A few weeks," Mother replied. "Not that you should care."

"How can you say that?" I snapped back at her. "You know how much I love Daddy."

"Yes," she replied. "You loved him enough to go gallivanting around California while he was dying. You two have always had such a special bond." Her sarcasm hissed through painted lips.

"Are you jealous?" I asked in a contemptible tone.

She didn't reply but sat staring at me.

"You are jealous!?" I continued raising my voice. "Because you have never had this kind of a bond with anyone have you, Mother, not even with your own daughter? You have no idea what it is like to really care about anyone."

"Don't start with me, Lovella!" she snapped back.

I went on.

"The one thing you never could stand was that Daddy and I were so close. You couldn't stand it that we cared so much about each other, but you also couldn't stand to let yourself be that close to anyone, not me, not Daddy, not your own parents, not anyone."

"Oh, you have such a special bond with your father," she snarled, "always taking up for him, protecting him, making excuses for him, while he drank himself to death. You see where it got him, Lovella?" She stood up and slung her hand toward Daddy, "You see?!"

"I cannot fucking believe you," I snapped back. "You are actually blaming me for Daddy dying. Oh my god what a pathetic lonely, old bitch you are."

"I tried to stop him, Lovella! You know I tried. You have watched me from the time that you were a little girl, trying to keep him from this. Why do you think I always insisted on having the car? I knew what he would do. If I had given him an inch he would have been dead in the gutter long before now. He would have been dead ten or fifteen years ago and you wouldn't have had your precious Daddy to moon over. Do you think I did that because it was fun? Do you think I had a good time being married to this man? I had to watch his every move to keep him from killing himself, or god forbid, somebody else. He got arrested for drunk driving when you were not even two years old. He almost ran over a child on a bicycle."

264

Confessions from the Pumpkin Patch

Her face became even more tense. Her jaw tightened, and she spoke through clenched teeth.

"I had to take responsibility because he was not going to, and when you were barely old enough to talk you started protecting him."

She hurled her hand back and forth in the air as though trying to erase the past, and then she went on.

"Do I think you killed him?" She paused and that same hand swooped back from the air and over her lips. "I don't think you drove the stake through his heart, but I think you certainly helped provide the hammer." She trembled and looked up at me.

"Oh, my god!" I thought, "She actually fucking believes this shit!"

In astonishment my jaw dropped as I was filled with shock and horror. There was a part of me that recognized she was at least partially right. I had stood between her and Daddy, and maybe by doing that, I had kept her from controlling his drinking, but I couldn't bear the thought that I might have been to blame for him dying. I thought I was protecting him because I loved him and I wanted her to leave him alone.

"You fucking bitch!" I hissed. "I loved Daddy more than anyone else in the world. I would have done anything for him, and he loved me. He was always warm and comforting to me and you were nothing but a cold, angry, pathetic block of ice."

"Well, isn't that sweet?" she growled in sarcasm. "You two were just two lovely little rotten peas in a pod."

"We are two peas in a pod," I taunted. "We love each other like you are not even capable of loving."

"Oh, for heaven's sake, Lovella!" she snapped. "He's not even your real father!"

"What? What the hell!" I shot back. "Are you going to stoop that fucking low? You want to hurt me so bad that you would tell that lie while he is lying here dying?"

"It's not a lie, Lovella." She spoke in a cold deliberate manner. "I was pregnant by another man when I married John. You can go back and check the marriage license against your date of birth. I can prove it."

"So you got pregnant before you were married," I announced. "Lots of women get pregnant before they marry. The only thing that proves is that you are not the bastion of perfection that you have always pretended to be."

"I can tell you who your real father is. You can go talk to him if you want. He might even own up to it. You can ask your Grandmother Claudella who I was dating when I got pregnant with you. John Fuchs was just a boy I knew in school. I never had any interest in him."

265

Karlyle Tomms

"Then why the hell did you marry him?" I chastised. "That doesn't even make sense."

"He had always had a crush on me and, since I was pregnant I needed a marriage to protect my reputation," she responded calmly and coldly. "Your real father was not going to marry me."

"Stop this nonsense!" I half shouted, half pleaded.

She taunted. "Your real father's name is Carl Whitmire. You might know him as Dr. Whitmire. He has a clinic there in New Bethlehem."

I feigned laughter.

"Our fucking family doctor is my biological father? Give me a fucking break, Mother."

"Where do you think you got your intelligence?" she went on. "You certainly didn't get it from John Fuchs because he didn't have it to pass on to you, and look at him. He is short and small boned. Compare that to your frame, Lovella. Have you ever thought about the fact that you don't look anything like him?"

I interrogated her. "Well, if Dr. Whitmire is my biological father, then why aren't you married to him instead of Daddy?"

"It's a long story," she said smugly. "I'll have to give you the details someday."

I felt Daddy's hand move slightly. I hadn't realized that I had held onto it through all that. I looked down at him, and he took a very deep breath with a gurgle in his lungs as he exhaled. Then he stopped breathing. I ignored Mother and began shaking him lightly at the shoulders. "Daddy! Daddy, breathe!" It was a couple of seconds at least before he took another breath. "Oh, my god, Daddy!" I shouted. "Mother, get a nurse."

"It won't do any good," Mother said tritely. Then she stepped to the door and called out in the hall, "Nurse. Nurse!"

Within a few seconds a pudgy short little nurse with permed, bleach-blond, hair came into the room and strolled over to the bed on Mother's side.

"He can't breathe!" I shouted to her.

She observed him and put a stethoscope to his chest. He continued to take one long breath every three or four seconds. The gurgle would come on exhale, and then he would stop breathing again. Each time, the breaths seemed to come further and further apart.

"I'm sorry," she said. "This is death breathing. Your father is passing away."

Tears filled my eyes and I began to tremble. I continued to hold Daddy's hand as the nurse stepped back from Mother's side. Mother placed one hand on the rail of the bed, but didn't come any closer.

Confessions from the Pumpkin Patch

"Oh, god, no!" I cried. I pleaded, "Daddy?—DADDY!"

The breaths came further and further apart. The gurgling sound seemed deafening, and in probably less than a minute more his breathing simply stopped. He became still and silent.

I waited, ten, fifteen, seconds. I watched for another breath, but it never came. The nurse leaned over the rail and placed the stethoscope back on his chest.

"I think he is gone," she said quietly. "We will have the doctor confirm." She looked up at me sweetly and said, "I'm so sorry."

"DAAADYYYY!"

I broke into heaving wales of grief. I don't know how long I cried. It felt like I couldn't stop crying. I felt like I couldn't breathe, and I couldn't make myself let go of his hand. Mother just stood there quietly, one hand resting on the bed rail. She said nothing. In my own grief, I could not tell if she shed a tear. She offered no comfort and I sobbed until I felt completely drained and exhausted.

A brief pause after my tears had quieted and she said, "Well—that's that."

I couldn't believe my ears. After nineteen years of being married to Daddy she brushed him off like a piece of lint on her shoulder. My grief switched to rage like the flip of a light switch. I grabbed the bed pan that was sitting by the night stand and flung it at her.

"YOU FUCKING BITCH!" I screamed at the top of my lungs as the bed pan, unfortunately empty, passed by her head, and clanged with metal force into the wall.

"YOU FUCKING, SELF-SERVING, SELFISH, HORRID BITCH!" I screamed as I fled the room.

Outside the room more nurses were rushing to calm the situation, leaving their posts to see what the matter was.

"GET ME THE FUCK OUT OF HERE!" I screamed at one of them and she led me quickly to the door.

I marched in angry determination to the elevator and frantically punched the button, not knowing, not caring, what Mother was saying, thinking, or doing. I only wanted out. The elevator was too damn slow. I spotted the stair exit sign nearby and made a bee-line for it. On the way down, my tears returned mixed with my rage, and I found myself hitting the wall and the rail as I descended. At the bottom of the stairs, I marched straight for the lobby, threw open the door and paced angrily through to the outside doors.

Earl was sitting in the lobby waiting for me. I didn't see him, but he saw me, as did everyone else in the lobby, when I flung open the hall doors. I

Karlyle Tomms

was neither quiet about it or apologetic. Alarmed, Earl stood up and followed me, "Lovella—honey—oh, my god!"

He followed me outside where I didn't stop. I stepped with determination around to the side of the building, having no idea where I was going, or what I was going to do.

Earl, following close on my heels, shouted. "Lovella, please stop, honey, please."

"LEAVE ME THE FUCK ALOOOOOOONNNNNNEEE!" I screamed.

He caught my sleeve. "Baby, baby, baby. Please, please, please, please stop."

I swung around and hit him, and began pounding on him with all the strength I had. "LET ME GO!" I screeched. "GODDAMN YOU! LET ME GO!"

In all the violence, he managed to put his arms around my back and pull me into him, close to his chest where I couldn't hit him any more except to reach my arms around and try to pound my fists into his back.

"Shhhhh, shhhhhh, shhhhh," he whispered as he held me tight to his chest.

Soon the violence stopped and the sobbing started again. I stood there whimpering into his chest as he held me. When the crying finally subsided, he led me to a nearby bench and we sat down. There he simply held my hand and was silent.

"I'm sorry," I said finally. "I didn't mean to go off on you like that. I know you were only trying to help."

"At that moment," he said, "the only thing you knew was hurt. It's okay."

"No, it's not okay," I said. "I shouldn't have hit you."

"Believe me, honey," he replied. "It's okay. I knew this was going to be hard for you."

"It's not just Daddy dying." I looked up at him finally and saw the tenderness in his eyes. "I feel guilty that I wasn't here, and it's her! I fucking hate her with every ounce of my being."

"I know you and your Mom have had a hard time getting along," he pleaded, "but surely you don't hate her."

"Do you know what she said after Daddy passed?" I questioned without waiting for an answer. "She said, 'Well, that's that' like she had just finished a housekeeping chore. Jesus Christ! I do fucking hate her."

"Oh, god," he sighed. "She doesn't have a clue does she?"

"A clue about what?" I snapped, "That she is a fucking bitch?"

"She doesn't have a clue how to be human," he replied. "She is so caught up in herself and her own anguish that she can't seem to understand

Confessions from the Pumpkin Patch

that other people have feelings."

It was a little comforting to know that he had this insight. I turned and stared across the parking lot and saw the sunlight glistening off windshields.

"Or maybe she is just an evil mean-spirited bitch." I said, finally.

"Now, I understand," he said after a long silence.

"Understand what?" I queried turning back to him.

After a long deep sigh he replied to my question.

"Do you remember that first time that you took me to visit your family over Thanksgiving and your father and I ended up in so many huddled conversations?"

"Yeah, I figured the two of you must have just hit it off but it was strange."

"Well, there was more to it than that," Earl went on. "Your dad must have known that he was going to die or something because he insisted on telling me your story. He made me promise that I wouldn't tell you 'til after he had died. I didn't even think you and I had dated long enough for him to even assume we would still be together, but he wanted to tell me this."

"What? What the fuck?" I exclaimed. "Is there some fucking mystery that Daddy kept from me?"

"More that the whole family kept from you," Earl replied.

"So they kept the god damned secret from me, but told my boyfriend," I ejected with sarcasm. "Doesn't that just put the fucking cherry on this shit parfait?"

"Well, *they* didn't tell your boyfriend. Your Dad did. He told me he was worried about what might happen between you and your Mom when he passed and he wanted to make sure you knew the truth. He said he was worried about both of you, and he didn't think you would get the real truth from your mother."

"Well, why the fuck didn't he tell me then instead of telling someone who, for all he knew, was going to be an ex fling in less than a year's time?"

"He was convinced that you and I would be more than a fling he said. He had always been under a lot of pressure from your mom and her family not to tell you," Earl continued, "and he wasn't sure how you would take it or how you would react. I guess he was a bit of a chicken too because he didn't want you to be upset with him."

"Oh, so he is dead now and I can't yell at him for the big, fucking, family secret!" I rolled my eyes and looked away. "Give me a fucking break!" I turned back to him. "I know Daddy is not my genetic father if

269

Karlyle Tomms

that's what you are getting at. Mother made sure that I knew that in the room up there while he was dying. She made sure to torture me with that at the very moment I was losing Daddy—yet, another reason on the long list of reasons why I hate her."

"Well, there is more to it than that," he implied.

"I also know that Dr. Whitmire is supposedly my genetic father, assuming Mother was not making that up just to hurt me. Who can tell when the bitch is telling the truth?" I got up to pace. "Who the fuck cares?" Nervous, I began talking to myself. "Where is my goddamn purse? I need a cigarette. Oh, fuck, I left it up in the room. Damn it!"

Earl reached into his shirt pocket and pulled out a battered pack of cigarettes. "I thought you might need these," he said as he fished in his pants pocket for a lighter. The first couple he pulled out of the pack were mutilated beyond any reasonable use, but he finally pulled one out that wasn't too damaged to smoke. He put it to his lips, lit it up and handed it to me. I drew a huge long drag into my lungs and let it out slowly.

"There's more to it than that," he went on. "Yes, your Daddy told me Dr. Whitmire is your biological father. Apparently your mom dated him once when she was twenty. She thought she was in love with him, but it sounds like he saw her more as just a fling. Maybe she saw him as a way to marry out of her roots. However, his family was well-to-do and didn't want him to marry someone they considered to be beneath him."

Earl stood up and walked over to face me.

"Your daddy said that your mom had always aspired to be well-to-do herself and wanted to move up in the world. She thought she could do it by marrying into money. Maybe she thought that getting pregnant would force this Whitmire fellow to marry her. It had the opposite effect. He refused to claim you as his own child and told your mother that if she tried to make this public he would accuse her of sleeping around and there would be no way to prove he was the real father. Apparently, his parents backed him up on this and told her the same thing. Her family didn't have the money to fight it, so there she was, a person who considered herself a good Christian girl on the one hand, trapped in her own manipulation on the other. Your father told me that he had always had a crush on your mom. She had been one class ahead of him in school, and they had also grown up as neighbors. He had tried many times to get her to go out with him and she would have nothing to do with him. Their families did know each other and she had not been opposed to cutting up with him, teasing him a little, but she wouldn't date him. When the pregnancy happened, she came to him and told him about it, and that her reputation would be ruined if she had a baby out of wedlock. Of course, he agreed to marry her. He said he

Confessions from the Pumpkin Patch

had been in love with her for as long as he could remember. He thought she was what he had always wanted, and he said that he would always love her. He wanted me to ask you to remember that she is your mother, and despite her problems, she has many fine qualities that deserve your respect."

"Fuck!" I exclaimed and paced a few feet away from him.

"I know. I know," he said. "I'm just trying to tell you what your dad wanted me to tell you. He assumed that your mother would tell you who your real father was when he died, and he wanted you to know how it really happened."

"John Fuchs is my REAL father," I exclaimed, "Not some goddamned sperm donor."

Earl sighed. "I agree," he said." May I continue?"

I nodded to him and puffed on my cigarette.

"Your dad told me that when you were born he could never have loved you more even if you had been his own flesh. He said that your mother adored you as well. On one hand, she wanted your love terribly, and on the other hand she resented that you had not been her ticket into the Whitmire family. Something happened to her after you were born. She kind of lost her mind, depression, or psychosis, or something. He said she took you around the neighborhood showing you off, and when people would tell her what a beautiful baby you were, she would tell them that your father was really this Whitmire guy. Your daddy said she kind of lost it. She had like a breakdown and spent some time in a mental institution. Apparently it happens to some women after childbirth that they get depressed, or crazy, or something. Anyway, while she was away, your dad and your grandparents took care of you. I think he would leave you with them when he went to work and then he would pick you up and take you home after work. When you were very little, you were around him a lot more than your mom. I guess she was hospitalized several times before you were maybe three years old. He said a couple of times she tried to kill herself. You bonded with your dad and when she came out of the institution she was angry and couldn't understand that you would cling to him instead of her."

"Oh, jeez!" I exclaimed. "I do remember when I was like three or four years old that for a long time it was just me and Daddy. And I don't remember Mother being around. I never even thought that was strange 'til now. Daddy told me she was visiting relatives in Kentucky."

I snuffed out the cigarette and asked him for another one. We sat down together on the bench and Earl continued.

"So, apparently, when you bonded with your dad, and wouldn't have much to do with your mom she just turned off and wouldn't really try to care about you. I guess before you started school she stopped having to go to the mental hospital and she was always home after that but the damage was done. She kind of resented that you were close to a man who wasn't your real father and not close to her. Anyway, so your daddy thought it was his fault that you never got along with your mom."

"It was her fucking fault we never got along, I exclaimed. "She's a bitch. I was a fucking little girl. Don't you think if she had tried just a little we might have had at least a slightly better relationship, and what is this shit about taking me to Whitmire as my doctor? Was she trying to shove me in his face so he would maybe change his mind? Apparently he just went along with it and pretended like I was any other kid to be treated for a cold."

Earl took my hand. "Your dad wanted you to try to have some understanding and compassion for her. He said you would understand if you talk to her and give her a chance."

"Oh, my fucking god!" I blurted as I tamped my cigarette out on the edge of the bench. "Give her a chance for what? A chance to be the fucking nut job that she is?"

"I'm just repeating to you what he told me," Earl replied.

"Is that it?! Give her a chance?!" I looked at him puzzled and angry.

"I don't really remember anything else I was supposed to tell you right now," he said. "I'll try to remember if there was anything else he wanted me to tell you. It seems like I've forgotten something, but I don't know." He placed his large warm hand over mine. "You want to go see if we can find your mom?"

"Hell, no. I don't," I replied. "Honestly, I don't give a shit if I never see her again. What she did up there in that hospital room was cold and heartless to me and to Daddy. She didn't care that he was dying and she didn't care that I was grieving. 'That's that,' she said, like she had just thrown out the garbage!"

"Maybe she didn't know what to say," Earl empathized. "She's your Mother. Doesn't she at least deserve a chance to explain herself?"

"You want me to fucking ask her what she meant by that?" I snarled. "I know what she meant by that. I know exactly what she meant by that. She meant that she wouldn't have to put up with Daddy's drinking any more. She meant that she wouldn't have to be constantly trying to control him. She meant that her self-proclaimed chore is over. I guess now she can devote more of her energy into trying to control me and make me into the perfect little daughter she thinks she deserves!"

"Lovella, there is going to be a lot going on over the next week or so,"

Confessions from the Pumpkin Patch

he pleaded. "Your family will be grieving. Your Grandmother Fuchs is going to be dealing with having a child precede her in death. Surely your Grandma and Grandpa Donner will have some grief for the son-in-law they had for nineteen years. Don't you think you could be civil to your mom for a little while?"

"You mean overlook her bullshit, pretend like it doesn't matter, that it doesn't hurt?"

"I guess you could put it that way," Earl reasoned. "I just don't think that your father wanted his funeral to be a fight."

Tears welled in my eyes when I saw in the distance that Mother was standing alone in front of the hospital. Earl turned to see what I was looking at. He turned back to me and took my hand. "Come on," he said, "Let's go talk to your mom."

Although I wanted to resist, to run away or maybe even to attack her, I rose with him and we walked around the building to the front where Mother was standing. As we approached, Mother looked up from fingering her purse.

"Hello Earl," she said softly and sternly without acknowledging me at all. She handed my purse to him.

"Hello, Mrs. Fuchs," he said, "I'm sorry about your loss."

He never turned loose of my hand. He gripped it tightly, but gently.

"Thank you." Mother responded. "He is being taken to Nash Funeral Home."

She then dug in her purse and pulled out car keys. She held the keys out to Earl. "Do you mind driving me there?" she questioned. "I don't feel up to driving."

"I would be happy to drive you," Earl said. "Do you mind if Lovella comes along?"

Mother responded with well-practiced flat demeanor. "Of course I don't mind if Lovella comes along. She is my daughter. I will need her input on the funeral arrangements."

Earl released my hand to take the keys and handed my purse to me.

Mother then turned on her heel and walked toward her car in the parking lot, never looking back, expecting correctly that we would follow.

273

Karlyle Tomms

Chapter 21

Sunlight glistened off the clean, polished enamel of the black hearse parked off the curb at the bottom steps of Mother's church. Daddy long ago stopped attending church, but there he was on his last day above ground finally attending church with Mother. I suppose it was only fitting that his funeral should be where Mother wanted. He would not have cared really, and since she had controlled him in life, why not in death. My part in the decisions was to pick the suit and tie that Mother insisted he wear— and insisted that I pick. She could barely ever get him to wear a suit in life, but in death she would finally dress him the way she always thought he should be dressed. He was never the man she wanted, but at least in death she could make him kind of look that way. It would have been more befitting of Daddy's style if he had been buried in a pair of khakis and a flannel shirt, but he would have given in to what she demanded anyway, so why not a suit. I didn't care. I only wanted it over.

Earl's parents had actually come down for the funeral. They took a hotel room in New Bethlehem. At first, I thought it might have been beneath them to stay at a little ramshackle hotel, but then I recalled that they didn't start rich and they had probably stayed in such accommodations before. There were no luxury hotels in New Bethlehem.

Earl and his father were civil to each other despite the conflict they had back in May. There was no mention of the argument they had. They treated each other as though it had never happened. I don't know that I could have done that. I would have had to have some word in, some dig to let the opposing party know that I remembered the injustice of disagreeing with me. I guess in that way, I was way too much like Mother.

All met on a Saturday afternoon for the funeral. Several of Daddy's friends from the factory were there with their wives. I watched them and wondered if their wives had been as displeased with their Friday night drinking as Mother had been with Daddy, but then they might not have taken it as far as Daddy did.

Mother and I stood in the foyer of the church greeting people as they came in and expressed condolences. I would rather have had a hand chopped off than to go through that, but there was the obligation for all the family that I must do it. Earl stood nearby, never letting me out of his sight, but not imposing himself either.

Confessions from the Pumpkin Patch

I gleamed a bit when I saw Gretta and her parents come up the stairs. Gretta's mom had Derrick, almost a year old now, straddling one hip. Her parents were more like aunt and uncle to me. They had known me, practically raised me since I was six years old. I met them in the middle of the foyer and held out two hands to Gretta. We touched hands and then hugged. "Oh my god I've missed you," she said.

I turned to her mom and gave her and the baby a joint hug then I touched Derrick on his little leg and said, "How's my little namesake besides growing like a weed?"

He buried his head in Mrs. Tannenbaum's shoulder as if to say, "I don't know this strange person and I'm not going to talk to her."

"Oh, he is wonderful!" exclaimed Gretta. "He is the sweetest, funniest boy."

"How's Tommy?" I questioned with concern. I knew that Gretta had moved home with her parents after Tommy was deployed to Vietnam. She had called me months earlier before I left for San Francisco tearfully exclaiming that he had been sent to combat duty.

She half smiled in an attempt to hide the worry that she wore on her face more often than she realized. "Oh, last we heard, he was maybe in someplace called Gia Binh. I don't know. We get bits and pieces, a letter once in a while. I know he is not telling me what's really going on. I know he sugarcoats everything—I just—I just pray a lot."

I squeezed her hand and hugged her. What else could I do?

I would have preferred to stay there talking to them, but I heard Mother clear her throat rather loudly and received the message clearly that I was to cut off this conversation and return to her side. I looked back over my shoulder to find her staring at me with stern displeasure.

"Maybe I can talk to you later," I said and returned to Mother's side. Gretta gave a brief salutation to Mother and then went into the sanctuary with her parents to find their seats.

I had not seen Grandma Fuchs in a very long time. She had moved to Philadelphia in the spring to live with my Uncle Raymond, Daddy's younger brother.

After having shaken the hand of some obscure stranger who was giving me some rehearsed bullshit of how sorry he was for my loss, I happened to look over and see Grandma Fuchs and Uncle Raymond coming up the front steps. She had always been thin, but she seemed even thinner. She wore a black dress with black lace around the hem and a lace overlay around her shoulders. Her thin white hair was pulled back into a French bun and she wore a little hat that would have looked a bit like a nursing cap except for the fact that it was black and also covered in black lace.

275

Karlyle Tomms

Uncle Raymond was a pudgy short little man with a round belly that sat over his belt like a sack of beans. Like Daddy, he was bald. He had thick black glasses that saddled his nose, and despite the fact that this was a funeral he wore a tan suit with white shoes. He had never married and had taken care of his mother off and on since the middle years of my youth after Grandpa Fuchs passed away. He moved to Philadelphia for a job about a year or two before I graduated high school and when Grandma Fuchs couldn't handle living alone anymore, she followed him.

Uncle Raymond held Grandma Fuchs' one arm as they walked carefully together up the steps. As I watched them approach I thought about the fact that I was her only grandchild and she must have known, like everyone in the family except me, that I was not her blood kin. Yet, like Daddy, she always treated me with the utmost love and kindness.

When they entered the foyer, Grandma Fuchs saw me and rushed across the room as best as she could at her age. She placed one hand behind my head and kissed me on the cheek. "Oh, my dear!" she said in a trembling little voice. "It is so good to see you. I have missed you very much. I only wish I could have seen you under better circumstances."

She spoke not a word about her own loss but looked me straight in the eye and said, "How are you doing with this?"

I felt the tears well in my eyes as I thought about how much love she had given me knowing all along that I wasn't even her own blood kin and how she had just lost the only child she had except Uncle Raymond. I sucked in my breath and tried to be strong. "I'm fine Grandma Doreen." I replied. "How are you?"

"Well, it's not very easy to lose your child," she said smiling sweetly with some hint of a tear in her own eyes. "But I keep myself reminded that my John is in God's hands now."

I noticed that Uncle Raymond was now standing beside me. He was slightly effeminate and light on his feet as though his girth was filled more with air than with weight.

"Hello, Lovella," he exclaimed as he spoke through his puckered little mouth. "My you have grown so much. Oh, my—what a lovely young woman you have become."

I suddenly found myself wondering if the timing and generational circumstances had been different would I ever have seen Uncle Raymond strolling down the streets of San Francisco with a tattoo over his ass that said, "Feels like pussy." I caught my drifting mind and brought it back to the moment. "Thank you, Uncle Raymond," I responded. "It is so nice to finally be grown up."

I caught a glimpse of Mother rolling her eyes at that statement. Then a

Confessions from the Pumpkin Patch

plastic smile crossed her face as she reached out a black gloved hand to Grandma Fuchs and said, "Oh, Doreen—we've lost our boy."

I thought I was going to puke. Emotional nausea filled me like a wave and I realized that there was absolutely no end to her hypocrisy. I wanted to throw another bed pan at her and would have thrown anything within my reach had it not been for my determination that I was going to address this event with dignity.

Grandma Fuchs seemed to realize the truth. I caught an interesting little smirk on her face as she heard Mother speak. She glanced over at me and back at Mother giving her a stern but gentle look. "And Lovella has lost the one *she* loved the most," said Grandma Fuchs.

"Bless us all," Mother said turning loose of Grandma Fuchs' hand with a quick little snap.

Raymond escorted Grandma Doreen Fuchs into the main hall of the church and they sat at the front in the area that had been cordoned off for family.

Eventually, there were no more people coming up the stairs. Mother, Earl, and I walked up the center aisle and took a seat next to Grandmother and Grandfather Donner who were also sitting in the family section. Earl sat on one side of me and Mother sat between me and Grandmother Donner. I could still smell breakfast bacon reeking off Grandmother Donner and imagined that she had not even bothered to change her clothes much less shower for the occasion.

Daddy's casket sat front center of the sanctuary. The fake copper lining shimmered in the overhead lights and tufted cream colored satin lined the top half of the lifted lid. Looking on, I couldn't help thinking how isolated it seemed from everything and everyone else in the building. We all sat together and Daddy lay there all alone. In many ways he had always been alone, even in his marriage. He lived in the same house with Mother. He loved her and adored her but he could never be close to her. She would never allow it.

The church at this time had yet another minister. I didn't pay any attention to him. He seemed to me to be any average looking man although I'm sure that Mother thought him to be something special. She thought any man with any kind of authority, expertise, or prosperity was something special.

The service was conducted as most any funeral service is conducted. There were songs sung by the congregation and Mother had picked some lady from the church, who sang a somewhat comical operatic version of "Nearer to Thee."

After all the hoopla and passing by the casket where Daddy lay

Karlyle Tomms

completely separated from us and from life, we crowded into cars for the processional to the cemetery where there was even more hoopla by the gravesite. When we arrived, I was escorted to the gravesite by some funeral home employee as though I would fall completely on my ass if he didn't have his hand to my elbow. Earl walked behind me. Mother was also escorted and took the opportunity to give the occasion her usual flare of high drama. Her black glove pulled a tiny white hanky to her eye where she pretended to have a tear.

We were seated in a row beneath a tent. Before us was the hole in the ground for Daddy's final rest and above it I noticed a double tomb stone already carved with Daddy's dates of birth and death on one side and Mother's date of birth with a blank left on the other side. I couldn't believe my eyes. Mother was going to play this ruse right up to the point of her own death. She was going to lay down beside him in death with the hope, I suppose, that all those left living would somehow be convinced that she actually did love him. I sat there praying to God that it would all be over quickly so that I could get the hell out of there. There was no way that it could possibly be quick enough.

Eventually the pall bearers carried Daddy's casket and set it on the apparatus designed to lower it into the grave. Then the minister gave a few more parting words. "Loving Father and husband—blah—blah—blah—a good man who would be sorely missed—blah—blah—blah—final resting place in the gentle loving arms of our Heavenly Father—etc."

I wanted so desperately to scream, "Shut the fuck up!" I wanted to grab Mother by her damn beehive and fling her into the grave. I wanted to run screaming, to somewhere, anywhere. I wanted a cigarette, a drink, some pot, acid, or arsenic. The last thing I ever wanted was to be there going through that.

As the casket was being lowered into the grave, the minister decided there needed to be one last prayer. I couldn't take it anymore. I didn't wait for the prayer to finish. I stood up and marched with rapid determination back toward Earl's VW bus which he had parked at the edge of the cemetery. I heard Mother call after me with a whisper yell in the middle of the prayer, "Lovella! Sit down!" I wanted to turn around and scream, "Fuck you! You two faced hypocritical cunt!" But I said nothing. I simply kept marching across the cemetery stopping at one point to pull off those damned high heels and fling them each in different directions.

Earl followed me silently, saying nothing, making no effort to stop me. When I reached the bus I tried to open the side door, and when it wouldn't budge I pounded the bus with my fists and leaned my head up against it, sobbing. Then I felt a big gentle hand on my shoulder. I turned and Earl

278

Confessions from the Pumpkin Patch

pulled me to him. I sobbed into his chest and he held me closely, stroking my hair but saying nothing. He didn't try to quiet me. He simply held me and let me cry. When at last I had cried enough, I pulled back and looked up at him. "I want to go home," I said.

"Sure, fine, Honey," he said. "Your Mother will probably be back there shortly too."

"No, I don't mean that," I exclaimed.

I had been thinking of our apartment back at State College. It had become home to me. It was more of a home to me than anything that bitch had ever provided. However, in that moment, I had forgotten that it was gone.

I took a flabbergasted breath. "I'm sorry," I said. "I was talking about the apartment back at State College. I guess I forgot that we don't have it anymore."

"Don't you want to go back to your home and spend some time with your mom before we think about what's next?"

"No! I don't want to be around her any more than I absolutely have to and that's not my home any more. She never gave me a real home!" After snapping at him I felt guilty and softened my tone. "I guess we don't know what's next, do we?"

I caught a glimpse from the corner of my eye and saw that Gretta was walking up to us. She had followed me from the tent, apparently leaving her parents to take care of the baby.

"Honey, are you alright?" she asked on her approach.

I didn't know if I was alright or not. The heat of the day had become unbearable. I reached out and took her hand when she was close enough.

"I'm fine," I said somewhat lying. "I had just taken all the bullshit I could stand in one day. I just had to get away from it."

"Listen," she said glancing back at her mother who was standing at a distance with the baby asleep in her arms. "Why don't you guys come by our house for a little while, take a load off, get away from family and just give yourselves some time to chill?"

"Oh, god! That sounds wonderful!" I exclaimed. "Earl, do you mind?" I looked back at him and questioned even though I already knew it would be fine with him.

"Sure, no problem," he said.

"Wonderful," Gretta continued. "You guys can meet us there in twenty or thirty minutes, okay?"

I turned back to Earl and looked up at him longingly. "Thank you." I sighed.

"You want to get your shoes?" he inquired as he glanced back across

279

the cemetery.

"Fuck the shoes!" I said. "Let's go."

"Let me go tell my mom and dad that I'll call them later at the hotel," he said. "I'll be right back."

Earl crossed the lawn to meet his parents. By this time, the ceremonies had completed and everyone was crossing back toward parking. Earl spoke to his parents briefly and then trotted back across the lawn to me.

"Get in," he said, opening the bus front door for me—and soon we were gone.

Tommy and Gretta had a modest but nice little house. We passed it on the way to the Tannenbaum home. The house was a little post war cracker box painted a light blue with white trim. The postage stamp lawn had a few flowers left from summer in the beds on either side of the steps, but most had begun to brown either from the heat or anticipation of the coming cold.

We pulled up to the curb in front of the Tannenbaum house and in short order they arrived. Gretta took Derrick while her Dad unlocked the front door. The baby's toys were scattered here and there in the floor. Derrick, having awakened from his nap was squirming to be let loose. Gretta sat him on the floor and he went waddling off toward one of the toys. She sat on the floor beside him and began to entertain him with a tiny stuffed giraffe

"Let me get you some tea," Mrs. Tannenbaum said as she departed for the kitchen.

Mr. Tannenbaum motioned to the couch. "Sit down and get comfortable," he said as he aimed toward a side chair. "Can you believe this heat?" he said when his butt hit the cushion.

"Yeah," I said, "I thought I was going to suffocate before that crap was over."

Mrs. Tannenbaum called out from the kitchen, "Anyone want lemon?"

We glanced around at each other continuing the question with body language. I shook my head no, and so did Earl. Mr. Tannenbaum shouted back, "No, Baby Doll, just plain iced tea for everyone."

"Well, I've already put some lemon in mine," she shouted back. Then, shortly after, she returned with serving tray in hand. We each took a glass and began to sip.

"Damn, I'm parched," I said. "Thank you."

"Jesus, honey," Gretta released as she got up and moved to the chair next to me. "Are you sure you're alright?" She reached over with a warm smile and touched my hand.

"Oh, you mean besides the fact that I would like to slit my mother's

Confessions from the Pumpkin Patch

throat and throw her in a well?" I replied with sarcasm. "Other than that, I guess I'm okay." I had not had a chance to talk to Gretta and fill her in on all that had happened.

"Well, I know you hate her, but I hope you don't hate her that much," she pleaded.

"Oh, it's fun to imagine," I smirked. "But I don't look good in shackles. There are so many more flattering accessories."

"Your mother told me a few weeks ago that you were spending the summer in San Francisco," Gretta ran her finger around the rim of her glass. "I hope you had a nice time."

I looked at Earl and he gave me a puzzled look then smiled.

"I guess you could say we had a very interesting time," I said. "I wish I had known that Daddy was so sick though. I probably never would have gone. Mother tried to tell me he was sick before I left, but he denied it and I didn't believe her. Then I was so pissed at her for insisting that she wouldn't *let* me go, I didn't call her all summer."

"You got back before your Daddy passed through—right?" There was a hesitation in her voice. I think she understood the guilt I was feeling.

"Just barely," I went on, tears welling up a little. "Daddy died in less than an hour after we got here. Earl dropped me off directly at the hospital doors." My voice trembled. "I might as well have not gotten here before he died. There was nothing left of him. He couldn't respond at all and I doubt he even knew I was there." A tear rolled down my cheek and I wiped it with my opposite thumb.

"Oh, honey," she soothed. "You know your daddy knew you were there. The two of you were too close for him not to feel your presence."

"Mother was horrible!" I continued. "She took the opportunity to tell me that Daddy is not my real father and that my real father is Dr. Whitmire. I mean how fucked up is that?"

Immediately I realized that I had just used profanity in front of her parents and looked up embarrassed. "I'm sorry," I said glancing back and forth between Mr. & Mrs. Tannenbaum.

"Sweetheart," Mrs. Tannenbaum smiled lovingly. "Profanity is the language of the heart. Sometimes it is the only thing that lets us express what we need."

My tears began to flow openly.

"Oh my god!" Gretta exclaimed. "Dr. Whitmire, your family doctor?" She motioned to her mom who left the room to return in a moment with a damp wash cloth. The cool cloth felt good against my face. Earl wrapped a comforting arm around me and everyone let me grieve. Thank god the baby was playing with one of his toys and didn't really know what was

Karlyle Tomms

going on.

I vented through my sobs. "Even if it is true, why would she even tell me that, especially as Daddy was lying there taking his last breaths? And, Jesus! How fucked up is it that the doctor she took me to for my whole life might be my real father! He had to have known. Earl, tell them." I nudged him on the leg.

Earl hesitantly began to tell them what he had told me outside the hospital. "Well, Lovella's dad—John—spoke to me at Thanksgiving and told me about this. He told me not to tell Lovella, that he didn't want her to know 'til after he was gone. I think I was supposed to have told her before her mother did. I don't think he wanted her mother telling her this stuff, and he wanted to make sure that she knew he loved her. I guess I messed up not telling her first."

"You didn't know," I exclaimed, defending him. Then I turned back to Gretta, "And how fucked up is it that Daddy pulls Earl aside to tell him the first damn time he met him and he never told me?!" The anger moved back to grief and I wailed, "He could have told me himself." Then the grief switched back to anger. "GODDAMN IT! HE COULD HAVE TOLD ME HIMSELF!" I screamed and slammed my fist against my leg with the wash cloth clinched in my hand.

Immediately, Derrick burst into tears frightened by the display. My anger switched just as quickly to compassion. "Oh, no—poor baby—,"I pleaded as I took a step toward him to give comfort. This only made him wail louder and Gretta rushed to pick him up.

"It's alright—it's alright, sweetheart," she cooed to him as she bounced him gently on her hip. "It's alright."

Compassion switched to guilt and the tears returned. "I'm sorry," I pleaded. "I'm so sorry. I didn't mean to scare him."

"It's alright." Gretta turned to comfort me. "Honey, don't worry. Sit down."

She made a quick glance to Mr. Tannenbaum and said, "Daddy, would you take the baby to the other room for a while?" Earl had stood up to catch my arm. I suppose fearing that I might lose control. Then, his warm hand moved to rest between my shoulder blades. Mr. Tannenbaum quietly took the baby from her arms and went toward the back of the house. Earl and I sat back down.

"I'm sorry," I cried.

"Honey—honey—listen." Gretta sat back down close enough to pat my knee. "Derrick is fine. He just got a little scared. It happens. Don't worry about it."

"Losing Daddy is bad enough," I sobbed. "But then that fucking evil

Confessions from the Pumpkin Patch

bitch has to lay this shit on me, and then she fucking expects me to come to the funeral and pretend like everything is just peachy! I tried—I don't know why I tried, but I tried to hold it together."

"Thank god you don't have to hold it together now," Gretta soothed. "You just let it out, honey. I want to hear everything you have to say."

I looked up at her astounded by her understanding. "You are the best friend anyone could ever have," I sobbed.

She smiled a comforting smile and said, "I'd better be a good friend. You might beat me up again. Besides, you taught me how to cuss."

I almost laughed. "Thank you," I said. "Thank you for giving me a place to let go."

"I suspect the letting-go won't be for a while," she replied. "I'm just giving you a place to rest. Speaking of which, where are you staying?"

I glanced at Earl. "I don't know. Earl's parents got a hotel room and paid for an extra room for him. As much as it killed me to do it, I spent the last few days since Daddy died with the bitch from hell to *make plans.*" I made quotation marks in the air with my fingers and slurred the last two words with sarcasm. I took a deep breath and went on. "I can't go back there," I said. "I just can't. As far as I am concerned, I never want to see her again. I don't really have any place to go. Earl's father stopped paying for the apartment. I haven't even thought about college. I should probably be registered by now if it's not too late. I guess I could move back in the dorm, but I don't know where that leaves us." I placed a hand on Earl's leg.

"We'll figure something out," Earl said giving a quick hug to my side.

"Well, you are welcome to stay here for the night," Gretta invited as she glanced back at her mom for reassurance. "We could sleep together just like old times when we were kids."

"That reminds me," Earl said. "I told the parents I would call them back at the hotel. Do you mind if I borrow your phone?"

"No problem," said Gretta, "It's in the kitchen mounted on the wall by the refrigerator." She pointed and Earl followed the direction of her finger.

When Earl had left the room, Gretta turned back to me and said, "Lovella, I'm more worried about how your heart is than where you are going to stay. I know all this simply had to have thrown you for a loop."

"Well, you know what they say about that which doesn't kill us," I said.

"It makes us stronger," she replied.

"It leaves scars," I said with a smirk.

"Honey, I have no doubt that you are going to have scars from this," she replied. "If anything, that's what I'm really worried about."

"I'll be fine," I went on. "Nothing that some alcohol and a few cigarettes won't fix. Jeez, can you believe I haven't smoked through all

283

this? I might have had one or two when I was staying at Mother's. I mean, if I was going to smoke it would have been there. I don't know what has happened. I just find myself disgusted by them all of a sudden. It's like of all the things that have happened and all the hurt I've felt for the last week—I get upset and think I want a cigarette. Then I take a few puffs and it's like I'm disgusted. I think to myself—that's not going to help. I'm almost as mad at the cigarettes as I am at Mother. I don't know why. I get angry when I try to smoke. Then, when I put it out, I'm mad. It's like I'm trying to smash it into the ash tray like it is something I want to hurt. I just don't feel like I can smoke anymore."

"Well, that's a reaction I never thought I would ever see," Gretta responded. "Maybe it's a good thing."

Earl returned from the kitchen. "Lovella, my parents offered to get a room for you too. They don't want us in the same room because we aren't married but they said they would be happy to get you a room at their hotel. We can probably figure out something else over the next couple of days. They are going back to Bradford Woods tomorrow, but they will be happy to pay for a couple of days for us."

"That's very sweet of them," I said. "Gretta, I hope I won't hurt your feelings if I take Earl's parents up on their offer."

"Oh, hell no. honey," she exclaimed. "A hotel bed has got to be more comfortable. We just might not fit in my bed as well as we did when we were little girls."

Earl continued standing. "Ah, I need to talk to my parents before they go back tomorrow. I would kind of like to go. Lovella, you can stay here and I'll come back later in the evening to pick you up."

"Oh that would be great!" Gretta interjected.

"That would be wonderful," I parroted. "What time would you be back to pick me up?"

"Nine or nine thirty sound all right to you?" Earl questioned.

Gretta and I glanced at each other and both said, "That's fine," at the same time She laughed at our synchronicity and reached out to pat my arm.

"I'll walk you to the VW," I said rising from my seat.

We walked out the door and down the walk to the curb. Earl turned and hugged me. "You going to be okay?" he questioned continuing the lingering hug.

"I'll be fine," I said, not breaking the hug with my cheek feeling warm and comfortable against his chest. "It's just that there's a lot to figure out now. I kind of wasted the summer not really paying any attention to going back to school and now I don't even know if it is too late to register for fall classes. I don't have much time to waste on that. I mean, I've got to get

Confessions from the Pumpkin Patch

with it first thing tomorrow and call the university. If I can't go back to school, I don't know what I'm going to do. I couldn't stand staying here or living with Mother. I might have to see if I can find a job somewhere."

He sighed and said, "We'll see."

He held me arms-length from him and looked at me. "Right now," he said, "you need to go back in there and have a much overdue visit with Gretta. I'm kind of in the same pickle where school is concerned but I'll bet Dad can pull some strings to get me in even if they have closed registration. He might be able to pull some strings for you too. That's why I'm going to talk to him. I'm going to have to eat crow, but the bottom line is that I need to finish college and if that means kissing the old man's ass, I guess I have to go back to kissing ass. We can't roam the country and live in the bus forever. Sooner or later we have to come back down to earth." He then nudged me toward the house and said, "Go on. We'll talk more when I come back to pick you up tonight."

I looked at him in wonder, not really knowing what to say, wondering what happened to the ugly hippie who took me to San Francisco a couple of months ago. Finally, I nodded in agreement and turned to walk back in the house. I was almost up the front steps when I heard him call, "Lovella."

I turned to see him turning back and coming around to the front of the VW bus. He looked down at the ground and then back up at me. He half smiled, hesitated and then said, "Do you think we can put this thing with Screech behind us?"

I had not thought about it in days. I had been so caught up in the whole event of Daddy dying that I hadn't even recalled much about San Francisco.

"Do you?" I said, stalling as I searched my soul for how I really felt.

"I know I'm damn sure going to try," he said. "I want to try, Lovella. I want us to be us again."

"I'm not very good at predicting the future," I said as I grabbed hold of the porch post for support. "But I'll try too."

He looked around as though searching for something to say, but in the end he said nothing. Finally he gave me a brief little wave, got in the bus, and drove away.

I stood there and watched the VW disappear up the street asking myself, Can I put it behind me? Can I pretend that this hasn't changed everything?

Karlyle Tomms

Chapter 22

Earl's father did pull some strings that got us both enrolled again for fall semester. However, the deal was that we both had to live in the dorms and Earl kept the VW for his transportation. His father sold the Ferrari. By early September we were both getting settled in for the next year of classes. The good news is that I didn't have Marcy for a roommate any more. My new room partner was a chubby, somewhat homely girl named Marlene Crenshaw from Dillsburg, a little town only two or three times bigger than New Bethlehem, which isn't saying much. Marlene was much to my preference. She was a quiet girl, an English Literature major, who kept her nose in a book even more than I did. It seemed her biggest delight was lying on her bed nibbling snacks and reading. The first time she met Earl and found out that his family owned Chum Snacks I thought she was going to fall to the ground and start kissing his feet. Earl took the hint and every time he went home he brought back multiple bags of crackers, nuts, and chips for Marlene.

I didn't get to see Earl nearly as often as I wanted. I missed living with him. I missed domestic life, cooking for him, and cuddling up on the couch together after dinner to watch a sitcom on TV. Earl poured himself into his studies that last year. It suddenly seemed as though he had started wanting to please his father.

On a Friday night in October we had made plans to go out for dinner. Earl was picking me up at five o'clock and we had made arrangements for me to wait for him by a tree on the northwest side of the girls' dorm parking. It was a little chilly that day and Earl was a bit late. I had been out there five minutes early and within a few minutes of standing in the cold wind, I was pulling my coat up around my collar. I was standing there prancing up and down trying to keep warm and watching the parking lot for the VW when I was startled by a loud and somewhat threatening voice behind me.

"Boooh Haaaaa!"

I screamed and jumped half out of my skin. I lurched to take off running across the parking lot when a hand caught my arm from behind and twirled me around. There was Earl standing in front of me laughing.

"Earl Titwallow! You asshole!" I exclaimed. I swatted him hard across the arms and chest with open hands.

286

Confessions from the Pumpkin Patch

It only took a moment for me to catch myself and realize what I was looking at. There was no more long hair! He was as clean shaven and well groomed as any business man. I stopped hitting him and stepped back with my mouth wide open in amazement.

"What the hell!" I exclaimed. "Who are you and what have you done with my ugly hippie?"

He laughed. "I wanted to surprise you."

"Well you could have surprised me without giving me a heart attack!" I snapped back.

"You like it?" he questioned as he smoothed one hand over his ear to the back of his head.

"Yeah, you look nice," I said. "But I never thought I would ever see you with short hair. What in the world ever made you want to cut your hair?"

"Come on, let's get warm," he said as he took my arm and led me back in the direction from where he had approached. The VW had been parked behind us and was still running.

"I was just thinking if I'm going to be finishing up a business degree this year, maybe I need to look a little more like a business man. I mean if I want to get a job when I get out of school. I have to be realistic. If my Dad and I get into it again and I don't end up working for the company, I'll have to get a job and who is going to hire me if I don't look the part?"

"It would be a shame if someone turned you down just because of how you look," I argued. "That wouldn't be fair. What about your talent and your intellect?"

"Hey, I agree with you," he responded. "But the truth is we live in a world full of prejudice and until the time comes that people look beyond the cover of the book to the content, we have to play the game. I have to give them an appealing book cover to even get them to look at the content."

"What happened to physics?" I questioned.

He opened the passenger side door and I got in, glad that he had left it running to keep the heater going. I felt immediately better just to have the wind chill off my face.

"I still like physics," he said as he closed the door. He came around to the driver's side and got in the van. "I like physics," he continued. "But I really don't think I have the talent it takes to land a job in physics that would pay my bills. I have to be realistic and realistic may mean that I end up doing what dad always wanted me to do."

"Do you think you can be happy doing that?" I pondered.

He put the VW in gear and pulled away from the curb. "I think happy is something I have to decide for myself. I don't think happy is going to

287

come from having things or doing things. I think happy is going to come from the decision and practice of keeping a positive attitude."

"Well, yeah. That makes sense I guess." I fiddled in my purse for a cigarette having gone back to enjoying a smoke once I was back in school. "But don't you think that having things and doing things at least contributes to the process?"

"It is a whole lot easier to face your problems with money in your pocket than it is to face them without it. There is no doubt about that," he went on. "But, ultimately, happiness comes down to accepting what you can't change and making the best of what you have."

"Damn! How profound," I said, with a slight hint of sarcasm as I pulled the cigarette and lighter from my purse. "Have you been studying the Buddha or something?"

"Well, more than anything, I've just been thinking about it all," he said ignoring my jab. He looked here and there paying attention to traffic and watching for his turns. "But—well, I do read a lot of philosophy and stuff along with other things, and I guess maybe I pick up things here and there from what I read."

"You're changing," I said as I lit the cigarette and cracked the window a touch to let the smoke drift outside.

"Maybe I'm changing in some ways, staying the same in others," he said, turning onto a now very familiar street. "Maybe I'm finding out who I was all along."

"Well, I've heard you say this kind of shit before," I said. "It's just that now you seem to be using it to justify pleasing your dad instead of using it to justify why you need to be free from the conservative industrial complex and the war machine. It's interesting. You used to argue so vehemently for standing up against *The Man*."

"I still believe in my principles, Lovella," he said. "But maybe I was standing up for my principles the wrong way. I mean, this summer, and this whole involvement with Screech kind of scared me in a way. I kind of need to turn away from that a little. Just because I wear a suit and work for The Man doesn't mean I'm giving up who I am. Besides, maybe I can work to change things from the inside, instead of trying to knock down the front door of the establishment. Maybe I could have more success at creating change if I sneak in the back door."

I looked at him for a moment trying to take in what I was hearing. I didn't really know how to respond. I finished the last drag of my cigarette as Earl pulled up to the curb in front of The Finer Diner. It was where we had our first dinner together and it continued to be one of our favorite hangouts. We walked hand in hand down the sidewalk and into the diner

Confessions from the Pumpkin Patch

where we slid into a booth near the door.

"I've come to love this place," I said as I took off my coat and tossed it over to the other end of the booth seat. "I think I like it more every time I come here."

"It grows on you," he said as he did the same with his coat. "Good food and service usually will win you and keep you."

It was not long before our bleach-blond, gum chewing waitress was there with the menus. She took the drink orders and pranced away in her colorful little uniform. We chit-chatted over the food choices for a while then placed our orders when she came back with the drinks. It was always fun to hear the waitress shout the orders to the grill cook in their own special diner language.

We sat there sipping on our sodas waiting for the order to arrive and I began to muster my courage to tell him what I had been needing to tell him for several of weeks. He was going on about some of the classes he was taking this year and how economics was, in some ways, similar to physics and more interesting than he had given it credit when I cut in on him.

"Earl," I said nervously stirring my soda with the straw. "We need to talk."

This stopped him in his tracks. He fell completely silent and he looked at me intently. "Oh god," he sighed. "You're breaking up with me. I know what 'we need to talk' means."

"No, it doesn't mean that," I said thinking he was being silly. "I have something I need to tell you."

"Is something wrong?" he bantered. "Something the matter with the family? Is your grandmother okay?"

"Would you just shut up and let me talk!" I said tersely, becoming a little irritated.

"I'm sorry. Okay. What?" He reached his hand across the table and took hold of mine.

I took a deep sigh, glanced out the window and back at him. "I'm late."

"Late?" he pondered. "Late for what?"

"I'm late you idiot!" I snapped. "Think—I'm late for my period."

His face went pale and a collection of emotions danced across his affect. "Oh—," he said finally. "Okay—well—humph—I don't know what to say." He sat for a moment and pondered. "So, we'll be having a baby?— you and I are going to have a baby—cool! That's cool!" His eyes rolled around as he did the math in his head. "Wow!—Ummmm—along about May, June?"

"Try early April," I said.

289

Karlyle Tomms

"April?" Confusion hit him. He thought I must have just missed my period and that I must be maybe about six weeks along.

I didn't wait for him to comment. "Earl, I haven't had a period for two months. This is the third time I've missed."

"Third time!" he snapped. "Why the hell didn't you tell me?"

"A lot of reasons," I said. "I wanted to be sure that it wasn't some fluke that I just happened to miss a period and maybe my cycle would start up again the next month, but—I was also scared."

"Scared?" he questioned. "Scared of what? You don't have to be scared of anything. You know I would take responsibility. You know I'm not going to leave you hanging with anything like that. You know me better than that, Lovella. I'll take care of you and the baby."

"That's not what I'm scared of," I returned.

The waitress brought our food and we began preparing ourselves to eat, moving the utensils around and placing our napkins. Earl began squirting catsup on the edge of his plate for his fries.

"Earl, do the math," I continued after the brief interruption. "You know when I got pregnant. It had to have been the end of July."

"So," he said as he dipped his fries into catsup and started to eat.

"Think about it," I continued. "What were we doing at the end of July just before we came back to Pennsylvania—what if the baby isn't yours?"

He stopped in mid-chew, frozen in time for a moment.

I continued. "What if this is Screech's baby?" I said staring straight at him.

"Ah—well—jeez," he stammered. "That makes it a bit more complicated doesn't it? I mean there are a lot more factors to consider. Screech would surely want to be a part of the baby's life if he knew it was his baby. At least, I assume he would."

"What do you think that would do to us, Earl? You and me?" I pressed him. "What do you think would happen to us if this is Screech's baby?"

"Goddamn!" he spouted with a full mouth as he put his burger back down on the plate suddenly seeming surprised. "Oh, shit. I don't know what it does to us."

He continued to chew trying to clear his mouth so he could talk. Finally he swallowed.

"I don't want it to do anything to us. I want us to be fine. I love you and I want to be with you, but if this is Screech's baby there is going to be some shit hit the fan, Lovella, with my family and yours, and probably also with Screech."

"Exactly," I said picking at my food, "and also with society. That's one of the reasons I've hesitated talking about it. I've been really scared about

Confessions from the Pumpkin Patch

what it might mean. I wanted to think about it. I mean, we have options. One option might be for me to drop out of college, go away, and have the baby somewhere, put it up for adoption, and then come back and pretend nothing ever happened. We could do that—maybe with your parent's help. We could do that and then go on with our lives."

"Oh crap, Lovella!" he popped. "Could you do that to your own baby? Could you throw away your child? Could you ever forget about it, knowing that you had a child out there somewhere? Wouldn't you wonder about that child, if it is safe, or loved?"

"I wouldn't be throwing away my child, Earl." I leaned my elbows on the table, folded my fingers together and rested my head on them for a moment. "I would be giving my child a chance," I whispered, then suddenly fearful that someone might overhear. "I don't know how to give a black child what it needs. Wouldn't the baby need to be raised by a black family; someone who understands what it means to be black, a family that knows how to deal with being black in a world of prejudice? I don't know how to deal with that."

"Screech's family is out of the question for adoption," he insisted bluntly.

I knew he was recalling, as was I, how terribly Screech had been abused as a child.

"Hell, for that matter, I'm not sure that Screech is not out of the question as well."

I hadn't even gone to the subject of Screech's family, or Screech for that matter. I had never thought about giving the child to one of its own biological kin. The stories Screech had told about them frightened me about ever giving them a chance to raise another child. I had figured I would go away, adopt the baby out, and maybe never even tell Screech. However, when I thought about it, I wondered how Screech would feel if he ever happened to find out that he had a child and was never brought into the conversation. I had such conflict inside me and such an incredible mix of emotions.

"Would it be fair for us to judge that?" I returned. "If Screech is the baby's father, would it be fair to shut him out? I admit I have thought about never letting him know, but would that be fair?"

"I just don't know how emotionally stable Screech is," Earl responded. "And, Lovella, you really don't know. He is much more into drugs than you ever realized. I love him. Part of me has to admit on some level that I was in love with him, but he's on a collision course with hell, Lovella, and he was starting to take me there with him. I was starting to do drugs way too much myself. In some ways, I'm really glad that we got away from him."

Earl reached thumb and forefinger to each eye to wipe back brief tears. He paused and collected himself.

"I don't think it would be fair for Screech to have anything to do with raising a child. I don't think he could handle it, and I don't think I could handle it if I thought the baby wasn't safe."

"That doesn't mean that he doesn't have a right to know about his own child does it?" I questioned.

"And if he knows about his child, then what is he going to do? Take legal action or something? Tie us up in court?"

He paused.

"You know, we are assuming a lot here. I fucked you a lot more than Screech ever did. You had sex with him one time. It is much more likely that you are carrying my baby instead of his."

"I know," I said. "I know the chances are slim, but we don't really know for sure do we? We won't know 'til the baby is born."

"So, what if you go away to have the kid somewhere and we have made arrangements to give it up for adoption— what if it's my kid?" he questioned. "I don't want my kid being given up for adoption. If this is my child, I want it. I don't want to think that I might have a kid out there somewhere that someone else is raising."

"People do it all the time, Earl," I argued. "At least if a child is adopted it is going to a home where the parents want it instead of coming into a situation where it messes things up and it is just going to be a problem. If I have this baby, I am not going to be able to finish my degree. I'll be stuck being a mother instead of having the career I want."

He sat completely still for a moment and pondered what I just said.

"Problem—a situation where it is just going to be a problem—not a person—a problem," he repeated. "What—if—this—is—my—baby? God forbid, I don't want my kid to be the only white child in a black family."

"We have to do something, Earl! We can't just sit back and do nothing!" I said, exasperated.

"You're not sure you even want this baby, are you?" he said softly.

"I'm not sure, Earl," I pleaded. "If I have a black child, how am *I* going to be treated? How will the child be treated? What will it be like for a black child growing up in a mean and prejudiced white world where nobody really tries to understand?"

My eyes filled with tears.

"What will it be like if I can't understand?"

"And if it is my child and you don't have to deal with any of that, then what?" he asked.

Confessions from the Pumpkin Patch

"Then I don't know," I said. "I am so confused and mixed up over this. It is not that I don't want to have your baby, Earl, I just don't want to have your baby *now*."

"So," he argued back. "When you adopt a child out, don't you have to make all the arrangements before the child is born? I mean, pick the family, or the family picks your baby, or something? What if you make arrangements for a black family to have this baby and it ends up being my baby? It's the flip side of the coin, isn't it? And, if the adopting parents aren't involved on the front end, where does the baby go? To an orphanage? I don't want my kid going to an orphanage, Lovella, not when there are two perfectly good parents to raise it. I don't want Screech's kid going to an orphanage either—not when there are two perfectly good parents to raise it. I don't like it, Lovella. I just don't like this adoption thing."

"So, what's the other option?" I pleaded.

"We get married," he asserted. "We get married right here this week, as soon as we can get the license. We get married and we keep the baby no matter who the father is. If it is my baby, wonderful! If it is Screech's baby, well—I love the baby's father and I will think of it as my own. I will love this baby like it came from my own loins even if for some reason it didn't."

"And if this is Screech's baby, what do you think that is going to be like?" I pressed. "How is your family going to react? I don't give a shit about how my family is going to react, they can all go to hell as far as I'm concerned, but how is *your* family going to react? How do you think your ultra-conservative father is going to respond when he comes to the hospital thinking he is going to be passing down his important lineage to another generation only to find out— whoops!?"

"I don't know how he is going to react," Earl responded calmly and precisely. "But I do know how I'm going to react. I know that I am going to finish my degree in May and, whether my father is with me or not, I'll have something I can use to parley a job sufficient to raise my family and I'm willing to do that. I will dig ditches if that's what it takes to put a roof over my family's head. I've decided, Lovella. I've decided right here tonight. I want this baby! I want this baby no matter what. The question is do you want this baby?"

I realized that I was suddenly feeling very sad. I found myself pondering his question, confronting in myself prejudices I had grown up with, mind-sets about boundary and place and how race fits into all that. I wanted to tell myself that I was not prejudiced, but I couldn't. In my heart of hearts, deep down in my soul despite all my preaching, and despite all my determination to see every human being as equal to myself, I found a fear. I found a fear that I might think of my own child as deserving less because of color. I found a fear of having people shout at me, judge me, condemn me, and call me names because I had a black child. More than that, I found a fear of how people might judge and condemn my child. I found myself vacillating back and forth in my emotions to what a happy and prosperous life I might have if this was indeed Earl's child, but how that would likely mean sacrificing my education and career. I knew in that case, that Earl's father would try to hand this baby the world on a silver platter. I thought about how wonderful that would be, but what if this wasn't Earl's baby—what then? Was I prepared to love a black child and stand by that child no matter what, even if society and our own families turned against us because of it? I wasn't sure. I couldn't be sure. I looked everywhere except at Earl and finally, I said, "Yes—I want this baby."

"No matter what?" he confirmed.

I sighed deep. "No matter what," I responded hesitantly.

Earl got up, came around the table to my side. He kneeled down next to the booth, reached out and took my hand. "Lovella Fuchs—will you take me, Earl Titwallow, as your lawfully wedded husband? Will you marry me?"

His behavior had drawn attention and we suddenly had an audience of the entire diner. I looked around feeling sheepish and shy—strange and unusual emotions for me. I felt my face flush with embarrassment. I looked at him and gave a hesitant smile.

Yes—," I said at last. "I will marry you."

The diner roared with cheers and applause. Earl reached out his hands motioning for me to stand up. When I did he swooped me up into his arms, twirled me around and kissed me. He sat my feet back to the floor and looked lovingly into my eyes. I found myself thinking: "Oh, shit! What have I done?"

I did not sleep that night, not because I was a blushing bride excited about planning my wonderful wedding but because I don't think I really wanted to get married at all. This was not because I didn't love Earl or because I didn't want him to be my husband. If the circumstances had been different, if I had not been pregnant, and it had been another year into our relationship, I might have been that blushing bride, but everything had changed.

Not only was there the potential that I was pregnant by a man other than Earl, it was the same man that Earl had fallen in love with. He admitted to me that night that he was in love with Screech. It might have been one thing if his involvement with Screech had been just sex, but it was more

Confessions from the Pumpkin Patch

than that. I could understand sex for sex sake. I might even have been able to understand sex for sex sake when it was a betrayal of the monogamous relationship I had with Earl up to that point. However, I was having trouble wrapping my mind around Earl being in love with Screech and in love with me at the same time. Maybe it was the sensibilities taught by my upbringing, but I had not considered that someone could be fully in love with more than one person at a time. It was obvious that Earl was in love with me too, but it seemed as though he was looking at this baby as though it was the love child he conceived through his affair with Screech. I just happened to be the one who was carrying it. In a way, I felt like a surrogate giving birth to someone else's child. I was very confused, mixed up, not only with my own feelings, but mixed up about what all this meant to Earl.

After lying there staring at the ceiling listening to Marlene snore for much too long, I sat up and dug through my purse for a cigarette. No one was supposed to smoke in the dorm rooms, but at that point I fucking didn't care. I fiddled in my purse, mostly feeling my way around, but also using the faint street light through the dorm window as my guide. Finally, I pulled out my cigarettes and lit one. I sat there on the edge of the bed, smoking and staring at the misty hint of light coming through the window.

Thinking, thinking, thinking, I was trying to make sense of it all and what it would mean for my life. Earl had said that he would call me the next day and we could define how we wanted to approach the whole marriage thing. We were supposed to go see his parents and talk it out. Before I lay back down, I determined that there had to be some rules. We couldn't just go on like mice in a maze turning this way or that to see where it would lead. We had to have some regulations about how we would relate to each other and to our child. Even if the baby had been fathered by Screech, it was still going to be our child. There was so much to think about that I didn't want to think about, but there was no way out. There was no such thing as not facing the problem that was before us.

Finally, very late into the morning, I felt a little drowsy and drifted off into a light sleep. I awoke not two hours later to the sound of Marlene milling around the room preparing to go take her shower. It was a Saturday, so no class, but she had an annoying habit of getting up early regardless of the day. There was no such thing as sleeping in with Marlene. She was a seize-the-day kind of a girl. At that point, I felt more like a seizure of the day kind of girl.

Marlene noticed that I had roused awake to look at her.

"Hey, sleepy head," she smiled way too cheerful. "The day's a-wasting. Don't you have something wonderful to do today?"

Karlyle Tomms

"No, not really," I mumbled through sleep tongue.

"Well, I am going to go downtown and see what shopping damage I can do with the fifty dollars my parents sent me this week," she beamed. "Want to go?"

"No, thank you," I garbled as I rolled away from her and buried my head in the pillow.

I didn't hear her leave and the next thing I knew someone was knocking at the door.

"Lovella," the girl's voice rang out. "You have a phone call."

"Fuck!" I exclaimed as I threw my face into the pillow.

"Lovella? Are you in there?" the voice chimed.

I used all the strength I could muster to yell back. "Be right there." Then I dragged my led body out of the bed, donned a robe and slippers to stagger down the hall to the phone."

The phone was dangling against the wall. I picked it up and gave a sleepy, "Hello?"

"Hey, you ready to go?" I heard Earl's voice call back from the receiver.

"Go where?" I responded.

"Remember last night we said we were going to drive up to Bradford Woods today and talk to my parents about the wedding," he chirped.

"Oh, shit!" I exclaimed. "Yeah, vaguely I remember. I just—I—."

My heart said, drop the phone and find some place to hide or run away, but I finally said, after moments of stammering, "Yeah, I'm almost ready, give me another thirty minutes."

I barely heard him say, "Sure, no problem," as I hung up the phone. I ran back to my room, stuffed a few things into an overnight bag and ran down the hall for a quick shower. The whole time, I was asking myself, "Why am I doing this? Why am I doing this?" The answer never came.

I tied back still-too-wet hair, skipped the makeup, and threw on a sweater and some jeans. I met Earl in the parking lot by the girl's dorm where he was sitting in the VW listening to music and patiently waiting.

"I'm sorry," I exclaimed as I pulled open the door and started climbing into the passenger seat.

"No problem," he soothed. Then he took my bag and tossed it over into the back. "We've got time. I called the parents last night and told them I wasn't sure exactly when we would arrive. It's all right. It's eleven or so now. We'll probably be there by three or four, no sweat."

Earl put the bus in gear and we began a journey that I never wanted to make, and never dreamed that I would ever have to make.

"Have you eaten?" he said, as we pulled out onto the street.

"No," I replied quietly.

296

Confessions from the Pumpkin Patch

"Deli sandwiches be okay?" he questioned.

"Sure," I replied with little emotion.

"Cool," he continued. "Teplitz Deli is on the way."

We stopped at the deli and picked up our sandwiches, then began the almost three-hour trip to Bradford Woods.

After finishing our sandwiches and engaging in idle chat for a while, I finally said, "Earl, I have some concerns."

"Oh, the parents will get over it," he quipped. "Yours and mine."

"No, that's not what I'm talking about." I turned sideways in the seat to look at him. "I have some concerns about us."

"I thought we hashed this out last night," he said.

"Well, we hashed a lot of things out last night," I said. "I agreed to some things, but I had a lot of questions in my mind after our talk and it kept me up most of the night thinking about it."

"What?" he contemplated keeping his eyes on the road.

"Well, we have kind of been drifters in our relationship don't you think?" I went on. "I mean we have just kind of gone where the wind has blown us and we haven't really had any direction. If we are going to get married, don't you think we should have some direction, some plan?"

"I guess so," he replied. "What direction?"

"Well, for instance," I remitted, "we have never really had any rules in our relationship. We have just gone on trusting that whatever happened, or wherever it took us, would be okay. We have never said what's cool and what's not cool, what we are comfortable with, or what we are not comfortable with."

"Are you uncomfortable about something?" he pondered.

"I—well—I am confused I guess," I stuttered. "I mean, we never really talked about whether it would be okay if we had sex with someone else or if we wanted to keep it monogamous. I guess despite all the fucking around that I did before I met you I just assumed our relationship would be monogamous."

"What the hell are you getting at?" he snapped suddenly.

I stopped, frozen in my tracks.

"I was hoping we could talk about this without getting upset. I mean I know—I—shit!" I turned away from him and looked out the window of the VW.

"I'm sorry," he said. "I shouldn't have snapped at you—am I right in thinking that we are both really scared?"

"You're right," I said, leaning my head against the window watching the roadside spinning by. "I'm really, really scared."

"Tell me what you're thinking," he considered. "Ask me what you need

297

to ask me. I love you and I want to know what you have to say."

"I know you love me," I said tears now streaming down my face. "I have no doubt that you love me. What I just can't seem to get through my head is how you could love me and someone else at the same time."

"What are you talking about?" he disputed.

"You told me last night that you are in love with Screech," I sniffled. "You had an affair with him all summer behind my back. You never talked to me about it. You never asked me how I felt about it. You just assumed that it wouldn't hurt me."

There was a very long silence and I waited for him to answer.

"I don't know what to say," he said finally. "I don't—I do love you both. I guess I didn't realize where I was going with that relationship. It just—it just kind of happened. I don't know what I was feeling. I mean—I'm straight, Lovella. Or at least I thought I was. If you had ever asked me if I thought I would ever have sex with another man, I would have said, 'Hell no,' but I did. I did, and fuck! For the life of me, I don't know why. There was always a part of me that knew it would hurt you when you knew, but I told myself that you were really liberal sexually and that you would be cool with it. I didn't give myself permission to think about what it would do to your heart."

Earl began to cry as well. I turned back to him; watched the tears roll off his cheeks.

"I have to stop," he said, as he pulled over to the shoulder of the road.

When he had stopped the bus and put it in park, he leaned over the steering wheel and sobbed. I watched silently as he cried and when he finally began to subside, I said, "You fell in love with him."

Without looking up he said, "But I never fell out of love with you, Lovella."

He lifted his head up, looked at me and reached out to take my hand. "I never, not for a moment, ever stopped loving you."

"That's kind of what confuses me," I said. "There is a part of me that knows you love me, but there is a part of me that asks, 'If you really loved me why would you deceive me? Why would you do this behind my back and never talk with me about it?' Earl—it's not really the fact that you fucked Screech that bothers me. What bothers me is that you deceived me. It's not the sex that hurts. It's the betrayal that hurts."

He caught a breath half way in a gasp as guilt crossed his face. He sat there frozen for a moment, not really knowing what to say. "I love you," he said at last. "I love you with every fiber of my being, and the last thing in the world I would ever want is to hurt you. I have no excuse, only the explanation that I was scared and confused because I love Screech too. I

Confessions from the Pumpkin Patch

don't know why. I just do—I didn't tell you because I was afraid it would hurt you. Maybe I thought—that night that we did the acid—maybe I thought that if Screech and I could bring you into it with us it would make it okay. Maybe in some delusion I thought I could have you both."

"We don't live in a world like that," I sighed. "We don't live in a world where egos don't get bruised, and insecurities don't get roused. We don't live in a world where anyone is so cool with themselves, so self-assured that they don't see an intimate involvement with someone else as a threat to themselves. I know I have portrayed myself as cool, Earl, but if you thought I was that cool and that secure, you were wrong."

Earl slumped in the seat. He looked out through the front window of the bus. A car passed behind him on the highway and he glanced backward for a second to watch it speed away. "Do you want to call this off?" he asked finally.

I reached down and placed my hand over my abdomen. "If this is Screech's baby, what will that mean to you?"

He took another deep, disjointed breath, and a single tear drifted from his eye to his mouth. "It means that I will love that baby with all my heart," he quivered as he spoke.

"Does it mean that this baby will be more important than me?" I asked what may have been a very unfair question.

"Can you both be important to me?" he questioned. "Can I love you both?"

I knew that he not only meant loving the baby as much as me, but he also meant loving Screech as much as me.

"Earl, where I get scared," I said, "where I get really, really scared is not that you will love anyone as much as me, but that you might love someone else more than me. Did you love Screech more than me?"

His eyes looked like terror when I asked that question. He looked terrified, not so much from what I asked as by the answer that he contemplated in his own mind at that moment. Tears rolled down his cheeks again and he gasped. "Probably, the hardest thing I have ever had to do in my life was to leave San Francisco and leave Screech, but I did that for you, Lovella. I chose you. I want you."

He reached out for me, buried his face in my shoulder and sobbed. I held him, silently, saying nothing. Finally he stopped crying and gradually pried himself away from me. He sat back into the driver's side seat and wiped his eyes on his sleeve.

After a while I said, "Earl, I have only one rule—honesty. That's it—that's all. Fuck whoever you want to fuck, but don't deceive me. Don't go behind my back, and if you ever fall in love with someone else and you decide that you want him—or her—more than me, come to me and tell me. Be clear and open with me. Don't leave me hanging or guessing. If you ever decide that you are not in love with me anymore or if you ever think that you will be happier somewhere else, please just have the balls to stand up to me and let me know. I want you to be happy with me. I don't want you to be unhappy with me. If you think you could ever be happier somewhere else, then go. I would rather you be happy somewhere else than to be unhappy with me. Hell, for that matter, I would rather you be unhappy somewhere else than to be unhappy with me. I want more than anything for you to be happy with me, but if you can't be happy with me, then at the very least—let me know."

"What do you want to do now?" he asked. "Do you want to go through with this?"

I eyed him up and down. "If you, in your heart of hearts, can tell me that you want to go through with this," I responded, "then I want to go through with this."

He stared at me straight in the eyes, unwavering, almost uncomfortable and said at last, "I want you for all of my life, Lovella. I want you. If I can spend eternity with you—I will."

The road noise of passing traffic filled my ears as I suddenly became fully aware of the moment.

"Then drive," I said. "Let's go talk to the parents."

Confessions from the Pumpkin Patch

Chapter 23

To say that Earl's parents were upset about me being pregnant out of wedlock would be an understatement. His mother was a bit nonplussed, but his father ranted for quite some time about what a disgrace he had brought upon his family. To my surprise, Earl sat there and took it quietly affirming here and there, "yes sir" and "no sir." His defiance was either hidden or gone. In the end, his father acquiesced after Earl promised to come to work for the company on graduation. Mr. Titwallow decided that he would let us move back in together when we were married, but after Christmas. He would foot the bill for a flat again just as he had before.

We were to be married early in November so as not to let this go any further, lest my showing tipped off all the neighborhood and our child would know him/herself to be a bastard. The decision was made against a formal wedding and we were to be married at a Justice of the Peace with only immediate family involved. This was fine with me as I knew Mother would have turned any formal wedding into her fest.

All the arrangements were made and we met on Wednesday, November first to the Justice of the Peace in Anderson County. We held it there primarily so Mother could attend, but she used the occasion to do little more than bitch.

"Lovella! I don't see why in the world you couldn't have a church wedding like normal people."

"Because—Mother—," I reacted, "you would turn it into *your* wedding instead of *my* wedding. It would be all about you and how you could show off your daughter getting married to a *rich* boy. I will have nothing of it! This is my wedding, my way, and if you don't like it you can fuck off and go home!"

"Ha! Lovella Fuchs!" she exclaimed, "how dare you speak to me in that manner!?"

"Ha! Mother!" I reacted mockingly, "how dare you make everything about you!?"

I wore a white knee length satin dress and carried a bouquet of yellow flowers that Earl's mother had bought for me. Earl wore one of the suits from his closet. We stood there nervous, side by side, in the Justice of the Peace office. The Justice stood up from behind his desk with the two of us standing in front of it and family on either side. He was an ugly man,

301

blondish, in his forties with a crew cut. He had a huge nose and, although he wasn't overweight, jowls flopped down on either side of his flat mouth. The Justice of the Peace obviously had a sense of humor. He looked at me first and said, as he pointed to Earl, "You like him?"

I said, "Yes."

He then spoke to Earl and pointed at me, "You like her?"

Earl said, "Yes."

"Then by the power vested in me by the great State of Pennsylvania," he exclaimed with authority in his voice, "I now pronounce you husband and wife."

We looked at each other waiting for him to say the traditional, "You may now kiss the bride" but he said nothing and finally after awkward silence, Earl gave me a nervous little peck on the lips. This brought Mother to clapping her happy little hands furiously together with moans of oohs and ahhhhs. I could only think that she took vicarious pleasure in the fact that I had accomplished quite by accident what she never could despite all her frantic effort. I married a well-to-do, upstanding man from a respectable family—or at least she thought.

After the ceremony we had a quick lunch at a little local cafe. Mr. Titwallow bought lunch for everyone. Then it was back to State College for classes on the following day. Earl and I had both skipped classes that Wednesday to get married but we had to be back in class by the following morning. I went back to my dorm and he went back to his. We really didn't see any use in a honeymoon or consummating the marriage as we had been consummating furiously ever since we had been together.

The weeks dragged on to the end of the semester. Earl's parents invited Mother to spend Thanksgiving and Christmas with us at their home in Bradford Woods. Mother was all too happy to skip out on Grandma and Grandpa Donner. After all, she now had a rich son-in-law and an opportunity to experience a bit of the good life that she had always thought she deserved. She reveled in having Nora wait on her hand and foot and she fussed over every little detail of etiquette to the point of exaggeration. Whenever she sipped her tea or coffee she made sure that her pinky finger was extended at full attention despite the fact that no one in Earl's family did anything similar and could have cared less.

In a conversation over Christmas dinner she looked at me squarely and questioned, "So—Lovella—dear—what have you decided to name the baby?"

I knew exactly what she was getting at, the 'ella' that had been traditionally placed at the end of every female's name in our family for

Confessions from the Pumpkin Patch

who knew how many generations.

"Well, Mother," I responded, "Earl and I have discussed it and if it is a boy, we plan on naming it John Gretton after Daddy and my best friend Gretta, and if it is a girl, we plan to name it Gretta Clarese after Earl's Mother and after Gretta."

"Oh—oh—what beautiful names," she twittered, "and how sweet that you would name the baby after *Earl's* mother. Of course Gretta is not his mother's name, and you are—after all—giving the baby her middle name, so I wonder if you might honor our side of the family's tradition by giving the child—if female—a name ending in ella? You know—Janella Clarese would be a lovely name."

I stared at her with a dead, stern look. I knew that she would try to control anything she could in my life for as long as she lived.

"Well—Mother—," I responded, "I am not particularly fond of 'ella' and since this is my baby I think I retain the right to name it whatever I please."

Earl's mother chimed in. "I think Janella is a lovely name, dear."

"You see! You see!" Mother leaped. "It is a wonderful name for a girl child."

"Mother—," I replied trying to maintain my composure, "Gretta has been my dearest and closest friend since I was in the first grade. She named her child after me, and I think it is only fitting that I should name my child after her as well.

"Well!" Mother said in a huff, "if you think some stranger you met in school is more deserving of a name than a tradition in your blood family dating back multiple generations then I suppose the family would simply have to bare that shame."

"What the?—." I caught myself before I said, "What the fuck" in front of Earl's family and sat silent for a moment thinking how I was going to respond to that.

In time I said, "Mother, I don't think naming the child after one of the people I love most in the world would bring any kind of shame to my family."

"Only that we would know that you were the one who broke the line," she quipped. "You would be the one who brought down a noble and honorable family tradition that for all we know could go back hundreds of years."

I wanted to scream, "Give me a fucking break!" but there were things that I might say to Mother in other situations that I would not say in front of Earl's parents and she knew it.

Before I could say anything, Earl's father chimed in with, "You know I

303

think your mother has a point there. There is something to be said for family and for tradition."

"Yes," I thought sarcastically but did not say—"that's why Mother is sitting here at Christmas having dinner with people she never knew a year ago instead of having Christmas with her own parents."

"You see, Lovella," Mother affirmed, siding with Mr. Titwallow, "there is something to be said, for the old ways, for tradition and family honor."

I sat there fuming wanting to strangle her and resisting the urge to climb screaming across the table. Earl, seeing my anguish gave me a little reassuring nod.

"Alright, Mother," I said, as I choked back my anger. "If you want 'ella' at the end of the name for a female, I will name her Vanilla."

Mother twittered, eyes darting, "Oh—oh—as in vanilla flavoring? I—I—I—don't think that would exactly be a fitting name for a child."

"Take it or leave it, Mother," I said firmly. "It's an 'ella' sound at the end of the name. It therefore meets the criteria for the family tradition. If the child is a girl—her name will be Vanilla Clarese Titwallow."

"Oh—well, but it's not a *normal* sounding woman's name with the ella on the end," she argued, "Not like—Janella."

"So and you think Claudella, Drucella, Cloella, etc., are normal sounding names!" I spit back. "No, Mother. If you insist that there must be an ella on the end of the name, then the name is Vanilla and to use your phrase at the point of Daddy's death, 'Well, that's that.' There is nothing more to say."

She sat for a moment fiddling with her napkin. She knew that I had her, that there was no real argument, and I had used the guilt card. She knew if she argued, I would point out to her that I had been willing to compromise and she obviously was not willing to compromise and ultimately had no say in the matter anyway.

In January, Earl and I moved back in together. We got an apartment very similar to the one he had when I met him. It was just up the street from his original apartment. By that time, I was practically waddling with pregnancy. I could feel the baby moving and it was not unusual that it would be rumbling around inside of me in the middle of the night when I was trying to sleep. I spent many nights falling asleep and waking again every time the baby shifted.

I hated trying to dress, even with maternity clothes. Nothing seemed to fit right. If it fit around my waist, it folded up under my belly and felt like I had a rope tied around me, and of course nothing would fit around my belly. Something fitting over the belly was totally out of the question. I

Confessions from the Pumpkin Patch

began to feel like my breasts were twenty-pound bags of water on each side and any kind of movement made them shift back and forth like the flow of the tides.

February was miserable. My stomach was as tight as a basketball and I felt like I couldn't sit down or stand up without the assistance of a fork lift. Somehow, with great care, I managed. I had stopped smoking by the end of November, not because I thought anything about any danger to the baby, but because it practically made me sick every time I tried to smoke. It was like the baby was saying, "No, I don't like that and I'm going to make you puke if you do it."

Earl was wonderful. He fussed over me like a mother hen, propping pillows to my back, bringing me tea and sitting up with me in the middle of the night when the baby was kicking and I couldn't sleep. Still, he kept up his studies, determined to graduate.

This went on throughout January, February and March. Then in the early morning of April 1st, 1968 about 4:30 AM, I woke with intense pain. I had gone to bed with a dull ache across my lower back and abdomen and had barely been able to get to sleep because of it. I finally slept more from sheer exhaustion than anything else. When I awoke, I noticed a sticky discharge mixed with blood that had come from my vagina and shortly afterward I began to have intense cramps in my abdomen.

"Earl! Earl!" I screamed. "Wake up!"

Earl popped up in bed like a jack-in-the -box. "What!? Are you all right?"

"Either I'm dying or the baby is coming!" I screamed.

He looked around confused. "Oh!—Huh!—Well!—." Then he leaped out of bed and began dressing furiously. He lifted me to the edge of the bed and wrapped my robe around me.

"Wait!—Ha—Ahh—Wait!" he exclaimed as he grabbed the suitcase we had packed for the hospital. He ran to the door with the suitcase, turned quickly raising one hand flat in the air like a traffic cop. "Wait!—Wait!" he exclaimed. Then he was gone.

Earl ran downstairs, threw the suitcase into the VW and came back for me. Then he walked me moaning and grimacing to the VW and sped away toward Hershey Medical Center. He was at the Penn State facility for Hershey in short order. Parking the bus in front of the emergency room he rushed in to grab a nurse and a wheelchair.

It was not long before I was in Labor and Delivery, legs in stirrups, panting, pushing and screaming. It seemed to me like it went on forever. The cramps would come and there would be waves and waves of them and then they would subside for a while only to come back with a

Karlyle Tomms

vengeance.

Earl went back and forth between checking on me and pacing the hall. He had called both sides of the family and told them that the baby was coming. Then at around 8:42 AM, Vanilla Clarese Titwallow was born. None of the family had arrived at that time. It was a two-and-a-half hour drive for Earl's parents and about a three hour drive for Mother.

I was taken to a room, exhausted, and needing to sleep. Vanilla was taken to the nursery. There was about a two-hour gap of time between the time that she was born and the time that family arrived. Earl had visited the nursery and then came to sit by my side in the recovery room. The nurse had brought me pain medications after delivery and an ice pack to go between my legs. I soon pulled the ice pack away as I felt it more uncomfortable than helpful, and then I slept for maybe an hour to an hour and a half. I awoke to Earl sitting by the bed holding my hand and staring lovingly at me.

"Hey, little mamma," he said, as I opened my eyes.

"Hey, big daddy," I responded. "Have you seen the baby?"

"Yep, I saw her," he said smiling. "She's beautiful."

"As beautiful as me?" I said jokingly.

"Just as beautiful as you," he said.

"How much does she look like me?" I questioned.

"Hard to tell at this stage," he responded. "But I think she has got your eyes and your cheek bones."

"How much does she look like you?" I continued, not really knowing how to ask and not wanting to be so blunt as to ask if she was black.

He reached his free hand over and pushed my hair back behind my ears and then stroked my face. He smiled and looked lovingly and reassuringly at me for a moment. "She doesn't really look much like me at all," he said.

My grip tightened on the one hand that was holding mine. A wave of emotion flowed over me. I trembled and a tear ran down my cheek for I knew exactly what he meant.

"Earl," I said, eyes searching his for whatever reassurance I could find. "What are we going to do?"

"We're going to love her," he said. "We are going to love her with all our might."

"What about our parents?" I questioned.

"They will just have to deal with it," he said. "They might have to challenge themselves to look beyond the limits of their prejudice."

He gently stroked my hair and the side of my face and I fell asleep again as he was holding my hand.

I awoke to a gentle tapping on the door. "May we come in?" I heard

Confessions from the Pumpkin Patch

Earl's mother say gently and sweetly from outside. I looked around the room and Earl was nowhere to be found.

"Sure—please," I responded. Then Mr. and Mrs. Titwallow glided gently into the room as though they had to walk delicately for fear of disturbing some fragile unseen barrier. Earl followed shortly afterward. Apparently he had waited at the entrance of the hospital to steer them first to the room and away from the nursery.

"I was waiting downstairs for Mom and Dad," he said in explanation. "They can visit with you for a while and I'll go back down to wait for your mother. I thought it would be nice if we could all be in the room together when they bring the baby in to see you."

"How are you feeling, dear?" Earl's mom asked as she crossed around the bed. His father sat down in a chair and said nothing initially.

"Well," I responded. "My—you know what— hurts like hell."

"Yes, dear," Mrs. Titwallow smiled reassuringly. "That's payment for all the love you are going to receive later."

Mr. Titwallow grunted at the comment.

"How are you, Mr. Titwallow?" I questioned.

"I'm very well, Lovella," he noted. "Thank you for asking."

We continued to make small talk for about forty-five minutes over various topics from how I felt about having a girl to the latest news and the weather. Later, there was another little knock at the door and this time immediately after the knock Earl and Mother entered the room without waiting for my invitation.

"Oh, Lovella, honey," Mother began. "You are just glowing. Doesn't she have that new mother glow?" She turned to Mrs. Titwallow.

"Yes, she is just beaming, isn't she?" Mrs. Titwallow responded.

Earl said, "I took the liberty of asking the nurse if she would bring the baby up in a few minutes.

My heart sank in the realization that the first time I would see my baby would also be the first time that everyone in the family would realize I had given birth to a black child. I was both exhilarated and terrified.

"Oh, wonderful!" spouted Mother, beaming all over Earl. "I'm just dying to see her."

I looked at Earl with both longing and terror. On one hand I had no problem with telling Mother to fuck off if she didn't like the way things had turned out, but on the other hand I wanted to be accepted and reassured.

In a moment, the nurse came into the room, walked straight over to the bed and began to lay Vanilla into my arms.

"Haaaah!" Mother gasped. "There must be a mistake. That's not her

Karlyle Tomms

child."

"This is Vanilla Clarese Titwallow," the nurse responded glancing up at Mother.

I took my baby into my arms, looked down on her, seeing her for the first time, tiny, wrinkled and helpless. A wave of love rushed over me as I witnessed my child for the first time. The nurse quickly left the room. Then I looked up. "This is *my* baby, Mother," I said.

"What!!?" Mother exclaimed. "Is this some kind of April Fool's joke?" She scanned the room as though a clown might leap out at any moment to shout, "Surprise!"

"What the hell is this!?" Mr. Titwallow blurted as he got to his feet. "Is this some kind of sick joke? If it is, it is not very damn funny."

"It is no joke," Earl stepped in. "This is our baby."

"There is no way you are the father of that child!" Mr. Titwallow demanded of Earl. "Now cut the shenanigans. Get that kid out of here and bring in my granddaughter!"

"Yes, Dad," Earl calmly replied. "I am the father of that child. This is the baby that Lovella and I had together. It is not a joke. This is our child."

"Well, maybe there is some nigger blood on her side of the family!" Mr. Titwallow argued as he pointed an accusing finger at Mother, "but there is damn sure none on our side!"

"There is no such thing on our side!" Mother snapped back.

"First of all," Earl continued, "I would appreciate it if you would not use *that* word. Don't ever say that word around my daughter again." His lips pursed as he emphasized the seriousness of that demand.

"Your daughter!" Mr. Titwallow exclaimed with Mrs. Titwallow holding and rubbing his arm trying to calm him down. "That is no more your goddamn daughter than Martin Luther King is my son!"

"Yes," Earl responded. "Yes, she is my daughter. She is my very own and I am legally her father."

"Over my dead body!" Mr. Titwallow bellowed.

"It's too late, Dad," Earl calmly continued. "My name is on the birth certificate. This is my child. I'm a legal adult. Vanilla is legally my child and there is nothing that you can do about it."

"I can cut your ass off from any penny you thought you would ever get out of my estate!" Mr. Titwallow snarled.

"Dad, if that is something you feel that you have to do, we are fine with that," Earl reasoned. "I will have my degree by the end of May and I'm sure that I can find work to support my family without your assistance."

"You are fine with that?" Mr. Titwallow bellowed. "You are fine with that!!? You are fine with knowing that you are going to live like a

308

Confessions from the Pumpkin Patch

goddamn pauper without a pot to piss in while you deny your own family so you can live with this nigger fucking whore and raise that little nigger baby!"

In a snap Earl had wadded up his fist and punched his father square in the face knocking him back into the wall. "DON'T YOU EVER FUCKING SAY ANYTHING LIKE THAT TO MY WIFE OR MY CHILD AGAIN!" he screamed. "YOU WILL RESPECT MY WIFE AND YOU WILL TREAT MY CHILD WITH THE SAME HONOR YOU WOULD GIVE TO ANY WHITE CHILD OR YOU CAN STAY THE HELL AWAY FROM ME AND FROM MY FAMILY! DO YOU FUCKING UNDERSTAND ME?!"

The baby began to wail at the noise and the anger. I sat there in bed rocking her, trying to sooth and comfort her. Mr. Titwallow regained his balance and looked at Earl with the utmost contempt. He grabbed Mrs. Titwallow by the arm. "Come on, Clarese," he said, "We are not welcome here."

As he began to pull Mrs. Titwallow toward the door she jerked her hand away from him. "Maybe you are not welcome here," she exclaimed, "but I'm staying here to share this moment with my son, his wife, and my granddaughter."

An amazing shock crossed Mr. Titwallow's face. He looked at her sternly and demanded, "I said, "Come on! Let's go!"

"No," she said calmly and firmly. "You can go if you want to. I'm sure I can find a way back to Bradford Woods if I need to but right now I'm staying here."

Mr. Titwallow's eyes darted between her, Earl, and me. "You can all go to hell!" he yelled and then he stormed out of the door.

After he left, Mrs. Titwallow took a deep breath. "Well—," she said, "What family doesn't have a few squabbles here and there." She smiled sweetly and nervously, glanced up at Mother and down to me and the baby. Earl walked over and hugged her. "Thank you, Mom," he said as he kissed her forehead.

To my surprise, Mother had kept quiet through all this. I knew that she was not the least bit happy about the fact that her first and only grandchild was black. I knew that prejudice ran deep in her, that it went all the way back to the Kentucky hills. I knew she had racist conditioning that had been subtly handed down generation after generation and that this probably had a lot to do with the struggles I found within myself. Yet, unlike Mr. Titwallow, for the most part she had held her tongue through all this. I suspected that part of the reason was the intensity of the situation and her desire not to get caught up in Earl's wrath as his father had been.

309

Karlyle Tomms

After Mr. Titwallow rampaged out of the room, Mother strolled over to my bedside, looked down at the baby and reached out a finger. Vanilla wrapped her tiny hand around Mother's finger.

"So this is my grandchild," Mother smiled looking down at the baby.

"Yes, Mother" I said. "This is Vanilla Clarese Titwallow, your granddaughter."

Mother looked down at the baby as the tiny hand was gripping her finger and said, without looking at me at all, "But she is not vanilla dear—she's mocha."

Confessions from the Pumpkin Patch

Chapter 24

I barely had Vanilla home from the hospital for two days when the most horrible thing happened. I had put her down for a nap and was relaxing, watching a little TV when the broadcast was pre-empted by a special report. Walter Cronkite, after some introduction, came on and announced, "Good evening. Dr. Martin Luther King, the apostle of nonviolence, of the civil rights movement, has been shot in Memphis, Tennessee."

"Oh, my god!" I cried aloud and held my hand over my mouth.

I watched in horror as awful descriptions of the assassination followed. My eyes filled with tears and my chest heaved as grief and fear flooded over me. I had seen this man speak at a march in New York only a year before. In many ways I felt almost as though I knew him personally. I questioned what all this might mean. The fears I had for my child growing up in a world where prejudice prevailed came rushing into my mind with a vengeance. I had images intruding on my mind of the KKK burning crosses on lawns and black people hanged in trees. I grieved and was afraid, alone. Earl was at the library and I wondered if he had gotten the news. I thought surely if he had, he would come home soon.

I found myself wondering if our child could be shot in cold blood for no more reason than inexplicable hate. I found myself thinking of Jesus and Mahatma Gandhi, how those who strive to bring peace and love into the world are the ones who are murdered and betrayed for it. I feared that hate was winning the battle over love for ultimate supremacy, and that the world would deteriorate into a Nazi-like hell. I worried for a sleeping baby only four days old, and I grieved for Dr. King and the entire black community. I grieved for my own guilt. Even though I had a black child, there were traces of prejudice that still found refuge in the deep recesses of my heart. My own conditioned intolerance troubled me. I so wished that Earl had been home as I sat there on the sofa watching the broadcast drag on. I was hanging on every detail—"shot in the neck—the bullet exploded in his face—rushed to a Memphis hospital where he died from a bullet wound in the neck—Mayor Henry Lobe has reinstated the dusk to dawn curfew he imposed on the city last week when a march led by Dr. King erupted in violence."

"What kind of world have I brought my baby into?" I wailed aloud as I watched the news.

311

Karlyle Tomms

I paced the apartment and watched the news until Vanilla awoke with the classic stilted crying of a newborn. I picked her up from the crib and held her close over my shoulder. I rocked her and paced the apartment. I repeatedly went to the window to see if I might find Earl coming up the walk. Little did I know there would be numbers of evenings where I would find myself at home with a child, waiting for him to come home.

Earl did not come back until late in the evening after finishing his studies. The news went through the campus like wildfire, so he heard about it. He had considered how it might be affecting me, but thought I could handle it while he finished his research. He was apologetic and affectionate when he came home to find me torn with grief.

"I never dreamed it would affect you this way," he said, as he put his arms around me. I was going to need a lot of comfort that year.

Nineteen sixty eight became the year from hell for me and for the nation. The presidential election was in full swing along with political ads on TV and radio. Race riots and war protests seemed to headline every newscast. There were no more peaceful protests. There was no more powder-keg. The powder-keg had blown and the country was exploding into violence. All of this made me even more terrified. I questioned whether there was any kind of future for my baby that would be worth having.

In June, Bobby Kennedy was assassinated in Los Angeles. When the Democratic National Convention was held in Chicago that August, riots broke out again. Every time something happened, I found myself becoming more anxious. I refused to take the baby with me if I went out anywhere. I would only go grocery shopping if Earl was home with her. I was terrified that someone of either race, white or black, might see me with a black child and attack me for it. I stopped talking to friends and stayed in the apartment with Vanilla day-in and day-out—isolated and anxious.

Of course Earl had graduated in May with a degree in business. Prior to graduation he had interviews set up in a couple of different cities. Both Pittsburgh and Philadelphia were on his list for jobs, but neither of them panned out so he got a job as a grocery clerk. He spent his days sacking and carrying groceries for old ladies, and when the store closed in the evening, he stocked the shelves and mopped the floors before coming home.

Earl and his father had not spoken since Vanilla was born. I guess his father took him at his word and decided that he could not be around us without being rude, so he chose not to contact us at all. Earl's mom called

Confessions from the Pumpkin Patch

frequently and on a couple of occasions she came up to spend the weekend so she could keep the baby and let us go out for much-needed adult time together. Even then, I felt uncomfortable going out.

Mother had even come up a few times to see Vanilla and baby-sit. She had shocked me with her response to the baby. I couldn't see that she acted any different toward Vanilla than if she had been a white child. I had expected Mother to throw just as big a fit as Earl's dad, at the very least to shame me about getting pregnant out of wedlock, especially by a black man. However, it never came. She never spoke a shaming word to me at all.

When the grandmothers were there to babysit, Earl would take me to the Finer Diner, but our dating hang-out no longer held appeal to me. I couldn't be in public without being constantly terrified that violence or racial tensions might break out at any moment. Earl assured me that he would protect me, but I didn't trust that he could. If someone decided to start shooting, how could he protect me from that? The images of violence on TV and the assassinations that occurred that year constantly plagued me.

The election was held in November and Richard Nixon won. This didn't do anything toward bringing me any peace of mind. Nixon had sworn that he would "crack down on lawlessness" but to what end? I did not see him having any real interest in ending the war, and I found myself certain that when it came down to it, he was a lot like Earl's father with a deep-seated but hidden prejudice, yet one that was far more insidious and evil.

I did not know that all this time Earl's mother had been working on his father to set aside his callow attitudes and reunite the family. If I had realized this, I don't know that I would have thought Earl could be receptive at that point. However, I suppose I underestimated both men. I think Mrs. Titwallow had been pushing a reconciliation with hopes to have something resolved before the approaching holidays.

Shortly after the election, Mrs. Titwallow called Earl and asked if he would come up to Bradford Woods and speak with his father. I was sitting on one end of the sofa nursing the baby when she called. Earl sat on the other end of the couch from me responding over the phone, "Well, if that's the case, why isn't he the one making this phone call instead of you, Mom?"

There was a silence as he listened to what ever argument she was giving. I had the feeling that she had done a lot of pleading with Mr. Titwallow long before she ever called Earl.

"Well, I don't care, Mom," he said into the phone. "If he is sorry for what he has done, then he needs to be man enough to call me himself.

313

Karlyle Tomms

Well, why can't he come to the phone and tell me that? Don't give me that crap about how busy he is. I don't care how busy he is. If this is important to him and he is genuinely sorry then he will tell me himself. No—no—Mom! I'm not going to come up there unless he asks me himself, not you—him. Well, you have him call me and tell me himself that he wants to meet with me and I'll be far more likely to consider it, but I'll tell you, the person he owes the biggest apology to is Lovella. The baby is too little to know any different, and I don't want her ever to know that her grandfather thought of her like this or ever treated his family like this,—well—fine, Mom. Have him call me—I love you too—okay, bye." Earl put the receiver back on the black phone that sat on the end table then turned to me.

"Can you believe that shit?" he said.

"What's going on?" I questioned as I watched Vanilla pulling on the nipple of her baby bottle.

"Mom put him up to this," Earl snarled. "I know the son-of-a-bitch never got the bright idea to apologize on his own. Apparently, he wants me to drive up to Bradford Woods so he can meet with me personally and give me an apology, but the asshole coward didn't even have the balls to call me himself! Besides, if he is going to apologize to anyone, he needs to apologize to you."

I continued to feed the baby and said nothing. About two hours later the phone rang again. By that time, Earl had taken Vanilla into the bedroom and laid down with her for a nap. I picked up the phone and said, "Hello." When I heard the voice on the other end of the line, I froze for a moment.

"Hello, Lovella." Mr. Titwallow spoke from the distance.

I stood silent and said nothing. I felt myself trembling.

"Hello?" I heard him question.

"Hello, Mr. Titwallow," I said finally. "I—am—fine," I said rather sternly and distant.

"Well, I'm glad you answered," he said. "I really need to talk to you."

Again, I stood at the end of the sofa holding the receiver in my hand and saying nothing.

"Lovella—," he hesitated. "I—I owe you much more than an apology."

In my mind I imagined Mrs. Titwallow standing there beside him with a gun to his temple hissing through clenched teeth, "Apologize to her, Daniel, or I'll blow your fucking brains out!" It was not at all her style, but it made for a nice fantasy.

"I—ah—I," he went on in divided segments of speech. "I was totally—out of line that day in the hospital—when Vanilla was born. —My—behavior—was scornful and wrong—and I have no excuse. I—hope that

314

Confessions from the Pumpkin Patch

you will see it in your heart to forgive me."

Again, I was silent for a moment. Offering no forgiveness at all I said, "I suppose you would also like to speak to Earl."

There was a brief pause and then he said, "Yes—thank you." I heard the misgiving in his voice. "I would like to speak to Earl please."

Earl heard the phone ring, had gotten up, and was leaning against the door frame to the bedroom. I looked up at him knowing that he had overheard the conversation. He looked at me for a moment with disdain and pried himself from the door frame to walk over and reach out for the phone. I silently handed the phone over to him and went to sit down.

"Hello, Father," he said formally. Then I watched him roll his eyes and occasionally grimace as he listened to the conversation. Apparently, at some point in his speech, his father wondered if Earl was still on the line or if they had been cut off. I heard Earl say, "Yes, I'm still here. I'm listening." Then he was silent again for several minutes.

"You will understand," Earl said at last, "that I have my doubts about your sincerity."

Earl switched the receiver from one ear to the other and glanced up at me while he listened to his father. I tried to busy myself with picking up magazines tossed about the living room.

"Well, that's on your turf," Earl responded a little later. "I think—if you are sincere and you really want to do this, then you are going to be the one to make the sacrifice and the effort to get together, not us."

While they were talking, I heard the baby stirring. I went into the bedroom to get her. Then I came back and stood nearby with Vanilla while I listened to the rest of their conversation.

Earl was silent listening to his father speak. Then he let out a deep sigh. "I don't know. —I'll have to discuss it with Lovella. I'm not sure that she will even be open to the idea. —Well, we will have to talk about it. —I'll let you know something in a couple of days. —Alright,—fine. —I'll let you know—bye."

"What's up?" I asked.

"If we don't want to come over to Bradford Woods for Thanksgiving," he said, "he would rent a house at Martha's Vineyard and we could all have Thanksgiving there."

"Can they get a house with such short notice?" I questioned

"He has connections," Earl said as he stretched out on the sofa, "and besides there is a house there on the beach that he and Mom used to rent for the family when I was a kid. He can probably get that and if I know him, he will take Ralph and Nora just so they can wait on us. The house has eight bedrooms so there is plenty of room, and there probably won't be

315

much competition to rent it over Thanksgiving. Summer is the busy time."

"So that means that he is really sorry?" I asked.

"Well, the house plus taking Ralph and Nora with us is probably going to set him back about $6 or $8,000 for the few of days we will be there." Earl grinned as he lay back on the sofa. "I'd be willing to bet that he is going to fork out more than that just so he can kiss ass and try to make up."

"Well, I'm glad he is willing to try," I said.

"Oh, Mom put him up to this," Earl noted. "I know she has been working on him since he made such an ass of himself when Vanilla was born. I kind of knew Mom would wear him down." He moved over next to me and took my hand. "So, what do you think?"

"It's good. I guess that he wants to apologize." My voice trembled as I continued, "But I'm really scared."

"Scared?" he questioned.

"Earl, the last time I saw your father he was screaming horrible things at me and the baby and you ended up punching him in the face."

My breath shortened to stilted gasps. I began shaking like a leaf in a heavy wind, and I could barely get the words out. "With—all—the—violence—out—there—and—the—hatred," Tears streamed from my eyes and Earl enfolded me in his arms. "I—don't—know—if—I'm—safe—anywhere—or—that—the baby—is—safe—especially—around—someone—who—has been—so cruel!"

"Shush, shush, shush," he said as he pulled my head to his chest and held me. "We don't have to go if you don't want to, and if you never want to be around my dad again, I understand."

"But—I—don't want—to break up—your family," I pleaded.

"You are not breaking up my family," he reassured. "If anyone has broken up my family, it's my dad."

I collected myself to look up at Earl and meet his eyes. "Do you think he still hates me?"

"I don't know what he feels," he said. "I have long ago stopped trying to figure my father out."

"Is it important to you that we go?" I questioned.

He looked away and thought for a moment. Then he looked back at me. "It's important to me that you are happy," he said.

"But it is important to you," I reflected. "I can tell by your response that it's important to you."

"You know—" He led me to the sofa to sit down. "I think I have wanted all my life to have some common ground with my dad, but I've never had it." He held my hand and sat close. "I do want peace in my family. I do

Confessions from the Pumpkin Patch

want some kind of reconciliation with my dad, but you are my family now, Lovella, and I don't want my dad appeased at the expense of your feelings."

"I don't know if I can handle it or not," I said. "I'm really scared of your dad now, but if it is important to you, I will go."

"We don't have to go, Lovella," he smiled reassuringly. "Honestly. It will be fine if we don't go."

"I just don't want to be alone with your dad," I responded, "and I don't think I could take it if he started screaming at me again."

"Then we won't go," he concluded.

"No," I continued. "We need to go. I just need to figure out some way to feel safe."

"You feel safe with my mother, don't you?" he asked. "Who else do you feel safe with? Do you want to ask Gretta to come along? You can invite anyone you want."

"Gretta will be having Thanksgiving with her own family," I noted. "It wouldn't be fair to ask them to leave their family holiday for this."

"Then ask the whole family," Earl said. "They can all come up. If there is not room in the house for everyone you want to invite, then Dad can start paying for hotels. Invite the whole fucking town of Climax if you want."

"Do you think it would be alright to invite Mother, and maybe Grandma and Grandpa Donner?" I asked.

Earl looked shocked. "I'm surprised," he said, "given the problems you've had with your mother."

"She has been pretty good since the baby was born. Don't you think?" I looked down at his hands which were still clamped firmly over mine.

He reached up to stroke my face with the back of his fingers. "Yeah, I do think," he said. "Go ahead and invite them, and Dad will just have to get over it. If you still want to invite Gretta and her family, he will just have to get over that too."

"I think I'll be fine with just my family." I said. "It will be nice to have an extra baby sitter or two, and as crazy as they are, Grandma and Grandpa Donner can be a fun distraction."

The next day, Earl called his father and told them that my family would be coming as well and that he expected him to pay for and arrange their transportation. To my surprise, Mr. Titwallow agreed and, like Earl, told me to invite whoever I wanted. I had not even called my family yet, but when I told them Mr. Titwallow would be sending a car for them and that all arrangements would be made, they jumped at the opportunity."

"Hell!" Grandma Donner exclaimed when I called her. "If I don't have

317

Karlyle Tomms

to cook all day, damn right we'll be there."

On the Tuesday before Thanksgiving, Earl's Dad made sure that a limousine was sent to Climax to gather up Mother and Grandma and Grandpa Donner for the trip to Martha's Vineyard. Since it was more than a ten-hour drive, he also put them in a luxury hotel in New York overnight. They completed the journey arriving on the Wednesday afternoon before Thanksgiving. He had also sent a limo for me, Earl, and the baby. Even though the limo from Climax could have stopped to get us on the way, Mr. Titwallow had sent a separate limo for us, and we actually arrived late on Tuesday evening. I had invited Grandma Fuchs and Raymond as well, but she was struggling with her age and health, so she didn't think that she would be able to handle the trip.

The house at Martha's Vineyard was a regal beach home that was both rustic and elegant. A porch went round three sides and there were views to the ocean on all but the backside of the house. Earl, Vanilla, and I were given a bedroom upstairs that had French doors opening to a balcony over the shoreline. The outside of the house was a pale yellow clapboard with white trim. Inside, rustic boards were washed with a light blue in most rooms so that the grain of the wood still faded through the color.

As predicted, Mr. Titwallow had brought Ralph and Nora. There was a separate apartment off the kitchen in the back of the house for them. When Earl and I arrived Tuesday evening, they were already busy with preparations for a Thanksgiving feast. Earl's Mom was waiting for us with news that his father would not be arriving until Thanksgiving morning.

On Wednesday afternoon, Earl and I cuddled up under blankets on the front porch to warm us in the fifty degree weather while his mom took care of the baby. The breeze coming off the ocean was almost too crisp, and the salt air had a sting, but we were determined that we were going to sit outside and enjoy the full open view. We had decided that nature had at last overwhelmed us and we were about to go back inside when the limousine with the rest of my family arrived.

Grandmother Donner did not wait for the limo driver to come around and open her door. She threw open the door and stepped out onto the driveway taking in the experience and the view. The driver, seeing that she had beaten him to his job opened the door on the opposite side for Mother who had patiently waited for her proper treatment.

Grandmother Donner was in her full bizarre regalia with a bright yellow wide brimmed hat that had a broad red ribbon around it. The ribbon was tied in a grand bow on the side of the hat with flowers drifting off the edge of the brim. She had on a blue and pink polka-dotted knee length dress

318

Confessions from the Pumpkin Patch

which wasn't long enough to cover the stocking rolls that clung to her fat little legs just below the knees. Her green jacket clashed loudly with the rest of her outfit as did the yellow and orange scarf that was wrapped like an ace bandage around her chubby neck. She stood by the door of the vehicle blocking Grandpa Donner from his exit.

"The Lord of Mercy!" she exclaimed. "Ain't this the fanciest damn place you ever saw in your life?"

"Get the hell out of the way, woman!" Grandpa Donner exclaimed from inside the car as he began pushing on her hips.

She slapped his hands but didn't move.

"Now don't you get frisky with me in front of strangers," she scolded.

"Go on, woman!" he pleaded. "Let me out of this damn car. I need to piss!"

When she wouldn't move, he scooted over to the other side and came out behind Mother who was also standing there looking at the house and the view across the ocean. Mother was dressed classically and neatly in a tasteful, conservative, tan dress. She was also wearing a tan pillbox hat with a rhinestone broach attached to the side. What I noticed immediately was that there was no beehive. I almost gasped in shock, but also was quietly delighted to see her hair flowing across her shoulders in the afternoon breeze.

Grandpa Donner grabbed his crotch like a little boy about to wet his pants and trotted up the porch where Earl and I were standing. "Where's the damn bathroom?" he exclaimed.

"Don't I even get a hello?" I giggled.

"Hello, now where's the damn bathroom?" he demanded again.

"Through that door," I pointed. "Mrs. Titwallow is in the living room. She'll show you from there."

By this time, Mother had come around the car and put her hand behind Grandma Donner's elbow to walk her to the porch.

"Oh, get your damn hands off me," Grandmother Donner exclaimed. "I may be old, but I can still walk, and I think I can see the way."

Mother immediately let go and walked ahead of her to the porch.

"Hello, Earl—Lovella," she said, formally, "How very nice to be invited for the holiday."

"Mother!" I exclaimed. "What have you done with your hair? What? No beehive?"

"Don't tease, Lovella," she responded. "It isn't seemly."

"I like it," I said. "I hope you keep it."

"Thank you," she said as she walked up the steps in her white pumps. I never realized until that moment that Mother was actually a beautiful

319

Karlyle Tomms

woman.

Grandma Donner was right behind her by this time, farting as she waddled up the steps almost beating Mother to the top.

"Oh for goodness sake!" Mother exclaimed to her. "Try to have some manners!"

"Hee. Yah!" Grandma Donner chided. "Has your ass got so tight that you don't even pass gas no more?"

Mother looked away and rolled her eyes. Earl and I showed them to the door. Nora came out to instruct the limo driver where to take their luggage. Mrs. Titwallow greeted them sweetly inside. She had never met my grandparents before and I was a bit worried that she might find them offensive, but if that was the case, there was never any indication of it.

We visited throughout the evening and the two families shared stories often of how Earl or I had behaved as small children.

The next morning Earl and I slept in late. It was so nice to have grandmothers doting over the baby so I could almost feel the freedom I had before she was born.

Since Ralph was busy preparing dinner for the family, Nora made an omelet for us which we shared so as not to get too stuffed before the big meal. The rest of the family was in the living room watching the Macy's parade. Grandpa Donner had his sock feet propped up on an ottoman just as he would have done at home. He had fallen asleep and there was an occasional snore. Grandma Donner was swigging on beer from a glass and making comments about the parade. Mother was holding Vanilla and cooing to her in such a relaxed manner that I could scarce believe it was her. Earl's mom sat there quietly and sweetly watching the TV, and his sister Anna was propped up on pillows on the floor with her nose in a book.

We sat down with the family and enjoyed the rest of the parade. By early afternoon, Ralph had prepared a sumptuous Thanksgiving feast with tweaks on the traditional such as roasted pine nuts topping the stuffing. Earl's dad still had not arrived by almost 1:00 PM when Mrs. Titwallow made the decision that we would go ahead and eat.

Grandma Donner did her usual Thanksgiving announcement and insisted that everyone go around the table and say what they were thankful for. When it came to Mother's turn she said, "I am thankful that I have a beautiful, intelligent daughter who has given me a beautiful grandchild."

"Who are you, and what have you done with my Mother?" I asked.

She looked up at me sternly.

"Oh, there she is," I teased. "For a minute there I thought we had lost her."

Confessions from the Pumpkin Patch

When it was my turn, I said, "I'm thankful for my loving husband and my beautiful daughter."

Nora had taken the baby to care for her in the kitchen while the family ate. I looked around as though I might find her standing there with Vanilla, as though I might also express gratitude directly to my daughter. In some ways it felt very strange that she was not with me.

When Earl's turn came, he reached over and took my hand. "I am thankful that I have a beautiful, loving wife, a beautiful daughter, and a wonderful family to share my life."

After grace, when we began to eat, Mother looked over at Mrs. Titwallow and said, "I do hope that Mr. Titwallow has not come to some harm. Is it like him to miss a holiday gathering?"

"I'm sure he is fine," Earl responded. "There were lots of times when we were growing up that he never made it to a holiday at all. He always had the excuse that he was working and couldn't even take time for his family. He is probably sitting in a bar somewhere convincing some grocery store owner that he'll be greatly benefited by stocking Chum Snacks."

"Earl," Mrs. Titwallow said, as she handed a basket of rolls, "Why don't you see if Lovella would like some bread."

The subject changed as was the intent. Although Nora usually served meals, Mrs. Titwallow had made the request that the meal be family style with everything on the table or on the sideboard for passing around.

After the meal, we retreated back to the living room waiting for the meal to settle enough to make room for dessert. The television had been turned off to allow for conversation and Nora served coffee.

Mother sipped her coffee with the saucer held carefully beneath the cup. She gazed out through the large bank of windows across the front of the living room which gave a view across the porch to the ocean beyond.

"This view is so amazing," she said. "I just feel so relaxed and at ease here."

To this Grandma Donner lifted one leg and farted. She snickered at Mother and said, in her best southern belle' accent, "Oh, pardon me. However could I be so rude? It is a lovely view out there isn't it? Does anyone have a fan? I do declare. I think I have—the vapors."

Mother said nothing and ignored her completely. I found myself at one of the few times in my life having compassion for her. I wondered how torturous it must have been growing up being taunted and ridiculed by her own mother. I was beginning to realize that a lot of the effort she had put into controlling me was to make sure that I did not turn out like her family.

Mrs. Titwallow, being her gracious self said, "Drucella, you should

Karlyle Tomms

come back to visit again. Daniel and I come out here once or twice a year usually. We would be very happy for you to join us."

"Thank you, Clarese," Mother responded. "I would love to come back if I ever have the opportunity."

We were startled at that point by a slam of a door in the back of the house near the kitchen. We then heard Mr. Titwallow's voice which was somewhat loud and a bit overbearing. "Nora, see if you can round me up enough leftovers to make a meal."

"Yes, sir, Mr. Titwallow," she responded.

We had all turned to the direction of the commotion. Shortly, Mr. Titwallow came somewhat staggeringly up the hall from the kitchen. It was rather obvious that he had been drinking. As soon as I realized that fact, I felt my muscles tighten and my breath quicken. I had trusted somewhat that he might be civil to me on this visit, but I began to doubt the possibility when I saw that he was not in complete control of his faculties.

"Hey! Hey! Hey!" he slurred loudly as he entered the room. "So glad you guys could all make it. I am so sorry I am late. I had some pressing matters at the office."

He then wobbled over to Grandpa Donner and extended his hand. "I don't believe we have met, sir," he stammered. "I'm Daniel Titwallow, Earl's father, and you must be Lovella's grandfather."

"Yes, sir," Grandpa Donner stood up and shook his hand, "Sid Donner. Very nice to meet you—and thank you for having us up to your place here."

"Oh it's not my place," Mr. Titwallow responded. "It's just rented, but you're welcome."

He then turned to Grandma Donner. "Now this beacon of beauty must undoubtedly be Mrs. Donner."

"Flattery will get you everywhere," she giggled as she reached out her hand to him palm down as though expecting him to kiss it. He gave it a brief little shake and then turned to us.

Lovella! Earl!" he spouted with inebriated charm, so sudden and loud that I startled. "It is so good to see you two. I have missed you."

"Thank you, Dad," Earl responded.

I glanced up and caught a milli-second contact of his eyes and then stared at the floor. "Thank you," I said, quickly and almost under my breath. I felt terrified in that moment. There was a part of me that realized that I was safe and that Earl would protect me no matter what, but I was also trying to fight off a full-blown panic attack. I asked myself where the gutsy, stand-up-to-anyone Lovella had gone. Perhaps she had been

Confessions from the Pumpkin Patch

subdued by a cumulative effect. It was not just the fact that Earl's father had screamed at me and called me a "nigger fucking whore" when Vanilla was born, it was the whole year, the death of Martin Luther King and Bobby Kennedy, the riots shown constantly on TV, and the isolation in our apartment where my mind had gone into fear overdrive.

Mr. Titwallow, despite his inebriation picked up on my discomfort. "Ah—Lovella. I—hmmm. I am going to go back to the kitchen and eat a bite, and then maybe a little later we could maybe sit down together and have a discussion. I—I'm also going to try to sober up a little bit so I don't make such a big ass of myself."

He retreated back to the kitchen and when he was out of the room, Earl turned to me and said, softly, "Are you alright?"

"I don't know," I said. "I don't know why I'm so scared. It's not like me to be scared like this."

Mrs. Titwallow came to sit on the opposite side of me from Earl. She reached out and touched my hand.

"Lovella," she said, so gently. "You know that I love you, don't you, and you know that I adore little Vanilla?"

"Yes, I do," I responded.

"Then believe me when I tell you that it is all going to be fine." She smiled and looked at me with such gentle eyes. "At this point, honey, Daniel is having to face something that he is finding very difficult. Please understand that he is just as nervous about this as you are. —Earl," she said, "why don't you take Lovella and show her the view from the crest."

"Sure," he responded.

We got our coats and headed out of the house. There was about a fifteen minute walk to the top of a little hill on the west side of the house. It was a bit steep but Earl held on to my hand to make sure I had my footing. When we got to the top, the view was magnificent. There was an inlet there and in the distance across on the other side the hills jutted down to the water's edge. Even though it was cold and breezy, the sun was shining in a perfectly blue sky.

"It's beautiful," I said, mesmerized by the sight.

Earl walked around behind me, wrapped his arms around me and held me close to his body to keep me warm.

"Anna and I used to love to climb up here when we were kids," he said. "We didn't have to do anything but just be here. There is something just so enchanting about it."

"Your mom must have known that I would relax if you brought me here," I said.

"We both needed to relax a little bit," he responded.

Karlyle Tomms

We stood there a very long time, saying nothing, just watching. Even on a cold Thanksgiving Day, there was the occasional boat that we would see. Gulls and other water birds sailed in the low sky, occasionally skimming down just above the surface. The sound of the waves lapping against the stones of the shore made a soothing rhythm and created a symphony accented by the horn-like cries of the gulls. After a while Earl asked me if I was ready to go. Then we navigated our way back down the hillside to the house.

When we came back in the house, it was very toasty warm. Mr. Titwallow had built and was in the process of stoking a fire in the fireplace. There was no one else in the living room except him and Mrs. Titwallow.

"Where is everyone?" I asked, suddenly feeling a little nervous again.

"There is a football game on the television in the den," Mrs. Titwallow replied. "We asked them if they would like to go back there to watch it. Besides, Daniel and I need to have a little time alone with just the two of you if you don't mind." I looked around at Earl for reassurance.

Mrs. Titwallow motioned for us to sit down. We sat on the sofa side-by-side. Mrs. Titwallow sat in a chair just off-center between us and Mr. Titwallow, who had come to sit in a chair that was opposite the sofa.

"Daniel," Mrs. Titwallow began. "I believe you have some things you need to say to Earl and his bride."

Mr. Titwallow almost looked as though he was scanning the room for a route of escape.

"Well, you see,—" he began finally. "I was far more out of line than I thought I was when I said, those awful things about you Lovella and about the baby. I—ah, —Well, it is wrong for anyone to say things like that. It was totally inappropriate, and Earl your mother has helped me to realize that I have no business judging anybody that way."

"Okay." Earl responded.

"Well—I—I'm sorry for what I said," Mr. Titwallow continued. "I know I can never take it back, but I want you to know." He looked up at me almost pleadingly. "I want you to know that I have changed my mind about such things. I've changed—completely changed."

"Well, why the big change, Dad?" Earl chided. "I've never known you to give up on a point. Hell, you demand that you are right when everybody else tells you that you are wrong, — when you know you are wrong. Why would you change your mind about this?"

Mr. Titwallow looked over at his wife. "You want to tell them, Clarese," he questioned.

"No Daniel," she replied. "I think you need to tell them."

324

Confessions from the Pumpkin Patch

He took a deep breath and let it out in a big sigh. "Well, ah—after I had acted like such an ass the day Vanilla was born, Clarese did her best to convince me that I was wrong and that I should apologize. Of course I refused, because like you said, Earl, when I think I'm right I refuse to listen to arguments to the contrary. Finally, she stopped talking to me about it and I thought we were getting back to normal."

He kept looking over at Mrs. Titwallow as though trying to gather some strength from his repeated glances.

He went on. "I felt that you had been totally out-of-line to hit me, son, and I kept telling her that you owed me an apology. I told her I was going to call you up and demand that you apologize to me. What I didn't know was that your mother had started doing some—research. I don't know what gave her the idea to do this, but she did. She even contacted the Mormon church to find out about how to do it."

"About what?"

Earl cut in glancing back and forth between his parents.

"About—our heritage."

Mr. Titwallow leaned forward and put his hands together. He stared down at them as though there might be some prompt written there.

"It seems that one of our ancestors was a plantation owner in Georgia before the Civil War and he had a habit of having sex with his slave women and then also maybe their daughters, his own biracial children. It turns out that maybe a generation or two down the line one of those daughters had become so light-skinned that if she was careful about it, she passed as white. She ran away and hid out, and was eventually able to find passage to Pennsylvania. She married your great, great, Grandfather Simon Titwallow. He apparently knew that she had black ancestry but helped her hide it. I guess it was never spoken of even within the family and after a while everyone forgot about having a biracial, great grandmother."

"Holy shit!"

Earl burst into laughter and stood up pacing back and forth.

"Holy fucking shit! This is too damn funny for words! Mom! How the hell did you ever find this out?"

Mrs. Titwallow then spoke. "Well, when Daniel insisted there was no Negroid blood on our side of the family, I thought, 'How does he know?' So I searched. I was able to trace records back and then look at lineages and how the family split off into different factions over the years. I got suspicious when I traced back to your great, great Grandpa Simon Titwallow and couldn't really find any information beyond that about his wife. When I traced it down the different branches of the family, I found a

325

Karlyle Tomms

distant cousin of Daniel's and contacted her to see if she might know why the information stopped with Simon's wife. She had a journal that had been kept by your great, great aunt identifying knowledge that her mother had black ancestry. Your cousin was kind enough to send me a photo copy of one particular and telling page of that journal. I then had the evidence I needed to sit down with your father and have a little discussion."

"This is so fucking funny!" Earl laughed. "The buzzards have come home to roost. They have found the skeleton in the old man's closet and have picked the last bit of meat off the bone! —So Dad, how does that feel? How does it feel for you to find out after all these years of being a bigoted asshole that you *are* the very thing you were judging?"

Mr. Titwallow was still leaning over his folded hands and said, "It feels very humbling son. It feels like I have been a hypocrite and that it is about time I learned to do a little listening instead of so much telling."

Then he looked up at me. "I'm sorry, Lovella," he went on. "I'm sorry that I judged you and I'm sorry that I judged my granddaughter. I was totally wrong. I hope you realize that I am sincere, that I truly want and need your forgiveness."

I sat looking at him for several seconds pondering what I was going to say. At last I was feeling once again back to my old self. I said calmly. "I forgive you, Mr. Titwallow."

"Thank you, Lovella," he said. "May I have a hug?"

I got up and walked across to him. He stood up and enfolded me in his huge arms. As we stood there I asked laughingly, "Do you think that history is why Earl has such a big dick?"

Without missing a beat, Earl's Mom said, "No, dear, that probably comes from my side of the family."

Confessions from the Pumpkin Patch

Chapter 25

On the following morning, the skies were a crystal clear cold blue with no clouds to be seen anywhere and sunlight reflected off the chilly earth like a mirror. Earl and I awoke to the sound of a light tapping on our bedroom door. When I stirred, it woke the baby as she had been sleeping quietly between us. Startled, Vanilla wailed at the morning. I picked her up quickly from the bed and began pacing in my gown rocking her and trying to quiet her as Earl went to the door. When Earl opened the door, there stood Nora, half bent at the shoulders and being careful not to peek in.

"I am so sorry to disturb you, Master Earl," she said in her classic British accent, "however, John has prepared breakfast and Mr. Titwallow requests that you join the family in the dining room before preparing for departure."

"Yes, um," Earl said sleepily. "We will be right down."

He closed the door behind him and turned to me. By this time Vanilla had quieted her crying to a gentle whimper. Earl immediately turned back around, threw open the door and called down the hall. "Nora. Nora." Realizing his nakedness he grabbed the sheet off the bed and quickly wrapped it around himself.

"Yes, dear boy," she said as she turned in the hall.

"Could you take Vanilla for a short while so Lovella can dress?" he asked.

"Certainly, Master Earl," she said and then walked into the room, straight to me. She diverted her eyes until I said, "It's okay, Nora." She then quickly took the baby and exited from the room.

As soon as she left, I threw on some jeans and a ruffled blouse while Earl hunted for the pants he had worn the day before. Once we were dressed, we threw our remaining clothes into the suit cases and went downstairs.

There at the dining table sat the whole family, all fully dressed and sitting about waiting, I suppose, for our arrival. Mrs. Titwallow sat to the side at one end of the table holding Vanilla, who was greedily sucking at a bottle. Mr. Titwallow sat across the corner from her at the head of the table. The places were set with silverware and napkins, but there were no plates. Most of the family did have bits of coffee sipped down to various

327

levels in their cups.

Grandmother Donner spouted immediately, "Hell. It's about time you two got down here. I thought I would plum starve to death before the two of you would make a showing. So, can we eat now?"

"I'm sorry, Grandma," I said. "You shouldn't have waited on us. Surely you could have started the meal."

"No, this is the last gathering before we all go home," Mr. Titwallow interjected. "We all need to share the time together. I'm sure your grandmother has not starved yet. Have you, Mrs. Donner?"

Grandpa Donner chimed in, "She ain't starved yet. Hell, look at her. She could live for two weeks just on belly fat."

Grandma Donner stared at him. "Shut up, Sid, before I start gnawing on your belly fat."

Nora had seen us enter. She motioned to John who had already begun to serve the Eggs Benedict. By the time we were taking our seats, plates were being placed in front of us. Nora came around to fill our coffee cups remembering exactly how we liked it. The food was plated as a work of art with slices of honeydew melon and strawberries to one side with a garnish of parsley topping the Hollandaise sauce that coated our ham-stacked English muffin.

When we began to eat, Mr. Titwallow announced, "I just want to say how truly happy I am that all of you could join us for this holiday, and most of all, I have to say that I am so glad to have my son back, and my family reunited."

Earl leaned over and whispered in my ear. "Shit, here it comes. Watch and learn how a true controller works."

I gave only a tiny nod to Earl and otherwise pretended that I didn't hear.

Mr. Titwallow continued. "I say we should make this a family tradition and all meet back here again next year."

"Here. Here!" Grandma Donner exclaimed as she raised her coffee cup into the air before bringing it to her lips.

"It has been truly wonderful," Mother said. "Daniel, Clarese, your gracious hospitality is greatly appreciated." She then threw a stare at me to let me know, as though I was still a little girl that manners would insist on an expression of gratitude from myself as well.

"Thank you, Mr. & Mrs. Titwallow," I said. "It was very sweet of you to have us."

"Well," Mr. Titwallow continued. "I have enjoyed this as much as any of you. I—I—ah—just hate to see my son go back and work for minimum wage at a grocery store."

"Told you."

Confessions from the Pumpkin Patch

Earl stifled a sarcastic tone under his breath.

"We are doing fine, Mr. Titwallow," I said defending Earl. "Honestly, we are quite comfortable."

"Well, I know you are doing okay," Mr. Titwallow replied. "It is okay. I mean, I started out at the bottom and worked my way into what I have now. In some ways, I think it was sheer luck as much as it was hard work for me to have built this business. I have done some soul-searching over the last few months, and even though I have mixed feelings about it, I do understand that sometimes it is important to feel like you have accomplished something on your own, that you have done it yourself without having it handed to you. I think somewhere along the way I had forgotten that."

Earl didn't say a word. There were some glances between him and his mother. After a moment, I spoke for him. "Thank you, Mr. Titwallow. It means a lot to us that you have come to realize our need for independence."

"I hope that I understand," Mr. Titwallow responded. "The truth is I would give you kids everything if I could, but I know I have to back off and let go. I know I haven't been very good at that in the past and Earl—I owe you another apology as well. I owe you an apology for trying to make you into what I wanted you to be instead of letting you be who you are. I have interfered in your life. I have pushed you and I have tried to make you into me. Instead of loving you for who you are, I have tried to make you into what I expected from a son. I'm sorry I did that to you."

Earl looked up from his plate and down the table at is father. His face was stern "I am not sure if I believe you," he said.

"I don't blame you if you don't believe me," Mr. Titwallow replied his own voice trembling. "I just want you to know that I love you no matter what you want to do with your life, but I also want you to know that I have options for you if you should ever decide that you want to accept them."

"Oh, here we go," Earl said not even trying to hide his hostile tone.

Mr. Titwallow drew a very deep breath and then leaned forward in his chair. "Son, I know you don't believe me when I say that I am leaving your choices up to you, but I swear to you this is the commitment I am making to you right here in front of these witnesses. I will not continue to interfere in your life. I want to help you if you will let me, but if you want to build a life on your own then I will bless you in that decision."

"What kind of options?" Earl questioned.

Mr. Titwallow sighed again and looked down at his plate. When he looked back up he said, "Son, I promise you that this is an invitation and

329

Karlyle Tomms

not an expectation. It is an offer and not a demand. If you tell me that you don't want to do this, then I will bless you in whatever choice you make."

"What is it?" Earl responded with a hint of hostility still in his voice. "You want me to come back to Pittsburgh and follow you around the office so I can learn to imitate you? You want to tell me what I need to do to protect your legacy?"

"No, Son," Mr. Titwallow said with an uncharacteristic softness. "I have already told you that I want you to be your own man. I mean that. I want you to be who you are, whatever that means to you. I know that doesn't sound like me, but I have had to do a lot of soul searching over the past couple of months. I have had to re-think a lot of things including my role as a father."

"What then?" Earl quipped.

"Like I said," Mr. Titwallow labored on. "This is only if you want to, only if you are willing to give it a try."

"What, damn it?" Earl snapped losing his patience.

Mr. Titwallow did not take the invitation to fight, also something he did not often do with Earl. Mrs. Titwallow was showing some anxiety at this point. Mr. Titwallow took a deep breath and went on. "You know that I have been building a warehouse distribution center in Nashville, Tennessee over the past couple of years. I have been expanding distribution into the southern states, Georgia, Alabama, Mississippi, and South Carolina. I hope to maybe include Arkansas, Louisiana and Missouri. Anyway, the facility is due to be finished in February, and I hope to have full distribution out of there by next summer. I would like for you to manage it for me."

"Manage it?" Earl questioned looking obviously confused.

"Well, you have a degree in business management, don't you?" Mr. Titwallow responded. "You should have some idea what it takes to manage a distribution center."

"I have a degree, Dad," Earl pleaded. "That's all. I have a degree. I've never managed anything in my life. I figured when I finally got a job it would be working for a few years probably in lower or middle management before I tackled anything remotely like a seven state distribution center. I don't know that I know how to do that unless what you mean by manage you want me to be your puppet in Nashville and do what you tell me to do."

"No—," Mr. Titwallow proceeded. "I don't mean that. I will be available to you if you want or need my advice as will several of my other managers. I mean for this to be yours. Yours to run as you see fit. Maybe you have learned something in school that I don't know. Maybe you might

330

Confessions from the Pumpkin Patch

have some creative ideas that I never considered. It will be yours. The company will supply the product. Then the markets and distribution you create for the product will be up to you and your own talent."

"You realize that you are taking a huge risk by doing that?" Earl defended. "What if I screw it up? It could mean millions. It is too big for me to fuck it up." He turned quickly to the rest of the family and said, "I'm sorry, please forgive my language."

"Oh, hell!" Grandmother Donner interjected. "We've all heard French before."

"I'm putting my faith in you," Mr. Titwallow said, as he looked intently and confidently at Earl. "I know that you can do this. I know you have it in you. If you don't want the job, I understand, but if you do take the job, you have my promise that I will stay out of the way and that I will give only the advice that I am asked to give."

"You are taking a risk that could potentially bankrupt Chum Snacks," Earl responded.

"I know," said Mr. Titwallow. "But I'm also taking a risk that could double or even triple the size of the company. Do you want the job? If you want it, you can have it."

"I'll have to think about it," Earl replied looking over at me. "We will have to think about it."

Mr. Titwallow took a bite of his breakfast and chewed it gingerly. "I am willing to start you out at $200,000 a year and give you a 20% bonus of any profit increases the company makes."

Mother dropped her fork and gasped.

I reached over and took Earl's hand. "Whatever you decide is okay," I said. Inside, my heart was pounding. I would accept if he said no, but my mind was already racing to what my life would be like with that much money. Unlike Earl, I was a transplant hippie. I agreed to a point with his causes but there was still a part of me that liked the finer things in life.

"How soon do you need to know?" Earl asked.

"Two weeks," Mr. Titwallow replied. "Does that give you enough time?"

Earl nodded and then changed the subject. He turned to my family and said, "So, are you guys looking forward to going home today?"

Grandma Donner said, "Hell, if I never go back to that rat-trap again it's fine with me. I would just as soon stay here and be waited on. I go back home, I gotta wait on this fat bastard." She slapped Grandpa Donner across the belly to which he responded, "Goddamn woman! Lighten up!"

I sat there snickering under my breath watching Mother who was obviously appalled.

331

Karlyle Tomms

"Well," Earl said politely. "I'm glad you enjoyed your stay here."

After breakfast, the limo drivers brought our luggage down from the house and stuffed it into the trunks of the cars. Then they stood dutifully to the side of the open doors waiting for us to descend the stairs like royalty and enter our gleaming black chariots. There were two limos to take us back just as there had been two to deliver us.

We said our goodbyes on the porch. Mr. and Mrs. Titwallow were going back in another car with John and Nora that afternoon.

Just as we were getting ready to leave, Mother approached me.

"Lovella," she whispered. "Do you mind if I ride back with you and Earl, at least as far as State College? I really don't think I can tolerate one more hour with the Donners."

I was shocked at her politeness and keenly aware of how she distanced herself from her own parents by calling them, "The Donners."

"I'm sure it would be fine, Mother," I said. "Besides, maybe you can hold Vanilla while Earl and I talk. It seems like we have a lot to talk about after this visit."

"I would be delighted to hold the baby," Mother said. She then shifted her attention behind her to tell Grandma and Grandpa Donner that she was riding back to State College with us. I heard Grandma Donner exclaim, "Can't stay away from that grandbaby, huh, Drucella? Hell, I don't blame you. Go ahead."

Mother came to me and took Vanilla from my arms before we even descended to the cars. We had no sooner pulled out of the driveway when Earl leaned his head against the window and said, with exasperation, "What the hell!"

I reached my hand up to touch his shoulder and he turned to me, "Can you believe this shit?" he said incensed.

"I believe what I heard," I replied. "I don't know how you are interpreting all this."

Mother sat quietly holding Vanilla pretending not to hear. The baby had easily fallen asleep in her arms.

"That's the problem," Earl replied. "I don't know how I'm interpreting it either. I don't know what to fucking think. I spent my whole life fighting with and resisting the control of my father, trying to give him what he wanted on one hand, but rebelling and trying to live my own life without his control on the other. Now he wants to play nice cause he found his roots, but I still don't trust him."

"Sometimes people change," I said. "Sometimes we realize things in retrospect that we just didn't see when we were in it."

Confessions from the Pumpkin Patch

"If it was up to you, Lovella," he stared at me intently, "if it was all up to you and it wasn't my decision to make at all, what would you do? Would you go to Nashville?"

"I don't think that's fair," I moaned. "It is not my decision. It's your decision."

"No," he affirmed. "It is *our* decision. We are a family. You are my wife. Whatever I decide affects you and the baby, so what you think about this is important."

I turned and looked at Mother who sat silent. She glanced at me briefly then looked away. I could scarcely believe that she wasn't chirping in with her opinions about this.

I turned back to Earl. "I have mixed feelings, too," I said. "On one hand I think, my god, with that amount of money I could buy practically anything I want for myself or the baby. On the other hand it might be nice to have all that somewhere besides Nashville, Tennessee."

"What's wrong with Nashville?" he questioned.

"Oh, jeez!" I quipped. "Minnie Pearl, Earnest Tubb, and the Grand Ole Opry for starts. I mean the whole town is about hicks and rednecks. If the TV shows and record stores are any indication, you would think that there is not a black person living within hundreds of miles. What are they going to think about or do to a family with a biracial baby, burn a cross on our lawn?"

"What about Charlie Pride?" he asked.

"Charlie Pride? Honestly, Charlie Pride?" I responded. "They have one token black country singer just to prove they aren't prejudiced. That's worse than prejudiced."

"Nashville is not like that," he said. "For Christ sakes, Vanderbilt University is there. It's an Ivy League university, and country music is only one of lots of different types of music recorded there. The Beatles even recorded there."

"Well, I've never been there," I said. "I just know the stereotype I guess."

"I'm sorry," Earl responded. "I didn't mean to sound condescending. I have been there. Vanderbilt was one of the universities I applied to. Nashville is much more metropolitan and much more sophisticated than most people imagine. It's even called the "Athens of the South." They have a full-sized replica of the Parthenon there."

"Okay," I said. "I never knew any of that stuff. You make it sound nice. So they have got a little culture, but it is still the south and I think about the prejudice in the south. I even worry about bringing up Vanilla in Pennsylvania. I think I would be even more worried about raising her in

Karlyle Tomms

Tennessee."

"We don't have to go," he said. "I don't want to make it sound like I want the job. I don't want the job—." He paused for a moment. "Well, I don't know if I want the job. Maybe I would like to have the job, but I don't know that I have what it takes to pull it off."

"Do you think you could be happy living in Nashville?" I asked.

He reached over and took my hand. "I could be happy living anywhere if I am with you."

"Oh, come on, Earl," I pleaded. "There's more to it than that. Cities have a soul just like a person does. Just as you might not like one person's personality but prefer another, you might not like the personality of a city. It needs to be something that draws you to it."

"I suppose," he said.

"Well, did you visit Nashville when you applied to Vanderbilt?" I questioned.

"Yeah," he responded. "I spent a few days there."

"Did you like it?" I continued. "How did it feel to you?"

"It's kind of cool in a way," he said.

"Is that it?" I pressed.

"Well, I guess there is kind of a mix there," he explained. "It's not just country music. You can find people there from all over the world, really."

"That's cool," I said. "What do you think it would be like to live there?"

He turned to face me as much as he could. "If we lived there," he said, "we would probably be living in Green Hills or Brentwood. They are sort of the nouveau riche areas of the city. I suppose we might live in Belle Meade, but that's old money, way old money. You have million dollar and multimillion dollar homes out there. I think a lot of the country music stars live in Green Hills. It's rich but newer, maybe not as rich. I don't know, Lovella. I don't know what I want. The thought of even considering living in places like that feels like I'm selling out. It feels like I'm giving in to the establishment."

"Lots of money means having the resources to help others more," I said. "If we had that much money and maybe if we didn't spend too much of it on our own luxuries, we could contribute to some good causes or maybe even create our own charities."

He took a very deep breath then turned to stare at the passing landscape that was flying by the window.

"The truth is," he said, fiddling nervously with a button on his shirt. "The truth is I feel guilty about having that much money. I've felt guilty about it most of my life. I mean we didn't always have the best. When I was really young, we had it nice, but not great and when we started having

334

Confessions from the Pumpkin Patch

more money, when Dad got dollar signs in his eyes, we moved into bigger and bigger homes with more opulence, and servants, but my friends didn't. I had to leave them behind. Dad didn't want me to be friends with the poor kids anymore, but fuck, what was he when he was growing up? He grew up poor just like them and then when he got rich it was like he was better than them and he expected us to act like we were better than them, but they were my friends, Lovella."

"Your Dad fought so hard to get out of poverty," I reasoned. "Maybe he hated poverty so much that he couldn't separate the poor person from the poor condition."

"He thought everybody ought to be able to just go out and make millions like he did," Earl snapped. "He thought anyone who didn't go out and make millions must be lazy, but he didn't think about the fact that a lot of those poor people working in our factories had hard times that he didn't face, medical bills or family tragedies that a minimum wage job was not going to cover. He didn't figure that some of them were working harder than he ever worked and were struggling paycheck to paycheck to cover their bills and raise a family with no real way to save. He didn't think about the fact that not everybody is as smart as he is or even if they are smart, they might not have the business sense that he has. He just flat out didn't think. He had the idea that if he could do it the whole fucking world should be able to do it, but it doesn't work that way. The American dream is not for everyone. There are people who can never have it no matter how much they desire it or how hard they are willing to work for it. It takes more than just hard work and know-how. It takes the stars being aligned just right for you. Otherwise you end up like the next poor schmuck who thought his life was going to be better. If you work your ass off but you can't afford to go to a dentist or see a doctor, then your health deteriorates. If you can't afford the good food that rich people can afford, and you can't afford the healthcare that rich people can afford, your life goes downhill faster. The next thing you know you are so sick you can't work and your own personal American dream becomes an American nightmare, and if you're lucky you can get on disability or some kind of pension plan. If you're not lucky you end up on the streets or in an institution. It takes more than hard work to be successful, and my Dad just doesn't seem to get that."

I glanced up at Mother and realized that she was paying very close attention to his speech. He looked at me, then back out the window. "I guess the difference between me and my father," he said, "is that I notice things. I watch how things work. I notice people and pay attention to all the factors, and my Dad gets a dollar sign in his head and can't see anything else. Like a horse with blinders on, he can't see anything but what is right in front of him. If that is a dollar bill, he will follow it like a carrot in front of a horse's nose all the way to the end of the road."

I sat there thinking for quite some time before I spoke. "I guess the question," I said finally, "is whether you want to cash in on the coat tails of your dad's American dream or try to create one of your own, and take the chance of ending up like one of those poor schmucks you are talking about?"

"Unless Dad goes bankrupt," he said, "I would never be one of them. He would see to it one way or another that I was taken care of. I might not be in the lap of luxury, but he would find a way to make sure my basic needs were met. I've already cashed in just by being his son. The only option I would have if I wanted to build my own dream would be to cut all ties and refuse any assistance from him at all. Even then, if I didn't disappear where he couldn't find me, he would find a way to sneak it in."

"Are you willing to do that?" I asked. "Disappear?"

A look crossed his face that I had difficulty interpreting. I think it was a mix of multiple emotions. Then he glanced quickly around the passenger cabin like a trapped animal trying to find a way out.

"I'm hungry," he quipped completely ignoring my question. "Are you hungry, Mrs. Fuchs? You guys want to stop somewhere and have a snack?"

"I'm fine," Mother said. "I would perhaps like to have something to drink however."

Earl reached over and pressed a button on the console and we heard the chauffer's voice come through the speaker. "Yes, sir?"

"Driver, please look for a place to stop and have a soft drink or a snack," he said.

"Would a Stuckey's be acceptable, sir?" the driver responded.

"Yes, any place like that would be fine," Earl said.

"Sir," the driver went on, "there is a Stucky's just over the Connecticut border a few miles ahead."

"Fine," Earl said. "Stop there."

"Should I inform the other car to stop as well?" the driver asked.

"No!" exclaimed Mother, half shouting.

Earl turned and looked at her with a strained curiosity then told the driver, "No, only this car will be stopping."

Earl settled back into his seat and we continued the ride sharing small talk. No more mention was made of Nashville. In about thirty minutes the limo pulled into the parking lot of the Connecticut Stuckey's on I-95. The driver got out and opened the rear doors for us and we all filed into the

336

Confessions from the Pumpkin Patch

building. Mother continued to carry Vanilla who was still quietly sleeping in her arms.

We strolled up to the Formica counter at the snack bar in the back corner of the building. I quickly spotted the restroom and told Earl to get me a coke and an order of fries. Then I went trotting off to the restroom and came in behind a middle-aged woman with reddish-brown hair. "Oh, excuse me," I said as I darted past her to one of the stalls. "Got to go really bad." She said nothing but as I was opening the door to the stall I heard the door to the bathroom slam. I turned and she was gone.

When I returned, Earl had ordered for everyone. We had our drinks and found a booth. Mother insisted on keeping Vanilla.

"Lovella, you will have her all to yourself when you get home, and I have a limited time with my grandbaby so go on and explore while I spoil this child," she said politely. I smiled back at her feeling a warmth that I rarely ever felt with Mother.

While we waited for the food I went strolling around the displays of trinkets and treats. I then saw that same middle age woman get up from a booth, stare at me, and then go to the bathroom. I thought her behavior was strange, but then I thought maybe she had one of those phobias where you can't pee if there is someone else in the room. I didn't notice when she returned.

In a short time we were called to pick up our order. I helped Earl bring it to the booth. Then as we were eating, Mother noticed a couple in a booth across from us who kept staring and whispering. "What are you doing?" I whispered noticing Mother's glances across from me.

"That couple over there," she whispered back. "They keep looking at us like we're some kind of circus show."

When I turned and looked, the same middle-age woman sat in a booth across the way from us. There was a pot-bellied man who appeared to be in his late forties. He was wearing blue jeans and a flannel shirt with suspenders that caused his belly to look even more pronounced. They were indeed whispering and casting disgusted looks in our direction.

"What the hell!" I said. Then I turned to Mother watching her struggle to sip her soda and hold the baby at the same time. "Let me take her, Mother," I said, getting up to reach for the baby.

"No, dear, I have her," she said. "Go ahead and sit back down."

I had no sooner taken my seat on the opposite side of the booth when Mother stood up and carried Vanilla across to the couple who had been staring at us.

"This is my granddaughter," she said smiling. "Isn't she beautiful? I noticed that you folks kept looking over in our direction and I can only assume that you were thinking what a beautiful baby we have."

"Ah, no, not exactly," the middle-aged woman said. "Wasn't thinking that at all."

"Hmmm," Mother sighed. "I wonder then what would cause you to be so interested in my family that you were constantly staring and whispering. You must have mistaken my beautiful daughter for a movie star then."

The red-headed woman's skin was aged from tanning and the crow's feet streaking across her eye sockets made her look mean and menacing. She snarled at Mother "Why don't you just take your little eggplant back over to your own booth, Miss Mammy, and leave us alone."

"Oh, dear," Mother said. "Surely you mean to be nicer than you sound. I just could not imagine why you would want to be inconsiderate or make a nasty remark about my beautiful grandbaby or me."

I had been watching this scene unfold with intrigue. Mother turned to walk back to our booth and had scarcely gotten ten feet across the floor when I heard the middle-aged woman say, "Nigger lover." In an instant, I felt red-hot rage inside of me that flipped into an anger like I had never felt before. No sooner had I realized what had been said than I was up out of my seat and across the room.

"WHAT THE FUCK DID YOU JUST SAY TO MY MOTHER?" I screamed. "WHAT THE! GODDAMN FUCK! YOU SELF-RIGHTEOUS, BIGGOTED, FUCKING, WRINKLED, OLD WHORE!"

The woman slid back to the end of the booth startled by my attack, visibly shaken at the violence of my temper. She had good reason to be shaken because I was on the verge of trying to rip her throat out.

"YOU APOLOGIZE TO MY MOTHER YOU FUCKING CUNT!" I screamed. "YOU FUCKING APOLOGIZE TO MY MOTHER AND MY BABY!"

Earl had gotten to his feet and come across the room to catch my arms and pull me back. "Come on," he said. "Let it go."

I struggled against him feeling an anger so deep and so vile that I could scarce contain it. "I AM GOING TO RIP HER FUCKING FACE OFF!" I screamed.

The man, who was with her, got to his feet and pointed an accusing finger in my direction.

"I THINK YOU NEED TO TAKE YOUR NIGGER-LOVING ASS BACK OVER TO YOUR BOOTH AND SIT DOWN NOW!" he yelled.

Earl turned loose of me and stepped between me and the other man. He towered over that pot-bellied old fool by a good foot or more. Grabbing him by the collar and yanking him up so hard that he came half up on his tiptoes, Earl commanded, "I think you need to apologize to my wife and

Confessions from the Pumpkin Patch

my family."

The man choked out a "Fuck you, asshole!"

Earl grabbed both sides of his collar and brought his fists up so tight under the man's chin that it tilted his head back.

"Now I think you need to apologize to me, my wife and my family," Earl said through clenched teeth. "Cause, if you don't, I might not let go of this cheap five-and-dime shirt of yours 'til you stop breathing completely." I noticed the manager frantically dialing the phone and was certain that the police were being called. I tugged on Earl's shirt now realizing the severity of the situation.

"Come on, Honey," I said. "We need to go, now!"

Earl barely noticed.

By this time the baby was disturbed and was wailing in Mother's arms. Mother bounced her gently and tried to quiet her with, "Shh, shh, shh, shh."

"Apologize!" Earl hissed grabbing the man's collar even tighter. The man nodded affirmation and Earl loosened his grip slightly. "Say it," he said.

"I am sorry," he said.

"You are sorry for what?" Earl insisted.

"I am sorry that I called—"

"Don't say that word again!" Earl interrupted, tightening his grip.

The man took a hesitant breath. "I'm sorry for what I said," he squeaked. "I was wrong."

"Thank you," Earl said as he loosened his grip slightly, but before he let go he turned to the woman who had cowered back to the edge of the booth, "You, too, bitch," he said.

"I, ah—I'm sorry for what I said," she replied shivering.

"Now," Earl concluded as he turned loose of the man, "I suggest you folks try to be a little more civil. After all, this is America where everyone is created equal."

He turned to look at me and Mother.

"Come on," he said. "I think we have had our break."

Earl came back to our booth, gathered up our coats and headed for the front door. Mother and I followed dutifully behind him. As Mother passed the booth where the couple had been sitting she stopped and said, "Hmmmm. You seem to think you are better than other people. Maybe you think the color of your skin makes you superior. That's interesting you should think that, 'cause I heard the same brown shit comes out of everybody's ass."

I turned and stared at her in amazement. She looked up at me, caught my astonished glare and cocked her head to one side, then followed me out of the building. We did not hurry, but strolled across the parking lot to our car. I wanted to hurry. I was as nervous as a cat, but Earl kept laying his hand on my shoulder, pulling me back and saying, "Calm down."

The chauffeur on spotting us got out of the limo where he had been waiting. He came around and opened the door to the passenger compartment. Earl waved at him to close the door. He then waited by the car about six feet from where we were standing.

"What are we doing?" I asked. "We need to go! Jeez!" I was pacing and felt like I was going to have another panic attack.

"The police will be here any minute," Earl said. "We are going to make sure that there are no surprises."

He handed my coat to me. I put it on then took Vanilla so Mother could put her coat on. Vanilla was well wrapped in blankets but I still nuzzled her under my coat.

"Jesus! I need a cigarette!" I exclaimed. I had not had a cigarette in a couple of months and I don't think I had even wanted one 'til that day. There had been no special reason for quitting. I just decided that I didn't want to smoke anymore. However, I quit many times before finally beating the habit.

Mother reached into her purse, pulled out a pack of cigarettes and a lighter. As soon as I realized what she had in her hand I was filled with a mix of emotion. I desperately craved a cigarette but on the other hand, I was angry at cigarettes, at a lot of things.

"I thought you quit," I said to Mother.

"I did," she responded. "I only started smoking again when your father died."

Another mix of emotions went over me and I was transported back to Daddy's death bed in the hospital and the cruel things Mother had said to me at that time. There were still too many unanswered questions, and though Mother was behaving very differently, I still had a hard time bringing myself to fully trust her. She started smoking again after Daddy died and that was when I began the process of quitting. I realized that I couldn't bring myself to smoke again, at least not then. I had felt abandoned on so many levels when Daddy passed. I guess I even felt abandoned by the cigarettes. Smoking didn't do anything for me anymore. It no longer seemed glamorous or cool. It just felt like a stupid thing to do even though I craved them when I was upset.

"No, put them away," I said. "I don't want to smoke around the baby anyway." I took some deep breaths and tried to make sense of the avalanche of emotions that had rushed back into my body.

Confessions from the Pumpkin Patch

Just as predicted, a State Patrol car soon pulled into the parking lot. We saw the manager meet the officer at the door and point in our direction, then back at the store. The officer went inside the building and came out a few minutes later. He strolled across the parking lot in our direction. He tipped his hat with his fingers as he approached. He was an older gentleman probably in his late fifties yet still looking quite dashing in his blue and gold uniform.

"You folks been having a little trouble here today?" he questioned.

"No, Sir," Earl responded. "I think we had everything well under control."

"The manager of the store tells me you had yourself a little physical altercation in there a few minutes ago," the officer continued.

"Well sir," Earl explained, "we did indeed have to ask a couple of folks to be a little more civil."

"Wasn't the way I heard it," the officer reiterated as he nodded in my direction. "Said, the young lady here was getting a little loud and out of hand and that you got a bit physical with those folks."

"Well, sir," Earl explained. "My wife usually doesn't have much of a temper but I think she got a little bit provoked today. I was doing my best to contain the situation."

"Provoked?" the officer questioned as he turned his attention to me. "Now how did you get provoked young lady?"

I looked at Earl questioningly and he nodded for me to go ahead. I pulled back my coat so the officer could see Vanilla's face. "My Mother was holding the baby and those people called her a—," I held my breath for a second and then forced myself to say the word I never wanted my child to hear, "A—nigger lover."

"Humph," the officer grunted. Then he looked back at Earl. "You are aware that these folks in there are within their rights to file charges for assault, and the store manager is within his rights to press charges for disturbing the peace?"

"Yes, sir," Earl quietly responded. "I don't think I could blame them if they did. Unfortunately there aren't any charges that could be filed for what they did to start the problem, and I don't think I would be much of a man if I stood by and allowed my family to be bullied."

The officer looked at him with inspection for a few long seconds. "Unfortunately," he said at last, "you get into these kinds of tussles often?"

"No, sir," Earl responded. "I can't say that I have ever gotten into this kind of tussle, except I punched my dad in the face for saying the same kind of thing the day my baby was born."

341

Karlyle Tomms

The officer looked at Earl sternly and then at me. "This is your baby?" he questioned.

Earl nodded affirmation.

"And this is your wife?" the officer continued.

Earl nodded again.

"So you had the baby before you married this fellow," the officer affirmed to me operating under the expected assumption.

"No, sir," Earl responded, reaching his arm out to me. "Lovella had the baby after we were married. This is our baby. She is my child."

A look of puzzlement crossed the officer's face, but he didn't ask any more questions. He looked down at the ground and then perused the three of us again.

"You folks wait right here. I'm going to go see if I can talk the manager out of filing charges. The people who were in the altercation have already said that they don't want to press charges."

He then turned on his heels and walked back to the store.

After a few agonizing minutes while we stood there in the crisp air discussing the situation, the officer came walking casually back across the parking lot.

"You folks think you can keep things under control and stay out of trouble?" he asked as he approached.

"Yes, sir," Earl replied.

"Where are you headed," the officer questioned.

"State College, Pennsylvania," Earl responded.

"Well, once you get out of the State of Connecticut you are not my problem," the officer commanded. "Just make sure I don't hear anything else from you before you cross that state line."

"Yes, sir," Earl said and then motioned us to get into the car. Before the driver could get to the door, Earl had already opened it for me and Mother.

We arrived back home late in the day with nightfall already started. Grandpa and Grandma Donner's car was waiting on the street by our apartment when we arrived. As soon as they saw us drive up, Grandma Donner got out of the car and came trotting back to meet us.

"Lord have mercy!" she exclaimed. "I thought something terrible must have happened to you. What took you so long?"

"Oh, we stopped to have a bite to eat," Earl responded as we stood on the street and waited for the driver to unload our luggage.

"Well, I guess we could have stopped," Grandmother Donner said as she pointed back to their limo, "but I packed up some leftovers for me and fat-butt to eat on the way."

"Where is Grandpa?" I asked.

342

Confessions from the Pumpkin Patch

"He's passed out asleep back in the car," Grandma Donner replied. She then looked around me to Mother and exclaimed, "Drucella! Let's get a move on!"

Mother ignored her, but handed Vanilla to Earl so she could oversee her luggage. The driver delivered Mother's luggage to the other car and our luggage to the apartment. We then had hugs and said goodbye.

When Mother hugged me I said, "Thank you, Mother."

"For what, Lovella?" she said standing back from me.

"For accepting my baby and standing up for her," I said. "You surprise me."

"We surprise each other, dear," she said and then turned to walk toward the other limo. "Take good care of my grandbaby," she said just before she slipped inside.

The driver closed the door behind her and each limo left in separate directions. Earl held Vanilla in one arm and put his other arm around me as we walked back up the walk to our building. Out of habit, I checked the mail when we came in. I realized that I had forgotten to check our box before we left. There was a letter that had been dated the week before Thanksgiving which must have arrived just before we left. There was no return address, but I noticed that it had been post marked in San Francisco. As soon as we got back in the apartment, I sat down and opened the letter. Earl put Vanilla in her crib and came back to sit across from me on the sofa. I read the whole thing silently.

November 17, 1968

Dear Lovella and Earl,

Sure hope you guys are loving it back in Pennsylvania. Dave and I have missed you guys. Hey, we know you were close to Screech and all, so thought we ought to drop you a line and let you know. Super bummer, I know, but about a week ago me and Dave went to pick Screech up for band practice and we couldn't find him. We went to his apartment and like walked around and called for him, but he never answered. Man we didn't even think to look in the bathroom. So, next two days, no Screech and nobody has seen him. Finally, we go back up to the apartment and start looking again and this time we found him in the bathtub. He had been gone at least three or four days. Man it was awful. He still had the needle in his arm from shooting up. We knew he had gotten hooked on heroin pretty bad, but nobody knew how bad. The coroner said he died of a drug overdose. No surprise though.

Karlyle Tomms

I'm really sorry. I know you guys were close. Thought you ought to know.

Hey, if you ever get back out to San Francisco, look us up. Dave and I would love to see you.

Peace,

Lorenda

My heart fell as I read the letter. I found myself questioning whether we should have stayed in San Francisco, whether maybe we could have made a difference. I heard myself asking the question, "What am I going to tell my daughter when the question comes up about her real father?" I wondered how Earl was going to react, and I hesitated.

Sensing my hesitation, Earl asked, "What's wrong?"

I simply handed him the letter.

As he read the letter, I saw his face melt into sadness. A single tear rolled down his cheek, and then another. He finished reading the letter and looked up at me with a profound anguish in his face. I moved over next to him and put my arm around him. Then he buried his face in my shoulder and sobbed.

"I loved him, Lovella," he cried.

"I know," I said softly. "I know."

After he had wept for a very long time, Earl pulled back from my embrace and wiped his eyes with his sleeve. He picked up the letter from the floor where he had dropped it, wadded it into his fist and said, "I want to go to Nashville. You want to go to Nashville?"

"Sure," I said, softly. "Wherever you go, that's where I will go. Whatever you want, that's what I want." It occurred to me in that moment that life often takes us where it wants us with only the illusion of choice. "I love you," I said softly.

"I love you, too," he said. "I want you to know I love you, too. I never stopped loving you for Screech. I love you from the depth of my soul, Lovella. I will never stop loving you."

Confessions from the Pumpkin Patch

Chapter 26

On a cold morning in January 1969 the phone rang early. I rolled over to look at the clock and realized that it was ten minutes before the alarm was set to go off at 6:00 AM. Earl stirred and took a deep fluttering breath, "Honey, can you get that?" he said in a sleepy whine. "Just a few more minutes." I had already started sitting up in bed when Earl made his request.

My heart sank when I looked at the time thinking there was no way anyone would be calling at this hour unless something was wrong, especially when it just kept ringing. We didn't have a phone by the bed and so I staggered across the dark bedroom to the phone beside the sofa in the living room. I picked up the receiver with one hand as I switched on the sofa lamp with the other. "Hello," I said almost breathlessly as I plopped myself on the end of the sofa with my night gown pulled over my now chilling feet.

"Hello, Lovella?" The tearful voice questioning on the other end of the line I recognized immediately. It was Gretta.

"Good morning, sweetie," I said. "What's wrong?"

"Tommy's coming home," she sobbed.

"Oh my god that's wonderful! Shouldn't you be happy about that?" I realized at the moment the words left my mouth that the tears could be about him coming home in a body bag. Too late to catch them, I blurted a quick, "I guess."

"I am happy," she wailed. "But he's coming home wounded. They are sending him to Walter Reed Medical Center in Washington from a military hospital in Germany."

"Oh my god," I gasped, "how bad?"

"I don't know. All I know is that he has been shot and thank God he's alive but he could still die, couldn't he? I just don't know what to do. I want to go to Washington to be with him, but I have the baby to take care of and I don't want to be away from the baby. I know Mom and Dad would take care of him, but I just don't know." The words came flooding out of her in a nervous barrage.

345

Karlyle Tomms

"Hold on. Hold on, sweetie," I tried to calm. "Let's not try to do too much at once here, one thing at a time. Do you know when he will be there?"

"He may already be there," she said. "I just got a strange call from some guy with the Marines late yesterday and I don't remember half of it. He said Tommy had been wounded and I just kind of blanked out from there. I know he is supposed to arrive there soon. I have worried about it all night. I don't know what to do."

"First of all," I scolded. "Stop worrying. At least he is coming home alive. Second of all, there has to be a number at the hospital and some kind of protocol for military families. I'm sure you can go there and probably take Derrick with you. Wait till after 8:00 when the business office opens, then call Walter Reed and call me back. Okay?"

"Okay," she whimpered. I heard the line go click—just like that. I knew she had to be nervous. She didn't even say goodbye.

By this time Earl was getting up. The alarm had gone off and he was getting ready for his day. We both had things to do and went about doing them. I was amazed Vanilla had slept through the phone ringing, but she had. I went to check on her to find her on her back in the crib, looking up at me googley-eyed and smiling.

"There's my little princess," I said as I reached into the crib to pull her to my shoulder.

The day went on from there and a little before noon Gretta called me back. When I answered the phone, I could tell there was a distinct difference in her emotional state.

"Lovella, hi, it's Gretta again," she said calmly. "I found out he is there. He is stable and the wound was not life threatening. Apparently though it is enough for them to give him what they call a medical retirement. He was shot through the hip or something. I think the doctor said the bullet split his pelvic bone. I don't know how much damage it did, but apparently it broke off the edge of his pelvic bone and did something to his hip joint on the left side. There will be probably more than one surgery and then he will have to go through some rehab before getting released."

"Oh, I am so relieved," I said. "I know you must be too."

"At least I know he is not going to die," she said calmly. "There are guest facilities there on base, so I am going to be taking the baby and going up to Washington tomorrow. Hopefully, I will get to see Tommy when I get there. I don't suppose there would be a chance you could go with me? You wouldn't have to stay. Maybe overnight. I have no idea how long I'll be staying. Do you think you could go with me?"

Confessions from the Pumpkin Patch

"Oh, honey, I don't know," I responded quietly. "Let me talk to Earl when he gets home. I think he will be getting out of class at 2:00." Earl had decided to take a couple of public relations classes post graduate before we moved to Nashville.

"You know I get so nervous about these things, big places, traffic and such," she stammered. "You have had so much more exposure to the city than I have. If you could just go up and help me get settled into the guest-quarters that alone would make me feel so much more comfortable."

"I'll see what I can do, sweetie," I said. "I'll call you back as soon as I have had a chance to discuss it with Earl. You are planning to go up to-morrow?"

"Yeah, if I can," she said.

"It is kind of short notice but I understand it is important," I mused. "I'll do the best I can, but will probably have to make arrangements with the baby and Earl in class. I don't know."

"Maybe you could come down and leave Vanilla with your mother for a couple of days and we could leave from here," she pleaded.

"Well," I pondered, "it is about a three hour drive to Climax and then almost five hours to Washington from there. If I could get out of here early enough this evening, maybe we could leave from there in the morning."

"Lovella, I would feel so much safer and more comfortable if you were with me," she begged.

"Well, let me call Mother and then I'll talk to Earl as soon as he gets home from class. He is usually here by 2:30."

"Okay. Okay," she said nervously. "Call me back."

"You know I will, sweetie," I said. "Love you."

"Love you, too," she parroted. "Goodbye."

"Goodbye."

I hung up the phone and immediately began wondering how I was going to manage everything. I knew I was fine with Earl. He was so easy going about everything. Mother had developed an adoration for her grandchild so I knew Vanilla would be in good hands. It was just a matter of planning and packing. I decided the best thing to do would be to have everything packed and ready to go by the time Earl got home. The problem was going to be that we only had one vehicle. Earl had sold the bus and his dad had gotten us a new four-door black Mercedes. He said the sports car was no good for a family and neither was the bus. This time, he put the title in Earl's name and that's when I learned to drive. With Earl teaching me, it didn't take long.

Mother was happy to keep Vanilla. Sometimes I thought she doted over my baby the way she couldn't dote over me.

347

Karlyle Tomms

When Earl came home he told me to take the car and go. He said he could take a taxi to class for a couple of days and not to worry about it. I never ceased to be amazed at how understanding and supportive he could be.

Just in case, I had everything packed for me and the baby by the time Earl got home that afternoon so I was out of the house and on the road by 3:30 PM. I was in Climax in plenty of time to spend the rest of the evening with Gretta. We made some phone calls and she was actually able to speak with Tommy over the phone to let him know we were coming up. He was somewhat groggy as they had done an initial surgery that afternoon, but able to ask about Derrick and clear enough to tell her that he loved her.

The next morning Gretta debated about it because she knew Tommy would want to see him, but finally decided to leave Derrick with her mom and dad. We had a quick breakfast with her parents and left very early for Washington. I drove the entire way. After stopping for an early lunch we arrived at Walter Reed Medical Center at about one o'clock that afternoon.

At first it was chaos trying to find the right building, and the right person to talk to in order to get Gretta settled with guest housing. After some fits and starts and a cross word here and there, we were finally able to navigate to the right government clerk who could help us. He was an older gentleman named Harold. He had a slight haunch in his back and thick black-rimmed glasses that almost looked like magnifying glasses. His messy hair was salt and pepper but mostly pepper. The darker hair didn't seem to match the age lines that cut trenches across his face. However, he was sweet and attentive as well as quite talkative. I noticed very quickly that his filler phrase when he couldn't think of anything else to say was, "Oh sure, sure, sure."

We met him at a counter in an older building having been sent there by a clerk who sent us to another clerk who sent us to a third clerk until we finally arrived at Harold. By the time we found him, we were both tired of trotting across the campus shifting this direction and that trying to figure out which building was which or what the instructions given by the last clerk actually meant. Finally, we found Harold and as soon as Harold listened to Gretta's request he responded, "Guest housing? Oh sure, sure, sure. We can get you into guest housing. So, you are the wife of Private First Class Thomas Smith. Sure, sure, sure."

He flipped papers around on a desktop far too small to contain it all and finally pulled one to the top which he eyed like a half blind owl.

"Oh, sure, sure, sure. You called last night didn't you, Mrs. Smith? Private First Class Thomas Smith was flown in with the wounded a couple of

Confessions from the Pumpkin Patch

days ago. Already has had two surgeries on that hip. Oh, sure, sure, sure. We have a room arranged for you and little Derrick Lo—Velllll—Smith."

"No," Gretta replied. "Derrick is not with us. I decided it would be best to leave him with my parents, but this is my friend, Lovella." She grabbed my arm and pushed me forward as though presenting me for inspection. "Is it okay if she spends the night with me before she has to drive back tomorrow?"

"Oh, sure, sure, sure. Lovella," Harold chirped in his squeaky little voice which was actually quite masculine given the high pitch and tonality. "She is not on the list. I may need to follow up with that and get clearance. I just need a little information." He stared at me until I caught on and gave him my status.

He immediately got up from the desk and disappeared through the back without so much as an "excuse me." or "I'll be right back."

Gretta and I chatted small talk and wondered several times if we should leave or see if we could find someone who might try to retrieve Harold. We must have stood there at the desk for another fifteen minutes. Harold finally came back and got around to giving us directions to guest housing, and a key to the room. By the time we got through that ordeal and had luggage in the room it was 3:30 PM. It took another thirty minutes to navigate our way to the medical facilities. We finally arrived at Tommy's bedside which was several counts down from the door in an open ward.

We walked up to the foot of Tommy's bed to see him sleeping in what appeared to be a very awkward position due to traction, or some other kind of apparatus, that was hooked around him and apparently kept his leg stabilized.

"Oh, he's asleep," Gretta half whined. "Maybe we should go. Maybe we should come back later. Do you think they might have him sedated?"

She turned to walk away. I grabbed her arm. "Stop right where you are," I commanded. "We have just driven five hours and have spent another three hours trying to get our asses settled into this disorganized mess they call a hospital. You have not seen your husband in over a year and you are just going to give up and walk away? No, I don't think so. You are not going anywhere."

"But what if they have him sedated?" she questioned.

"Well we are going to find out," I affirmed. "Wait here."

I left her standing there looking helpless like a lost puppy at the foot of Tommy's bed and went to find an orderly. It only took a couple of minutes to find out that Tommy was just sleeping and that it would be fine to wake him. I came back and ordered Gretta to wake him.

"But?" she protested.

Karlyle Tomms

"Wake him," I demanded. "It's okay."

I walked around the bed to the side behind him where he couldn't see me. I motioned to Gretta to go around to the other side of the bed. By this time the orderly I had talked to came to stand at the foot of Tommy's bed.

"Go on," I said.

Gretta looked up at me and then back at the orderly as though asking permission.

The orderly nodded to her. "It's alright," he said softly.

Gretta then nudged Tommy gently on the arm, but he didn't stir. She looked up half frightened and half wondering what she should do then. I reached over from behind, gave his arm a good jostle. Startled, he opened his eyes. As soon as he realized where he was he looked straight at Gretta and said, "Hi, honey. What are you doing here?"

She burst into tears and Tommy reached out to her as best he could, given his confinement and said, "Baby—Baby—what's the matter? Don't cry."

She sobbed even louder and then began to take air in big gulps. "I—ugh—ah—thought you—ugh—ah—had died."

"Oh, sweetheart," Tommy said trying to reach for her. "Here I am. I'm okay."

"No—ugh—ah—you're not," Gretta sobbed. "You're hurt—ugh—ah—ugh—ah—I never wanted to ever see you hurt."

"Please—sweetheart—come here," Tommy pleaded, and she fell into his chest with huge waves of tears. He let her cry. Fight as he might, the tears began rolling down his cheeks as well, silent, stealthy, little rivers that drifted off his eyes and into her hair.

He still didn't know I was there. I held it together pretty well myself, allowing Gretta her moment with her husband and letting her have her feelings, but when I saw the tears come across Tommy's face as well, I couldn't hold on anymore. I fought to hold it back and keep silent but a yelp slipped past my lips and the tears began to stream down my own face.

Hearing this, Tommy cocked his head back toward me. As soon as I saw him move I quickly pulled one finger over my lips to let him know to stay silent. Then I mouthed the words, "I'll be back." I slipped past divider curtains and motioned the orderly to the aisle so I could ask him where to get a cup of coffee. The orderly directed me to a rather sterile looking guest lounge. I got my cup of coffee, sat at a table, and watched as families visited with injured soldiers who were able to ambulate. I sat there thinking for a long time and one of the things I thought was, "There, but for the grace of God, go I." If my behavior had been a little different, if

350

Confessions from the Pumpkin Patch

circumstances had not been what they were, or if I had gotten pregnant when I was fooling around with Tommy, that could have been me by that bed letting out all the fears and pent up worries stuffed over almost a year of my husband's deployment to Vietnam. It could have been me worried sick that my husband might never be able to work again or worse yet that he still might not survive his injuries. I began to realize how much our experience in life is created not by the choices that we make, but by the choices that others make. I understood what a huge impact Tommy's decision to join the military was going to have on his whole family. Derrick was never going to remember a father who wasn't disabled. Gretta was going to have to work harder to take care of her family than she ever would have had it not been for Tommy's decision. In some ways, I felt glad that I wasn't Gretta and in other ways I felt guilty. After about an hour, I went back to the ward to find Gretta sitting by Tommy's bed holding his hand and laughing.

"Well this is a different picture than the one I saw last," I said as I walked up.

Gretta, still giggling, turned to see me and said, "Hi, sweetie. Tommy was just telling me about this guy he was with in boot camp who was a really funny kid from Idaho."

"Well, it's good to see you both laughing," I said as I searched around for a chair.

I finally found a little metal chair and pulled it up beside Gretta. We sat there talking, laughing, and reminiscing through Tommy's dinner being served and for an hour or so beyond.

Finally, the orderly came by, "If you folks would like to have dinner, you might want to head over to the cafeteria. They are gonna stop serving in about thirty minutes," he said glancing at his watch.

"You go on, Lovella," Gretta said squeezing Tommy's hand. "I'm not really hungry anyway."

I gave her a stern and motherly look and said, "Honey, you need to eat."

She looked back at Tommy and he said, "Go on and get something to eat and then go on back to the guest house and get some rest. We can talk tomorrow."

Gretta hesitantly let go of his hand and said, "Okay then." She leaned over the bed and hugged him. "Good night, honey," she went on, "I'll see you in the morning."

I walked over behind her and leaned over to hug him as well. "Take care of yourself, asshole," I said. "You got a family to go home to."

He looked up at me a bit forlorn and said, "I know."

I smiled, "I love you. You know that—right?"

Karlyle Tomms

"Yeah, I know," he replied. "I love you too."

I took a deep sigh and squeezed his hand. "I probably won't see you for a while. I'll be going back in the morning. We will see how visits go after that. If you guys need anything, let me know."

Gretta hugged him one more time and we headed off to the cafeteria. We had a pleasant enough meal as hospital cafeteria food goes and then headed back to the room. There was only one bed in the room that we had to share and Gretta's excitement kept her awake. She kept talking about everything from whether they would have to make changes in the house to accommodate if Tommy would be in a wheelchair to how we used to sleep together when we were kids to what she was going to fix Tommy for his first meal when he got home. I finally said, "Gretta—shut up, honey. I have got to drive home in the morning."

"Oh, okay." she said with disappointment obvious in her tone. "I'm sorry."

"It's okay, sweetie," I replied. "I know you're excited, but we have got to get some sleep."

The next morning we had breakfast at the same cafeteria after I packed the car to go home. I left from there and told her to give Tommy my love. Gretta's parents were going to come up with Tommy's parents on the following weekend and bring the baby. I knew she would be fine. She just needed me to support her through the initial jitters.

The drive back to Climax was uneventful, a bit boring and a bit lonely. Mother had enjoyed her time with Vanilla and had made her a cute little bonnet to wear. I stayed only a short while to visit with Mother and then headed back to State College with Vanilla.

Back home, I went back to our normal routine. Earl's classes and working at the grocery, more for his own satisfaction than necessity, kept him busy. I was home most of the time with the baby. I got calls from Gretta periodically with updates and apparently Tommy was healing fairly rapidly. His injuries were not so severe that it would be completely debilitating but they were severe enough for him to be released from the military. Apparently, he was eligible for a partial service-connected disability based on the damage to his hip and pelvic bone. He would not get 100% disability, but it sounded like it might be able to apply for enough to somewhat offset the fact that he would not be able to work as he had before. He was also getting a Purple Heart medal, but that wouldn't pay his bills. Until Tommy could use the GI bill to re-train or figure out some other type of job, Gretta was going to have to work. I felt bad for both of them and felt just as helpless.

Confessions from the Pumpkin Patch

The 23rd of February was a very lazy, cold, and dreary Sunday. Early in the afternoon, I had put Vanilla in her crib for a nap. Then Earl and I took time to do something that was one of the things I most loved to do with him. We lay down together for an afternoon nap. I so loved being cuddled up next to him, drifting in and out of sleep, feeling his warm body next to mine and just knowing that he was there. I was just getting up to get the baby when the phone rang. Earl was still lying down but heard Vanilla start crying so he went to get her while I went to the phone.

"Hello," I said as I picked up the receiver and sat next to the phone. I already had a feeling that it was Gretta and I was right.

"Hi, sweetie," the voice crooned from the other end of the line.

"Well, hi back," I responded. "How's your Sunday."

"Still a little too cold for my taste," she said, "but not bad. How's yours?"

"Earl and I just got up from a very nice afternoon nap," I said.

"Perfect day for it," she went on. "Guess what? They are discharging Tommy this week. He said he thinks they are going let him come home in a few more days and I was wondering if I could ask a favor."

"You know if I got it, honey, it's yours," I said.

"Well," she continued, "next weekend I was thinking about having a coming home party for Tommy, that is, if they release him like they say they will. I was thinking you could maybe come pick us up while our parents fix up our house for the party so when we get there it will be a surprise. Just a few people you know, you and Earl, your Mom, our parents, and maybe one or two friends—very small."

"When were you planning to do this?" I questioned.

"I was thinking maybe next Saturday," she half whispered as though Tommy might overhear.

"Where are you?" I inquired.

"I'm at a pay phone near the cafeteria," she responded. "Why?"

"Is Tommy there?" I continued to interrogate.

"No, of course not," she said. "He's back on the ward. I wouldn't have him here to plan the party. I wouldn't want him to over-hear."

"Then why are you whispering, sweetie?" I demanded.

"Oh, ah," she giggled. "I didn't realize I was whispering. I guess I'm just excited. So do you think you could do this for me?"

"Give me a sec," I said then I called out to the other room. "Earl."

"Yeah, Baby," he called back.

"Do we have any plans for next weekend?" I called.

"Ah—no—I don't think so," he called back. "Give me a second. I'm just finishing up a clean diaper."

Karlyle Tomms

I went back to the phone. "Earl says he doesn't think we have plans."

"Oh, wonderful," she exclaimed.

About that time Earl came into the living room rocking Vanilla on his shoulder. "What's up?" he questioned.

"Tommy is getting out of the hospital this week," I said with the receiver held out slightly from my face. "Gretta wants to know if I can come pick them up while her parents set up a surprise party for him."

"Okay. That's cool," he replied. "I'm sure the kid and I will be just fine having a weekend to ourselves."

I heard Gretta on the line say, "Well, I want Earl to be there too."

"Gretta wants you at the party," I said. "Either you could go up with us and we could all ride back together or maybe Mother could come pick you and the baby up on Friday while I go get Gretta and Tommy."

"Whatever you want to do is fine," he said. "You know I'm pretty cool about stuff."

"Yes, I know you are sweetheart," I smiled. "That's one of the things I love about you."

I turned back to the phone. "You heard that right?" I said.

"Every bit of it," she replied. "So how are we going to do this?"

"Give me some planning time," I replied. "The best thing will probably be to have Mother come pick up Earl on Friday unless you want his parents to come take him down there. Are they invited too?"

"Well, I don't mind if they come," she responded. "But Tommy doesn't really know them."

"Then, let me call Mother and make arrangements. I'm sure she will be okay with it. I think she has forgiven Tommy for that incident in the laundry room." We both laughed.

"Oh my god!" Gretta teased. "I hope she can deal with it."

"Mother has changed a bit I think," I resumed. "I think she will be fine—so listen. Go ahead with your plans. I will come up to stay the night on Friday and on Saturday we will take Tommy home. Call me on Wednesday to finalize and see if I have run into any problems, but I'm sure it will be fine."

"You're a darling," she said. "Bye now."

"Bye, sweetie," I said and hung up the phone.

Mother had only minor complaints about coming up to State College to pick up Earl and the baby. The phone call on Wednesday went fine. I left on Friday morning for Washington and Mother came to get Earl and the baby Friday afternoon. I arrived in DC about 3:30 PM and went to guest housing to meet up with Gretta.

Confessions from the Pumpkin Patch

I knocked on the door to Gretta's room and it swung open very briefly after I knocked.

"Oh, Jesus! I'm glad you're here!" she exclaimed. "It is so good to see you. Come in. Got any luggage in the car?"

"Nope, this is it," I responded. "Only needed an overnight bag. Earl is taking a few things down to Climax for me."

"Listen," she said, "Tommy is almost officially discharged. He is going to spend one more night in his bed on the ward but his doctor said it would be fine if he went off base and I was thinking maybe we could all go out to dinner instead of eating cafeteria food again. What do you think?"

"I'll bet you are both sick to death of hospital food," I said smiling. "Sure, sweetie, we can go to dinner. You have someplace in mind?"

"Well one of the other wives told me about an Italian restaurant that is only a few blocks from here," she gleamed. "I don't think I've ever really had Italian food that wasn't out of a can or the freezer. Do you think we could go?"

"That sounds wonderful," I said as I set my bag next to the bed.

Gretta grabbed my hand and we sat down on the bed together. "Oh, Lovella," she twittered, "I have met some of the most wonderful people since I've been here. The other wives and I have gotten to spend a lot of time together and I think I have made some new friends."

We sat there for the next couple of hours with Gretta going on about the experience of being there for the past few weeks. At 6:00 PM we left for the ward to meet Tommy who had been signing papers that afternoon and would be good to go the next morning. We walked up to his bed to find him sitting there in his dress uniform on the side of the bed.

"Well, damn!" I exclaimed. "You look a hell of a lot better than you did the last time I saw you! Don't you look handsome in your dress blues!?" I turned to Gretta teasing, "Are you sure you want him? I might want to take him back."

"No, I don't think so," Tommy quickly replied as he reached for Gretta's hand. "Nothing against you, Lovella, but I think I have already found the love of my life."

"Well the love of your life and the fuck of your life are going to take you out to dinner," I laughed. "Are you ready to go?"

"Ready and able," he said as he reached for the cane that I had not noticed leaning against the side of the bed. He got to his feet slowly leaning partly against the bedside table and partly against the cane. I reached to help him and he simply responded, "Nope."

Gretta said, "He doesn't like for anyone to help him."

355

Karlyle Tomms

"I've got to learn to stand on my own two feet again," Tommy affirmed as he stood upright. "Let's go." He limped on his cane to the end of the bed and started walking toward the ward door. One of the orderlies said, "Private First Class Smith!" Tommy stopped and turned in his direction. The orderly went on. "We do have a wheelchair available. You can always walk from the front door to the car. Nobody has to know but us."

Tommy took a couple of more painful steps then turned back to the orderly and nodded. The orderly brought a wheelchair. After Tommy sat down, the orderly tapped the back and then said to Gretta, "Just fold it up and leave it inside the front door. I'll come get it in a few minutes."

Gretta stepped behind the wheelchair and we rolled Tommy down to the front. I went ahead and brought the car around close to the door. Tommy got up from the chair at the front door half stumbling at first then walked to the back door of the car. He could stretch the leg out in the back seat which would have been a tall order in the front.

As promised, just up Georgia Street, a little past the post office, was a corner brick building with an Italian restaurant, *Bienvenuto*.

It looked as though there was street parking only. I had to go up a block and turn around so Tommy would not be having to cross the street and could get out curb side. I was lucky enough to find a parallel spot about fifty feet from the door.

When we stepped onto the side walk, the wafting smell of Italian cooking filled the air all around the restaurant. Tommy pulled himself up and out by the car door and we walked slowly down the street to the restaurant. Within ten or twenty feet we met a couple of hippie looking women who were walking from the opposite direction. I noticed that they got a disgusted look on their faces and began talking to each other as they approached. Then just as they got to us, one of them spit at Tommy's feet and shouted "Baby killer!"

"WHAT THE HELL!" I exclaimed as Tommy simply looked shocked.

I turned and followed the women down the sidewalk. "What the hell did you say?" I shouted knowing full well what she said.

I heard Tommy exclaim from behind me, "Lovella, it's okay. Let it go."

The woman who spit at Tommy's feet turned around and shouted. "I SAID HE'S A FUCKING BABY KILLER, BITCH! ARE YOU ONE TOO!?"

"Why would you say something like that and spit at the feet of a total stranger?" I demanded.

"Give me a break!" the woman demanded. "How many innocent babies did he kill in Vietnam? Look at him! This country has no business being

Confessions from the Pumpkin Patch

there. All it does is benefit the fat cat establishment! It is slaughter, man, total slaughter of innocent lives."

The woman with her tugged her sleeve. "Come on, Jane, let's go."

"First of all bitch, the only thing you know from looking at him is our own judgment and so what?" I continued, "You think that everyone who went to Nam is some evil bastard, don't you? You think the innocent boys who were drafted out of their homes and off their jobs enjoyed going over there in the that god-forsaken rat-hole to get shot at, bombed, watch their friends die, or die themselves? What a fucking ignorant bitch!"

"What the hell do you know about it?" she retorted. "Look at you in your Miss former-prep-school designer dress outfit with Mister dressed-blues over there."

"What the hell do I know about it?" I shouted. "And what the hell do you know about me or any of my friends? Have you ever done anything truly meaningful? Have you? I have. He has. He tried to do what he thought was right for his family and his country. I was at the anti-war protest in New York in April 1967. I heard Martin Luther King speak. I marched to protest this meaningless war. Were you there?"

"No, but—," she began.

"No but, FUCK YOU!" I shouted, cutting in. "You don't know shit and you are going to be so fucking arrogant that you will walk up the street and spit at someone you don't even know just because he is wearing a fucking Marine uniform? FUCK YOU! Did you stop to think that he has already been wounded enough? FUCK YOU!"

I pointed back to Gretta and Tommy who knew me well enough to let me go.

"You know what?" I went on. "I don't happen to agree with his politics but that does not stop me from respecting his right to believe differently, or stop me from loving him for who he is. These are two of the finest people god put on this earth and you owe them, you owe us; especially this man here, an apology! Do you think he went over there and got wounded, disabled for life, in that fucking piss-hole to come home and have people treat him like he is a fucking pariah? He deserves more respect than you are capable of giving and all you can do is denigrate him? FUCK YOU BITCH!"

"I'm sorry," she said sheepishly, suddenly changing her tone. "I was out of line."

"Don't say it to me, bitch!" I shouted. "Say it to him!" I pointed at Tommy who was now leaning against the wall of the restaurant just a few feet away.

357

The woman looked at me, at Tommy, and back at her friend who was just standing there observing at this point. She then looked down at the ground, looked up and marched directly over to Tommy. "I'm sorry Mr. ah—?"

"Smith," Tommy filled in.

"I'm sorry, Mr. Smith." The woman continued. "I was out of line."

"Thank you," Tommy said softly and looked away.

The young woman said nothing more. She looked around and walked back in my direction. She looked up at me as she passed and I stared her down. "Sorry," she said quickly and softly as she passed by dropping eye contact. She then met up with her friend and walked quickly on down the sidewalk.

I turned and walked back to Tommy and Gretta. "I'm sorry, Tommy," I said as I approached.

"It's okay," he said with a half laugh and half exhausted release of air.

"Let's go eat," I said, and the two of them joined me in our slow trek down the sidewalk to the front door of *Bienvenuto's*.

The restaurant was quaint with limited space. The tables were all covered with red and white checkered cloth and the waiters were dressed in black and white with black bow ties and black aprons. The food smelled good but the company had been tarnished by the events out front. Tommy seemed distant and detached. He scrutinized the restaurant as though staking out a heist and then asked the hostess, "Can we pick our seating?"

"We can make arrangements for you," she responded.

Tommy pointed to a booth at the very back next to a window. "Can we have that one?"

"Certainly, sir," the hostess responded. She clutched the menus to her bosom and turned. "Right this way."

I reached the booth first and started to sit at the back near the wall when Tommy said, "Lovella? Do you mind if I have that seat?"

"Sure," I said stepping back, feeling curious about behavior I had never seen in him before.

He made Gretta sit on the inside of the booth and he sat with his back to the wall where the only activity was staff coming in and out of swinging doors about ten feet away. I noticed he would often flinch when a waiter came through the door.

As our dinner lingered on Tommy joined the conversation here and there, but often seemed to drift off in thought. At one point when I saw him staring out the window as though he was seeing something off at a great distance, I asked him, "Are you okay?"

He did not respond at first.

Confessions from the Pumpkin Patch

"Tommy?" Gretta called and reached out to touch his arm.

Gretta had only lightly touched his arm and he startled as though the devil himself had just reached for him.

"Ah! What?!" he half shouted.

I said nothing and let Gretta do the comforting. "Are you okay, baby?" she questioned softly.

He took a deep breath and sighed, "I'm fine—fine." The embarrassment on his face was luminous. He reached out to the basket on the table and tore off a piece of bread and said, "The bread is really good. Anyone want more bread?"

This was not the Tommy I knew. His behavior back at Walter Reed had been more like the old Tommy, but after that incident on the sidewalk, it seemed like something changed and he withdrew into himself.

We finished our meal and lingered over strong Italian coffee for a little while, then headed back to the base. By about 9:00 PM, we had Tommy settled back on the ward for one more night. Then Gretta and I went back to the guest quarters.

It was another night in which she wanted to talk more than sleep. She seemed somewhat oblivious to Tommy's behavior at the restaurant and was completely focused on how wonderful it would be to have him home, how her parents had gone down to the house to fix it up and get it ready for the surprise party tomorrow, and that his dad had talked about finding a way to hire him back at the feed store, at least part time. She went on and on with me grunting the occasional, "Yeah. Uh huh, or, ahhh."

Finally, as I had done before, I rolled over to face her and said, "Honey, shut up. We need our sleep." Gretta dutifully obliged and the next thing I knew it was her snoring that was keeping me awake.

We got up early on Saturday morning and picked Tommy up at the hospital by 7:00. By timing the trip just right, we should arrive at their house about noon. Gretta had already gotten on the pay phone to call her mom and make sure that everything was going as planned.

The trip was essentially uneventful. We had one stop to fill up on gas and let everyone go pee. I was happy to see that when Tommy came around from the bathroom on the side of the gas station to the front to buy a soda, the older man who was attending the station noticed him. He walked straight up to Tommy as he was standing by the soda machine, reached out his hand and said, "Son, thank you for your service."

Tommy smiled and shook the man's hand and said, "I appreciate your kindness." They nodded to one another and Tommy limped back to the car with his cane in one hand and the soda in the other.

Karlyle Tomms

When we got near home, I noticed that Tommy was very quiet in the back seat. I glanced up into the rear view mirror to see that he was not asleep but had his head leaning against the window and was peering out across the landscape. I didn't say anything. I was not going to engage in the redundancy of asking him again if he was alright. I knew that he wasn't. Gretta chattered about re-claiming the flowerbeds around their little home and that this is the perfect time to do it with spring seeming to come a little early this year.

When we got to their little blue house, I noticed that there were not any cars parked around. At first, I wondered if there might have been some mistake and if everyone had forgotten that there was a party. Then I realized that they must have parked around the block or something so Tommy wouldn't notice and they could keep the surprise.

Tommy did fine up the sidewalk, but struggled a little bit up the four steps to their tiny little front landing. Gretta excitedly fumbled to get the key in the front door and I wondered if her anxiety and giddiness was going to give away the surprise. Finally she opened the door and said to Tommy, "You first, sweetheart." He no sooner stepped into the living room than eight people, all waiting inside, shouted, "SURPRISE!"

Tommy let out a yelp like Satan had just landed with cloven hooves, snarling in front of him. He lunged backward and almost fell, perhaps would have, had it not been that Gretta and I were right behind him. He quickly caught himself and realized that he was looking at family and close friends. Then he laughed, "Boy! Howdy! Ah—," he said nervously. "You guys scared the hell out of me."

Everyone gathered around him wanting hugs. I watched him stiffen and barely respond even when his mom and dad were hugging him. I watched as his breath quickened and he said, "Boy, it's a little stuffy in here. You guys mind if I step back outside for just a moment and get some fresh air?"

He pushed his cane out from his side and limped back toward the front door. In my mind, I saw him rushing off down the walk as fast as his cane and bad hip would allow him, but he stepped out onto the landing and leaned one side against the house. I saw him through the open door and said to Gretta, "Why don't you go see if your mom needs some help in the kitchen?"

She trotted off still oblivious and I stepped out onto the landing with Tommy. I stood back about two feet behind him, but I know he knew I was there. Finally I spoke. "You had it pretty rough over there didn't you?"

Confessions from the Pumpkin Patch

For several seconds he said nothing. Finally he said quietly without turning around, "I guess so."

I took a deep breath.

"Tommy, I have no idea what you have been through or how you feel, but I know you are not the same man who left here two years ago. I can see that you are pushing it to be able to tolerate things you used to revel in."

"It's just too much, Lovella," he clamored barely looking up. "I'm kind of overwhelmed here. I needed some peace and quiet. I needed a little time to get used to things again."

"I know," I said. "It's not just your hip that's wounded, it's your heart. I figured that out last night. Gretta still doesn't have a clue. She is so happy to see you and so thankful that you are home alive."

"I love her so much," he said, "but I just don't know if I can take this."

"Well, a couple of things," I went on. "First of all, you are here with people who love you to the depth of their soul, who only want the best for you. You have to get through this afternoon to get your peace and quiet. Second of all, I don't know if Gretta is going to get it. You are going to have to spell it out for her. Make it clear what you need from her, what you can handle and what you can't."

"That's just the thing," Tommy responded. "I don't know. I don't understand this myself. I just know I feel like every nerve in my body is set on high alert. I don't know what I can tolerate or what I can't."

"Then you are going to have to teach Gretta as you learn," I said. "Make sure you communicate to her. Make sure she knows how you feel at the very least and if possible let her know what you need."

A crisp Pennsylvania breeze swept through the yard and chewed the warmth from our faces. Tommy pushed back from the side of the house and turned around. He looked at me warmly. "You know you're my best friend don't you?"

"Hell, I am about everybody's best friend," I grinned. "If I'm not your best friend, I'm probably your best enemy."

The front door of the house creaked and Tommy's father stuck his head through. He looked at Tommy and then over at me where I was standing on the opposite side of the landing. Tommy didn't see me wink at his dad as he tentatively checked out the situation.

"Son," he said, looking back from my direction toward Tommy, "Aren't you hungry? These women have got enough food in here to feed your whole platoon. I have been resisting the urge to go ahead and tear into it, but it just wouldn't be the polite thing to do if I was to go to the table before the guest of honor."

361

Karlyle Tomms

"Yeah, you know I am a little hungry now that you mention it," Tommy said as he turned his cane and reached out the opposite hand to motion me ahead of him. As I walked through the door, I felt his warm hand rub between my shoulder blades and I felt the love that he didn't need to express further.

Inside there was a big banner across their tiny dining room surrounded with balloons that said, "Welcome Home!" Three tables had been pushed back against the wall in a "u" shape to make more room for food and they were covered with meats and casseroles, salads, breads, and desserts. Tommy hobbled up to the group left standing around: his parents, Gretta's parents, Mother, Earl, and a couple of friends Tommy and Gretta used to hang out with before he joined the military.

Gretta's dad stepped forward from the group and raised his hands to lead everyone in what had obviously been rehearsed. As his raised hands fell, they all began to sing, "For He's a Jolly Good Fellow." When the song ended, they all stood there silent as though waiting for applause.

"Wow!" Tommy exclaimed. "This is really something. I want to thank you guys so much. I love you." His voice cracked and he fought tears as he finished. "I love you all."

"Yeah, yeah, yeah," I exclaimed, coming to his emotional rescue. Then I moved over by Earl's side, put my arm around him and demanded, "Let's eat!"

"Yeah!" Tommy echoed. "I don't know about you guys, but I'm pretty hungry. He ambled toward the table where Gretta intercepted.

"I'll hold your plate, Sweetheart," she said gleefully. "You just tell me what you want as we go around the table."

Gretta grabbed a plate and stood beside him as he moved around the u-shaped formation selecting food. After that, others joined in.

We all sat around the living room with food on our laps. Extra chairs had been brought in and there was barely enough room between them to set our drinks on the floor. Earl and I took turns holding the baby while the other one ate.

Tommy had not seen Derrick in so long I think at first he might not have recognized him. Derrick was testing his walking and was wobbling around the living room. Suddenly, Tommy took notice.

"Oh my god! Derrick!" he exclaimed as he handed his plate to Gretta who was beside him on the sofa. He reached his hands out to the baby and exclaimed, "Come here little man. Let daddy give you a hug."

It then became obvious that Derrick didn't recognize Tommy because as soon as he saw Tommy's reaction he recoiled into frightened tears. The

362

Confessions from the Pumpkin Patch

look on Tommy's face was a combination of horror and sadness as he realized the implication of that moment.

I was about to move over to pick up Derrick when Gretta's mom came to him first. She whisked him up into her arms and began to coo to him. "Ooooohhh, now, now, now. What's the matter, sweetie. You want to go see daddy, don't you? Let's go see Da Da. Can you say Da Da?"

Mrs. Tannenbaum brought him over to Tommy and sat him down on the floor in front of him. Gretta discretely pinched the side off a cookie and handed it to Tommy.

Derrick continued to cry as Gretta's mom sat down on the floor with him at Tommy's feet. Gretta nudged Tommy and motioned for him to give the cookie piece to Derrick.

Tommy held the cookie out to his son and said, "Here, little man. You want a cookie? Want a goodie?"

Derrick wailed, turned away and buried his face in Mrs. Tannenbaum's bosom.

I watched from across the room and my heart broke as I saw the tiny secret emotions flowing across Tommy's face. He stuck it out though and they continued to work with Derrick until he first took the cookie from Tommy's hand and later allowed Tommy to pull him up into his lap. I sat there wondering if Tommy had really thought it through when he joined the Marines. I know he thought he was planning for his family's future. I know he was dreaming the dreams that some recruiter had fed to him, but his reality had turned out to be harsh.

Tommy held his son for a fair amount of time and then put him down to go to the restroom. Several of us got up to cart paper plates and empty Dixie cups to the trash and then meet in the kitchen for clean-up. I noticed that Tommy was gone for what seemed to be an extreme amount of time. Later someone went down the hall to knock on the bathroom door and I heard Tommy call back from inside, "Just a minute." I knew he was escaping as much as he possibly could.

I heard the bathroom door click open and looked down the hall to see Tommy's dad entering. I made several passes back and forth between the living room, dining room and kitchen and each time I glanced down the hallway to see Tommy just standing there at the end of the hall with one arm on his cane, the other against the wall and his head buried in that arm.

At one point, I saw his mother standing beside him in the hall with her head tilted to his shoulders talking to him. He wasn't looking at her. He kept his head buried in his arm. She stood there for a short while with him and I could only imagine the conversation they might be having.

363

Karlyle Tomms

Earl did his best while caring for Vanilla to pick up things here and there and help with the clean-up. Finally, I said, "Sweetheart, just go sit down and enjoy your daughter. We'll take care of this."

He did as he was told.

In short order we had it all cleaned up. Family members said their goodbyes and gave their hugs.

Earl and I were going to spend the night in Tommy and Gretta's spare bedroom and go back to State College on Sunday morning, so we stayed behind after everyone else had left.

After all the clamor was over, Tommy sat back down on the sofa in the living room. Gretta came to his side, grabbed his arm and hugged him from the side. "I'm so glad my man is home!" she exclaimed.

Tommy reached over and put his arm around her. It was almost as though none of us knew what to do after the party was done. I knew Tommy would want to have some time of peace and quiet, but we sat in the living room chatting as the sun fell into evening. Derrick tottered around here and there and would now occasionally go to Tommy of his own volition.

In early evening Gretta announced, "Who want's leftovers?" She rose and headed for the kitchen.

"That sounds good," I said as I handed Vanilla to Earl so I could go with her.

"Oh, no, no, no." she exclaimed. "You sit right there. I'll call you if I need you. Besides, I think I might want to get creative and see what I can make new out of old leftovers."

Gretta had not been in the kitchen more than three minutes when we heard her slam the door of a cabinet. Bam! The sound resonated through the house and in a normal household such a sound would have been taken as commonplace. Maybe one might startle a little at first but would quickly realize someone is just slamming a kitchen cabinet. However, not this household, not anymore.

Tommy was off the sofa and onto the floor the instant he heard the sound. He shoved their coffee table across the room. His arms stretched out in front of him on the floor as though he was holding a gun. He began screaming, "TAYLOR! TAYLOR, GET DOWN, GOD DAMN IT! GET DOWN. DAWSON, GRAB HIM! GRAB HIS FEET. PULL HIM DOWN. TAYLOR! WHAT THE HELL!"

Tommy then covered his head and face into the floor as a blood curdling cry came out of him, "OH JESUS FUCKING CHRIST! OH CHRIST! GOD DAMN IT TAYLOR! OH CHRIST!"

Confessions from the Pumpkin Patch

Gretta ran back from the kitchen with a horrified look on her face. Derrick and Vanilla both hit a full throttle cry and Earl was trying to tend to both of the children. I jumped up and ran across the room to grab Gretta. "Don't touch him!" I yelled. "Let him be."

Gretta was immediately in tears heaving, "What!? What's—Ha—Ah—Ha—the matter with him?"

"Just wait," I admonished. "Wait it out."

"What is the matter?" she pleaded.

"I've read about it, honey," I said. "I think he has got what they call shell shock."

"What?" she pleaded and pulled toward him but I held her back.

Tommy continued to cover his head with both hands with face flat into the floor sobbing as loud and as hard as I had ever heard in my life. "JESUS! OH JESUS CHRIST! TAYLOR!" he continued to wail.

We all stood there watching, waiting, as he cried. Finally, he got still and the crying stopped.

Once again, Gretta pulled toward him. "Don't touch him," I said. "Just gently call his name."

She moved tentatively toward him as Tommy lay still on the floor, breathing in deep intermittent gasps.

"Tommy?" she called softly. "Tommy, it's me, Gretta."

"Tommy?" she kept calling, gently.

Finally, he said, "Yes."

"Can I come over there?" she said, looking back at me for reassurance.

"Yes," he responded.

She came to her knees beside him. He still had his face to the floor.

"Can I touch you, sweetheart?" she sighed.

"Yes," he said again.

She reached out to put her hand on his back and at first he winced but then relaxed as she gently rubbed her hand up and down his back. At last he turned hesitantly over and looked at her.

"I'm sorry," he said fighting back tears again.

"Oh, baby, baby," she said as she leaned over onto the floor to hug him. "It's all right."

"I didn't mean to cause a problem," he whimpered.

"It's no problem, honey," she responded. "What happened?"

"I don't know. For a minute there it felt like I was back in Nam," he answered. "I felt like I was dreaming, but it felt like it was really happening too."

"What happened?" she queried.

"Oh Jesus, I can't tell you," he said. "I don't want to put that on you."

365

Karlyle Tomms

Tommy sat up on the floor and Gretta sat beside him at his knees facing his direction.

"Who's Taylor?" she asked.

Tommy heaved, his breathing quickened, and tears pooled in his eyes. Immediately Gretta reached out and took his hand. "It's okay," she said. "It's okay. You don't have to tell me. It's all right."

"Hey," I said. "Why don't we all sit down and play a game of Scrabble after dinner?"

Earl picked up on the distraction and chimed right in. "Yeah that sounds good. I don't remember the last time I played a game."

"How about that, sweetheart?" Gretta inquired as she squeezed Tommy's hand.

"Yeah," Tommy responded in an obvious and deliberate attempt to lift his spirits out of the hell where they had been. "Scrabble sounds good."

Gretta helped him get to his feet and lay his leg out on the sofa. "Damn that hip and leg hurt!" he groaned.

"Want me to get you some aspirin?" she asked.

"No, the doctor gave me something for pain when I left Walter Reed," he replied. "Can you check my bag?"

Gretta went to his bag in the back bedroom. We could hear her scrounge a bit and then she returned with a medicine bottle. "Is this the one?" she asked. "It says it's for pain."

"Yep, that's it," Tommy replied as he took the pill bottle from her hand.

I had already gone to the kitchen for a glass of water while she was in the bedroom.

"I'll get you some water," she exclaimed turning around to see me standing there with the glass.

"Wow! That was easy," she chimed as she took the glass from my hand and handed it to Tommy.

"Come on," I said. "Let's get dinner ready."

Gretta and I retreated to the kitchen. She went to the refrigerator, pulled out a covered dish and set it on the counter top."

She then took a deep sigh and leaned over the sink. I walked up behind her and placed my arm around her shoulder and said. "I kind of had the feeling it would be hard."

"Damn it, Lovella!" she said. "I am so mad at him for doing this. I am so mad at him for joining the fucking military and at the same time my heart breaks for him. I don't know what to do?"

"Honey, right now what you do is grit your teeth and get through it," I admonished.

"I can't," she whispered.

Confessions from the Pumpkin Patch

"Yes you can, sweetie," I affirmed. "You can. You have to. You both have to be strong 'cause there is a lot more wounded in him than just his hip. He is going to need you to be strong."

"Lovella, what do I do?" she asked as she turned around and leaned back into the counter top. "I don't know what to do."

"First of all," I commanded, "you go to the library and you read everything you can about any diagnosis they give him. You read everything you can about shell shock, and then you make sure you don't let go 'til the cows come home. You hold them accountable. Don't be afraid to question every doctor. You contact the VA and find out what he qualifies for and you ask for any kind of assistance or services you can get. If they tell you that you can't have it, read their literature about it, and educate yourself about their rules. Then go back and ask again. Find out if there are counseling services available for you and for him or for the two of you together or if there are other programs to help vets besides the VA. Persist, sweetie—persist."

She looked at me sternly. "This will go on for the rest of my life won't it? It will go on for the rest of our lives."

I sighed and looked back at her with as much compassion and understanding as I could muster. "Yes, honey," I said. "I'm afraid that it will."

Gretta looked to the side and a tear rolled down her cheek. "I just wanted us to be happy," she said. "Is that too much to ask? I just wanted us to be happy."

"It has to get better, sweetie," I said as I reached for her hand.

She sniffled and turned back around, pulled herself upright and exclaimed. "Let's get dinner ready."

The next morning, Earl and I drove back to State College. Vanilla lay cooing in her back seat bassinette or would drift off to sleep. I was glad to relax on the passenger's side and occasionally tend to the baby.

"You ever wonder," I said, "why life seems to turn out so good for some people, even without them really trying, and it turns out so shitty for others?"

"Yeah, I know," he said staring off down the road. "It's strange isn't it? Some of it has to do with the choices we make or that we don't make, and some of it has to do with the choices that others make which affect us. For instance, that first day we met in the library at Penn State. I was messing with you and teasing you. You could have told me to fuck off and that would have been that. Both our lives would have turned out completely different."

367

Karlyle Tomms

"Well, actually you may recall that I did tell you to fuck off," I smiled. "But that's just it, why didn't I make you fuck off? I mean, you're not my type, really." I giggled as I teased him. "You were the only man I ever met who tried to seduce me instead of the other way around. I never really gave them a chance to seduce me. I would give them first base and a home run before they ever had a chance to swing the bat. Jeez!" I exclaimed as I thought about it, "I am so fucking lucky I didn't get pregnant, or worse, syphilis."

"You took precautions, didn't you?" he consoled.

"Yeah, but still," I went on, "the more guys you fuck the more you increase your chances of getting in trouble even if you do take precautions."

I reached over and lay my hand on his leg. "I think I am glad to be with just one guy. Just one sweet guy who loves me back, and who isn't messed up like Tommy is going to be for the rest of his life."

"I know," he responded. "Poor guy."

"His own choice put him there," I said.

"He gambled and lost," Earl evaluated. "He thought he was going to be able to have a military career and be able to have a better life for his family. He knew there was a risk. He just lost. In the long run, it is the ones who are willing to take some risks and work for it who are most likely to win."

"I haven't really taken any risks," I replied. "Neither have you really. You inherited the options you have and I was lucky enough that you fell in love with me. What risk?"

"We all take a risk every day when we get up in the morning," he explained. "We take a risk when we go to sleep that our heart will still be beating when the alarm goes off. We take a risk when we have a meal in the restaurant that the cook washed his hands after he took a poop and we are not going to get sick. There are daily risks and there are risks that we take when we gamble for more. We are taking a risk to move to Nashville. I might not be a good manager. The distribution center might fail. My dad's business could go bankrupt. Tommy took a risk to do what he thought was right for his family. It's just a shame that our government would send innocent guys to their death for an obscure and really unexplainable cause. For what? Support the military industrial complex so some fat cats in the arms industry can get even fatter on the carcasses of the nation's young men? I mean, you know, I think it is a crock of shit, but what can we do? Vote? Protest? Assassinate? I mean, Jesus, to assassinate another person because they don't think the way you do has to be the ultimate injustice. Who gave that person permission or the audacity to think that they have the right to impose their will on other people? They killed

Confessions from the Pumpkin Patch

JFK. They killed Bobby Kennedy and Martin Luther King. Hell, for that matter, they killed Jesus because he threatened the status quo. They killed him for not thinking the way they do. Our government committed mass assassination by drafting young men to fight a war that they didn't want, that most of the fucking country didn't want. They got away with it for a long time before people began to catch on and vote and protest. But hell, the ones who died are the lucky ones. It's the guys like Tommy who are the real victims. He will have to fight their fucking war for the rest of his life unless some genius somewhere, sometime, can come up with a treatment, a way to lead these poor souls out of that hell."

"Do you believe in fate?" I asked.

"Kind of like reincarnation?" he questioned. "Some folks are just destined to have more shit to deal with than others?"

"Yeah, kind of like that," I said.

"Well, I think some people obviously have more shit to deal with than others," he pondered, "and obviously through no fault of their own. I guess what matters is how skillfully you deal with the shit you have, whether you face it and conquer it or whether you let it drag you down. Maybe it's like lifting weights. When you are lifting that weight, your muscles feel queasy and you don't feel very strong at all, but if you keep lifting that weight you build muscle. You don't realize that you are stronger than you think. The more you lift the stronger you get so the really strong people are the ones who have dealt with more shit. They have lifted that weight off themselves, so to speak."

"Interesting," I said. "So in the long run, Gretta and Tommy may end up stronger emotionally and spiritually than us because they have to face more challenges and figure them out."

"If they don't run from the challenges," he continued, "if they face them."

"Maybe that's the genius you were talking about," I said. "The genius to heal it is to hit it head on and keep hitting it 'til you develop the strength to deal with it. Make sure you don't pull the rug over it and pretend it isn't there. Talk about it. Face it. Feel it. 'Til you heal it." I leaned back into the seat of the car. "Hmmmmmm," I pondered. "I need to talk to Gretta and Tommy about that. You are a smart man Earl Titwallow."

"You are a smart woman Lovella Titwallow."

"Why do you say that?" I asked.

"You married me didn't you?" The grin on his face ran from ear to ear. I lay my hand on his leg as we both watched the Pennsylvania highway - rolling far off into the distance before us.

CHAPTER 27

In May of 1969 Earl and I moved to Nashville. This was a total change for me in so many ways. For one thing, I had never lived in such opulent settings. In those days, $200,000 a year went a very long way. By today's standards it would be equivalent to over a million a year. We bought a very nice modern ranch home in the Green Hills area of Nashville off Franklin Road near the Governor's mansion. The driveway curled up the side of the hill to a basement garage on the side of the house. The large windows in the living room overlooked that little hill, and across the road there was a grove of trees. Faintly through the trees could be seen the white columns of a rather stately mansion which I learned later belonged to the Grand Old Opry star Minnie Pearl. This was an adjustment for me as well because I never expected that she was playing the part of Minnie Pearl for the TV cameras. I thought she was really like that, the backwoods hick. The elegance of her home told a different story. I learned later that the elegance of her character was even more impressive.

Earl was gone a great deal of the time and I wanted to finish my education, so we needed someone to help with Vanilla. We interviewed for a nanny and a maid so that my time could be freed to go back to school, hopefully starting in the summer session. I was going to try to get into Vanderbilt, but I wasn't sure if I could. If not Vanderbilt, then there were a few other options and a state school in Murfreesboro, a city not far away.

We hired a middle-aged black woman by the name of Elmira Shanks as our nanny. I came to love her. She had a rounded face with black eyes that looked at you as though they contained the love of Jesus. Her smile was full of perfect teeth and was heart-warming to experience. Her countenance was as sweet as anyone I had ever met. The first time I saw her with Vanilla, I knew that she was right for the job. She had not always been a nanny. Yet, when her last daughter left home after finishing a degree at Fisk, a black college in Nashville, Elmira decided that she needed something to do with her time. She never asked why we had a black child, but the surprise on her face was evident when I took her to meet Vanilla.

A little over a year old now, our daughter was clamoring around on bowed little legs and frequently getting into things where she didn't belong. One day when Vanilla had gotten her hand caught between the

Confessions from the Pumpkin Patch

slats of a heating vent Elmira freed Vanilla's little hand and was rocking her on the hip, wiping her tears when she scolded me. "Lovella, you have got to baby-proof this house. There is just too much for this baby to get into."

"Baby-proof?" I questioned.

"Lord! Miss Lovella," she responded with shock. "Don't tell me you don't know anything about prepping a home for a baby."

"No, Elmira," I said. "I am afraid I don't. I never really had children before and never expected to, so I have a lot to learn, I guess."

"You never expected to have children?" she questioned. Still, she didn't ask how it came to be that two rich white kids from Pennsylvania had a black child.

"No, ma'am," I responded. "Vanilla was a bit of a surprise. I guess it is different when they are still in the crib than when they start becoming mobile."

"Mmmmm. Hmmmm," Elmira moaned as she rocked the baby. "Well, there's a lot of things around here that need some attention. Those cabinets in the kitchen are way too easy to open for one thing, and there is stuff under the sink that can hurt a baby. You need to get that stuff up out of the way."

"Well, if you will show me what to do," I pleaded, "I'll see if I can get someone to fix it."

"Miss Lovella," Elmira educated. "With the kind of means that you and Mr. Earl have there is no reason why you can't get someone to just come in here and take care of it all. You might get over there and look through the yellow pages. I'm sure there are people in town who will come in and take care of those kinds of things for rich folks. If there ain't, you give me the money and I will go to the hardware store and do it myself."

I took the phone book to the dining table and with Elmira's help soon found a handyman to come in and baby-proof the house. I knew that Vanilla was in good hands with Elmira and I trusted her completely.

Our maid was a pretty little country girl by the name of Linda Clark. She had come to Nashville to try to break into country music. So when she wasn't working with us, she was trying to pitch herself as a singer and find gigs to play. But the truth is she had been in Nashville for five years by the time we hired her, and the chances of achieving stardom appeared increasingly slim. She came to Nashville at eighteen and she was twenty-two when we hired her. Her drawl was as thick as a fence post, and her naive manner caused others to overlook the fact that she was a very intelligent person. She was very good at keeping the house clean and presentable. She worked 8:00 AM to 5:00 PM, Monday through Friday most of the time but adjusted her hours if we had dinner plans for anyone. Earl was frequently calling and asking if we could have dinner ready for a potential client or someone he wanted to hire into an executive position. For the longest time, I tried to cook these dinners myself, but it soon became evident that I could not pull off preparing the meal and playing the gracious hostess at the same time, so we hired a part time cook. More and more I came to think that there was nothing for me to do except exist.

All that money was going fast. Earl bought me a new Mercedes as well as one for himself. His was black and mine was maroon. We had a large house payment and then hired three servants. I was beginning to feel rather worthless and un-needed. I didn't clean the house. I didn't cook. I didn't even take care of my own baby. When Earl was there sometimes he was attentive and affectionate and at other times he was just as buried in his work at home as he was in the office. Love-making became a dull routine. Three or four nights a week he would crawl into bed and start feeling my body and kissing me. Then with very little foreplay he would climb on, rock and fart 'til he climaxed and then roll over and go to sleep. It stopped feeling like I was making love to him and started feeling like I was servicing him. I barely enjoyed it anymore.

I didn't start college that summer. I didn't even try. I started smoking again a few months after we moved to Nashville. I didn't have to worry about smoking around the baby because Elmira had her well cared for somewhere else in the house. Much of the time, I sat in the living room looking out that big window at the beautiful view, puffing away, feeling drab and useless. In the past I would have absorbed one book after another, text or fiction, and I had stopped reading. I did nothing but stare out the window and smoke. Our sofa sat near the window with a side table on either end. I pulled a chair up to the side table where I could set my ashtray and gaze across the yard as I smoked.

At times I would go out shopping and spend some of Earl's money on dresses or jewelry—so much for the hippie chick. I was back to dressing the way the real Lovella would have dressed, except I found myself picking more and more classic lines like Mother would have done. Occasionally, I would buy a nice gift for Elmira or Linda just because I wanted to.

I tried joining some women's clubs, but I found them totally inane. Here were grown women talking like Mar-ceeee and Sta-ceeee back in the college dorm. Most of the time, they talked about their husbands and from time-to-time pictures of children went around. I found myself hesitant to show a picture of my child. I didn't feel ashamed of her, but I was ashamed of having had her the way I did. I knew the kind of response I

Confessions from the Pumpkin Patch

was likely to get. The fear of being judged permeated my emotions.

One day as children were being discussed, one of the women at our card table said, "Lovella, you have a child, don't you? Why don't we ever get to see pictures of your baby?"

I froze. I didn't know what to say. I stammered and finally said, "Well, it seems to frighten her when we take a picture so we haven't taken very many."

"Oh, my goodness," one of the women said. "You don't take pictures of your baby? Surely not! How old is your baby now?"

"She is nineteen months," I said, shyly.

"Oh, surely you have pictures of your baby," another woman said.

"Well, I—

The words barely came out of my mouth 'til someone else said, "I'm sure she's adorable. Let's see."

I reluctantly reached into my purse and took out my wallet. I pulled a snap shot of Vanilla from the picture compartment and handed it to the woman next to me. The look on her face was a rapid sequence from scorn to pretended congeniality.

"Why, she is a beautiful baby," she said, after the wave of what might be interpreted as nausea crossed her face. "Is she adopted?"

With the most intense ambivalence I said, "No, she is mine."

"Oooohhhh," the woman said almost sarcastically as she passed the picture on to the next person, casting a look at her that in my mind said, "You are not going to believe this."

The picture went around the table and the response was essentially the same. I wish it had not been what I had expected, but it was. I felt in that moment that the only thing worse than being black in 1969 was to have a baby by someone who was black. I could have told them the story of Earl's grandmother being an escaped slave, but I doubt that it would have made any difference. In fact it might have lowered their opinion of him and I felt such a need to protect him, his business. At least they could look on him as the benevolent man who chose to marry and give a home to the slut who had a black child. The picture came back around to me and I put it back into my wallet. Afterward the conversation was trite and stilted. It didn't take long for someone to suggest that we call it a day.

When I got home that afternoon I went immediately to my lone perch in the living room and lit a cigarette. As I sat staring out the window across the manicured lawn through the trees to the white ornate gate of the Minnie Pearl property a tear dripped from my eye. I felt terribly alone. My mind went back to high school, to friends in Climax, and how I had pretty much wasted the opportunity to make more friends by trying to screw practically every boy in high school. I had such grand, though immature plans for my life, but they had all been derailed. So much for being a research scientist. The grandeur of my surroundings meant nothing to me in that moment.

Elmira walked into the room, "Miss Lovella, I have put Vanilla down for her nap and I was wondering—."

She stopped cold in her tracks seeing the tears streaming down my face and the mother in her kicked in. She came across the room and sat on the end of the sofa next to my chair. She didn't say anything for a moment and then she said, "You know some folks think a little age gives you wisdom that you don't possess when you are young."

I glanced over at her and she gave me that sweet smile as she said, "You know I do have the age and I might have a little wisdom if you want to share your troubles."

I took a drag off my cigarette and blew the smoke toward the window. "I don't know if there is anything that can help," I said blotting the spent cigarette into the ash tray.

"Well, how about you just start by telling me what has got you so upset," she smiled.

I reached into the pack for another cigarette and said, "I don't think counselor is in your job description."

"Well, no it ain't, Miss Lovella," she replied "and I won't go on if you don't want me to, but I have long had mother in my job description. I raised up six children and there have been many times I've had to come to the rescue of a broken heart."

I lit the cigarette and looked away from her. "I am ashamed of even having these feelings, Elmira. I would be especially ashamed of discussing them with you."

She leaned toward me. I heard her move and turned back around. Her eyes met mine and she said, "One thing I know, Miss Lovella, shame never solved a problem anywhere in the world. There has not been one single time that lookin' back with remorse ever made anything better."

I sat there, silent, looking at her.

"Tell me what has hurt you, child." Her voice was soft with compassion.

Finally, I gave in. I sighed and stared out the open window, unable to look at her.

"I was at this stupid luncheon and bridge game," I said. "They started asking me to see pictures of my daughter." Tears made my voice tremble with the next words. "I was ashamed to show them pictures of my own baby. Then when I showed them the picture, I could see the disgust on their faces. They asked me if she was adopted. There was a part of me that

Confessions from the Pumpkin Patch

wanted to say—yes. There was a part of me that thought it would be so much easier to deal with if they thought we were this benevolent couple who adopted a poor black child, but I couldn't say it. I couldn't make myself lie. I told them that she is my baby and then they were even worse." I wiped tears with the back of my hand and continued. "It's like they could have accepted it if I adopted a black child but they were disgusted that I gave birth to her. I wanted to tell them she was adopted, but I couldn't make myself. I don't know why I didn't stand up to them. I mean I cussed out this old bitch in Connecticut for making snide remarks about my baby and my family, but I couldn't stand up to their disgust behind their smiles. It would have been easier if they had attacked me and called me names instead of pretending congeniality. At least then I would have had something to fight."

Elmira reached out a comforting hand to touch my arm. "You are new at this," she said. "Black folks have been dealing with this kind of thing for two hundred years but it's all brand new to you. One thing I can tell you is what them women think don't have nothin' to do with you. Judgment tells something about the person doing the judging. It don't really say nothin' about the person being judged. Condemnation and gossip is what a lot of southern women do. Many southern white women are like brightly-colored spiders: Just because they smile pretty don't mean they won't bite."

"I was just trying to make some friends," I sniffled.

"And what you found out was these people ain't your friends." She patted my arm. "When we face tough times in life that teaches us who our real friends are, but it also shows our enemies."

"But Elmira," I countered. "I have to be around these people. I have to live here and deal with this prejudice. I have to put on a face for Earl's job and the company reputation."

"Darlin', I have lived here my whole life," she said "You think I haven't had to deal with uppity white folks who think they are better than you just 'cause their skin is a little lighter? Yes, you have to live with them, and you have to deal with them and their attitude. That's true. But their attitude don't have nothin' to do with you being proud of yourself. You can be proud of who you are in spite of what they think, and you can smile right back at 'em and be as fake as they are when you're around them knowing that you matter even if they think you don't. Then you come home and be real with the folks who really know you matter."

I smashed another cigarette into the tray. "That's just the problem," I said. "I don't have anything to be proud of. I have given up my dreams, and my life has become totally different from what I planned. I haven't finished my education. I don't even take care of my own daughter."

"You always have something to be proud of," Elmira responded. "Be proud of the fact that you are a child of God."

I laughed sarcastically. "I have never been much on God," I said. "Mother forced me to go to church. I always thought it was more of a show and a social event. I can't say that I ever really got anything out of it, or that I ever thought there was any more to religion than control and appeasement."

"Well now folks go to church for all kinds of reasons," she replied, "and it ain't always to praise the Lord. When the Bible says, 'narrow is the way and few there be that enter there in' it means some folks get it, and some folks don't. Don't matter what church they go to. Some folks get it and some folks don't."

"Well, I guess I never got it," I said feeling uncomfortable that the conversation was swinging toward religion. As far as I was concerned, religion was something to be avoided.

"Well, let me sum it up for you," she said. "God is Love, and God is Holy, and God made you in his image. Now what does that make you?"

"A person," I said, nervously trying to figure out a way to get out of the conversation.

"It means that you are made in the image and likeness of pure and perfect holy love itself," she went on. "Can't nothin' ever change that. Nothin' nobody ever said or did can change what God created, and no mistake you ever made can change what God created. You are a child of God. But you see, God made everybody in his likeness. He made us all the same. The Bible says God ain't no respecter of persons. That means he don't favor nobody over someone else no matter what the color of their skin or who they are or what mistakes they have made with their life or whether they think they are good or bad. It also means he loves them uppity prejudiced white folks as much as he does you and me. So we have to learn to forgive 'em 'cause they don't know what they do. They don't get it. Now do you understand?"

"I guess so," I said, relaxing a little and reaching for another cigarette.

"Child, I am telling you that you don't have to do anything to *be* special." She leaned forward a little more and patted my arm to call my attention. When I turned to look, her eyes met mine with a gaze of pure love. "You are already special," she went on. "You don't have to get an education to be special, but you can if you want to. You don't have to cure cancer to be special, but if you do the world would be grateful. God don't make nobody who ain't special. It means we are all equal in his love. There is no way around it. If you believe that his love is real, then we are

Confessions from the Pumpkin Patch

all equal in it. You hold your head up high. Don't you worry about what anybody thinks about you. What they think don't have nothin' to do with you. You had a baby with the same worth as any other baby. If somebody else don't think so, then that's their problem. When the Bible says 'Judge not, lest ye be not judged' it means the first person hurt by his own judgment is himself."

"Yes, but they can create problems for us," I countered.

"They might," she said. "Sometimes people do bad things, but you can't spend your life worrying about what bad things they might do, and you don't need to spend your life letting prejudice define you. You define yourself in this world. God defined you before you got here. If people sit around worrying about what other people think of them instead of getting on with their lives, nothing would ever get accomplished."

"That's the problem," I replied. "I'm not accomplishing anything. I'm not even raising my own child. You are."

"No, I'm not," she snapped. "I am like a grandmother giving you a little help to get by. You are the one that child bonded with. I have watched you with that baby and I have watched that baby with you. I see you when you put her down for a nap and when you hold her close to your bosom. Somebody else might feed her once in a while or change her diaper, but that don't mean she ain't yours. I know you love that baby. I see it every day."

"I haven't ever really taken care of her except for here and there," I snapped back. "Earl's mother has taken care of her. My mother has taken care of her. Earl has taken care of her and you have taken care of her. I probably have less to do with her than anyone."

Elmira sat back into the sofa and smiled. "How much do you want to take care of her?"

The question caught me off guard. A hot flush of embarrassment filled my face and I realized I had just passively stood by and let other people have my baby. Maybe it was because there was a hint of shame there, an embarrassment that she wasn't really Earl's biological child, embarrassment about that night with Screech. I asked myself if maybe I didn't want her, if maybe I resented her and I realized that there was a part of me that wished she wasn't there, a part of me that saw her as a barrier to what I thought I really wanted in life. I knew I had a choice. I could go on with the way things were. I could actually go ahead and pursue my career, or I could be a mother to my child. No matter what choice I made, I realized in that moment that I had to grow up. I fiddled with the bracelet on my arm as Elmira sat silent waiting for my answer.

"I want to be a real mother to my baby," I said at last. "Will you show

Karlyle Tomms

me how?"

Elmira leaned forward and said, through her beautiful smile, "Honey, I would be proud to teach you everything I know."

Confessions from the Pumpkin Patch

Chapter 28

My daughter grew, to use an old cliché, by leaps and bounds. By the time she was three years old, I was pregnant with my second child. This one I knew belonged biologically to Earl. Elmira, true to her promise, taught me a great deal about being a mother. I forgot about going back to college because I simply couldn't see a reason for it anymore. The Chum Snacks Company grew and Earl's income increased to the point that we could have practically anything we wanted any time we wanted. He was busy, but I didn't care. I knew I still loved him and I extended that love to my child in his absence.

Earl would come home in the evening, whenever he was able to get away early enough, and would delight in Vanilla's company. The two of them had a joyful time together and I realized that he meant it when he saw her as his own child. I realized that she was somehow a link to the love he had felt for Screech and in some way maybe she kept that love alive for him. I wasn't jealous anymore because I knew that he loved me just as much as he had ever loved Screech. It had been a moment in his life that caught him off guard, caught both of us off guard really. I doubt that he ever expected in a million years that he would fall in love with a black man from Alabama or would meet him in San Francisco. I certainly never expected to become pregnant by that same man. We were young, dumb kids out for an adventure. The fact that the adventure became a turning point that totally changed life for both of us was more of a comfort now than a regret.

I had learned to play chit-chat with rich Nashville women while I ignored their gossip and cutting little digs in the disguise of humor and I found a couple who were genuine friends. On a few occasions, I had attended church with Elmira and that certainly was an experience worth having. It made Mother's church seem like a piece of stale toast next to a banquet of soul food. Although I appreciated it and I knew that I was welcome, it never quite fit with my personality. Besides, Elmira encouraged me that I had two reasons to go to church. The first and foremost reason was to develop my spirituality, to emulate Christ, and try to live as he lived with the given exception that I was not about to hang out with twelve guys and be celibate. The second reason was that I needed to attend church for show, for community, to play the role that would be

379

Karlyle Tomms

expected of me as the wife of a wealthy businessman in a southern town.

I attended several different churches trying to see which would best serve the dual purpose recommended to me and finally settled on a large Evangelical church near Brentwood: Evangelic Temple. The drive was not that extended from Green Hills and the church was filled with people who obviously came from money. As well, it was a little bit fun in addition to often being enlightening. I certainly didn't mind it. I even convinced Earl that he should go. I could drop Vanilla at the church daycare when we went in on Sunday, and pick her up on the way out. After a while I volunteered to help with weekly church business such as preparing and printing the bulletins for Sunday morning service. I would normally go in on Thursday or Friday to type up the bulletin information and get it ready to be printed for Sunday. Unfortunately, it was more of a challenge than I thought it would be to curb the nasty edge of my tongue which was all too prone to snap with profanity. I was constantly catching myself half way into cursing the typewriter when some little screw-up occurred.

The minister was a very nice man by the name of Pastor Wilkes. He was tall, about 6'4" and was a very healthy man for his late forties. In person, he was soft spoken, gentle, and respectful. In the podium, he was a fireball of energy and enthusiasm. His sermon, which he delivered with a deep powerful voice, resonated to the back walls of the church.

On a Thursday afternoon in late May he approached me and asked if I had ever heard of a pastor by the name of Ronald Dennison.

"Oh," I said, "Isn't he that TV preacher who has the Sunday morning broadcast?"

Yes," Pastor Wilkes replied. "Pastor Dennison actually has a couple of TV shows and has been very well known around this area for his work in the use of media to reach the faithful and convert the fallen. He has become a national figure in the evangelical movement."

"Uh huh," I said smiling. "I happened to catch his broadcast a couple of months ago when Vanilla was ill and I stayed home from church that day. He is quite a speaker and a very striking figure of a man as well."

"Well," Pastor Wilkes continued, "Pastor Dennison is going to be broadcasting from our church on Sunday, June 20th."

"How wonderful!" I spouted smiling. "I will look forward to that."

Pastor Wilkes ignored my somewhat less than sincere enthusiasm and said, "I was wondering if we might impose upon you to meet with Pastor Dennison regarding his program for that day and work with him to set up the service according to his specifications. Would you be willing to be in charge of the bulletins?"

I knew that a broadcast was going to take a lot more than bulletins.

Confessions from the Pumpkin Patch

There would be camera crews, sound techs, producers, and they would be in and out of the church for the upcoming weeks preparing for the broadcast.

I nodded, "Of course."

"We are quite honored to have Pastor Dennison come to our church," Pastor Wilkes continued. "We want to present with our best foot forward, and having seen your work, Lovella, I trust that you will prepare a very nice program for that service."

"I am honored," I replied.

"When do you think you might be able to meet with Pastor Dennison?" he questioned.

"I can make myself available at any time," I answered.

"Wonderful. I will contact Pastor Dennison and give you a time that would be convenient for him. You may have to meet with him at his studio. Will that be okay with you?"

"Of course," I said.

"It is not uncommon for Pastor Dennison to speak before crowds of five or six thousand," he explained. "We are not sure how many additional parishioners we may have for that day. We may have to have extra bulletins for the day and be prepared in case there might be any surprises."

"I don't understand why he would want us to complete the bulletins," I reflected. "I would assume that he has a whole collection of staff for that sort of thing."

"He would prefer that the bulletins be printed in the usual manner customary to each church," Pastor Wilkes responded.

"Just let me know when," I said and went back to my work on the typewriter.

The next day I received a call at home from Pastor Wilkes informing me that Pastor Dennison wished to meet with me on the following afternoon at 2:00 PM. I accepted the appointment and affirmed to myself that I would be there and on the following day dressed in my finest. The hippie days were completely gone now and I was back to classic lines and make up. In those days I tended to wear my hair in a French roll with a clip. I thought it made me look a bit thinner and I could show off my earrings since I was accumulating quite a collection. I dressed in a pale green, sleeveless, tube dress with a slight flare around my knees. It had a mock turtle-type of collar with a little loop below which showed just the hint of cleavage. My earrings were small diamond-studded gold crosses. I was sparing with the eye shadow but liberally applied a burgundy colored lipstick. All finished, I looked at myself in the full-length mirror to see my fourth month of pregnancy protruding out slightly beyond the curve of my

Karlyle Tomms

dress. "I am going to have to start wearing maternity clothes," I thought to myself. "But I don't have time to deal with that now."

It was already 1:30 when I backed out of the garage. I only had thirty minutes to make it to Briley Parkway on the south end of town and find the studio. Of course I was late. I went clamoring up to the receptionist at a quarter after two.

"I'm Lovella Titwallow," I said half breathlessly. "I have an appointment with Pastor Dennison."

"Oh, yes," she said grinning from ear to ear. "He has been expecting you."

She was a middle aged woman who looked to be perhaps older than my mother. Her hair was fairly short, obviously colored, and permed in large round curls like a grass helmet. Her ample glasses sat securely over her pointy, little nose. She presented as sweet but I had the distinct impression she could be quite tough.

"I'm sure he has," I quipped, "especially since I'm late."

"Oh, you are fine, darlin'," she said sweetly with a country drawl. Then she reached over to press a button on the intercom, and said, "Mrs. Titwallow is here to see you Pastor."

I heard a man's voice return with, "Send her in."

The receptionist got up to lead me and said, "Right this way, sugar."

She led me down a short hall to a large, ornate, wooden door where she tapped lightly and waited to hear "Come in." She then opened the door, ushered me through, and closed it behind me.

Pastor Dennison rose from his high-back leather office chair and came around the large mahogany desk that sat near the middle of the room. He was a man in his mid-to-late thirties, of average to slightly small stature, but he was a strikingly handsome man. He had a full head of thick dark brown hair and swimming pool-blue eyes that topped off the dimples on either side of his square jaw. He was dressed in a black suit with a white shirt and a solid pale blue tie. No sooner did he see me than his eyes lit up like he had just seen a long lost loved one returning home.

"Mrs. Titwallow," he exclaimed with a sing-song tone as he approached me and took the hand I extended for a handshake between both of his large hands. "How good to see you!"

I looked down at the hairy backs of his thick, full hands to see the wedding band wrapped ornately around his finger. He held my hands for a few seconds and looked at me like I was an ice cream cone he wanted to lick.

"Come. Sit down!" he said with vigor.

He gave a slight tug with both his hands still over mine leading me to

382

Confessions from the Pumpkin Patch

the chair without losing physical contact. Just before I reached the chair, he turned loose and motioned for me to sit.

"Would you like a soda or a cup of coffee?" he questioned as he went back toward his desk. As he passed by he removed his suit jacket and laid it across the front corner of the desk without turning around. He walked on toward the wall behind his desk where I noticed a coffee pot and a small refrigerator. I couldn't help also noticing that he had a firm round ass perfectly outlined by his suit pants.

"Yes, please," I said. "Coca Cola if you have it."

"Ice?" he questioned as he bent over and pulled a bottle of coke from the fridge.

"Yes, if you have it. Thank you," I said.

"I certainly do have it," he responded. He pulled a glass from a nearby shelf and opened a drawer on what appeared to be a small ice maker. He put a scoop of ice in the glass and brought both the glass and the opened bottle of coke back to me. "Don't worry about setting it on the furniture," he said as he turned and went back to the fridge where he poured a soda for himself as well.

I poured the coke into my glass and sat patiently waiting for the foam to clear before adding more.

"So, Mrs. Titwallow, what brings you to Nashville?" he questioned, assuming I guess that I was not from the area. Mother's insistence that I articulate probably eliminated any hint of an inherited Kentucky drawl.

I cleared my throat. "My husband is the district manager for the Chum Snacks Company I replied. "His father owns the company, and we moved here about two years ago after they built the distribution center here."

"Well, you must be from fine stock indeed," he quipped. "At least you certainly look like you came from very fine stock."

The little kick of a grin up one side of his mouth and the look in his eyes led me to believe that he was coming on to me. I dismissed it initially as my imagination.

"My mother's family is from rural Kentucky," I said. "And my father was an alcoholic factory worker. I just happened to meet the right boy when I went to college."

"Do you love him?" he questioned.

I felt suddenly uncomfortable with his questions becoming a bit too personal. I avoided snapping that I thought we were here to do the bulletins for his service, not pry into one another's personal life. Instead, I responded, "Yes, I do. I love him very much."

"Well, good! Good!" he spouted. "A woman ought to love her husband. Any children?"

383

Karlyle Tomms

"Yes," I replied quietly. "We have a daughter aged three."

"And one on the way looks like," he said, smiling as he glanced down at my belly.

"I'm sorry," I said, feeling suddenly embarrassed and covering my belly with my hand. "I should have gotten into maternity clothes before now."

"Oh, don't be sorry," he said. He moved around to the front with his soda in hand, leaned back on his desk, and crossed his legs at the ankles. He leaned back on his desk eying me like a steak dinner. "Pregnancy is when a woman is at her finest and most beautiful," he went on. "You should be proud that you are with child."

"Well, I am proud," I responded. "Earl and I love our daughter very much, but we have been looking forward to this baby as well."

"May I?" he said as he dismounted the desk and came to kneel beside my chair. He held his left hand over my belly about six inches away and rested his right arm across his leg.

I felt very odd at that moment. This was an extremely personal and intimate thing for even family to do, much less a man I had never met before. I felt almost violated. Yet, on the other hand, I felt enticed. I looked over at him and met those amazing blue eyes gazing directly at me. His look was both inviting and questioning.

I nodded, and his hand went smoothly to my belly while he maintained his gaze into my eyes. I felt the warm masculine touch of his hand flow over my belly, and then around to my waist quickly like a test before moving back over my stomach. I looked down at his hand, but his gaze toward my face never wavered. Now, I knew he was coming on to me. It felt really strange to be the one who was being seduced instead of being the one doing the seducing. Only Earl had ever seduced me. Pastor Dennison was not exactly subtle, but much more subtle than I ever had to be when seducing boys. Most men are easy, especially if you are pretty.

I watched his hand move around my belly and made no effort to pull it away. I had a mix of feelings at that point. On one hand I had taken on the quest to be a good Christian, to do the right thing, and I wanted to be faithful to Earl. On the other hand the old me was still in there. I felt my groin begin to crave. Yet I felt guilt that I was betraying Earl and my family. The fact that this was a powerful and beautiful man made the temptation even more enticing. The fact that the fruit was most assuredly forbidden made the craving sweeter. I lifted my head and met his eyes again.

"You are so beautiful," he whispered, smiling. "Your lips are like sweet red wine. They make me want to take communion with you. I want to drink the sweet nectar of your lips. May I kiss you Mrs. Titwallow?"

Confessions from the Pumpkin Patch

That felt so strange for him to call me Mrs. Titwallow. I said nothing but sat looking at him, not knowing what to do. A part of me wanted to get up, slap him and leave, but a part of me wanted to protect him, his role as a pastor and his reputation. I did want him to seduce me. I wanted him to make love to me. Yet there was a voice in my mind telling me that it would be very wrong. Although I very much loved Earl, it had been forever since we had really made love. I enjoyed our contact, but more often than not it was over briefly and it had become increasingly mundane as our marriage progressed with Earl becoming more involved in the company. Earl had become his father in so many ways. As much as I hated it, and as much as I wanted it to be different, it often felt like my role as a wife was to service him, pleasure him and keep him going while he did the work that he had to do. Still, I never talked to him about it because I had also become like his mom, at least in her youth. I played the dutiful wife who gives in to her husband's needs without questioning or thinking of her own.

Pastor Dennison leaned in ever closer to my lips. He did not ask again if he could kiss me and I never told him that he could not. Coming slowly closer, at long last, his lips touched mine ever so lightly and then pulled away. A second later his lips maneuvered skillfully over mine then pulled away again, but only for the brief second that he gazed into my eyes. Then he moved back to gently cover my mouth with his own. The expertise of his kiss felt as though he could have picked up a single grain of rice with those lips. The sensuality of it was amazing. He kissed me gently, covering my mouth, consuming my mouth with a ravishing hunger. I closed my eyes and melted into his kiss.

His hand moved from my belly to my breast. He caressed it as if he was petting a cat, gently moving his big hairy hands across to my nipples. I felt them harden as his thumb moved back and forth gently over one nipple. I felt his other hand move to the back of my neck. Electricity surged throughout my body. I felt sensual tingling from my neck through my lips to my breasts and to my groin. I felt myself gasp in pleasure as his lips moved to the nape of my neck. Never had a man touched me that way before, not even Earl. Never had a man filled me with such longing and intensity. I had fucked boys repeatedly since I was a young teen and had never experienced anything like this.

He lifted me up gently, his hand firm against the back of my neck. I rose with him like the assistant in a magic show, levitated, floating. He kissed me the whole way, moved his lips across my neck as he caressed my body. We moved across the floor to his desk never losing contact. I felt him press his stiff erection into my belly, and his hands moved across my body like he was playing a harp. He stopped, gazed into my eyes, and cupped his mouth over mine again. He pulled a pillow from the chair with one hand while his other held firm around my waist. He placed the pillow on the desk to cradle my head as he tilted me back onto the desk. He pulled my hips to the edge of the desk, and reached up under my dress to pull my hose and panties down over my legs and to the floor. My high heels popped off my feet to the floor as he pulled panties past my feet. He pulled my naked feet up beside his ears and pressed his firm crotch against my buttocks while his mouth made love to my feet. I felt the pulse of his erection through his pants as he pressed it against my ass. His lips went down my legs to my knees, along my inner thigh to the muff-dragon. I felt myself gasp, head tilted back into the pillow as he made contact with those skillful lips. I couldn't breathe. I gasped as pleasure shot through me like a bullet. My head felt suddenly light as an orgasm rushed over me like a tsunami. He worked his way back up my legs to my feet, licking around my ankles. He unfastened his pants and dropped them to the floor. He never lost contact with my body, all the while loosening his tie and the top button of his shirt. He ceased contact with me only for a brief moment as he deftly and quickly pulled his shirt, undershirt, and loosened tie all together up over his head and cast them to the floor. I looked up to see what I expected, a chest full of gorilla hair covering his body all the way down to his ample presentation.

He pressed against my groin, then leaned forward and pushed himself inside of me. One solid hand went behind my back. Then he picked me up from the desk and used the opposite hand to move the pillow from behind my head to my hips. After he positioned it firmly behind my hips, we slammed together wildly between brief intervals in which he would stop to run tender fingers across my lips. He would change his motion and sometimes lean me backwards until he was pressing straight upward into me. I surged with another climax, one like I had never felt before. It was like my pelvis was convulsing in rapid vibrations that then radiated upward and outward into my entire body.

At last I heard his breath quicken, felt his rhythm alter and knew that he was nearing climax. He began to quiver almost like a baby bird as he continued to thrust. Then he exploded as though demons were rushing out after the exorcism of a possessed man. I feared that security guards would hear his screams and come rushing in thinking he was being murdered. In a few seconds he fell silent, breathless, still inside of me but not moving. A second or two later he quaked again like a surging rush of electricity ran suddenly through his body. He shivered once more, still inside me, still holding me, when one last smaller wave went through him and he pulled

Confessions from the Pumpkin Patch

back.

"I'm sorry. I'm sorry," he said pleadingly and immediately. "God forgive me. I'm sorry."

I was taken aback. I had just had one of the most spectacular sessions of sex ever in my life and this man was telling me he is sorry.

"What for?" I asked.

"I have sinned! I have sinned against God and against you."

He began to cry, huge tears rolling over his distorted face.

"I am a worthless no good sinner!"

He started to turn around apparently forgetting that his pants were still around his ankles. He tripped over them and fell sideways onto the floor.

"The Lord has struck me down!" he cried as he buried his face into the floor. "I deserve to be struck down. I deserve to be punished! I am a miserable worthless sinner."

"Your pants struck you down," I quipped as I got up from his desk and collected myself. I realized that my dress was now wrinkled and there was a little wet spot at the hem on the back side. I knelt down beside him and put a comforting hand on his shoulder. "Pastor Dennison," I said, "it's okay. It's just sex. Excellent sex, but just sex. I very much enjoyed it. Thank you."

"Don't call me Pastor!" he wailed. "I don't deserve to be called Pastor!"

"Uh—Okay—Uh—Ron?" I said after fumbling for what to call him. "You have to pull yourself together now."

"I am a God-forsaken sinner!" he bellowed into the floor.

"Well, doesn't God forgive?" I questioned.

"Yes, but I keep doing it over and over. I can't stop doing it. I have to seduce women, especially women with beautiful lips. I can't stop myself! I can't! I would spend every waking hour doing it if I could. I am a weak and worthless man."

"There is no such thing as worthless," I said quoting Elmira. "God made everyone equal."

"God punishes the sinful," he wailed. "You have no idea how sinful I am. All I want to do is have sex, seduce women. The devil keeps my mind constantly on women. I have had so many women. I have defiled so many poor helpless females. I have corrupted the sanctity of the church!"

"Well, it kind of felt like you might have had some practice," I grinned. "But come on. I am not poor or helpless and I had a choice in this— defiling. I am as responsible as you are."

"You are responsible!" he shouted looking up at me. "You are a Jezebel! A whore!"

"Well, I wouldn't take it that far," I said. "I never got paid for it, but I

387

Karlyle Tomms

have been a bit of a slut in my day. I like sex too. That doesn't make me a bad person."

"You *are* a bad person!" he bellowed as he buried his face back into the floor. "You're a seductress. You lured me into sin! But I am worse! I am called of God and I allowed myself to be lured into sin. I am lower than the belly of the serpent! I am worthless scum on the shoes of the righteous."

"No you're not," I argued. "Look, I'll prove it to you. God is love, right?"

"Yes," he quietly responded.

"And God is holy?" I went on.

"Yes," he said again.

"And God made you in His image?"

"Yes."

"Then what does that make you?"

"A miserable, worthless sinner," he persisted.

"It means you are made in the image and likeness of pure and perfect Holy Love itself!" I argued. "It means there is no such thing as worthless!"

"But I have sinned and fallen short," he continued.

"Well join the fucking club!" I blurted, losing patience with him. "Who hasn't?"

"I already have joined the club." He burst into tears again. "The club of eternal hell-fire and damnation!"

By that time, I had enough.

"We have got work to do," I commanded. "Get up! We have got to get you ready to present at Evangelic Temple on the twentieth."

"I should throw myself into a furnace and burn myself so I know what hell feels like. I deserve to burn in hell," he cried.

I found myself wondering what happened to the self-assured, determined man I had met when I came in.

"It doesn't matter what you think you should do," I responded. "It only matters what you have to do. Now get up." He didn't move. I stood up at that point and commanded firmly, "RONALD! I SAID GET UP!"

"Yes," he said, responding quietly to the authoritarian tone. "Yes, I need to get up. We have work to do. There are things I need to do." He rolled over but did not get up.

I couldn't help feeling a surge of power as I stood over him looking down at his now limp dick and his naked body. He looked up at me like a little boy looking at a scolding mother. "GET UP," I commanded again.

He sat up, rolled over to his knees, put one arm on the chair to pull

388

Confessions from the Pumpkin Patch

himself up and into it where he began the task of pulling his pants up. I watched him with curiosity. A few minutes before a commanding masculine man had given me the best fuck of my life and now he looked sheepish and child-like. He spoke in soft, frightened, child-like tones.

"I need to get up. I have work to do," he said as he stood up, pulled his pants the rest of the way up, and fastened them. He then retrieved his shirt and tie and began to put them on.

I found my panties and hose, slipped back into them and asked, "Do you have an adjacent restroom?"

"Over there."

He pointed quietly to a door near the back right corner of his office.

I went in and took a look in the mirror at the mess on my face. My burgundy lipstick was now smeared across my face and down my neck. My hair was a fairly easy fix with a few bobby pins, but the makeup took a little more time. I washed away the excess lipstick with some soap and the hand towel. Then I noticed that there was a little dab of it on my collar. That was not going to come off so easily. Finally, I re-applied my makeup and stepped back into the office to find Pastor Dennison fully dressed back in his suit and sitting behind his desk.

When I initially saw him he had his face buried in his hands, but as soon as he heard me re-enter the room he looked up and smiled as though nothing had ever happened. The persona of Pastor Dennison was back and the sinful little boy who needed to be punished was gone. He stood and came around the desk just as he had done when I had first been ushered into his office. He began to speak with the same masculine commanding voice as he reached out and took my hand between both of his just as he had done when we met. "Mrs. Titwallow—" he crooned, "How good of you to come by my office today. I hope this was not inconvenient for you."

I stood there looking at him thinking, "What the hell?"

"I think we may be out of time this afternoon," he went on as though all we had done was sit there sipping soda pop talking about church. "If I write notes for the bulletin format by hand, do you think you might be able to decipher my chicken scratch to put the material together?"

"Uh, yes," I said. I was now thinking that the man was totally nuts. To say that his behavior was bizarre would be an understatement and why did he even want me to come to his office if all he had to do was write notes for me? The next week I concluded from a conversation with the church secretary that he had set it up. After seeing me in a picture of church volunteers he decided he wanted to fuck me. Putting the bulletins together was just a ruse to get me into his office.

Karlyle Tomms

While he was fucking me I had found myself hoping that we might be able to do it again. It was so good. It certainly would have been nice to make a habit of it since I wasn't getting much from Earl anymore, but I was also breaking my own rule about honesty. Then I found myself thinking that he was such a nutcase I would rather keep my distance.

"Good," he smiled congenially. "I'll have Miss Smith bring the notes to you tomorrow. Will you be at Evangelic Temple tomorrow afternoon then?"

"Yes," I replied. He continued to hold my hand and I found myself looking at him as though I was examining some strange animal on display at the zoo.

"Good. I will have Miss Smith see you out." He finally released my hand and turned to the intercom on his desk.

"That's okay," I said quickly. "No need to involve Miss Smith. I don't think it is so complicated I can't figure it out."

I walked confidently to the door and opened it. To be a little mean I turned back to him and in my best ditzy girl voice said, "See you later, honey." I gave a dainty little wave and a backwards kick of my heel. Then I left the door open behind me. As I walked past Miss Smith at the reception desk, she looked at me with an interesting, smirking smile. "She knows exactly what he does," I thought to myself as I passed.

That evening at home was typical. Earl got home from work about 7:00. We had a quick dinner and played with Vanilla for a while before we put her to bed. Often he would tuck her into bed himself, but this time I went with him. After putting her down together we went back to the living room where he flipped on the TV and sat on the sofa. I went right behind him and turned the TV off. He looked at me curiously but said nothing. I guess he could see the seriousness on my face. I sat down next to him and put my head on his chest. I hugged him, looked up, and said, "I love you. Do you know that?"

"I do know that," he responded. "I love you too."

"Then why don't we act like we love each other anymore?" I queried.

He sat up and turned toward me. "What do you mean?"

"Earl," I said, calmly. "We've become your parents."

A brief moment of shock went across his face, then he sat another moment in thought, and then the realization of what I was saying hit him. "Goddamn!" he exclaimed. "What do you think we should do about it?"

"Well, for starters," I said, "tonight, I want to sit here, cuddle with and talk to my husband instead of staring at the boob tube. Maybe we might have a glass of wine. Then later, we could go to bed and make love the way we used to make love instead of just having a quick hump."

Confessions from the Pumpkin Patch

He smiled, cupped my face in his hands, and kissed me. "I am so glad you are my girl," he said.

He got up from the sofa and headed for the kitchen. Over his shoulder he asked, "Riesling?"

"Riesling," I affirmed.

CHAPTER 29

I never told Earl about my tryst with the crazy televangelist. I mulled it over in my head many times, but decided that it would do nothing to improve our relationship and that ultimately he was the man I loved and the only one who I wanted to spend the rest of my life with. I was never unfaithful to him again. I stopped going to Evangelical Temple and decided that the Presbyterian Church was more to my liking. Earl really didn't care where we went to church or even if I went. He thought the whole idea of church for show or for business was a bit of hypocrisy anyway. However, Elmira had taught me to appreciate spirituality and that there was wisdom to be gained no matter what church I attended. Earl went with me for a few years and then decided he would rather sleep in on Sunday morning. I took the children for as long as they wanted to go. When they each reached the age of ten, I allowed them to choose whether they wanted to go or if they wanted to go to a different church. Both of them decided they would rather stay home and sleep in like daddy.

On October 24, 1971 our son, Andrew Daniel Titwallow was born. As had been the case when Vanilla was born, the families gathered. When Earl's father learned that we had named the child after him, tears welled in his eyes but he looked away trying to hide the fact that he was touched. We would call the baby Drew for short, but Mr. Titwallow always understood that this, his only grandson, was his namesake and they grew close as Drew matured. Earl commented more than once that his father was more understanding and nurturing with Drew than he ever had been with him. Each time he commented I would smile and say, "Well, I guess he has learned a few things over the years."

Over time, I began to understand what family is really about. Sure, there are squabbles and disagreements, mess ups, and misunderstandings, but ultimately it is about coming back to the love, hanging on to the love, no matter what else happens. I wondered if my kids would put me through what I had put mother through. I wondered if they would misunderstand my intentions and my love for them or if I would be able to be the kind of mother they would love and respect.

As Vanilla got older she had questions about why she looked different from the rest of the family. We told her we would explain it to her when she was old enough to understand. I was thankful that she was close to

Confessions from the Pumpkin Patch

Elmira and that she learned from her how to be black and proud of herself for who she was instead of what others thought she was. At last when she was fourteen and began asking questions about sex we explained to her a little bit about her genetic father and that we had both loved him very much. Earl explained to her what he loved about her father as a man. He emphasized Screech's strength and said nothing about his insecurities or his problems. We told her only that he died of mysterious causes. Eventually when she was an adult, we told her the whole truth.

Vanilla had been a little jealous of Drew when we first brought him home, but she soon fell into the role of little momma, wanting to hold the baby like the adults. For safety, Earl would hold them both in his lap, Vanilla in his arms and Drew in hers. Earl wrapped his long arms around them both and bantered with Vanilla as she looked back and forth between him and Drew saying, "Baby?"

"Little brother, bubba, Drew Drew," Earl would say. He loved both his children more than life and that only made me love him more. He was determined, despite the business, to be the father that Daniel had failed to be to him. He was not about to make his career more important than his children and he always managed to find time for both.

On September 14, 1974, right after Vanilla had entered the first grade, Elmira answered the phone about 2:00 PM. Drew was almost speaking complete sentences by that time. He loved Elmira and followed her around the house like a lost puppy calling her "E-my,"

When Elmira picked up the phone, a serious look came across her face. Drew wrapped his little arms around her leg and must have felt her tension when she said, "Miss Lovella, I think you best come to the phone." No sooner had she said the words than Drew burst into tears.

I had been reading a book by the window having finally given up cigarettes entirely. I learned to enjoy the window better with a book than with a smoke. When I turned to look, Elmira's face was stark with apprehension.

"Elmira, what is it?" I said folding the book closed.

"I think it best they talk to you," she said holding the receiver in my direction.

My heart sank and fear rushed over me. At first I thought that something must have happened to Earl. I no sooner took the phone from Elmira's hand than she bent over, picked up Drew, and began to console him. She stood back with the baby as I put the receiver to my ear and said, "Hello."

"Is this Lovella Titwallow?" I heard a woman's voice on the other end

Karlyle Tomms

of the line.

"Yes," I replied.

"Mrs. Titwallow," the voice followed. "My name is Brenda Patterson. I am a nurse with Armstrong Memorial Hospital in Kittanning, Pennsylvania. I regret to inform you that your mother, Drucella Fuchs, has been involved in a serious accident."

"Accident," I questioned. I could see Elmira nearby rocking Drew on her hip and watching pensively.

"Yes," the voice responded. "Your mother was involved in a serious automobile accident this morning. We have no idea why she crossed the center line into on-coming traffic. There is some suspicion at this point that she may have passed out or that she might have had a seizure."

"Oh, my god!" I winced. "Is she alright?"

"No, Mrs. Titwallow," the voice went on. "I'm afraid your mother has been seriously injured. She crossed over the center line into the path of a semi-truck. No one else was injured seriously, but your mother has had a near fatal accident and has suffered significant brain trauma."

"Oh, Jesus!" I exclaimed. "Is anyone with her? Where are my grandparents?"

"Your grandparents are at the hospital," Brenda Patterson informed. "However, the accident is potentially fatal and your mother is in critical condition. Your grandmother felt that she was too distraught to call you herself and asked that we contact you. She said she knew you would want to be here."

"Yes. Yes," I said, feeling dazed and confused. "I will get there as soon as I can."

I hung up the phone without thinking while the voice on the other end was still speaking. I must have looked totally lost when I turned to Elmira.

"Go pack a bag, honey," she said. "I will call Mr. Earl and let him know. Has your momma been bad hurt?"

"Bad," I said,

"Don't you worry about nothing," Elmira said as she walked over to place a comforting hand at my cheek. "You know I will take good care of everybody down here. You feel up to driving?"

"I don't know," I whispered.

I was too shocked to cry. The tormentor of my childhood had in my adult years become at least congenial with me. She had been good to Vanilla and had, to some extent, redeemed herself. Yet, I still did not trust her, and now knowing that she might die, I had a mix of feelings rushing over me.

"Well, you go on and start packing. Pack for Mr. Earl too. While you

394

Confessions from the Pumpkin Patch

are doing that, I am going to call him and tell him he needs to come home and drive you to Pennsylvania."

"He has got too much to do," I argued. "I can drive."

"Miss Lovella, that company has got plenty enough money that he can take some time off to drive you over to see your sick mother," she argued back. "Chum Snacks is not gonna go out of business cause Mr. Earl took a little time away. Now go pack."

I did dutifully as she had told me. She called Earl and of course he came home immediately. By 4:00 PM we were on our way to Kittanning. Elmira would take care of the children while we were gone. I had no worries about that, but it was a long and tedious trip made worse by worry about Mother.

We arrived in Kittanning about 2:00 AM, exhausted and irritable. Earl pulled his Mercedes into the almost-empty parking lot of Armstrong Memorial.

"You know, they are going to have the hospital locked down at this time of night," he said. "Why don't we just get a hotel room and come back in the morning?"

"Take me around to the emergency room," I said, "I can talk to someone there."

He drove around to the emergency entrance. I got out of the car and walked in alone. There was a reception window in a lobby beside double-doors leading back to the treatment rooms. A skinny older nurse with mouse-blond hair sat behind the window. As I approached she looked up. Her cheekbones squared under her gray eyes as she fixed them on me and said, "May I help you?"

"My name is Lovella Titwallow," I replied. "My mother is Drucella Fuchs and she is in critical care here. We just got in from Nashville. I was wondering if I could see her."

"Visiting hours are not in the middle of the night," she affirmed.

"Look," I responded maintaining my temper, "My mother could die tonight. Are you going to deprive me of possibly my last opportunity to see her alive?"

For a moment her gaze fixated on me like a raccoon in a flash light. Then she said, "I'll call up to that floor and ask."

She closed the sliding glass on the window and I saw her on the phone for a couple of minutes. Afterward she opened the glass again and said, "Your mother is not conscious but she is stable. She probably wouldn't know you were there. Apparently your grandmother is in the room with her. They said they looked in on them just about ten minutes ago and your grandmother was asleep. Why don't you find a place to stay for the night

Karlyle Tomms

and come back in the morning? There is a nice hotel about a mile from here on Glade Park East. If you will go up Nolte this direction and turn left on Glade Park, you will see it just a couple of blocks down." She pointed in the general direction that we were to take.

"Thank you," I said, too exhausted to argue.

"Call us back when you get there with your room number and we will contact you if there is any change in your mother's condition." She smiled and scribbled a note on a piece of paper. "Here is the hospital number and the name of the night nurse on your mother's floor. Call her and let her know how to reach you." She handed the paper to me through the sliding glass window.

"Thank you," I said again and walked out.

I got back in the car and gave Earl instructions to find the hotel. It was almost 3:00 AM by the time we checked into our room. We were both exhausted, but I couldn't sleep. I called the hospital to give the night nurse our room number, and then called the front desk for a wake-up call at 7:00 AM. Most of that four hours, however, I lay there in the dark staring at the ceiling while Earl slept.

The next morning I called the front desk and canceled the wake-up call before they had a chance to ring the room. I showered and dressed and left Earl a note that I had gone back to the hospital. I knew if I woke him he would want to go with me. I thought it best to let him sleep. At least he could.

It was a very short drive back to Armstrong Memorial. I got there right after they brought a breakfast tray for Grandma Donner and just before the doctor made rounds. Mother lay unconscious on the bed with a respirator and tubes poked in everywhere. I thought surely that she was going to die. I assumed that this would be the last I would see of Mother and that she would never even know that I had been there.

Grandma Donner's behavior was significantly more subdued than usual. She quietly ate the breakfast while I asked questions of the doctor. He explained that Mother had a skull fracture to the front left side and lesions in her left frontal lobe. She had also had the type of injury where the brain is rocked back and forth in the skull so she had damage to the back part of her brain as well. He explained that this affects the autonomic nervous system and was why the machine was having to breathe for her.

"Ultimately," he said, "we don't know long-term. Right now we have to get her stabilized and then we will see what happens after that. There are a lot of factors that will determine how well her brain heals. She also has some fractured ribs and narrowly missed a puncture to her lung."

I realized after the discussion with the doctor that I wouldn't be going

Confessions from the Pumpkin Patch

back to Nashville for a very long time. I was torn between my mother and my children. I felt like they both needed me, and there was no way I could split myself between both places. Earl stayed with me for about a week in the hotel room and then had to go back. We went to a local rental company and rented a car for me to drive while I was there. I checked out of the hotel and stayed at Mother's house. It felt so strange to be back there especially alone. Even though I had grown up in that house and my childhood pictures dotted the walls I felt like I was intruding into the life of someone else.

For the next two months I went back and forth between there and the hospital and made one short trip back to Nashville, but only for a day. I dropped off the rental car there and brought my own car back to Pennsylvania. Earl brought the kids up for a weekend a couple of times but I still felt torn between them and my time at the hospital.

While I was there, I went through Mother's papers and tried to figure out what she did and did not have in the way of insurance, burial policies, bank accounts, etc. There was so much to think about and to figure out. It felt as though I was in a vice with the pressure constantly tightening.

In a little over eight weeks they moved Mother out of critical care. She was breathing on her own, but just barely. They still had her on oxygen. She appeared coherent at times and it seemed as though she could carry on a normal conversation, but within minutes she could not remember who had been there and who had not.

The holidays were fast approaching and Thanksgiving would be in just a couple of weeks. I had no idea how I was going to handle that, but it came and went as usual, just another date on the calendar. Earl took the kids to his parents for Thanksgiving Day, and then brought them to spend the weekend with me. Grandma and Grandpa Donner came over and brought food that Saturday and I baked a pumpkin pie in Mother's kitchen.

A few days after Thanksgiving weekend, Mother spiked an infection and regressed considerably in her condition. I went back to sitting with her in the hospital instead of visiting a couple of times a day. She became fitfully delirious and had to have restraints. On the following Thursday afternoon, one week past Thanksgiving, I was sitting in her room watching her cycle in and out of sleep and delirium when I heard her begin talking about something that sparked my curiosity. I could scarcely hear what she was saying at first, but when I heard a particular name, I got up and leaned over her bed.

"Carl! Carl!" she said, fitfully, "Stop. No. No, I don't want to."

I recognized the name. She had told me that Dr. Whitmire, Carl Whitmire, was my biological father. I didn't believe her. Then there were

397

Karlyle Tomms

the things that Daddy told Earl before he died. I never knew what to believe really. My home life and my childhood had become a mystery. What I had thought to be the truth came into question and I wondered if I would ever really know what the truth was. Daddy told Earl his side of the story and who knew if Earl remembered it correctly.

Mother fell silent, then after a minute or two she began thrashing around again. "Carl, I'm a good girl, good girl. No!"

She was in and out. At one point it seemed as though she had quieted down and I went back to my chair. In a few minutes she began again. "I don't want to get pregnant. No, Carl—we're not married. Stop, Carl! Stop, you're hurting me! Sttoooooppppppp!"

I rushed back to the bedside and took her hand to comfort her. "Shh, shh, shh. It's okay, Mother. You're okay."

I stood there with my mind reeling. Was this a hallucination or a flashback? Did he rape her?

She went on calling off similar things for a couple of hours. Over that time, I heard my name called. I heard the words 'pregnant' and 'abortion'. I heard the full name: Carl Whitmire.

About 7:00 that evening Grandma Donner came to the room. She was dressed in her usual gaudy garb, but there wasn't much fire or spunk in her like I had seen my whole life. The humor and spit had gone out of her. Having become a mother I had some idea what kind of pain she must have experienced in watching her daughter suffer.

"Hello, sweetheart," she said, walking up to me and giving me a quick sideways hug. She turned toward Mother and said, "How's she doing today?"

Grandma Donner walked over to the hospital bed and looked down at Mother before waiting for my answer.

"She's still delirious," I responded. "She has been saying all kinds of things but there seems to be a theme."

Grandma Donner looked down at Mother pitifully and patted her on the shoulder. "Lord have mercy." she lamented. "No momma ever wants to see her baby girl go through something like this. God forbid." Her voice trembled. "I think she is gonna die."

"We don't know that," I encouraged. "For all we know, she could have a complete recovery."

Grandma Donner looked up at me and I could see the pain on her face with her eyes floating in little wells of tears that refused to spill across her cheek. "Honey, it sure don't look like it to me," she said mournfully.

I didn't know what to say. I sighed and reached out a hand over her arm. She patted my hand and smiled. "Anything new?" she asked.

Confessions from the Pumpkin Patch

"She has been calling out Carl Whitmire's name," I said.

"Oh, mercy," Grandma Donner exclaimed and moved quickly to a chair.

"What do you mean, oh mercy?" I asked, following her.

"What has she been saying?" Grandma Donner questioned back.

"She has been saying things like 'stop you're hurting me, and I don't want to get pregnant'," I replied.

Grandma Donner's face looked stunned and she turned away from me.

"What do you know that I don't?" I pressed.

She said nothing but kept her face turned away from me.

"Grandma, what?" I persisted.

Still she said nothing.

"Grandma!"

"He raped her," she said finally without turning around. "Nobody ever wanted you to know."

I sat silent taking it in, memories going back to things said, and things done from the time that I was a little girl. At last I said, "Tell me, Grandma. I want to know."

She turned slowly around and said, "Baby, Carl Whitmire is your real father."

"What the fuck!" I exclaimed. "I know that, but sometimes I just didn't want to believe it. He raped her? Why isn't the fucker in jail!?"

"She was on a date with him," Grandma Donner explained. "How are you going to prove it was rape and she just didn't consent to it? Besides, he was a medical student from a wealthy family. They had the money to hire lawyers. We didn't."

My mind burned with rage. No wonder Mother was such a prude. No wonder she tried to make me perfect. She tried to control Daddy to protect him from his drinking, and maybe she tried to control me to protect me from what she went through. Her attitude toward men was totally different than mine, maybe because she got raped. She may have loved Daddy, but she was never in love with him. She idolized men, but never let anyone get close to her. I could see her never wanting to have sex again after something like that. I could also see her resenting men and maybe resenting me because I was the product of her rape.

"How did Daddy come into the picture?" I asked.

Grandma Donner smiled a little. "That man—he had been in love with your mother for as long as he had known her and that went back to the first grade. He would have lassoed the moon for her if he could. She wouldn't have anything to do with him though. He wasn't good enough for Miss Priss over there who had in mind she was gonna marry herself a rich man. That's why she went out with Whitmire. He was smart, and his

399

Karlyle Tomms

family had clout, but your daddy struggled to graduate high school.

When she got pregnant she went and told Whitmire about it and he told her he would pay for an abortion. She told him she could prove it was his baby and he was gonna marry her. He told her he had plenty of friends who would testify that they had slept with her and he would ruin her reputation; told her he could fake paternity results. He blew her off and told her to get lost.

Your daddy was always coming around doing things for her, buying her stuff. He didn't push himself off on her too hard so she kind of tolerated it, pretended she didn't like it, but truth is she wanted the attention. Your daddy worshiped her. If that girl ever had a tear to fall your daddy would have caught it in the palm of his hand before it ever hit the ground. He knew her like a road map on his heart. He saw her getting depressed, and he noticed when she first started to show. He cornered her about it one day and she told him. First thing he wanted to do was rip Whitmire's head off but they both knew there wasn't really anything they could do. The next thing he did was convince her that nobody had to know. They was out of high school by then—grown. They could do what they wanted. He told her if she married him he would love you like you was his very own and nobody ever had to know the difference. He did love you, honey, like you was his own blood. He convinced her to go over into Maryland with him and get married. That way, if anybody asked they could say they got married in Maryland and could lie about when they got married.

When you were born, lord you were a beautiful baby, but she had postpartum and went a little nuts for a while. When she started hauling you around and showing you off to everybody in town we had to intervene. That was the first time your momma went into a nut hospital. Your daddy took care of you in the meantime and you bonded more with him than with her. I think that totally broke her heart. A couple of other times she went to the hospital, but by the time you was four or five years old she was stable enough to stay home and take care of you."

I sat there and listened quietly until she stopped talking.

"What about Daddy's drinking?" I asked. "When did that start?"

"Your daddy was an alcoholic plain and simple," she replied. "Ran in his family. He was probably hooked the first time he took a drink. Some people can handle their liquor and some can't. Your daddy never could handle liquor. One drop and he was off on a binge. His drinking didn't have anything to do with any of this. It had to do with the fact that he was what he was. It wasn't so bad early on, but the older he got, the worse it got. The worse it got, the more your momma tried to stop it. Hell, she was no more in control of it than he was, but she damn sure tried. You can't

Confessions from the Pumpkin Patch

make a silk purse out of a pig's ear, and damn, she wanted that silk purse. She never got what she wanted. You got what *she* wanted and without even half trying. At first, I think she was a little jealous of that, but then I think she was proud that you got there even if she couldn't. She started to lighten up a little after your daddy died."

The more I thought about what Grandma Donner said the more rage I felt. I left Grandma to sit with Mother for a while and went home for the evening. I remembered seeing a curious deposit when I went through Mother's papers. Every month, like clockwork, there had been a deposit for $200 but I couldn't find any receipt for deposit anywhere. Now my curiosity had changed to suspicion. I knew Mother kept meticulous records, so that evening I went home and headed straight for the shed. I turned on Daddy's little shed heater and went to work. I pulled out boxes of records and started going through them. I found every bank statement going all the way back to the month of my birth and before. About six months before I was born, the deposits started. The months before that, there had been nothing.

On the following morning, I went to Mother's bank and asked about the deposit. They knew me. They had known me all my life just like almost everybody else in town. There was no problem getting a look at the records because they knew me and they also knew that Mother was critically ill. Mr. Simmons, the bank vice president, sat down to talk with me about it. I found that the deposits came from a fabric company in Kittanning.

"Mr. Simmons, why would Mother be getting regular deposits from this company?" I questioned.

"Well," he began. "All the deposits are from a trust established through the company. We assumed that your mother must have had some deceased relative who had stock in the company and had set up a trust."

"There is no such deceased relative that I have ever heard of," I said. "Who owns that company?"

"From what I understand," he replied. "The company is owned by the Whitmire family."

I know that my face must have turned the color of a tomato as my rage broiled. I then knew what the money had been for. There it was, the pay off, the hush money; support for the bastard child that Whitmire refused to claim, but more than that, hush money that continued long after I was an adult. A wildfire of rage ignited inside me.

"Thank you, Mr. Simmons." I said, politely.

I left the bank and drove straight to the Whitmire clinic. As I walked by the sign on the building that said, 'Carl Whitmire, MD, I spit on it. I burst

401

through the door, walked firmly up to the receptionist and asked, "Is Dr. Whitmire in?"

She was a new hire, someone I had not seen before. I judged that she was some, fresh out of high school little twit who had nothing more than a receptionist job to look forward to in life. It wasn't fair to judge her, but at that moment, I felt negative and judgmental toward everyone in my path.

"Are you a patient?" she asked.

"Yes, I am," I said, through teeth about to clench. "Is he in?"

"Yes," she replied, "If you will just have a seat, I'll—."

She didn't get a chance to finish her sentence. I dashed through the door to the medical area before she had it out of her mouth. A nurse in the hall looked up at me with shock on her face. She was a nurse who must have been on the edge of retiring at the time. She had worked in the clinic for as long as I could remember. She knew me, but she had never seen me like that.

"Where is he?!" I insisted.

"Lovella," she said, attempting to be calm. "Is there something I can help you with?"

I didn't respond but started throwing open every door as I brushed passed her down the hall. By the time I got to the third door, there he was, bent over a pregnant woman with her legs in stirrups doing some kind of exam on her twat. He barely had time to recognize who I was before I crossed the room and slapped him as hard as I could.

"YOU FUCKING LOW LIFE PIG FROM HELL!" I screamed. "YOU FUCKING SELFISH IMMORAL BASTARD. YOU RAPED HER YOU GODDAMN BASTARD! THEN YOU HAD THE FUCKING NERVE TO TREAT ME AS ONE OF YOUR PATIENTS MY WHOLE GODDAMN LIFE KNOWING I WAS YOUR DAUGHTER!? WHAT THE FUCK! HOW COULD YOU? HOW COULD ANY DECENT MAN EVER DO ANYTHING LIKE THAT?!"

He put his hands up and backed away from me. "Lovella, I'm sorry. I don't know what you are talking about," he said.

"YOU ARE INDEED SORRY!" I screamed. "YOU ARE A SORRY LOW LIFE MOTHER FUCKING BASTARD AND YOU _DO_ GODDAMN KNOW WHAT I AM TALKING ABOUT! I KNOW THE TRUTH MOTHER FUCKER! GODDAMN IT! I KNOW THE TRUTH! I HAVE PROOF THAT YOU FUCKING SENT HUSH MONEY TO MY MOTHER'S BANK ACCOUNT EVER SINCE I WAS BORN 'CAUSE YOU ARE TOO MUCH OF A FUCKING CHICKEN SHIT TO TAKE RESPONSIBILITY FOR YOUR OWN CHILD!"

The poor woman in the stirrups lay there frightened and helpless while I

Confessions from the Pumpkin Patch

continued my barrage.

Whitmire was obviously taken aback. "Lovella, how about we step into my office and discuss this?" he pleaded.

"SO YOU CAN KEEP ANYBODY FROM FINDING OUT THE TRUTH ABOUT YOU? HOW ABOUT YOU KISS MY ASS MOTHER FUCKER!" I slapped him again.

By this time the nurses and other employees had gathered at the door. The older nurse who I passed in the hallway attempted to sooth me. "Lovella, honey," she said sweetly. "Let's go sit down and talk about what has you so upset." She reached out and touched my arm.

"DON'T FUCKING TOUCH ME!" I screamed at her as I jerked away. Then I turned back to her. "DO YOU KNOW WHO THIS MAN IS," I questioned. Then I went on without giving her a chance to answer. "THIS MAN IS MY FUCKING RAPIST SPERM DONOR! HE IS MY GODDAMN BIOLOGICAL FATHER. HE RAPED MY MOTHER AND THEN DIDN'T HAVE THE FUCKING BALLS OR DECENCY TO DO THE RIGHT THING WHEN SHE GOT PREGNANT SO HE FUCKING PAID HER OFF FOR THE LAST TWENTY-SIX YEARS OF MY LIFE!"

I turned again on Whitmire.

"AND DON'T FUCKING CALL IT CHILD SUPPORT MOTHER FUCKER! IF IT WAS CHILD SUPPORT IT WOULD HAVE STOPPED WHEN I WAS TWENTY-ONE AND IT WOULD NOT HAVE STARTED SIX MONTHS BEFORE I WAS BORN. YOU ARE STILL PAYING YOUR GODDAMNED HUSH MONEY. I KNOW IT CAME FROM YOU. I TRACKED IT DOWN TO YOUR FUCKING FAMILY TRUST! WELL GUESS WHAT MOTHER FUCKER, THE HUSH IS OVER! IT'S OUT! MY MOTHER MAY HAVE KEPT HER MOUTH SHUT, BUT I AM NOT GOING TO! I AM GOING TO TELL EVERYBODY I CAN TELL THAT CARL WHITMIRE—M. D.—IS A FUCKING RAPIST LOW LIFE BASTARD WHO WOULDN'T EVEN ACKNOWLEDGE OR TAKE RESPONSIBILITY FOR HIS OWN GODDAMN CHILD!"

I turned and pushed my way past the nurses who were standing in the doorway. Then I turned around and went back for one more rant.

"YOU ARE NOT A FATHER!" I screamed, sticking my finger in his face. "YOU ARE A FUCKING FORCED SPERM DONOR. MY REAL FATHER LOVED ME 'TIL THE DAY HE TOOK HIS LAST BREATH. HE WAS WHAT A FATHER IS SUPPOSED TO BE. THERE WAS NOT A SINGLE ATOM OF HIS GENETICS IN MY BODY BUT JOHN FUCHS WAS MY REAL FATHER. HE MAY HAVE BEEN AN

Karlyle Tomms

ALCOHOLIC FACTORY WORKER, BUT HE WAS MORE OF A MAN THAN YOU WILL EVER FUCKING DREAM OF BEING! YOU SHOULD HAVE GONE TO PRISON FOR WHAT YOU DID, AND YOU DESERVE TO ROT IN HELL!"

I turned to leave again, then whirled back around one more time.

"BY THE WAY, MOTHER FUCKER, MY HUSBAND CAN BUY AND SELL YOUR WHOLE GODDAMN FAMILY FIFTY TIMES OVER AND NEVER MISS A FUCKING PENNY! WE DON'T NEED YOUR GODDAMN MEASLY TWO HUNDRED DOLLARS A MONTH!"

I turned on my heels at that point, marched out of the building, got in my car and left. When I walked through the lobby the stares and shocked faces of patients there made me realize they had heard enough to end the secret. As I was pulling out of the parking lot, a police car pulled in. I kept going. I suppose the asshole could have pressed charges against me, but nothing ever happened.

CHAPTER 30

I never heard anything of Carl Whitmire again. I didn't care. In short order, I had no reason to go back to that part of Pennsylvania ever. Mother improved over time, but she never recovered. About six months after the accident we moved her to a nursing home in Nashville so I could visit with her and keep an eye on her care. There is where she spent the rest of her life. Within about a year, she got to the point where she could walk with a walker, but she was never fully coherent again. The damage to her brain created something like dementia. There were times when I would go to see her that she would recognize me but there were times when she was lost in her memories, and other times when she was clearly hallucinating.

The years passed. My children grew up, and Mother's hair turned to a lightly peppered white. Beyond the point of her accident, she never knew her grandchildren. She never got to see school plays or go to ball games. On Christmas, Earl and I would take the children to the nursing home to visit her. We would take her a present, but she seldom even recognized it as a Christmas gift. One year she accepted the package and said a polite "Thank you." Then she sat with the box on her lap doing nothing with it. After a while Earl said, "Here, Drucella. Let me open that for you." But she held tightly to the box and would not let it go. We left that day with Mother still sitting there, holding the box in her lap. A week later, I went back to see her and the gift sat on her bedside table still unopened. From that point on we didn't bring gifts. We only tried to do for her what she needed.

My kids grew tired of going to visit. There was no one left for them to relate to. Mother was gone and in her place was a lost and confused spirit. I didn't blame the kids, and I never tried to force them to do something that they found uncomfortable. There were times that I found it difficult to go as well.

The kids were both close to Earl's parents and Drew especially loved his great Grandma Donner, so it wasn't like they didn't have grandparents at all. We made regular trips to Pennsylvania and Earl's parents made fairly frequent trips to Nashville. It was apparently very convenient to make a business trip that also included seeing the grandkids. If Earl and his father had their noses in the company, Clarese and I would be taking the kids to the park or a museum.

Karlyle Tomms

Many times we paid for Tommy, Gretta and their kids to come to Nashville. When Derrick was four they had another son who they named after the two grandfathers. In time, Tommy was placed on 100% service connected disability. His trauma reactions improved very little and try as he might, he could not work. Even when they visited we had to be careful of loud noises. He drank heavily for a time but in the end decided that his family was more important than the liquor, and it didn't really help anyway. Until Tommy got full disability, they never lived exactly well. Earl and I supported them as much as we could but there was an obvious shame that Tommy felt about taking any kind of financial help and eventually he stopped accepting it.

"We will make do," he said one day as Earl tried to hand him a 500 dollar bill. I could see that he was torn. I never knew what his circumstances did to him inside his own mind but it didn't take a genius to figure out that he was a tortured man. He never talked about it. It was one thing to vacation with us and allow us to pay for that. It was something else entirely for us to pick up overdue bills. There is a pride that is lost when a man can't work and a sense of dignity that can't seem to be substituted by anything else. There were times that I think he might have committed suicide if it had not been for his kids. Thank God he found a reason to keep going. After Tommy got his full disability they did okay, not great, but okay.

Gretta ended up going to nursing school to get an LPN. She took a job at the hospital in Kittanning making a little more than minimum wage but it became her passion and her career. When the boys were in high school, she went back to school to get her RN. I have no idea how she took care of home and family while going to school, but at least with Tommy being at home he could watch the kids while she studied or was in class.

When Derrick graduated high school he went to Penn State. He got a degree in social studies; then went on to law school. I was very proud of him. I know that Tommy and Gretta were proud of him too but he never was able to get close to Tommy. From the day that Tommy returned from Vietnam and Derrick saw him go into that first flashback he had always been a little afraid of his father. There were other things he witnessed over the years and Tommy's drinking never helped matters. However, Tommy insisted that the use of pot helped both his physical and emotional pain and Derrick must have witnessed that it brought him some kind of comfort. In time Derrick figured things out. He understood and was able to develop a compassion for Tommy but he could never seem to feel the closeness to his Dad that many boys experience. Nonetheless, maybe for his father's sake, he devoted himself to getting medicinal use of cannabis legalized in

406

Confessions from the Pumpkin Patch

Pennsylvania.

Grandma and Grandpa Donner became increasingly feeble as they aged, so we took the kids to them at least three or four times a year, however, often only on holidays. In 1982, Grandpa Donner died of a sudden heart attack. After that Grandma Donner seemed lost. As much as she bitched about him all those years, she needed him and loved him. When he was gone, she didn't know what to do with herself. She came to live with us for a while and then decided that it was time for her to move into the nursing home. I don't know that she really needed a nursing home, but I think there were times that she felt like she was in the way at our home. She moved into the same room as Mother and doted over her until her own health began to deteriorate and she could no longer "help" the nurses. Mother died first and I don't think Grandma Donner could deal with that. Not three months after Mother passed Grandmother Donner fell ill with pneumonia and passed away as well.

I became comfortable in my role as housewife and mother. I did piddle with the occasional college course if it piqued my interest. I got involved with charity events and various social clubs around town. I worked out regularly and even tried my hand at Community Theater, although I have to say I do much better as a back stage hand than as an actress.

The kids grew up way too quickly, and I was so thankful that my fears about having a black child in the south were only that. Other than the initial problems with the wrong women's club, it was never really an issue, at least not one that I picked up on. As she got older, Vanilla had questions, and some of them were difficult, but Elmira helped get us through those emotional hurdles. Her wisdom was not only a frequent soothing comfort to me, but was a comfort for Vanilla as well.

Vanilla graduated from Vanderbilt medical school in 1991, and Drew got a bachelor's degree in film making from UCLA. Despite my attitudes about sex and all the escapades of my youth, I regretted that he chose to work in pornography. None the less, he made an exceptional income and apparently got laid a lot. He liked that, but I worried about him. Things like AIDS were not known in my day. You might get something that would require penicillin or would be problematic but not life threatening. It was not until the early 1980's that sex became deadly.

Vanilla completed her residency at Vanderbilt with a specialty in cardiology. I don't know how much Grandpa Donner's heart attack might have influenced that decision, but she was only fourteen years old when he died and she took it pretty hard. She continued to work for Vanderbilt heart services on graduation and became a well-respected physician, known for her research in cardiac pharmacology.

Karlyle Tomms

When the kids were gone it was a lonely time. Then it was just me and Earl, but that was a good thing. Over the years we began to fit into one another like nesting dolls. We had staff in and out at various times, but when the kids got a little older and our cook finally quit, we didn't hire anyone else. I got out my Julia Child cookbooks and went back to the kitchen. We didn't have business guests in the house as often, but I delighted in throwing dinner parties for our friends. To see someone's obvious pleasure over a meal I had prepared was like a drug to me, and thankfully Earl very much enjoyed the socializing.

Several times while the kids were growing up we took them to various places around the world. One summer Clarese and I took them on a tour of Europe—from Ireland, over to England, up through Scotland to the Netherlands, Sweden and Norway down through Germany and Austria, over to France, to Portugal and Spain and then across to Italy and Greece before coming home. We were gone for their entire summer vacation. I think it was as much a thrill for me as it was for the children.

Earl had made a commitment that he was never going to be like his father and he kept to that commitment. In fact, Daniel changed himself. He stopped drinking so much and spent more time with his family. Earl commented once that he spent more time with his grandkids than he ever spent with his own children. Earl's sister married a stock broker and moved to New York. They only had one child, a daughter named Simone who pretty much followed in her father's footsteps on Wall Street. Daniel spent less and less time with the company as he got older and more and more time visiting his grandchildren. Earl, unlike his father, never allowed the company to become his obsession. He hired competent executives and trusted them to handle the business without him having to micro-manage. As a result, he was home and we traveled, or devoted attention to our charity, The John and Drucella Fuchs Prosperity Center, to teach people in poverty and the lower middle class how to start and manage businesses. Earl also changed policies at Chum Snacks so each employee got an option of an annual bonus in cash or company stock. Many who chose the stock retired with one or two million dollars in their account.

After medical school, Vanilla married another doctor, a very handsome man by the name of Stacy Winters. She debated keeping her maiden name but decided in the end that she wanted to become Vanilla Winters. They decided together that they were both too busy for children but by the time Vanilla reached the age of 32 she re-thought the whole thing and decided that she wanted to have a child before she got too old. Their son Griffin was born on June 13, 2000 with Down's syndrome. It was easy to see that they were both heartbroken.

408

Confessions from the Pumpkin Patch

After Griffin was born, their marriage began to go downhill. Stacy blamed her for his son's disability and would often scream at her that he never wanted to have children in the first place, "and now look what I'm stuck with."

Vanilla responded with, "You are stuck with a beautiful child who deserves your love as much as any other."

Vanilla was determined to love her son, no matter what, to make no difference between him and a child who had not been born with special needs. In time, he became a delight to her, but she was never able to convince Stacy and in 2005 they divorced.

Drew continues to work in pornography, even though the internet has completely changed everything. The industry has changed even in the last ten years. He keeps hoping that he will find some work in mainstream productions and has a possible opportunity to work with LOGO the Gay network.

The world has changed so much and yes has stayed so much the same. We went from the assassinations of the 1960s to planes flying into the World Trade Center, from Viet Nam to Iraq and Afghanistan. Technology has changed, but prejudice and hatred still abound if not toward black people then toward Mexicans or gay people or Muslims, Christians, Buddhists, or whatever. Sometimes I wonder if we will ever truly be free, and I know in my heart that so long as any human being seeks to control another we will never be truly free, and as long as any one of us is in chains to another person's ideology then none of us are free.

Sometimes I think of all the billions of people in the world and how each one has his, or her, own unique story and how those stories seem to unfold only partly because of our intent. We are all like boats on an open sea with no sails and only limited maneuverability. The slightest bump can often completely change our course. When those bumps are big the course change is often impossible to avoid. I wonder sometimes how many people have lives that turned out exactly the way they wanted and how many people live, or even continue to want, the dreams that they dreamed in youth. The world is not only an ever changing place, but our perceptions of it are ever changing as well. When we seek more to understand the truth than to defend what we believe then will come the true dawn of freedom.

I look back on all of it now and realize that there is always a veil of illusion over the truth. I doubt that anyone ever sees reality as it truly is. Everything is clouded by judgment and perception, by belief systems, and emotions.

One day as I sat looking out that picture window at our house where I had found my comfort after we first moved to Nashville, I looked out across the way to what used to be Minnie Pearl's house. But it is no longer her house since she has long since passed away. I wondered if the person living there now had the same vision for the house that Minnie Pearl had or if decorators had come in and changed everything. I thought about how we each have our own vision of things, our own idea of what is beautiful and what is not. Then I thought to myself, "No one else in the world sees what I am seeing at this moment. No one else in the world is having this experience. Only me. Even if someone were to come and sit exactly where I am sitting, even if some scientist could calibrate their head into exactly the same position as mine, they would see something different. If for no other reason, it would be because there would be a difference in time. Some bird on a limb would have flown away. Some car would pass that is not there now." I realized two things in that moment, that no one can ever see the world the way that I see it, and no matter what I look upon, the very next second, it has changed.

I have learned to understand that my perception is not the truth and I have come to know that even though I can have empathy, I can never truly walk in another person's shoes. I can never know what it feels like to be inside of that person. I think one of the most horrible things someone can say to another person, especially if they are grieving is, "I know how you feel." The truth is I only know how I feel and how I feel is colored more by my own judgment than by any event that ever happens in my life. I now know that I had no idea what it felt like to be my mother. I learned the story of her life, but I never really knew her. I try to imagine why she made some of the choices she made, but I will never fully understand. I now know that pain was there, which I never comprehended when I was growing up. There was a real person there who I never truly came to know.

They say that any life worth living is worth living well. I have come to know with all my heart that every life is worth living. Every life matters and every life has reason. I may not know that reason, but in the long run, does it really matter? When I was a little girl, I saw my mother as a tyrant bent on controlling everyone around her. I realize now that all control is born of fear. We have no need to control when we trust. Mother simply did not trust that life would be safe, that I would be safe or that Daddy could continue to support us. I don't know if she ever came to love him, but Daddy sacrificed himself for the one person he thought he loved most. I find myself speculating. Did Daddy drink because he knew he could never truly have the woman he loved? Was I his emotional substitute?

It's all confusing, but that is the one thing that can be said of everyone's life. It's all confusing. No one ever has all the answers. No one lives

Confessions from the Pumpkin Patch

without mistakes or without regret. If anyone says they have no regrets, either they are a saint, a liar, or totally insane. We are all where we are by destiny and by choice. Destiny is everything we can't control and choice is the only thing that we can. We choose based on what we think at the time. We choose based on our belief about ourselves, and all that is around us. The belief itself has more to do with how we think and behave than any circumstance. We are handed what we are handed and then we are left to choose based on the belief that is dominant in our mind at the time. If I, as that rebellious child, could have seen the world differently, then this story would have been totally different. If Mother could have only made sense of what happened to her instead of giving in to fear, maybe we could have been close. That I suppose is a story in some distant parallel universe. The truth is, Mother made the best choices she knew how to make with the destiny she had been given. I made the best choices I knew how to make with mine.

For as long as she lived, I went to see Mother at the nursing home every Wednesday and Sunday afternoon. Much of the time was spent just sitting there. Sometimes we talked, which meant that I would respond to whatever gibberish she was spouting on that particular day. Most days I simply sat and held her hand. About a month before she died, I walked into her room to find her sitting in the wheel chair and smiling. She looked up at me as I approached and said, "Oh my, aren't you a beautiful girl."

"Thank you." I said. I walked over and patted her hand. "How are you doing today?"

She did not respond to the question but said, "I had a daughter who was beautiful like you. Her name was Lovella and I don't know what ever happened to her."

I patted her arm again and knelt down in front of her face to face.

"Mother. It's me. I am Lovella."

Her eyes never met mine but she continued.

"My daughter was a little rambunctious. Sometimes she was a little defiant but that's because she had spirit and spunk, and oh my goodness was she smart."

"Mother," I said again, "It's me....Lovella."

Her head turned to one side. She looked as though gazing off into a very great distance. Then she said only one last thing.

"I loved her with all of my heart."

THERE IS NO SUCH THING AS
THE END